PRAISE

"I will read anything Susan Stoker puts out . . . because I know it's going to be amazing!"

—Riley Edwards, *USA Today* bestselling author

"Susan Stoker never fails to pull me out of a reading slump. With heat, action, and suspense, she weaves an incredible tale that sucks me in and doesn't let go."

—Jessica Prince, *USA Today* bestselling author

"One thing I love about Susan Stoker's books is that she knows how to deliver a perfect HEA while still making sure the villain gets what he/she deserves!"

—T.M. Frazier, *New York Times* bestselling author

"Susan Stoker's characters come alive on the page!"

—Elle James, *New York Times* bestselling author

"When you pick up a Susan Stoker book you know exactly what you're going to get . . . a hot alpha hero and a smart, sassy heroine. I can't get enough!"

—Jessica Hawkins, *USA Today* bestselling author

"Suspenseful storytelling with characters you want as friends!"

—Meli Raine, *USA Today* bestselling author

"Susan Stoker knows what women want. A hot hero who needs to save a damsel in distress . . . even if she can save herself."

—CD Reiss, *New York Times* bestselling author

THE
SOLDIER

DISCOVER OTHER TITLES BY SUSAN STOKER

Alpha Cove Series

The Soldier
The Sailor (March 2026)
The Pilot (August 2026
The Guardsman (March 2027)

Game of Chance Series

The Protector
The Royal
The Hero
The Lumberjack

Ace Security Series

Claiming Grace
Claiming Alexis
Claiming Bailey
Claiming Felicity
Claiming Sarah

Mountain Mercenaries Series

Defending Allye
Defending Chloe
Defending Morgan
Defending Harlow
Defending Everly
Defending Zara
Defending Raven

Silverstone Series

Trusting Skylar
Trusting Taylor
Trusting Molly
Trusting Cassidy

SEAL of Protection: Alliance Series

Protecting Remi
Protecting Wren
Protecting Josie
Protecting Maggie
Protecting Addison
Protecting Kelli (September 2025)
Protecting Bree (January 2026)

Rescue Angels Series

Keeping Laryn
Keeping Amanda (November 2025)
Keeping Zita (February 2026)
Keeping Penny (May 2026)
Keeping Kara (July 2026)
Keeping Jennifer (November 2026)

The Refuge Series

Deserving Alaska
Deserving Henley
Deserving Reese
Deserving Cora
Deserving Lara
Deserving Maisy
Deserving Ryleigh

SEAL Team Hawaii Series

Eagle Point Search & Rescue Series

Delta Force Heroes Series

Protecting Cheyenne
Protecting Jessyka
Protecting Julie (novella)
Protecting Melody
Protecting the Future
Protecting Kiera (novella)
Protecting Alabama's Kids (novella)
Protecting Dakota

Seal of Protection: Legacy Series

Securing Caite
Securing Brenae (novella)
Securing Sidney
Securing Piper
Securing Zoey
Securing Avery
Securing Kalee
Securing Jane (novella)

THE
SOLDIER

SUSAN
STOKER

Text copyright © 2025 by Susan Stoker

Published by Montlake, Seattle

www.apub.com

Amazon, the Amazon logo, and Montlake are trademarks of Amazon.com, Inc., or its affiliates.

EU product safety contact:
Amazon Media EU S. à r.l.
38, avenue John F. Kennedy, L-1855 Luxembourg
amazonpublishing-gpsr@amazon.com

ISBN-13: 9781662527296 (paperback)
ISBN-13: 9781662527289 (digital)

Cover design by Hang Le
Cover photography © FTAPE LIMITED
Cover image: © JHON CLAUD / Shutterstock

Printed in the United States of America

THE
SOLDIER

PROLOGUE

Chad Young stood leaning against the side of the house where he'd grown up, amazed and awed at how many people had come for his father's celebration of life today. It seemed as if the entire town of Rockville was there. Sam, the butcher; Mrs. Lakeworth, his fourth-grade teacher; lobstermen who'd taken the day off from fishing to attend; and of course all their nearest neighbors were there, as were his mom and dad's best friends. Hell, he even thought he'd seen some of the selectmen, representing Rockville's form of government.

Pretty much the entire town had shown up to pay their respects to his father and to let his mother know they were there for her. There were lots of reasons Chad had left Maine years ago to join the Army, but this sense of community was one thing he'd definitely missed.

"How're you holding up?"

Turning toward his older brother, Lincoln, Chad shrugged. "Not good."

"Yeah," Lincoln agreed as he took a swig of water from the bottle he was holding.

"How's Mom doing?" Chad asked.

"'Bout as expected."

Chad sighed. Evelyn Young was doing her best to play hostess. She was putting on a brave face, but losing her husband of fifty years was hitting her harder than she was letting on. As good as it was to see his brothers—his two younger siblings were milling around the yard, greeting people and keeping an eye on their mom at the same time—Chad hated that their little family reunion was because of their dad dying.

"Did you get a chance to talk to the doctor who treated Dad in the emergency room?" Chad asked.

"Yeah. Said he didn't suffer. That he'd definitely had a stroke when Mom called nine-one-one. There was nothing they could do when he had that second stroke after arriving at the ER."

Chad stared out at all the people in the yard and blinked back tears. It was impossible to think of his dad as anything other than larger than life. At six foot five, he'd been an imposing figure. But he was also a gentle giant. Memories of his booming laugh echoed in Chad's head. It was devastating to know he'd never hear it again.

Austin Young had been the best father growing up. Patient yet stern. He insisted his four boys study hard, but he also made sure to teach them the importance of having fun as well. Balance. His dad had been all about balance.

Chad and his brothers had a great childhood. They tinkered on every engine under the sun—motorcycles, ATVs, snowmobiles, cars, trucks, lawn mowers. There wasn't an engine his dad couldn't fix, and he'd taught all his sons everything he knew. They'd camped, boated, hiked . . . spent as much time as possible outside.

But it wasn't all fun and games. Both his parents worked their butts off to provide for their family. They'd bought a chunk of land when they were newlyweds, naming it Lobster Cove. It was right on the water, fairly large, at five acres. And over the years, they'd built businesses on the property, starting with boat storage facilities for the winter. Then Dad began contracting for the county, plowing roads, as well as helping friends and neighbors clear their drives.

The auto shop was the biggest moneymaker for his parents, however, and his dad, even at seventy-three, had worked in the shop until the day he'd died.

Their last business venture was building and renting two guesthouses on the property. They weren't large—one was a two-bedroom cabin, and the other a one-bedroom—but they were fully booked every summer from Memorial Day to Labor Day. Most years beyond that as well.

His mom had taken responsibility for that particular business. She cleaned the houses, managed reservations, greeted guests, and helped new visitors figure out what to do in the area, and she made complimentary baked goods for each arrival.

Thinking about what would happen to Lobster Cove now that their dad wasn't around made Chad's stomach clench. His dad had run the auto shop and the boat storage businesses . . . and he had a feeling his mom would be significantly impacted by the loss of the income if they both went under.

His younger brothers approached with slight frowns on their faces. Ten years separated the oldest from youngest, but many people often thought they were all much closer in age. They looked similar, and all of them had decided to go into the military after graduating from high school, which meant they were comparably fit and muscular as well. But they'd all taken separate paths, joining different branches of the military. It was an ongoing good-natured rivalry within the family.

At the moment, Chad didn't feel like ribbing Zach about the Army-Navy football game, or making jokes about whose branch of the military was better. It was all he could do to keep his composure when everywhere he looked around the property, he saw echoes of his dad.

"Dad loved Lobster Cove so much," Zach started without preamble after joining his brothers.

"Yeah," Lincoln agreed. "He did."

"I heard Victor asking Mom what she was going to do with the property, now that Dad's gone."

"Are you serious?" Lincoln hissed. "At Dad's memorial? What an ass!"

Chad agreed. It was no secret that their neighbor had always had his eye on the Youngs' land. He'd been trying to get their dad to sell part of it to him for years. And apparently he thought it was appropriate to approach their mother about selling when she was at her most vulnerable.

"What are we going to do?" Knox asked.

"About what?" Lincoln asked.

"About Lobster Cove. Mom can't run everything on her own. She doesn't know anything about the auto shop, and we all know that if she ever got behind the wheel of a plow, nothing good would happen."

Everyone chuckled. Their mom was notorious for being a terrible driver. She'd been in more car accidents in her lifetime than was normal for any one person, and their dad had refused to ever let her operate the plow for fear she'd take out one of the houses. It was another running family joke that seemed more sad than funny, now that Austin Young was gone.

"Otis is staying on, right?" Zach asked. Otis was their dad's longtime best friend. About five years younger, he did the accounting and payroll for the various businesses their parents owned. He also managed their personal investments and did their taxes each year. He was invaluable to Lobster Cove, and their mom would need his help, now more than ever.

"Yes. I talked to him earlier, and he reassured me that he wasn't going anywhere," Lincoln said.

"That's a relief. And Barry and Walt?" Knox asked. The two mechanics who worked with their dad would be key to keeping the auto shop running.

"They're staying too. At least for now," Lincoln said.

Chad's mind spun. Everywhere he looked around the property, he saw things that needed to be done. It was mid-April, and winter was finally waning. There were the normal maintenance items—the yard needed tending, the dock needed to be put back in, the kayaks taken out of storage for the summer guests to use at their leisure, and owners would be wanting the boats that had been stored over the winter.

But more than that . . . the longer he looked, the more Chad realized many things had been neglected.

One of the guesthouse porches was sagging. The roofs on both needed replacing. His mom had mentioned the oven in the one-bedroom wasn't working right and the whole-house generators hadn't worked for a while, probably because mice had gotten inside them again and chewed through wires.

Lobster Cove was looking . . . tired.

He didn't blame his parents; they were in their seventies, and it was a lot of work, keeping the businesses operating in the black. General maintenance clearly hadn't been a priority.

Which made Chad wonder what his parents hadn't been telling him and his brothers.

He felt guilty about not asking more questions, about not visiting more often. It was obvious his dad had been slowing down physically, and he hadn't been able to do some of the repairs that needed to be done around the property. But such vital things as structural maintenance . . . ?

Now Chad wondered if the businesses weren't doing as well as he'd thought and his parents didn't have the money to pay for bigger expenses like new ovens or hiring contractors to repair the roofs.

Without thought, he blurted, "I'm moving to Rockville."

As soon as the words left his lips, a huge weight seemed to lift from his shoulders.

"What?"

"You are?"

"Wow."

He wasn't surprised at his brothers' reactions. It was an impulsive decision, after all, and he'd shocked even himself.

"Mom can't run Lobster Cove by herself. She can't live out here on her own. And I don't trust fucking Victor Rogers not to do something shady to get his hands on the property. We all know how much this place is worth. Mom and Dad bought it for a song, but waterfront property in this state has skyrocketed over the years. Mom needs help. I can do what Dad did. Take over the auto shop, help with maintenance around this place. Maybe even see about taking over Dad's plowing contract with the city."

The more he talked about it, the better the decision felt.

"What about Carissa?" Lincoln asked.

Chad shrugged. "We broke up a couple of months ago. I've got nothing keeping me in Virginia. Mom needs me." A thought struck him then, and he looked each of his brothers in the eye. "She needs *us*."

He let those three words sink in for a minute.

"Can any of you tell me you're really happy where you're at? Professionally or personally?"

It was Zach who spoke first. "I didn't want to chapter out of the Navy. I loved what I did. But those two surgeries on my knees made it impossible to get around the ships without pain, and standing for hours in the galley was no longer an option."

"You could move to Rockville and open a lobster shack," Chad suggested.

Zach rolled his eyes. "As if the forty-three already in operation aren't enough."

"Fine. Something else, then. You know as well as I do that there aren't enough good restaurants in the area," Chad said. He turned to Knox. "And the Coast Guard is just as busy up here in Maine as it is in Florida."

Knox snorted. "Um . . . no, it's not."

"All right, fine. It's not. But I have no doubt *training* is just as important here as it is there. You told me not too long ago that you were looking for more of a challenge."

"Yeah," Knox mused.

Taking a deep breath, Chad turned to his older brother. He had a feeling Lincoln would be the most difficult to convince.

After high school, Lincoln had gone into the Air Force Academy in Colorado Springs and had flown jets for their country . . . until something went terribly wrong on a mission, and he'd had to eject over enemy territory. Chad still didn't know all the details—Lincoln never talked about it—but he knew his brother had spent a week evading enemy forces and walking about ten miles a day toward the border before he'd been extracted. By that time, he'd lost twenty-five pounds and injured his shoulder so badly, he could no longer fly the jets he loved without pain. He'd been medically retired a couple of years ago and was living the life of a recluse out in Montana.

"Linc, you can't tell me that Maine is all that different from Montana. It's rural as hell, you get as much snow as we do here, but there isn't any decent seafood for a thousand miles," Chad joked.

Lincoln didn't even crack a smile. "Rockville doesn't get nearly as much snow as Montana," he deadpanned.

The two brothers locked gazes, and Chad struggled to understand what he was seeing in his brother's eyes. He took a deep breath and decided to lay his feelings on the line.

"I miss you guys," he said. "Growing up with all of you . . . it was amazing. Lobster Cove was our home base, but the entire state was our playground. I didn't realize how much I missed it until now. And Mom *does* need us. Sure, I can attempt to step into Dad's boots, but we all know it'll take more than one of us to do everything he did. To make Lobster Cove flourish."

He held his breath as his brothers thought about what he was suggesting. It was a huge step. Uprooting their lives and moving back to their hometown. But as far as Chad knew, none of them were in serious relationships. It wouldn't be easy to find someone to settle down with here in Maine, and they were all well past the age their parents had been when they got married. Maybe that wasn't their destiny.

Maybe Lobster Cove would be their legacy.

Chad pushed away the cynical thought about what the point was in making their childhood home flourish if there was no one to leave it to.

"I'm in," Knox said suddenly. "You're right. I *was* already thinking about finding another contractor position. It'll be a nice change to be up here where my balls aren't sweating at six in the morning."

Everyone chuckled.

"Fine. I'll come too. But I'm not opening a fucking lobster shack," Zach said.

Everyone's gaze swung to Lincoln.

Their oldest brother stared at the people milling about on the property. Then he sighed. "*Someone* has to keep you assholes in check."

Chad smiled as contentment spread through his veins. He was suddenly excited about the future. About being able to spend more time with his brothers. He'd missed them. Yes, they were all adults now, and they'd changed a lot since they were kids, but blood was blood. When push came to shove, the Youngs stuck together. Family first.

They had a lot of details to figure out. Where to live—it wasn't as if there were apartment buildings on every block in Rockville—jobs, division of responsibilities at Lobster Cove . . . but they'd figure it out.

"Love you guys," Chad blurted. It wasn't something they said to each other a lot. But their father dying so suddenly had made them all understand the fragility of life. Of letting those you loved know how much they meant to you before it was too late. He couldn't remember the last time he'd said the words to his dad, and he'd regret not saying them to him more often for the rest of his life.

Lincoln grabbed him by the back of the neck and pulled him into a tight embrace. Zach and Knox crowded in, putting their arms around each other's shoulders. All four of them huddled together, cementing their commitment to each other, their mother, and their family legacy. Lobster Cove.

This was a new start for all of them. There would be bumps in the road, that was guaranteed, but as a family, they could get through anything.

CHAPTER ONE

Chad wiped a hand across his brow and took a deep breath. His back hurt. His knees hurt. His shoulders hurt. Hell . . . everything fucking hurt. At thirty-seven, he wasn't exactly old. But he was feeling every forty-mile march he'd done in the Army. Every shift he'd done as a sniper, lying motionless on a roof, in the dirt, in the cold or the heat for hours on end.

He'd been damn good at what he did, and Chad was proud of his service to his country. But he was also glad to have moved on. Killing people, even if they were the worst humanity had to offer, wasn't exactly a job he could talk about freely in polite society.

Being home, working with his hands in a whole different way, was just what he'd needed.

The salty breeze blowing in from the water, still cool though summer was coming up fast, rustled his dark hair, reminding Chad that he needed to get it cut. But he'd been too busy. He'd moved back to Lobster Cove the first weekend in May, and for the two weeks since, he'd been working nonstop.

Today, he was cleaning up the grounds around the houses. There were sticks to be picked up from the many winter storms, leaves to mulch, grass to mow . . . and then there was the *inside* work. The guest cabins needed some pretty extensive repairs. And on top of all that, he'd also been helping Walt and Barry at the auto shop as much as possible.

His brothers were going to be arriving in a week, and Chad would be glad for their help. He'd known there was a lot of work to do at their childhood home, but he wasn't prepared for exactly *how* much needed to be done.

"Chad?"

Turning toward the main house, he smiled at his mom. She was standing on the porch holding a plate and a glass of what looked like lemonade.

"It's time for a break. I made your favorite cookies!"

Without hesitation, he dropped the bundle of sticks in his hands and headed for the house. His mom was the reason he was here, and he'd never *not* take the opportunity to spend time with her.

Evelyn was struggling. Outwardly, she smiled and said all the right things, but it was more than obvious how much she missed her husband. And who could blame her? She and Austin had spent decades together. Her world had been turned upside down, and she was trying to figure out how to go on without him. It would take a lot of time.

Chad made a mental note to fix the porch stairs as they creaked ominously with every step. He didn't hesitate to barge into his mom's personal space and hug her when he got close enough.

"Chad! You're going to make me spill!" she protested with a small laugh.

He pulled back and took the glass and the plate from her hands, placing them on a small table between two rocking chairs on the porch.

"What? A son can't hug his mom?" he asked as he urged her to sit. He had no doubt she'd been working just as hard in the house as he'd been while he was outside.

"He can, but you hugged me last night. And this morning . . . three times."

"So there's a limit on hugs now?" Chad asked as he lowered himself into the other rocking chair. Memories of his parents sitting in these same chairs, watching him and his brothers roughhouse in the yard, hit him hard. The pain of losing his dad was so fresh, and being here at

Lobster Cove didn't help, because everywhere he looked were memories. Good ones, but still, if *he* was feeling so much pain, his mom had to be feeling it tenfold.

"I'm okay, Chad," she said softly. "I know you think I'm going to fall apart, but I'm not."

"I don't think that," he said, genuinely shocked. "You're the strongest woman I know. Even at seventy, you're more resilient and tougher than me. Which is why I'm never getting married. What woman could ever live up to you?"

"Oh, son," his mom said, sounding extremely sad. "Don't say that. She's out there."

"Who?"

"The woman made for you. The time just hasn't been right for you to meet her yet."

"But now it is?" he asked, amused.

"I think so." His mom nodded. Then she stared at him for a long moment.

"What? What's that look for?" Chad asked.

"I just . . . I'm so happy you're here. I've missed you. And your brothers. When you all told me you were moving home, it didn't feel real. Your dad and I talked about it a lot, you know. Wondered if any of you would ever find your way back home."

Talking about his dad was difficult, but it also felt good. "Yeah?" he asked, encouraging his mom to keep talking.

"Uh-huh. I fretted that none of you would *ever* come home. That you'd get married and we'd only get to see our grandbabies once or twice a year."

Chad resisted the urge to roll his eyes. For years, his mom had been on him and his brothers to have kids. She wanted grandchildren to spoil and never hesitated to ask them about the possibility every chance she got.

"He'd be bursting with pride if he knew how you were all stepping up."

Chad nodded. His dad *would* be proud. He'd also probably be overbearing and bossy about what his sons should be doing around Lobster Cove. He'd be overseeing their every move, critiquing their every decision.

"How are you really?" he blurted, needing reassurance that his mom would be all right.

Evelyn sighed. "I'm tired. And sad. I miss him. Nothing's the same, and it's hard to find the energy and will to get up each morning and continue on without him."

Alarm coursed through Chad. But then his mom went on.

"But I will. Austin would be pissed at me if I stayed in bed and moaned about how hard my life is without him. The truth is, life is *never* easy. It's full of ups and downs. It's how you deal with the downs that shows the true measure of a person. Your dad and I . . . we vowed a long time ago to not let the bad times outweigh the good. Do I wish he was still here? Of course I do. But that doesn't mean that I can't be happy ever again. I'm happy *you're* here. That your brothers will be here soon. Everything else, I'm taking one day at a time."

Love for this woman swept over Chad. She was the backbone of Lobster Cove. She was also his biggest supporter and had always been there for him. "I love you, Mom."

"And I love you too. Now . . . finish up your cookies and get your butt back out there. Those sticks aren't going to pick themselves up."

Chad chuckled. "Yes, ma'am."

She smiled at him from across the small table. "You going into town today?"

The change in subject was obvious, but Chad didn't mind. There was only so much emotional stuff a person could take at one time. "Yeah. I need to pick up a few things from the lumberyard and stop at the hardware store. You need anything from the grocery store?"

"Actually, yes. I have a list," his mom said, leaning to the side and pulling a piece of paper from her back pocket. The familiar move made him smile. He'd seen her do that countless times over the years. She always kept a piece of paper in her pocket so she could jot down items she needed throughout the week, then gave the list to his dad when he went into Rockville.

Chad reached for it and glanced at the items. She had a lot of cleaning supplies on there, as well as staples such as sugar, flour, and rice. Next week, the first guests would arrive at the rentals, and his mom always made cookies or muffins to welcome them to Lobster Cove.

"I could set up an app on your phone that would make this easier," Chad told her. "You could type in what you need instead of having to keep track of a piece of paper, then text me the list."

She smiled lovingly at him. "I've been doing it my way for so long, there's no way I could change now," she said matter-of-factly.

His mom was definitely old fashioned. She had a cell phone, but she lost it around the house more than she used it. She'd set it down and forget where she put it. Or the battery would die because she hadn't used it in so long. Evelyn was smart; she simply didn't feel the need to change a routine that had worked for years.

"All right, but if you change your mind, let me know," Chad told her.

She gave him a look that clearly told him she wouldn't be changing her mind anytime soon.

"I'm going to talk to Walt and Barry before I head out. Call me if you think of anything you forgot on your list."

"I'm making taco casseroles for them to take home today," his mom informed him. "Can you please remind them to come up to the house before they leave?"

Chad was well aware it would be useless to remind his *mother* that the mechanics weren't teenagers or college kids, and they didn't need her to send food home with them every Friday night. As she'd said earlier, her routines were her routines, and nothing was going to change that.

Besides, Walt and Barry would never turn down a meal from his mom. She was an amazing cook, and her love language was food.

"All right, Mom. Anything else before I head out?" Chad asked.

"Be safe," she said quietly. "The tourists are starting to come back to town."

"I will." He could've assured her that nothing would happen. That he'd survived situations overseas she wouldn't even be able to comprehend, and there was no way he was going out in a car crash in his hometown.

But he knew better than anyone how life could turn on a dime. Was more aware than ever of how precious life was. Since his dad had died, he was already taking fewer risks than he had before.

Standing, Chad kissed his mom on the cheek, crossed the open expanse of property for a quick stop in the auto shop, and then headed for his dad's pickup truck. It was older than dirt but purred like a kitten. His dad had kept her running smoothly and perfectly. His mom had given him the keys when he'd arrived, saying Austin would've wanted it to be used and not kept parked in the garage, rusting away.

Driving it made Chad feel closer to his dad. He particularly remembered the ride to the airport, just the two of them, when he'd left home to join the Army. The memory was bittersweet. But each recollection was just a little less painful than it had been when he'd come home to Lobster Cove for his dad's funeral.

Heading into town, however . . . that still felt a little surreal as he drove down well-known roads, took in the beloved scenery. He'd been home for just two weeks, but the familiarity somehow made it feel much longer.

Rockville was a large town for this part of Maine, though tiny compared to the Norfolk area in Virginia, where he'd moved from. It didn't take long to get anywhere, and mom-and-pop shops still thrived. Two weeks ago, he couldn't drive two miles without seeing a Starbucks or some other big chain restaurant. Dunkin' Donuts was king here in Maine, but there were only a small handful of them in a thirty-mile radius around Lobster Cove.

Nope. Most of the chain stores had settled along Route 1, which made sense, because that was the road most tourists took on their way to Bar Harbor and Acadia National Park.

But Chad didn't mind the lack of mainstream businesses. He loved supporting local shops, even if they were a bit more expensive. The quality was better, and the fact that someone knew his parents almost everywhere he went was a bonus. He never knew when he'd be treated to a conversation with someone who wanted to share one of their favorite memories of his dad, or pass on their well-wishes to his mom.

Even after being gone for so many years, he still felt at home here. Chad was well aware the rural life of Maine wasn't for everyone. It took some getting used to. Everyone knowing your business. Many restaurants and businesses closing on Mondays. The lack of convenience. But the fresh air, the trees everywhere he looked, and how freaking beautiful every view was made up for everything else.

Chad turned into the small lumberyard, mentally calculating what he needed to fix the porch steps on the main house. He figured he also might as well get enough supplies to fix the steps on the guesthouses, since they were probably in need of some TLC as well.

He was walking toward the doors when yelling caught his attention off to his right.

Turning, he saw a man standing next to a small brown Toyota Corolla, leaning toward a woman and jabbing his finger right in front of her face, as if to make his point clear. Because apparently his raised voice wasn't enough.

Before he could think about what he was doing, Chad started walking toward the couple. He had no idea what the argument was about, but the body language of the woman clearly indicated that she was uncomfortable.

As he approached, he studied her in detail. She was wearing a pair of jeans and a T-shirt. The jeans looked old and worn, and the tee was one of those cheap garments sold in tourist shops everywhere in the state. It had the word *MAINE* in bold letters at the bottom of the graphic, with trees and a huge sun in the middle.

Her hair was pulled back in a ponytail, and it honestly looked as if it could use a good washing. She wore no makeup, and if he wasn't mistaken, he could see a streak of dirt on her cheek. She was fairly tall—he estimated she was around five-nine or so—and slender. Her lips were full, her nose just a touch crooked, as if it had been broken at some point in her life.

She also seemed exhausted. As if she hadn't slept in ages. The dark circles under her eyes gave her a haunted look.

For some reason, the entire picture she presented bothered Chad. He had no idea who this woman was or where she was from, although the license plate on her car was from Georgia. She was most likely a tourist, and definitely a long way from home if she really was from the South.

"Is there a problem here?" he asked as he approached. He didn't recognize the man, which wasn't a surprise, since he'd been away from his hometown for so long.

Turning, the man ran a hand through his hair in agitation. "Yeah, there's a problem! This chick's been camping out in the parking lot. She can't do that. We aren't a fucking campground."

Chad's gaze flicked to the Toyota, and he saw what he hadn't noticed before. It was full. There were bags and boxes filling the back seat all the way to the ceiling. Shifting slightly, he saw the passenger seat was also filled with her belongings.

The woman sighed wearily. "And as I told you, I'd be happy to move on, but my car won't start. I don't know what's wrong with it."

"That's not my problem, or my manager's. You need to be off this property in an hour or we're calling the cops," the man barked. Then he spun and stomped back toward the store without a backward glance.

Chad turned his gaze to the woman. She sighed again and her shoulders slumped, but she lifted her chin almost defiantly as she stared back at him. As if bracing herself for whatever derogatory thing she expected him to say.

"You want to pop the hood? I can take a look for you."

She blinked, frowning. "What?"

"The hood," Chad repeated, gesturing to it. "I know a thing or two about cars. I'll see if I can figure out what's wrong with it."

"Oh, um . . . I don't have much money to pay you," she stammered.

Chad waved his hand. "Just being helpful," he told her. "Don't want any money."

"Okay. Thanks. I appreciate it." The woman opened the front door and leaned in to grab the lever that would open the hood.

Chad couldn't help it—he let his gaze stray to her ass. The woman might look a little rough, but she had a back end that would make *any* man take notice. And he was no exception.

Shaking his head at the inappropriateness of his thoughts, Chad moved to the front of the vehicle. He propped up the hood and leaned over the engine and forced himself to concentrate on figuring out why her car wouldn't start.

"I'm Chad," he said, without looking at her. As he hoped, she reciprocated.

"Britt."

"Short for Brittney?" he asked.

"No. Just Britt."

"You're not from around here." It wasn't a question.

"Nope."

She wasn't very talkative, but he was a stranger, so Chad didn't take it personally. "You passing through or staying in the area?"

She didn't answer right away, and Chad turned to make sure she was still there. She was. She was staring at him with a look of indecision on her face.

"Sorry, I don't mean to be nosy. Just trying to be friendly. I can shut up."

"No, it's just . . . I don't know why you're helping me. For free."

Slowly, Chad straightened. The woman was extremely distrustful. On one hand, it made no sense . . . he'd just met her. She had no reason to suspect there was evil intent behind his very simple conversation.

On the other hand, it made perfect sense . . . he'd just met her. Had no idea who she was, knew nothing about her background. For all he knew she was currently in an abusive relationship, or she had some trauma in her past related to men.

Whatever the case, it bothered him on a visceral level that she *expected* him to be an asshole.

"Name's Chad Young. I grew up around here. Just returned to the area to help my mom, because my dad recently passed away. He taught me to be respectful and to lend a hand when and where I could. Not for money. Not to gain a marker of any kind. But to be a decent human being.

"I don't know your story, Britt, but I'm telling you that you can trust me. I'm helping you because you need it. Because that asshole scared you by getting in your face. Because you look like you could use a break, and sleeping in a car sucks. Because I have the knowledge to figure out what's wrong with your car without charging you a thousand bucks to do it. And because my mom would whup my butt if I *didn't* help you."

He stared at her for a long moment before turning his gaze back to the engine. He already knew what was wrong, and thankfully it was an easy fix. He wasn't sure how it had happened—which made him uneasy—but he was taking one issue at a time here.

The first? Putting Britt at ease.

"Britt Starkweather. And no, I'm not from around here. I'd like to stay in Rockville, but I don't know if that's going to work out."

It wasn't a lot of information, but Chad would take it. He straightened once again and said, "It looks like your battery's been disconnected, which is why your car won't start . . . assuming you have gas?"

She nodded. "Half a tank."

"Okay."

"Um . . . can you fix it?" she asked uncertainly.

"Yeah. All it'll take is a quick turn or two of a wrench, which I've got in my truck over there," he said, gesturing behind him toward his truck. "My bigger concern is how it happened. Have you been mucking around under the hood?"

She scrunched her nose in an adorable expression that made him smile.

"No. I wouldn't have the slightest idea what to do under there."

"Right. So, sometimes the bolts can be jostled loose over time . . . but it's rare."

She stared at him for a beat. "What are you saying?" she asked bluntly.

"I'm wondering if someone deliberately loosened the bolts so they'd become disconnected at some point and strand you, like you are now."

The expressions flitted across her face so quickly, Chad couldn't discern one from the other. Then her lips pressed together, and she swore long and low.

His brows flew up at the colorful words coming out of her mouth. He was working on curbing his own habit of cursing. He'd picked it up in the Army, but his mom hated any kind of swearing, so he was making a conscious effort to stop.

"Sorry," she said. "I just . . . my ex. He's a dick. I could totally see him doing something like that just to make my life harder."

"He still around? Are you in danger?" Chad asked, glancing around the lot, even though he wasn't sure what the heck he was looking for. Someone hiding in the trees, waiting to jump out and attack?

"No. He left. We moved up to Maine together. Wanted a fresh start. At first things were okay. But he decided he wanted to go back to Georgia. I didn't. So he left."

Chad frowned. "Just like that?"

"Just like that," she confirmed. "We hadn't even found a place to live yet. It was a lot harder than we thought it'd be when we moved here, and Cole wasn't totally truthful about some things. I also couldn't afford to stay in the motel we were in any longer. I haven't found a job yet . . . even though I've been trying really hard."

Now *that* was a lot of information, and suddenly Chad was having a hard time taking it all in. "How long were you two here before he decided to bail?"

"Two weeks."

He blinked. "Two weeks? That's it?"

"Well, *he* was here two weeks before he bailed, I've been here for three. He didn't like that he couldn't get his Taco Bell when he wanted it. Didn't like how much it rains. Didn't like how cold it is here, and he got frustrated because there aren't apartment buildings like there are back in Atlanta. Basically, he didn't like *anything* about Maine. So . . . he left."

Three weeks. That meant they'd both gotten to the area around the same time. Although Chad was well aware that their circumstances couldn't have been more different. And her boyfriend just left her? What an idiot. "Did he do any research about the state before he decided to move?" Chad asked.

Britt shrugged. "Well, yeah, of course. We both did. Before we made the decision to move up here, we checked out the economy, the average temperatures, job market, things to do, stuff like that. He said he was cool with everything. He also swore he already had a house lined up for us to rent . . . but that was obviously a lie. Like just about everything else he told me."

Chad bit back the question, "Like what?" that he really wanted to ask. But it was none of his business. And regardless, Britt was now obviously stuck in a shitty situation. "What about you?"

She frowned. "What about me, what?"

"You want to go back to Georgia too?"

"No," she said without hesitation. "I love it here. I *like* that there aren't fast-food restaurants on every corner. I love the fresh air and all the trees. I don't mind it being rural, and living by the water has always been one of my favorite things." She shrugged. "And generally, most people I've met have been very nice. Besides . . ."

She hesitated, her cheeks suddenly coloring. Chad waited her out, saying nothing.

Finally, she sighed before continuing. "He took all the cash we'd saved together for the move when he left—the money we could've used for first, last, and security on a rental. He didn't care that half of it was mine. And of course he didn't pay for the motel before he took off in the middle of the night. I had enough in my account to pay our motel bill for the two-week stay, but not enough to stay any longer. Which is why I've been sleeping in my car . . . and why I couldn't go back to Georgia even if I wanted to."

Chad hesitated for a moment, then made a decision that felt right. "You hungry?"

Her head tilted at the question, and he could practically see her shields sliding back up. "Why?" She was on guard now, and he couldn't blame her.

"It'll take me ten seconds to reconnect your battery. Assuming that's the only thing wrong with your car, it should start, and you can be on your way. I recently moved home, as I told you, and I'm helping my mom get our property prepped for the tourist season to start again. She's been lonely since my dad died, and if you don't have plans, I'm sure she'd love to meet you. Feed you. It's what she does best. She's constantly trying to fatten me up. I'm sure in a few months, I'll be a blimp."

Chad was talking fast, but the more he thought about it, the better he liked the idea. His mom needed someone to talk to, and Britt needed a place to get back on her feet. She could help out around the house and property, and his mom would have someone to take care of, the way she'd cared for her husband.

He could see Britt was interested. It had to be exhausting, living in her car. She was probably constantly on edge, hoping the wrong person didn't spot her in that dark parking lot at night. Worried about where her next meal was going to come from and where she was going to live, how she was going to survive from one day to the next.

But she also wasn't stupid. He was a stranger. It wouldn't be smart to just go with a man because he offered her a meal.

"That's very generous, but I don't think—"

"Let me call my mom. Prove to you that I'm not luring you to my lair to have my wicked way with you," Chad interrupted. "That I'm being honest. That I *do* have a mother, and she'd be more than happy to meet you and spend an afternoon getting to know you."

She still looked skeptical, but she must've been more desperate than he knew, because she reluctantly nodded. And that made Chad all the more determined to help her.

He immediately pulled out his cell phone and dialed his mom's home number. He didn't bother calling her cell—because she probably wouldn't answer it, and it was probably dead anyway.

He didn't know anyone else who still had a freaking landline, but he smiled thinking of the black phone hanging on the wall in the kitchen, just where it had been for years and years.

"Lobster Cove, can I help you?"

Chad smiled wider at hearing his mom's "polite voice," as he called it.

"Hey, Mom. It's Chad."

"Hi. Is everything all right?"

"Of course. I met someone. A woman. And I invited her back to the house to visit with you and have a meal, but she's understandably nervous because I'm a stranger."

"Give her the phone," his mom ordered.

Chad was still smiling as he held his cell out to Britt. "She's kind of bossy," he warned, knowing his mom could hear him, and not caring. "And half the things she'll tell you about me are lies . . . especially if she tells the story about the time my brothers and I decided we wanted to sail to China and the Coast Guard had to rescue us when a storm came up."

He loved the small grin that appeared on Britt's lips.

"I'm just going to go grab a wrench while you talk to my mom." As soon as she took the phone from him, he turned. He heard Britt say "Hello?" as he walked away.

It took him a moment to find the correct-size wrench he needed from the toolbox in the back of the truck, and when he returned to her car, Britt still had his phone up to her ear and was nodding at whatever his mom was saying.

She didn't say a lot herself as the conversation progressed, but Chad wasn't surprised. His mom could be a chatterbox, and he suspected she was even more eager than he'd guessed to have the company of another woman. She had tons of friends in the area, but she'd always been surrounded by men at Lobster Cove. His dad. Walt and Barry. Otis, who stopped by all the time to shoot the shit and work in the office at the auto shop.

And now, Chad and his brothers. There was a lot of testosterone in her life, and he had no doubt whatsoever that she'd open her arms without hesitation to a woman in need. Even if he hadn't said as much, his mom was intuitive enough that she'd quickly realize Britt was *definitely* in need.

It didn't take him long to fix the battery, but he continued to tinker under the hood, giving Britt all the time she needed to come to a decision as she talked to his mom.

Finally, she asked, "Do you want to talk to your son again?" She laughed lightly at whatever his mom said in reply, then added, "Okay. Yes. I'll see you soon. Thanks. Bye."

She clicked off the phone and held it out to him.

"So you'll come?" Chad asked.

"Yeah. She's . . . nice."

"She is," Chad agreed. "But she's also sneaky. She has a way of getting you to agree to do things you had no intention of doing." He smiled when he said it, so as not to freak her out. To his relief, she chuckled.

"Yeah, I can tell."

He shut the hood of her car and nodded toward the driver's seat. "You want to give her a crank? See if she'll start?"

Britt moved to the door and sat behind the wheel. She turned the key and beamed at him when the engine turned over immediately. "It works!"

Chad couldn't help but stare. The wide, surprised smile on her face made Britt shine. She still looked tired and stressed, but something about that smile had him transfixed.

"Chad?" she asked, the smile disappearing, only to be replaced by a frown.

He gave himself a mental shake. "Sorry. If I give you the address to Lobster Cove, will you be able to get there?"

"Um . . . Lobster Cove?"

"Sorry, that's what we call our property. We've got Lobster Cove Rentals, Lobster Cove Auto Body, and Lobster Cove Boat Storage. It's a whole thing. It's a little cliché, but when in Maine . . ." He let his words trail off.

He was rewarded by that smile again, the one that had him so mesmerized.

"I was thinking I'd send you straight there, but since you don't seem sure about where it is . . . would you mind waiting while I did some errands? I don't have many. Then you can follow me home."

"That works."

Chad nodded. "I was going to grab some wood here, but I think I'll go somewhere else."

"Why?"

"Because that asshole was rude to you. And it was uncalled for. Think I'll give my money to someone else."

She stared at him for so long, Chad was worried he'd said something wrong. Finally, she simply nodded. "Okay."

"Okay," he agreed. "I should be able to get what I need at the hardware store, then I have to make a quick stop at the grocery store. That work?"

"Sure."

Chad gave her a chin lift, then thumped the hood of her car and turned to head back for his truck before he did something stupid . . . like invite her to ride with him. She trusted him enough to come to Lobster Cove, but he didn't want to push his luck. As he pulled out of the parking lot, he glanced in his rearview mirror and saw Britt was right on his tail.

A warm feeling spread through him. He wasn't sure why. But he liked it. A lot.

CHAPTER TWO

Britt had asked herself what the hell she was doing at least a hundred times since following Chad Young out of the parking lot of the lumberyard. She was being stupid, she knew that, but she needed a break. The last few weeks had been horrible.

When she'd decided to move to Maine with Cole, she'd been full of hope. Her job wasn't anything she was emotionally attached to—she'd worked retail all her life, which was tough, but something she could do anywhere. So when Cole brought up the idea of moving to Maine, she was more than all right with the idea of shaking things up in her life.

But during the few months while they'd prepared for the move . . . she should've paid heed to the little voice inside her brain that told her she was making a mistake.

Cole was everything a boyfriend should be—on the surface. He was good looking and smart and funny. He came from a nice middle-class family and made decent money working as a car salesman.

The latter was what should've made her hesitate to move across the country with the guy. He could sell sand to someone dying of thirst in the desert. Thankfully, Britt had insisted on driving her own car instead of selling it and simply going with Cole, like he'd proposed.

Nothing had gone the way he'd expected once they'd arrived in Rockville. He'd expected to walk into any car dealership of his choosing and have them begging him to accept a job. Instead, he'd discovered jobs weren't nearly as plentiful here. And because he was a stranger, the local Mainers didn't have a lot of trust in his abilities—or his will to stick around. And they were right.

Two short weeks. That's all it took for Cole to call it quits . . . and for his true colors to shine through. Everything she'd told Chad about why her ex had decided to go back to Georgia was true. He'd bitched about *everything*, all the time. Those two weeks were mentally exhausting.

Britt, however, was charmed by the small town of Rockville. They could've settled in Portland or one of the other larger cities in the area, but for some reason, Cole was determined to be by the coast . . . which was fine with Britt. The area was so freaking gorgeous. Every morning when she woke up and saw all the trees and the beauty of the land around her, she was in awe.

The evening before Cole up and left, they'd had a huge fight. He'd decided they were leaving, but Britt didn't want to go. She'd been looking hard for work but was having the same issues as Cole . . . she was an outsider, and jobs weren't exactly abundant, especially since it wasn't officially tourist season yet.

She'd suggested that they stick it out a little longer. Argued that they hadn't given the move a fair shot. That something would come up for them both, they just had to be patient.

Cole turned on her. Yelling at Britt in a way he'd never done before. He called her a mooch, said she was lazy and pathetic. Said that even if she *did* find a job, it wasn't going to do much toward putting a roof over their heads, since her only skills were in retail. He claimed it was *his* money that was keeping them afloat, and he was sick of carrying her "deadweight" around.

Britt had been stunned. True, things hadn't been great between them since they'd arrived, but the vitriol in his tone was shocking. He'd never once brought up the differences in their backgrounds or education or financial status. He'd never made her feel "less than" for not making as much money as he did. Until that moment.

It was also total bullshit. She'd contributed her fair share to the move. After rent on her apartment and other bills, she'd saved every dollar she could, and she'd had a few thousand dollars in cash when they'd left Georgia. Even though Cole earned more money, he also loved to spend it, so in the end, he'd left the state with little more than Britt.

She wasn't deadweight, and she deeply resented Cole trying to make her feel as if she was using him.

She'd been so pissed that night, she'd left the motel and taken a long walk, giving them both space and time to cool down. By the time she returned, Cole was already in bed. She'd wanted to wake him to talk, but she knew from experience that he was a grump when woken up.

So she decided to put off the discussion they obviously needed to have until morning. She'd fallen asleep shortly after.

And when she woke up early the next morning, Cole was gone.

He'd literally slunk off in the middle of the night.

And he'd taken all their cash with him.

Britt knew immediately he wasn't coming back. All his things were gone from the motel room. It was as if he'd never been there. She'd tried to call him, only to find he'd blocked her number. The asshole had left her high and dry in Maine and gone home to Mommy and Daddy.

Britt thought about following him. About going back to Georgia herself . . . but she didn't really want to. The people she'd met around town had mostly been nice and pretty welcoming, except when it came to giving her a job. They'd been a little standoffish in that regard, but that was understandable. Most had lived in the area their entire lives and were probably used to tourists coming and going.

Then Britt discovered that Cole hadn't paid for the motel. After paying for gas to get to Maine, as well as other miscellaneous expenses—no matter what Cole said, she'd been contributing to their living expenses by picking things up at the big-box store and paying for groceries—she'd had just a couple of grand left in her account. She had to use the bulk of it to settle the room bill.

With no luck finding a job, she'd resorted to sleeping in her car. It was humiliating and humbling. She'd passed by homeless people time and time again back in Atlanta and hadn't really thought too much about their circumstances. Sure, she gave spare change to them when she had some, but she often assumed those people were mentally ill and couldn't hold down a job, or drug addicts who'd use the money she gave them to buy their next hit.

She felt awful about that now. Every night for the last week, she'd had no choice but to sleep in her car. Yup. Definitely humbling . . . and it got more and more difficult. Her back hurt, she was hungry more often than not because she had to be so careful with her remaining money, and she felt filthy. It wasn't as if there were free showers at the beach . . . not that there were really any beaches at all. Not like in the South. The waterfront was different up here. More rugged. Stark. The water a lot colder.

And like she'd told Chad, even if she wanted to go back to Georgia, she was stuck. She didn't have enough gas money for that trip.

She had half a tank of gas at the moment, and she needed to find a place to park that wasn't too remote, so she'd be safe, but was within walking distance of somewhere she could use a bathroom. She'd meant to wake up earlier than she had that morning and be gone before the lumberyard opened, but that hadn't happened.

Instead, she'd been awakened by a man tapping angrily on her window, yelling at her to get the hell out of the lot or he'd call the police. She'd tried to start her car to leave the lot, and to her horror, nothing happened when she turned the key in the ignition.

So, on top of everything else, it seemed her car was apparently toast.

She'd tried to explain her predicament to the angry man yelling at her, but he wasn't willing to listen. And then Chad had stepped in.

Britt had no idea why he was helping her, but she was grateful. She hadn't been living in her car for all that long, not really, but she wasn't too proud to accept help when it was offered.

Thinking about what he'd discovered about her car made her pissed at Cole all over again. She could *totally* see him loosening her battery connections before sneaking off in the middle of the night, stranding her. He probably thought it was hilarious. She didn't know the first thing about vehicles or how to fix them when something went wrong.

He was a complete dick. And she was better off without him.

Her life had been turned upside down in the last month or so, and Britt simply needed a break. Of course, she was well aware that following a man she'd just met to his home was incredibly stupid. It would serve her right to end up on *Dateline* or some other true crime show. The woman he'd claimed was his mother could be a psycho lying in wait for her to arrive.

For some reason, a picture of one of those Venus flytrap plants came to mind. The second she set foot in the house, the door would shut, and she'd end up the sex slave to a depraved couple who kidnapped unsuspecting tourists for kicks.

But she was tired. And hungry. And desperately needed a vacation from her life. If Chad Young and his mother, if that was who she was, were in cahoots and killed her . . . well . . . so be it.

Deep down, however, there was something about the man that made her want to trust him. He'd seemed so earnest. And the way his voice changed when he was talking to his mom was kind of adorable. And Evelyn Young talked a mile a minute, reassuring her that her son was a good man and that he'd take care of her and would she please come to the house so she could meet her?

She hadn't been able to get much of a word in, and in the end had agreed because Evelyn just seemed so excited. When was the last time anyone had shown that kind of enthusiasm at the idea of meeting her?

So she'd followed Chad around Rockville as he did his errands, opting to stay in her car while he shopped. A small tickle of unease hit as they drove out of town toward his home, the place he'd called Lobster Cove. The road curved this way and that, and before long, it seemed as if they were in the middle of nowhere.

Just when Britt was ready to bail, she saw Chad put his blinker on. A large sign with a red lobster in the middle and the words *Lobster Cove* around it was mounted on poles among a group of trees just starting to get their leaves back after the long winter. The sign was weathered and rustic . . . and Britt loved it at first sight.

Which was stupid. Who loved a sign? But for some reason it put her doubts to rest. Would a serial killer name his killing fields Lobster Cove? She didn't know any serial killers, but she didn't think so.

The gravel driveway wound through the trees, and even though it wasn't exactly warm, Britt lowered her window. The smell of pine immediately filled the car. And she could hear the ocean.

Chad took a sharp curve—and Britt's eyes widened. Holy crap, the place was beautiful! It was everything she'd ever dreamed of when she thought about living in Maine.

To her right was a view of the water that photographers around the world would clamor to capture. The land sloped downward to what she thought was a pebbled beach.

Also to her right, a large house was positioned with its back facing the bay, the front facing the drive and an open expanse of property, as well as various buildings. A porch stretched across the front, where a woman was sitting in one of two rocking chairs near the door, waving at her and Chad. The two-story structure had navy blue siding and white shutters, and it looked like a lot of the homes she'd seen while driving through the small towns in Maine and Massachusetts on her way north. Old and full of character.

There were pine, aspen, and maple trees sprinkled around the property, and she assumed in the summer they'd give off a good amount of shade. She could see a smaller blue house to the left of the main home, through the trees, which seemed to also have a view of the water. A little farther back from the water was a third, even smaller house. She assumed those were the guesthouses Chad had mentioned briefly.

To her left were several long rows of boats, varying in sizes, each with a tight white cover that looked like some kind of shrink-wrap.

There was a garage close to the main house, and a longer building to her immediate right, set just inside the long driveway, with three garage bays—all occupied with vehicles—parking spaces that were obviously for customers, and a few cars, motorcycles, and ATVs parked around the building. Clearly it was the auto shop. She didn't need the sign above the door that said Lobster Cove Auto Body to tell her that.

The grass swayed in the breeze, birds chirped, and salty air filled her lungs. Britt took the place in, eyes wide. Chad grew up here? Why the hell had he left? This place was . . . idyllic. Perfect. Everything she never knew existed while growing up in a trailer in Atlanta.

A short honk made her jerk, and she saw Chad sitting in his truck, looking at her with concern. "You good?" he called through his open window.

Mentally shaking herself, Britt nodded. She hadn't realized she'd stopped her car at the head of the drive while she was gaping at the property. She crept forward and pulled up next to Chad's truck. He'd parked in front of the garage.

Instead of feeling nervous or uneasy about what was to come, Britt somehow felt as if she'd come home. It was totally ridiculous, but she couldn't help it. *This* was what she'd envisioned when Cole had suggested they move to Maine. Of course, she'd never in a million years be able to afford a property like this. Especially right on the water. She'd browsed a few real estate sites and had quickly realized places half the size of this, and with way fewer buildings, were on the market for a million dollars or more. She couldn't even imagine what this place would go for if Chad and his family were ever to sell.

"You gonna sit there all day, or are you gonna get out and come meet my mom?"

Britt looked to her left and saw Chad standing near her door. Not crowding her, not making her feel uncomfortable with his presence, just faintly smiling at her. He had the bags from the grocery store in his hands, which was what finally made Britt move.

She got out and reached for one. "Let me help."

"I got it," he said, turning and heading for the big house. His mom had stood up from the rocking chair and was waiting for them with a huge grin on her face.

"Hey, Mom," Chad said as they climbed the steps.

To Britt's surprise, the older woman ignored her son and made a beeline for her. "You're gorgeous!" she said, as she engulfed Britt in a tight, warm hug.

Britt froze for a moment, as it felt as if it had been forever since she'd been touched in such a heartfelt and honest way. Cole wasn't a hugger. Wasn't much for public displays of affection. And when they made love—the last time had been before the move to Maine—he performed almost routinely, and there certainly wasn't cuddling afterward.

The genuine affection this grandmotherly woman showed her almost brought Britt to tears.

"Welcome to Lobster Cove! I'm so happy you're here. Chad, just drop those bags on the counter, I'll put everything away."

"She thinks I mess up her organization," he told Britt with an affectionate smile toward his mom.

"That's because you do. I have things exactly how I want them, and when you come in like a bull in a china shop, you move everything around and I can't find a thing. Don't you have some work or something to do?"

"I thought I could show Britt around the place," he said.

"She's hungry and should eat first," Evelyn told her son.

"Mom, let her take a breath."

But Evelyn turned to Britt and said, "You're hungry, aren't you? Let me feed you before Chad force-marches you all over the property."

Britt wanted to laugh. The truth was, she *was* hungry. Starving. She couldn't remember the last time she'd had a good meal. Though she didn't want to offend Chad in any way.

But he chuckled. "Fine. Am I allowed to eat too? Or are you gonna starve me?"

Evelyn rolled her eyes. "Whatever. I forgot how much you boys eat. You had five pancakes this morning, along with three sausage rolls, several pieces of bacon, and two biscuits. I don't think you're in any danger of wasting away."

Britt's mouth watered at the thought of all that food.

Instead of being embarrassed about his large breakfast or irritated that his mom was basically kicking him out of the house, Chad merely sighed dramatically. "Fine. I'll go check in with Walt and Barry. I need to fix the steps out here too. I'll get started on that if there's nothing I need to do at the shop."

Evelyn flicked her hand as if shooing him away, then turned back to Britt. "I can't wait to get to know you. It's so nice to have a woman around here. Love my boys, but the testosterone gets pretty thick sometimes. Come on."

She put her hand on Britt's arm and pulled her toward the door with surprising strength.

"I'll be in later," Chad said, meeting her gaze. "If you need anything, I'll be out here."

Britt wasn't sure what she'd need, but she liked the feeling that he was concerned about her. Maybe liked it a little bit too much.

No boys, she told herself as she let his mom pull her inside the big house. She was done with dating for a while. A long while. A guy was why she was in her current predicament in the first place. Broke, living in her car, stranded.

The door shut behind them, and Britt stopped in her tracks as she looked around the foyer of the house. It was open to the second floor, and a grand staircase curved around in front of her. It was majestic and stately and obviously well loved.

"Wow," she breathed.

Evelyn laughed. "A little pretentious, but my Austin loved it the first time he laid eyes on it. The house was built a century ago, and we were lucky to stumble across this place when we were first married and looking for a place to settle down. Come on, I need to see if Chad got everything on the list, and put everything away."

Britt followed Chad's mom, doing her best to take the house in as she went. The wooden floors creaked under their feet, and the smell of lemon was strong, as if someone had just cleaned.

They walked through an arch, and once again, Britt's eyes widened as she took in the main living area. There were huge windows all along the back wall, facing the water and a huge deck. The sun glinted off the water, almost blinding her. The room was warm and cozy, and all Britt wanted to do was curl up on the couch and stare at the view for hours on end.

"It's nice, isn't it?" Evelyn said gently.

Turning to look at her, Britt could only nod.

Evelyn smiled, and the expression was a little sad. "This is my favorite room in the house. Some people don't like living this far north. They say it's too cold. Too remote. But for me, it's home. It's where I raised my family, and where the love of my life and I spent fifty years together. We would sit on that couch and watch rainstorms, snowstorms, windstorms, or just be amazed at the beauty of the sun shining through the windows, like it's doing now."

Britt studied the older woman. Her skin was wrinkled, her back a little rounded with age, and her slender frame made her seem as if a stiff breeze would blow her away. But the strength in her embrace proved she was no frail old lady.

Her shoulder-length hair was gray and tucked behind her ears. Her smile warm and welcoming. Britt could see the resemblance between mother and son. They had the same shade of russet brown eyes, the same bone structure in their faces, the same full lips.

But more than that, the resemblance in their *personalities* was loud and clear. Chad might bitch about not being able to eat with them, and Evelyn might gripe about her son not putting groceries away to her liking, but it was obviously familiar chiding done in jest on both their parts.

And there was an underlying respect and love between them that made Britt's heart hurt.

She wasn't close with her mom. Mom had always been too busy working. Fobbing Britt off on others to babysit—then leaving her to raise herself *long* before she was capable—far too often for mother and daughter to form much of a bond. Britt didn't blame her mom, though. Being a single parent was tough, and she'd done what was necessary to keep a roof over their heads and food on the table. Still, it had a disastrous effect on their relationship, one that Britt regretted to this day.

The truth was, her mom had always been somewhat resentful of her only daughter. Therefore, she also wasn't especially supportive. She'd warned Britt that she was making a mistake moving to Maine with Cole, which turned out to be correct . . . but she'd also told her not to come crying back to her when the shit hit the fan.

"You want to sit there and enjoy the view? Or I can give you a tour of the house. Or I can get you a snack while the pot pies are finishing cooking."

So *that* was what smelled so freaking amazing. She desperately wanted to see the rest of this house, but she also wanted to simply sit and soak in the beautiful view. "I can help you in the kitchen," she said instead.

"Bless you, honey. But I've got it. Why don't you just sit there and relax for a bit. I'll call you when lunch is ready."

Britt nodded and stood where she was until Evelyn was busy in the kitchen, digging into the bags Chad had carried in. She slowly sank down onto the couch cushion and stared out at the water. The property was located on what looked like a protected bay. The water was calm, and from where she was sitting, Britt could see the beach, a dock to the left, and a few kayaks sitting on the bank, ready to be put into the water. There was also a picnic table in a grassy area just above the rocks on the beach, and farther down the shore was a bench.

It was truly a beautiful place, and Britt felt honored to be seeing it. She was lost in thought for so long, she jumped a little when Evelyn called her name and told her lunch was ready.

Britt leaped to her feet and hurried into the kitchen. It was just as dreamy as the little she'd seen of the house already. The counters were granite, the appliances stainless steel, the farmhouse sink was a dream, and the cabinets were a deep navy blue, which matched the color of the siding on the outside of the house.

"You want to eat outside?" Evelyn asked as she stood next to the six-burner stove. There was a double oven beside it, from which she'd obviously just pulled the bubbling pot pies.

"Oh, isn't it a little chilly?"

Evelyn laughed. "Hon, this is Maine. Sixty-four is practically balmy. And the sun will make it feel warmer than it is. But we can bring out blankets to stay comfortable as well."

"Then yes. I'd love to eat on the deck," Britt said eagerly.

Thankfully, Evelyn let her carry the plates while she carried a pitcher of lemonade and two glasses out to the expansive back deck. The breeze from the water *was* a little chilly, and Britt was glad for the fuzzy blanket she wrapped around her waist as she sat at the surprisingly large table on the deck.

"My husband insisted we needed this huge table out here," Evelyn said, a small smile curving her lips upward. "He said that if we were going to have dinner as a family, we needed somewhere for all of us to sit. And he was right. It felt empty after the boys all moved away. And since Austin's passing, I couldn't bear to sit out here . . . but now that Chad is home, it's better. And the rest of my babies are coming soon too. I can't wait."

"They are?" Britt asked, then blew on the steaming pot pie on her spoon. It was all she could do not to ignore the heat of the dish and shove it in her mouth. It smelled so good, and she was so hungry, it took all her control not to act like a heathen.

"Yeah. My oldest, Lincoln, was a fighter-jet pilot in the Air Force. My youngest, Zachary, was in the Navy and won several awards for culinary excellence. They aren't serving slop, you know. It takes skill to be able to cook gourmet meals for thousands of sailors while on the high seas. And my third-born, Knox, was in the Coast Guard. No surprise, since he was the fish in the family. Now he's working as a contractor for them.

"And Chad's certainly no slouch. He was in the Army, where he was a sniper. Some moms wouldn't be too proud of that, but he was damn good at what he did. And again, I'm not surprised, because that kid could lie perfectly still for hours and not move a muscle while playing hide-and-go-seek with his brothers in the woods. They could never find him." She chuckled fondly. "And they're all coming home," Evelyn continued. "I know it's because they feel sorry for me, but I don't care. I'll just be happy to have them close."

Britt reached over and put her hand on Evelyn's. "I'm sorry about your husband."

"Thanks. Me too. But it's not as if we can live forever. We have to take pleasure in the small joys in life when we can. And I had fifty years with the man I love. I have to be content with that. And with whatever time I have left, I'm determined to keep Lobster Cove up and running to the best of my ability. Austin put his heart and soul into this place, and it's where we were happiest."

"It's beautiful. And I haven't even seen a fraction of it. This is the kind of place I've only dreamed about living. It's perfect. Absolutely perfect."

There was a glint in Evelyn's eyes that Britt didn't understand. She leaned forward. "So . . . you came to Maine with a boy and things didn't work out?"

Britt snorted. "That's putting it mildly."

"You have a place to live?"

"Um . . . not really." She doubted Evelyn would count her car as "a place to live."

"You have a job?"

Feeling uncomfortable for the first time, and a little ashamed, she squirmed in her seat. "No, but I'm working on it."

"Hmmm," Evelyn said, taking a bite of her chicken pot pie.

Britt didn't know what that meant, but since she didn't really want to keep talking about her failures, she asked Evelyn about the history of the town of Rockville. To her relief, that turned the conversation away from Britt's current situation. The pride and love for her hometown came through loud and clear while Evelyn chatted happily as they finished their meal.

When they were done, they continued to sit where they were and talk. After a while, a sound behind her had Britt turning. Chad had opened the door and was walking toward his mom.

He leaned over and kissed her cheek. "It's chilly out here. Mom, are you cold?"

But Evelyn waved him off. "I'm fine. How're Walt and Barry?"

"They're good. Busier than ever. It'll be good when the others get here so they can lend a hand. I've started working on the front steps. You'll need to use the side door for another day or so until I'm done."

Evelyn nodded. "Did you get some lunch?"

For all her poking fun at Chad's large breakfast, it was obvious she still worried about him eating enough, and she wanted to feed him.

"Yeah. Love your pot pies."

"I know," Evelyn said with satisfaction. "I think it's time you gave Britt the grand tour . . . since she'll be working here with me."

Britt's eyes widened as she gaped at Evelyn. "What?"

"She is?"

She and Chad spoke at the same time. Suspiciously, he didn't sound all that surprised. But Britt was too busy trying to understand what Evelyn was talking about to wonder why.

"I've decided. She doesn't have a place to stay, and she needs a job. I need more help around here. You know as well as I do, Chad, that I'm getting too old to take care of the cabins by myself. We have a full reservation schedule this summer, with more short-term rentals than long, and that means more cleaning and laundry and making sure they're stocked. Britt can help me with all that, as well as welcoming the guests and taking care of their needs while they're here."

Britt blinked in surprise.

"She can stay here at the house. There's plenty of room for all of us, even if your brothers decide to live at home too. But I'm guessing all you boys will want your own places soon. In fact, I think Knox and Zach both mentioned they've already found apartments. Britt, you can stay here as long as you'd like. In fact, it would be a huge help if you at least stayed throughout the summer. Oh, and I guess you need to know what kind of salary you'd be earning before you say yes or no."

She gave her a number that made Britt's eyes widen even further.

She had no idea what to say. The offer seemed too good to be true. It wasn't quite as much as she was making before she'd moved, but since she wouldn't have to pay rent—which was a huge draw—it was more than fair.

But surely Chad had to be concerned that his mother had invited a stranger to live in her house and had decided to hire her without talking to him about it first.

"That sounds great."

Now she turned to stare at *Chad* in shock. He was *okay* with this? Her mind spun.

"So? Will you take the job?" Evelyn asked, actually sounding unsure and a little nervous.

"Yes!" Britt blurted. In the past, she would've wanted to take more time to think about it. But honestly, she had no choice right now. And besides . . . she was already in love with Lobster Cove.

"Come on," Chad said, holding out his hand. "I'll give you the tour."

Britt was a little baffled. Why wasn't he freaking out? Why wasn't he asking more questions? This made no sense.

"Go on, honey. I'll take care of these dishes," Evelyn said with a satisfied smile on her face.

Without thinking, she reached for Chad's outstretched hand and stood. As soon as his fingers closed around hers, she knew she was in trouble.

She immediately felt as if everything would be all right. Like she was safe. It was the weirdest sensation. One she'd never experienced before. It should've freaked her out. It did a little, but more than that, she felt an overwhelming sense of relief. She hadn't let herself think about what she was going to do after her *literal* last dollar was gone. How she'd afford gas for her car. How she was going to eat.

And now, she'd been given a gift. One that had fallen right into her lap.

She wanted to cry, question Evelyn, ask if she was sure. Instead, not one word passed her lips. She simply followed Chad as he strode back into the house and headed for what she assumed was the side door. "I'll give you a tour of the shop, the garage, the boatyard, then the guesthouses, and we'll end up back here at the house, where we can grab your stuff from your car and move it in."

Before she could agree or disagree, they were outside and headed for the auto shop. Chad hadn't let go of her hand, and Britt was glad. She felt off kilter and unsteady.

How was this happening? She wasn't about to look a gift horse in the mouth, though. She couldn't. She was just going to go with the flow.

There was a chance this was all a setup, and Chad and his innocent-looking grandmotherly mother were serial killers after all. That they'd sneak into her room in the middle of the night and stab her in the heart with a huge eight-inch butcher knife.

But there was also a chance they were exactly what they seemed . . . two generous souls who wanted nothing more than to help a woman down on her luck.

She hoped and prayed they were the latter and not the former. Time would tell.

CHAPTER THREE

Chad could tell Britt was confused. He'd hustled her out of the house before she could protest and tell his mom "no thank you" for the job. She needed Lobster Cove. He felt that down to his toes. How, he had no idea, but he did.

He'd called his mom on the way home and brought up the possibility of hiring Britt . . . if she and his mom hit it off, of course. She *did* need help. And yes, his brothers coming home would lighten her load, but they would have their plates full just with the maintenance needed around the property. The roofs all needed replacing, probably some of the siding as well. The guesthouses were overdue for renovations, which would have to be done between reservations, making them tricky. They'd have to do the larger projects in the fall and winter, but in the meantime, they could patch holes, fix broken tiles, make sure the appliances were in working order, cut down trees that were dead or dying . . . all on top of keeping the other businesses going.

And of course, Knox also had a job lined up, and Zach was going to launch a business. So the time they could devote to Lobster Cove would be limited.

But Chad would take what he could get. He'd been overwhelmed since he'd arrived, and as far as he was concerned, his brothers couldn't get there soon enough.

Until then, he was counting on Walt and Barry to carry the biggest load at the auto body shop, Otis to keep the books, and his mom to continue doing what she did with the guesthouses. Britt being there would be a huge help—and a load off his mind. His mom was pretty spry for seventy years old, but he still worried about her.

It was a perfect solution, and he was thrilled his mom had gotten along with her enough to offer her the job. Though "offer" wasn't the right word. It was more than obvious she'd sprung the job on Britt. That she'd practically *ordered* the woman to move in with her and help out around the place.

So despite stealing her away so she couldn't turn down the position, he realized he'd have to tell her more about it. Give her some details. Reassure her that he and his mother hadn't lost their minds. That they didn't usually pick up random strangers in town and drag them back to Lobster Cove and force them to accept job offers. Hell, he was surprised she hadn't jumped back into her car and hightailed it out of there.

He was *also* surprised Britt hadn't dropped his hand. But their hands felt good, wrapped together . . . so he wasn't going to be the one to pull away first.

"So, this is the auto shop. That's kind of a misnomer, because we work on pretty much any kind of engine. Lawn mowers, ATVs, snowmobiles, cars, trucks, boats . . . if it's got an engine, we can usually fix it," Chad told her, gesturing to the building they were approaching with his free hand.

He walked them into one of the bays and called out to the guys.

"Under here!" Walt called out.

Looking toward the red pickup truck in the first bay, Chad saw a pair of legs sticking out from under the engine. Grinning, he pulled Britt in that direction. "Come out for a second, Walt. I want you to meet Britt."

At that, Walt moved with more quickness than Chad had seen since he'd known the man. Walt was around forty and had what he called a "fireman's mustache." It was large and bushy and curled downward on either side of his lips. He was a big man with a loud, booming voice, which sometimes was a bit over the top, but the guy was truly a gentle soul.

"A girl? You brought a *girl* home?" he asked as he stood up.

Looking over at Britt, Chad saw she was blushing. "Not in the way you're thinking, but yes, we met in town, and she was looking for work. Mom could use some help around here with the guesthouses, and with stuff in general."

"It's nice to meet you. I'm Walt. You need anything, feel free to ask. We're a pretty laid-back bunch around here, and it'll be great to have a pretty face amongst all of us ugly mugs."

Chad noticed the way Walt's gaze flicked to their hands. But since she didn't seem bothered, he didn't loosen his grip. "Is Barry here?"

Instead of responding, Walt turned his head toward the door that led into a small room they used as an office, and yelled, "Barry!"

Wincing and shaking his head at the mechanic, Chad said, "Jeez, Walt. Tone it down a bit, would ya?"

"Sorry. Just wanted to make sure he heard me."

"They heard you up in Bangor," Chad told him.

Walt chuckled, a hearty sound that was becoming extremely familiar. In the two weeks since Chad had moved back to Lobster Cove, he'd heard the man's laughter echo around the property at regular intervals.

The door to the office creaked as it opened, and Barry stepped through. He was a little younger than Walt, and his opposite in almost every way. He was only about five-seven, with red hair and green eyes, and he was slender enough to look as if a stiff breeze would blow him over.

But the man was a genius with engines. He didn't talk much, but he was a hard worker and loyal as hell. From what Chad understood, he used to work on a lobster boat but after a scare in a bad storm, he'd decided it would be safer to change professions. He had a wife and three kids who Evelyn loved to have over for visits, claiming that since her own sons hadn't given her any grandbabies yet, she'd have to make do spoiling Barry's kids.

"You bellowed?" Barry asked as he joined them.

"This here's Britt. She's with Chad. She'll be helping Miss Evelyn at the house," Walt said, taking over the introductions.

"Ma'am," Barry said politely with a nod.

"Oh, please, it's just Britt," she said quickly.

"That's her Corolla near the house. Can one of you please take a look at it? Someone loosened the nuts on the battery, making it disconnect. I fixed that, but I'd feel better if we made sure nothing else was wrong with it."

"Keys?" Walt asked, holding out his hand.

"Oh, um . . . it's okay now," Britt said.

"Walt will make sure of it," Chad answered reasonably.

"I . . . Chad, I can't afford to have any work done on it right now," she said quietly, sounding embarrassed.

He mentally kicked himself. Of *course* she was worried about her finances. He opened his mouth to reassure her that it wouldn't cost anything, but Walt beat him to the punch.

"You're one of us now," he boomed. "A Lobsterite—that's what I've dubbed us. The people who work here at Lobster Cove. And Lobsterites don't pay for shit like tune-ups and oil changes. Hand me your keys, sweetheart, and we'll make sure she's purring nice and good before you head out."

"Take your time," Chad told him. "Mom invited her to stay at the big house for as long as she needs."

Walt's eyes sparkled and his grin widened. "Did she? That's great! Welcome to Lobster Cove then, Britt. As I said before, you need anything, don't hesitate to let us know. If something breaks at any of the houses, Barry's your man to take a look. The washing machine, fridge, vacuum . . . you name it, he can fix it."

"Um . . . thanks."

"Keys?" Walt asked again, holding his hand out once more and wiggling his fingers.

For a moment, Chad wondered if she'd refuse to give in. Then she reached into her pocket and pulled out a key ring with a single key. For some reason, the sight of the lone key on the lobster-shaped key fob made him sad. He had at least a dozen keys on his—which was a pain in the ass—but it underscored how privileged he was to *need* keys to so many different locks.

"Lobster. Seems as if you being here was meant to be," Walt said with a wink as he palmed the key ring.

Britt shrugged. "I saw it when I first got here in a tourist shop and thought it was cute."

"And now here you are at Lobster Cove. Kismet," Walt said.

"You guys about done out there?"

Turning, Chad saw Otis Calvert standing in the doorway of the office. He hadn't realized he was here. "Otis! Come meet Lobster Cove's newest employee," he called out.

The older man had met his father over twenty years ago, and they'd clicked immediately. As far back as Chad could remember, Otis had been in their lives. Joining them for lobster bakes, fishing, drinking beers on the deck. He was as much a part of Lobster Cove as the rest of his family.

Like a lot of people, Otis had endured his share of financial struggles, and Chad's father had helped him out by giving him more and more responsibility in regard to Lobster Cove. To hear Austin Young tell it, Otis's long-ago divorce had been ugly, and his two kids struggled, having to split their time between parents. It affected them both deeply.

Otis's daughter had been in a string of bad marriages and was currently in Portland, living on the streets. He'd done everything he could to help her, but she had no desire to return to this "backwater town," as she called Rockville. She actually preferred the streets and living with her junkie friends over getting a job and working for a living.

Chad thought he remembered his dad telling him at one point that she suffered from mental illness, which didn't help the situation.

Camden, meanwhile, had fallen in with a bad crowd in his teens and done more than his fair share of time in prison. Otis had drained his savings trying to help his son through various legal issues. For the last ten years or so, he seemed to have gotten his shit together somewhat. He was living with his dad and staying out of trouble, working part time at Lobster Cove in the auto shop.

And Otis had long since become responsible for all the accounting for Lobster Cove, which wasn't a small job. He did their taxes and made sure their investments were working as they should.

At one time, he'd worked in the lobster-fishing industry, as had many men and women in the area. But lobstering wasn't an easy job. It was physically demanding and very time consuming, not to mention dangerous. He'd quit when he was nearly thirty, going to college and majoring in accounting.

Chad's dad had hired him sometime after Otis had started his own accounting and investment business, and the rest was history. He'd kept the books at Lobster Cove ever since. He was basically family.

"New employee?" Otis asked as he approached. "*I* didn't know anything about this."

Chad couldn't tell if what he was hearing was disapproval . . . but he didn't like his tone. And he didn't want Britt to feel anything but welcome. "Well, Mom just extended the employment offer ten minutes ago, so unless you've learned how to read people's minds, I'm not surprised you didn't know," he replied.

Otis's grin was contrite. "Sorry. I didn't mean to sound upset. I just need to know these things so we can set up payroll and get her on our insurance."

"Insurance?" Britt asked in surprise.

"Yeah, Austin and Evelyn always wanted to be competitive," Otis explain. "They didn't want to hire good employees only to have them leave because they needed what other, more traditional jobs offered.

So, we finagled things so they could offer not only good insurance but retirement as well."

"Wow, that's great."

"It really is," Walt agreed. "This is hands down the best job I've ever had, and I'm never leaving. I'm gonna be eighty and still puttering around out here in the garage."

Everyone laughed.

"Anyway, welcome to the team," Otis said, holding out his hand.

Britt shook it and gave him a small smile. "Thanks. I still can't believe this is happening. I really needed a job. And to find out it comes with insurance, housing, and retirement? That's more than I ever expected."

"She's staying here?" Otis asked.

"Yeah. Mom insisted," Chad told him.

"That's wonderful. It'll be so good for her to have some company in that big house. Uh, that is . . . other than *you*. I mean, *girl* company," Otis said, stumbling over his words.

"I know what you meant. As a son, I don't count," Chad said, rolling his eyes. "Everything all right here? You need anything?"

"No, everything's good. Just going over inventory with Barry," Otis said.

"All right. I'm going to continue Britt's tour of Lobster Cove. Let me know if anything comes up."

"I'm guessing nothing should. I've got things under control, like always," Otis told him with a laugh.

After promising to take good care of her car and let both of them know if he found anything, Walt pocketed Britt's key and turned back to the truck he'd been working on when he was interrupted. Barry and Otis said their goodbyes and went back to the office.

"Ready?" Chad asked her.

She nodded, and they headed out of the garage bay, toward the boat storage area. The rest of the tour went by fairly quickly, and Britt seemed charmed by the two guesthouses. They'd been decorated in a way that looked like lobsters threw up inside, but the guests seemed to love it. There were illustrated pictures of lobsters on the walls, and his dad ordered plastic cups with their Lobster Cove logo on them, for guests to take with them when they left. There were lobster rugs, shower curtains, knickknacks, and even throw blankets in the small living areas, which were each adorned with a huge lobster.

It was too much for Chad, but then again, he'd grown up in Maine, and lobsters weren't anything special for most locals. But Britt seemed enchanted. The smile on her face as she looked around the cabins was amused and carefree, which Chad loved.

As they toured the houses, which would be occupied sooner rather than later for the start of tourist season, Chad realized how much more work needed to be done in both. The structures were solid, but all the standard upkeep things had obviously been put off for too long.

The rooms smelled a little musty, and the walls could use new paint. He wanted to replace the carpets in the bedrooms with hardwood floors. There was a small stain on the ceiling in the one-bedroom that needed a closer look. And of course the roofs needed replacing. One deck needed a new coat of paint, at the very least, and the other could use a complete overhaul.

They were walking along the water's edge after the tour, approaching the bench seat, when Britt tentatively asked if they could stop for a moment.

"Of course," Chad said, gesturing to the bench.

Britt sat, her gaze glued to the calm blue water. Lobster Cove was named after the body of water the property sat on, a protected inlet that was fed by the Atlantic Ocean. But because it was a cove, they didn't get the destructive waves during storms. When his parents first bought the property, the water froze almost every winter, but these days they rarely saw such extreme weather.

Chad had spent his childhood swimming, kayaking, paddleboarding, and goofing off in and around the cove. The swing he and his brothers had used hundreds of times to fly over the water, jumping in when it reached its peak, was still hanging from a large tree at the water's edge.

He hadn't realized that the ocean could actually be warm until he'd gone to a beach in Florida on vacation one year.

Every direction he looked brought back good memories of a wonderful childhood.

He'd spent his fair share of time staring out at this body of water . . . so he turned his attention to the woman next to him. He loved experiencing Lobster Cove through her eyes. It made him appreciate all the more what he and his family had.

"It's so beautiful," she whispered after a moment.

"Yes," Chad said, not entirely referring to the view.

"You're very lucky."

"I know." And he did. Chad tried not to take the things he had in his life for granted.

Britt turned to him, and the serene expression on her face morphed to one of concern. He'd been expecting this. It was one of the reasons he didn't hesitate to agree to stop for a moment. So they could talk.

"Don't get me wrong. I want to stay. I want to work here. I *really* need a job. But it doesn't seem as if your mom really needs me. Especially since your brothers will be coming home soon. I don't want to take advantage of you or your family."

Her concern only further convinced Chad he'd made the right decision in inviting her back to Lobster Cove. If she was a different kind of person, she wouldn't care about anything but what *she* needed and wanted.

"We *do* need you. My mom might seem like she's doing just fine, but she's struggling. She's spent the last fifty years with my dad by her side. He was ripped away very suddenly, and she's having a hard time figuring out how to navigate this new phase of her life without him. You being here today, even for the short time you sat with her, has already made a difference. I saw a spark in her. She seems more interested in what's going on around her, in Lobster Cove, in life."

Britt gave him a skeptical look.

"Sorry, that sounded pretty heavy handed. Mom's . . . okay. Sad about Dad, but determined to keep the land and businesses they started together running smoothly. I just meant that I could tell how much she enjoyed spending time with you. I think you working here will be good for both of you."

"I don't want to be a mooch," Britt said softly.

Chad laughed.

"I wasn't kidding," she said, sounding a little perturbed.

"I'm sorry, I wasn't laughing at you. But you saw the guesthouses. This isn't a fake job or some pity offering. We really do need you. We have guests coming soon, and if they see the shape of those cabins, they'll never come back. We need help. *Mom* needs help. You'll earn your paycheck, have no doubt about that."

"Honestly, having a roof over my head and a safe place to sleep is enough."

"No, it's not. Are you okay with the salary Mom offered? I could talk to her if you don't think it's fair."

She stared at him with big eyes. "You're kidding."

"No, why? It's not enough?"

"Chad! I'm getting room and board, and apparently a tune-up for my car. That's already too much!"

"This is Maine. Things are more expensive here. For the record, I do think it's a fair salary, but if you want to negotiate, as I said, I can talk to Mom."

She turned back toward the water, and Chad saw her bottom lip quivering. He gave her the moment she so obviously needed to regain her composure.

Then she took a deep breath and looked at him again. "The salary is perfect. I'm going to be the best housekeeper, companion, concierge . . . *whatever* . . . your mom has ever had."

"I know you are." And he did. This woman wasn't one to take charity. To take advantage of others. How he knew that, he had no idea, but she practically oozed sincerity.

"Will your brothers be upset that she hired me without talking to them about it?"

"No." Of *that*, Chad had no doubt.

She looked skeptical again.

"Trust me, they aren't going to care. All they'll care about is Mom. Making sure she's content and safe."

"Will they be moving into the house when they get here too?"

Chad wasn't sure if she had trepidation about living with so many strangers, and men at that. "I'm not positive of their plans yet, but I don't think so. And even if they were, you have nothing to worry about. You can trust them. Me too, for that matter. In case you've had concerns, I didn't bring you here to seduce you or haul you to some underground lair we Youngs had built to imprison innocent women for our nefarious purposes."

Britt giggled. Which made Chad smile in return.

"Believe it or not, I *did* have a few moments where I wondered . . ."

"I'm a good guy, Britt. I swear. And I think if you let it, Lobster Cove can heal whatever hurts you have. Your ex? He was an idiot. And an asshole. I can't believe he just up and left you behind, sticking you with that motel bill. You're better off without him, and if you give Maine a chance, it'll sink into your soul and you'll wonder why it took you so long to get here."

"I hope so. Even with all the uncertainty in my life recently, I've found I really like it here. It's . . . serene. Back home, everyone is always on the go. Pissed off about traffic, ignoring trash they see on the sidewalks as they walk past, not caring about anyone but themselves. I found myself getting sucked into that same mindset, but when I got here, it seemed to melt away.

"And I know things won't be perfect here. There's still crime, still jerks who think it's okay to throw their trash out the window as they drive down a rural road, still bad people around. But somehow it feels . . . muted. If that makes sense."

"It does," Chad agreed. "I couldn't wait to leave. Wanted to see the world, so to speak. And now that I have, Maine, Rockville, and Lobster Cove seem even more perfect."

"Does your beach have those little pieces of glass that are all smooth and stuff from the water?"

It was an abrupt change of topic, but Chad didn't mind. "Sometimes. Since we're in a protected cove, we don't get as much sea glass as places like Fortunes Rocks Beach in Biddeford, or Pebble Beach on Monhegan Island. The waves bring in the glass that's been tumbled around in the ocean for years, decades even."

"It's weird that something that offends me so much, trash being put in our oceans, can create something so beautiful that people obsessively search for."

"I hadn't thought about it like that. But I think I'm still on the side of not littering," Chad said.

"Me too. But I'm not opposed to cleaning up beaches by picking up those pesky pieces of lovely glass." She grinned.

Chad wasn't even freaked out by the way he was already thinking of places he could take Britt to search for some sea glass.

"I could sit here all day," she said after a moment.

"You say that now, but when the wind picks up and you're freezing your butt off, you'll be happy to be inside in front of the fire, snuggled under a blanket."

"True," she said with a laugh. Then she sighed. "Chad?"

"Yeah?"

"Thank you." The words were soft and almost carried away by the wind.

"You're welcome. Come on, let's go see what trouble my mom's gotten into. She's probably broken out the whiteboard she used when I was a kid to assign us chores. We hated that damn thing."

"No, you probably hated doing chores," Britt countered.

Chad chuckled. "Yeah, you're right."

He wanted to take her hand again, but it felt a little awkward now. Then something occurred to him, and he wanted to make sure he cleared up this little detail *now*. "You don't work for me," he blurted as they stood.

"What?"

"I'm not your boss. You don't answer to me, you don't have to account for your time or what you're doing with me or any of my brothers. I just wanted to make sure you knew that."

She scrunched her forehead. "Um . . . then who do I work for?"

Chad shrugged. "I guess my mom. But she's never going to see herself as your boss either. I'm sure in her eyes, you're just another member of the family."

He could see Britt struggling to maintain her composure.

He said softly, "I just wanted to make sure you understood that this isn't a typical working environment. But on the other hand, if anyone ever makes you uncomfortable—guests or the others who work at Lobster Cove, my brothers included—you absolutely should *not* put up with that. Tell me, or any of my brothers, or even Otis. We might not have an official HR rep, but no one will tolerate anyone feeling unsafe or uneasy. Okay?"

"Okay. This still doesn't seem real," she mused as they continued down the path toward the main house.

"It will when you're irritated at my mom because she's forcing more food on you, or when you have to clean one of the cabins after an inconsiderate tourist leaves, or when you're so tired after a long day that you can't keep your eyes open."

"Oh, trust me, that'll be nothing compared to asshole ex-boyfriends who make you feel like shit for enjoying something as simple as a lobster key chain, or dealing with customers around the holidays in retail."

Chad smiled. "Welcome to Lobster Cove, Britt. We're lucky you're here."

"I'm the lucky one," she countered.

Chad had the thought that perhaps *he* was the lucky one, getting to work with her, see her every day, live with her.

It was that last thought that had him tripping over his feet. Britt grabbed his arm, as if she could keep him from face-planting on the rough trail. Thankfully he got his balance and didn't take her down with him.

He was thirty-seven years old, and he'd never lived with a woman. His mother didn't count.

But the thought didn't make him anxious. Instead, it had anticipation swirling through his blood for some reason. He had a feeling the idea of living with any other woman might already have him regretting his part in encouraging his mom to hire her.

But living with Britt? Getting to know her? He was looking forward to it.

CHAPTER FOUR

A week later, Britt knew that Chad hadn't been kidding when he'd said she'd earn her paycheck. She was exhausted, but in a good way. Every day, something new seemed to pop up that needed doing. The first guests of the season had arrived, and her experience in retail came in handy, as they seemed to have a hundred questions every day.

She'd given them her cell phone number—a cell phone that had been provided by Otis, who'd told her she should be reachable at all times, now that she was working and living on the property. And the guests hadn't been shy about using it. They wanted to know the best time to go kayaking, where the nearest Starbucks was located (about an hour and a half away, in Brunswick), and recommendations on where to find the best fresh lobster.

She'd also worked really hard before the guests arrived, ensuring the houses were as comfortable and clean as possible and making them look luxurious, at least at first glance. The more time she spent there, the easier it was to see the work that needed to be done. Work that Chad was doing his best to take care of. But as with her, something more important always came up that demanded his attention.

A tree coming down in a windstorm one night, emergency repairs to the heat pump in the two-bedroom guesthouse, boats that needed to be prepped for pickup by their owners. Lobster Cove was a busy place—and it was more than obvious why Chad was excited for his brothers to arrive today.

Britt was nervous. Even though they all knew about her, about how she'd come to be working and living at Lobster Cove, meeting the rest of the Young brothers seemed daunting.

She was sitting on the front porch having coffee with Evelyn when a blue Ford Explorer pulled up in front of the house. Evelyn let out an adorable little squeak and lurched out of her chair, hurrying down the newly repaired steps.

Britt stood and stayed where she was. Part of the reason she was nervous was because if Chad's brothers protested her being here, she'd be out. She had no doubt about that. And the longer she was here, the more she wanted to stay.

Evelyn was everything she'd ever wished her own mother could be, and Lobster Cove was possibly the most beautiful place she'd ever seen in her life. If she hadn't been keeping Evelyn company while she waited for Zach, Britt would've been on the back deck, watching the sunrise. It was one of her favorite things to do. It was chilly in the mornings still, but she didn't care. She bundled up in a blanket and sipped coffee while watching the world come alive.

She'd also never seen a loon in her life before coming to Maine, and now she could recognize their distinctive call and tell the difference between the eider ducks and the loons that swam around the cove.

But it wasn't just Evelyn and the view and the wildlife . . .

It was Chad.

She was appreciative of his help, of his kindness. But the longer she was around him, the more she realized gratitude wasn't the only thing she felt for him. They had a type of chemistry that she'd never experienced with a guy . . . ever.

She'd been pissed at Cole for leaving her, but not devastated like someone who was deeply in love with a partner would've been. She'd moved with him to Maine not because she couldn't live without him but because she wanted to get out of Georgia. It was a crappy reason to move halfway across the country with a man, and she wasn't proud of herself for using Cole in that way, but even with the trouble she'd had . . . she didn't regret going outside her comfort zone and upending her life.

With Chad, she didn't feel as if she had to put up a front, to pretend to be someone she wasn't. He'd seen her at her worst that day in the parking lot of the lumberyard, and he hadn't been turned off. She could still recall the way her hand felt in his as he gave her that original tour of the property. Walking with him had simply felt . . . right.

As if he'd brought her exactly where she was meant to be.

She'd tried to turn that feeling off since then, but it was impossible. Even when things went wrong, or when she messed up, she didn't feel as if she was about to be fired or like anyone was upset with her. Around Lobster Cove, shit happened, same as anywhere else, but everyone rolled with the punches. It was a nice way to live . . . not to be on tenterhooks, worried that she might be kicked out without a chance to defend herself.

But now that the other Young brothers were arriving, she'd be the outsider once more. They had every right to say who could and couldn't live here, and if she did anything they didn't like, they were sure to side with each other and give her the boot.

Britt opened a local bank account this week the second Otis presented her with her very first paycheck, and it felt really good to see a balance that wasn't so close to the negative. But if she had to leave, the money she'd been paid so far wouldn't last long.

Those thoughts were swirling around in her head when the door to the house opened. Turning, she saw Chad step out. He was wearing a pair of blue jeans, a black T-shirt, and black work boots. His brown hair was wet; it was obvious he'd just gotten out of the shower. He'd been up before dawn that morning, working on a lawn mower down in the body shop before Walt and Barry arrived.

Instead of walking down the stairs to greet his brother, Chad stopped next to Britt. "Morning," he said quietly.

For some reason, goose bumps shot down Britt's arms at hearing his low, gravelly voice. "Morning," she replied. When he didn't move, she asked, "Aren't you going to go greet your brother?"

"When Mom's done fawning over him, he'll come up here. I saw him not too long ago and talked to him last night on the phone. He stayed in Boston overnight. That's why he's here so early. He's a morning person, which is annoying."

Britt couldn't help but chuckle. "Um, I hate to break it to you, but you're a morning person too, Chad."

He turned his head and grinned at her. "Yeah, but Zach's *really* a morning person. He used to have to get up around oh three hundred to start cooking when he worked for the Navy, and even now he gets up at the ass crack of dawn. Leaving his hotel before six in the morning is nothing out of the ordinary for him. Even as a kid, he was always the first one up . . . used to drive my parents nuts, especially on holidays when he wanted everyone else up with him."

Britt loved hearing stories about when Chad was younger. Evelyn was constantly talking about her sons and husband and life at Lobster Cove. They had such an amazing legacy here, and she was so happy for them.

"There's no need to be nervous, you know," he said almost nonchalantly.

Britt glanced up at him.

"They're not going to kick you out."

She had no idea how he knew she'd been worrying about that exact thing. "I'm a stranger you picked up off the street. I'm guessing they're going to be a little worried about my intentions and whether I'm a danger to your mom."

"You aren't."

Britt huffed out an annoyed breath. "True. But *they* don't know that. For all they know, I'm hoarding the silver in my bags and I'll abscond with the goods in the middle of the night."

Chad laughed, and the sound rumbled through Britt, making her uneasy with how much she loved hearing pretty much any sound from this man.

He didn't get a chance to respond, because Zach was making his way toward them.

"Good thing you got here early. I want to get up on the roof to check out how bad it is, so I know how much time we have to replace it. I could use some help," Chad said.

Zach rolled his eyes but didn't hesitate to give his brother a hug. "Not even a 'Hey, how was the drive?' before you start cracking the whip?"

"Hey, how was the drive?" Chad deadpanned when he pulled out of the short brotherly embrace.

Zach punched his brother in the arm. "Introduce us," he ordered, turning his attention to Britt.

Forcing herself to not fidget, Britt smiled at Chad's youngest brother. He was tall, even for her. She knew he was six-six and got his height from his dad. He had hazel eyes and a square jaw. His lips were full and currently curled into a friendly smile. His dark hair—not quite black, but not a true brown either—was cut in a military style, short on the sides and a little longer on top. He had on a pair of khaki pants, a polo shirt, and sneakers. He looked more like a preppy stockbroker than the master chef she'd heard about.

"Zach, this is Britt. Britt, this is my annoying little brother—well, one of them—Zachary."

"It's nice to meet you. I've heard a lot about you," Zach said formally.

Which could mean just about anything. Not that Britt thought Chad was talking bad about her behind her back—and Evelyn certainly wasn't—but she was still worried. "Same," she told him.

"How do you like our little homestead?" he asked, waving a hand around to indicate Lobster Cove in general.

Now *that* was a topic Britt was comfortable talking about. "It's amazing. Like a dream. So beautiful."

"Until a foot of snow is dumped on us and we have to dig everything out," Zach said with a chuckle.

"Oh, I bet it's even prettier with snow!" Britt exclaimed.

"Come on inside," Evelyn ordered as she joined them. "Why are we standing around like heathens on the porch when we could be eating breakfast?"

"Please tell me you made your special waffles," Zach begged.

"Are you gonna leave if I say we're having Greek yogurt with strawberries and low-fat bagels?"

Zach scrunched up his nose, clearly letting his mom know what he thought of that menu.

She giggled. "Of course we're having waffles. They're your favorite."

Zach put his arm around his mom's shoulders and gave her another hug. "*You're* my favorite," he told her.

"And you're *my* favorite," Evelyn returned.

"Hey!" Chad protested.

Britt looked on with a grin. It was obvious the conversation was a running joke in the family.

"Actually, I think Britt is now my favorite," Evelyn said. "She's been a godsend. Works her butt off too. Did you know she spent the other day scrubbing the floors in the small guesthouse kitchen and actually got those pesky water stains out that have been there since the place flooded a few winters ago?"

"Yeah?" Zach asked as he steered his mom toward the door.

Britt could feel herself blushing. It wasn't as big a deal as Evelyn was making it out to be. Although it had been a lot of hard work, scrubbing the floor was cathartic. She'd taken out all her harsh feelings about her ex on the poor tiles.

"Yes. And *she* doesn't complain about having to fold laundry, like some people I know." Evelyn elbowed her youngest son as she hurried into the house ahead of all of them, toward the kitchen.

Britt thought Zach would crack a joke or say something lighthearted, but instead he turned to Chad and said softly so their mom wouldn't overhear, "How's she doin'?"

"Good. Well, as good as can be expected. Britt being here has made a huge difference. I think she was lonely and overwhelmed. Having Linc and Knox home will make her feel even better, I'm sure."

"They're still getting here later today, right?" Zach asked.

"As long as nothing happens, yes. Lincoln said he'd pick up Knox at the airport in Portland on his way through. He's shipping his car and the rest of his stuff from Florida. You know Lincoln, he won't get in a plane if he's not behind the controls, so he's driving all the way from Montana."

"Stubborn ass," Zach muttered. Then he turned to Britt again. And the happy-go-lucky guy she'd interacted with a couple of minutes ago on the porch had morphed into a serious, skeptical, protective son. "So . . . I'm going to want to hear the story about how you finagled your way to Lobster Cove."

Britt's stomach dropped, but she lifted her chin. She hadn't done anything wrong. Hadn't begged Chad to give her a job. But she understood Zach's concern. She was a stranger who was living in the same house with his vulnerable widowed mother.

"Zach," Chad warned.

"No, it's okay," Britt interrupted. She met Zach's gaze without flinching. "My car wouldn't start, and I was stuck in the parking lot where I'd been sleeping. One of the employees was yelling at me to get off the property when Chad intervened. He helped me get my car started and invited me here to have lunch. Your mom offered me a job, and since I had exactly a dollar and forty-three cents to my name, I agreed."

"I told you what happened already," Chad said.

Britt didn't take her eyes from Zach's. He might be the youngest brother, but he was obviously no pushover.

"I love my mother. She's the most important woman in my life and always will be. I'll move heaven and earth to make sure she's happy. And I won't hesitate to do whatever's necessary to keep drama out of her life."

"She's lucky to have you. All of you," Britt told him honestly. "I'm not going to hurt her. In just the week I've been here, she's treated me more like family than my own mother ever has. I'll prove to you, and the rest of your brothers, that I have nothing but the best intentions in being here. I'm not going to steal from her, or from anyone. I don't have a hidden agenda. I just want to work hard and earn my keep."

Zach stared at her for a long, uncomfortable moment, then he nodded.

That nod wasn't exactly approval, but it still made Britt's muscles relax a fraction.

"Are you done interrogating her?" Chad asked in a tone she hadn't heard from him before. Glancing at him, Britt saw a muscle ticking in his jaw and one of his hands clenched in a tight fist.

"I wasn't interrogating her. Just getting to know her," Zach protested.

"Give me a break. If that's your idea of 'getting to know her,' I feel sorry for any woman you might date in the future. What you were doing was questioning my instincts in encouraging Mom to hire her, and you were trying to make Britt feel uncomfortable," Chad countered.

Zach frowned. "I trust you. I just worry, and I had to make sure she knows that we aren't going to tolerate any funny business."

Britt couldn't help it. Her lips curled up at hearing this preppy-looking, obviously physically intimidating man say "funny business."

"What? Want to share the joke?" Zach asked. Thankfully, he didn't sound mad.

Britt shared a look with Chad and saw him grinning as well. He stepped in, saving her from having to explain. She had no idea how he knew what she was thinking, but as she'd found often during the last week, they seemed to be on the same page.

"*Funny business?* Who says that?" he asked his brother.

To Britt's relief, Zach chuckled. "Right, it sounded better in my head than it did in real life."

"Enough of giving Britt the third degree!" Evelyn shouted from the kitchen. "Get in here and eat or I really *will* feed you yogurt!"

Britt frowned, not liking the idea that Evelyn knew they were talking about her in a roundabout way behind her back.

"Mom has a way of knowing everything that goes on in this house," Zach told her when they all turned toward the kitchen. "I used to swear she and Dad had hidden cameras around here."

"But they didn't. And don't," Chad was quick to say.

"Must be a mom's instinct," Britt said, letting them both know she wasn't worried about cameras.

"I guess. But it was a pain in the ass growing up. Remember that time when I was making out with my girlfriend on the couch, and Mom yelled—all the way from her bedroom—for me to keep my hands to myself?" Zach asked. "It was embarrassing as hell."

"I wasn't here. I was already in boot camp, so I don't remember, but I can commiserate. It's like the time I was smoking weed out in my car with a friend, because I wanted to see what the fuss was all about, and Dad came out of nowhere and threw a Twinkie into the open window, telling me it was for when I got the munchies later," Chad said with a laugh.

"He did? He wasn't mad?" Britt asked.

"He wasn't thrilled," Chad admitted. "But we had a long talk the next day, and he said he was relieved that if I needed to try something like that, I was doing it in a safe place and that I wasn't driving." He sighed. "I miss him. He had a great way of making me think twice about stupid shit I was doing without sounding preachy."

"Yeah," Zach agreed.

Not for the first time, Britt regretted that she hadn't had a chance to meet the man. He sounded awesome.

Breakfast was delicious, as usual. Evelyn had gone all out since Zach was home. Just as Britt finished eating, a text came through on her phone. It was one of the guests in the two-bedroom house, wanting to know if she had any suggestions for a good seafood place.

Evelyn had given her a list of the best restaurants in Rockville and even farther out, just in case anyone wanted to explore the area a little. She kept it on her phone—updated to include phone numbers and websites—so she texted it to their guest. But she decided it couldn't hurt to take a walk over to make sure the guests in both cabins had everything they needed.

"It was nice meeting you," she told Zach as she stood from the table, then turned to Evelyn. "I'll do the dishes when I get back."

But the older woman waved her off. "There are two perfectly capable men here who can wash a dish or two. I know Otis wants to see you, so he can get your insurance paperwork filled out this morning. After you visit the guests, you can go see him at the auto shop."

Britt reluctantly agreed. She took her dishes to the sink, still feeling guilty for leaving them there, and headed for the front door.

Chad followed her out.

"You good?" he asked.

Britt frowned. "Why wouldn't I be?"

"Because I know you were nervous to meet Zach, and he was kind of harsh."

Britt shrugged. "Harsh? No, he's a concerned son worried about his mom, and whether a stranger who'd moved into her house might be taking advantage of her. I'd actually be more worried if he *didn't* question my being here."

Chad stared at her for a long moment.

"What?" she asked, feeling uncomfortable with his scrutiny.

"Nothing. I just . . . thank you."

"For what?"

"For being here. For not being offended with the questions. For helping. All of it."

"I'm the one who should be thanking you," she told him.

"How about we call it even?" he suggested.

"Deal."

Neither moved. Britt felt drawn to this man, and she didn't understand why. But it eased her mind that he seemed to feel the same way, if his reluctance to part was any indication.

"I guess you need to go," he said.

"Yeah."

"Wanna meet up later for lunch? I thought I could show you the secret trail my brothers and I made when we were growing up."

"Does it lead to a secret fort in the trees?"

"Of course."

Britt had no idea if he was kidding or not, but she wasn't going to pass up the chance to see a real live fort in the woods . . . or be alone with Chad. Any thoughts she had about him or his family inviting her to their lair to do her harm had long since disappeared.

They stood there staring at each other for another beat. It was a loaded silence filled with . . . anticipation? Nervous energy? Uncertainty?

All of the above.

Finally, Britt backed up a step. Then another, without losing eye contact.

"Don't let them give you any shit," Chad told her.

"The guests? They're nice."

He simply shrugged. "Give an inch, they'll take a mile."

He wasn't exactly wrong, so Britt nodded anyway.

"See you later."

"Bye," Britt told him. Then she forced herself to turn and walk down the front steps. She couldn't help but look back when she was halfway to the guest cabins. Chad was still standing on the porch, watching her.

Butterflies swam in her belly and her lips curled up as she continued on her way.

CHAPTER FIVE

"Was she really living in her car?" Zach asked Chad a bit later, after they'd both climbed onto the roof of the main house to see if any of it could be salvaged.

"Yeah. There was just something about her that got to me. A quiet dignity, maybe. She was down on her luck, hungry, desperate, and yet she didn't beg me for money. Didn't ask me for *anything*. But I think it was the surprise in her eyes when I offered to take a look and see if I could figure out what was wrong with her car that really hit home. Like she was shocked anyone would do something nice for her. I actually can't believe no one else offered to help. Things have changed around here."

"Things have changed everywhere," Zach countered. "People fake vehicle problems all the time to lure in unsuspecting victims they can rob, or worse. And while there are still plenty of people out there who're willing to be charitable and help out, they aren't stupid either. They don't want to just give money to someone, because the possibility that the money will be used for drugs is high. They don't want to give someone down on their luck a job, because they might get taken advantage of.

"It's easier for people to mind their own business. And I can't say they're wrong, especially when it's hard enough for most of us to just take care of ourselves. The more things cost, the harder it is to make a decent living, so people hoard what they have. Of course, that means those without are even *more* desperate."

Chad stared at his brother with a frown. "That's pretty pessimistic," he said.

Zach shrugged.

"You're too young to be that cynical. Are you saying that you'd ignore a young woman getting berated by a much larger and stronger man in a parking lot?"

"Probably."

Chad didn't believe that for a second. Zach might be seven years younger than him, but they'd both been raised by Austin and Evelyn Young. Two people who believed down to their core that others were generally good. Deserved the benefit of the doubt. And they'd passed those beliefs on to their sons. Encouraged them to do the right thing. To stand up for those who were weaker and needed a champion.

"I know being a cook is hardly the most difficult job in the military, but I still saw some bad shit," Zach said as he stared out over the water. "I wasn't a SEAL or Special Forces. I didn't have to deal with the aftermath of bullets and bombs and what those things can do to the human body. But when we were in port, I always volunteered to deliver food to organizations that handed it out to those in need. The things I saw . . ." His voice trailed off.

Chad sat quietly and waited for his brother to continue. Zach, as the baby in the family, had been spoiled, and he'd gotten into his share of trouble in school. He'd obviously grown up a lot in the Navy.

"Men pushed women and children out of the way to get to the food. They'd grab it out of the hands of little boys and girls and run off. Women weren't much better. Desperation does horrible things to people. The slightest sign of compassion, of trying to help someone else, could mean a beating or having all your belongings stolen. Trying to do right by my fellow man just showed me it's a dog-eat-dog world out there . . . and honestly? I'm exhausted by it."

Chad reached out and put a hand on his brother's shoulder. He sincerely hoped being back home in Rockville would help heal Zach's battered psyche.

He had his own demons from his time in the Army, but he'd been able to push most of the bad shit so far down that he didn't think about it much anymore. And no matter what Zach had gone through, Chad knew down to his bones that if his brother had been in that parking lot and seen Britt with that asshole from the store, he would've stepped in the same way Chad had. He might not have invited her home for lunch, but he wouldn't have allowed her to get verbally assaulted.

"You like her," Zach said suddenly, turning his gaze to Chad's.

"What?"

"You like her," he repeated.

His belly churned, and Chad shrugged. "Sure. She's been great with Mom and a huge help."

"Right, but that's not what I'm talking about. I can tell, bro. In the way you watch her when you're in the same room together. Just be careful, all right?"

Irritation coursed through him. "She's harmless."

"Uh-huh."

"She *is*," Chad insisted.

"Okay, no need to get huffy," Zach told him.

"I'm not huffy. I just don't want you to think the worst of her before you even get to know her."

"So if I got to know her and decided to ask her out, you wouldn't mind?"

His words were a gut punch to Chad. His first instinct was to blurt "No fucking way!"—but he resisted the urge.

"Yup, you like her," Zach said for a third time. "I'm just curious as to how she's gotten under your skin so fast. Is it because you're living with her? Have you seen her prancing around in her undies and gotten all hot and bothered?"

That pissed Chad off. "What the hell, Zach? No, she doesn't walk around in her underwear. Jesus! You're being a dick."

"Then explain it to me," his brother said calmly.

Chad was well aware of what Zach was doing. He'd done it all the time growing up. He was like a dog with a bone. Once he wanted to know something, he didn't let up until he got his answers. And he managed it basically by annoying the crap out of whoever was enduring the questions, until they gave in and answered.

Or if he wanted to learn how to do something, he'd read whatever he could get his hands on about the subject, or just go out and *do* whatever it was he wanted to learn. Dogged persistence through and through. That was Zach.

"She's . . . different," Chad said lamely.

"In what way?"

"I don't know, she just is."

"You've known her a week. How do you know she's different? Maybe you're just horny."

Jeez, his brother was annoying! He'd been happy to see him, but now he wanted to throw him off this roof.

"She just is!" Chad said way too loudly.

Zach chuckled. "Okay, okay. No need to get mad about it."

Chad took a deep breath, irritated that his little brother could still get to him the way he used to when they were growing up. "Honestly? I really don't know. She's just . . . calming. Nothing ruffles her feathers, which is so different from women I've dated in the past. They got so excited about every little thing, it was exhausting. But Britt is even-keeled, doesn't get upset when things don't go her way or when a guest is rude.

"Like . . . the other day, Mom was getting a casserole out of the oven and dropped it. The dish shattered, and food and glass went flying everywhere. I heard it from my room, and by the time I got downstairs—which didn't take long, trust me—she'd gotten Mom out of the kitchen and was making sure she wasn't cut by flying glass. She wasn't freaking out, was focused on reassuring Mom that it wasn't a big deal."

"Hmmm," Zach said.

Chad wasn't sure what that meant, but he kept talking.

"She'd been scrubbing that damn floor in the guesthouse all day, had already skipped lunch—which I only found out later—and had to have been starving. But she made sure to take care of Mom first, then set to work cleaning up the mess. I was going to help, but Mom was really upset. I think it was mostly just grief bubbling to the surface, but I had my hands full reassuring her. By the time she calmed down and I could help Britt, she'd already cleaned the kitchen and was making grilled cheese sandwiches for all of us to eat. I can't recall another woman I've dated who would've stayed so cool under pressure."

"You've been dating the wrong women, Chad."

"Obviously. But that's not all. It wasn't until after we'd eaten, and she'd done the dishes and was on her way to her room, when I saw blood on her leg. She'd been cut by the glass and hadn't said anything about it. Granted, it wasn't as if she'd cut an artery or something, but still. That's just one example, and not a very good one . . . but it's hard to explain how I feel when I'm around her. I'm still trying to figure it out in my head. And *yes*. I like her."

Zach nodded. "I still think you should be careful. You don't really know this woman, even if she *is* good with Mom and the guests. But I'm willing to give her the benefit of the doubt. If you say she's different and that you like her . . . I can go with that."

"Zach, nobody knows *anyone* when they first start dating. They learn about them during the dating process. That's how it freaking works. I do appreciate your begrudging support, as weak as it is, but please keep an open mind about Britt."

Chad was well aware that there was still a lot about their new houseguest that he didn't know. He wasn't ready to propose and run down to the courthouse and get married, but he was enjoying the feeling he got deep inside when he was around her. Time would tell where it would lead, if anywhere.

"What do you think about this roof?" Chad asked, wanting to change the subject.

"It's fucked," Zach said with a sigh.

"Yeah, that's what I thought too. Damn. What do you think about replacing it with a metal roof?"

"Was going to suggest that myself," Zach said. "I'm thinking we can save some money if we install it ourselves. Or at least help with the process."

"I agree. Otis isn't happy about how much things are costing to fix up Lobster Cove."

"Mom and Dad weren't hurting for money, were they?" Zach asked, sounding alarmed.

"I never thought so. But I've learned in the last few weeks from Mom that money's been tight. I've been trying to find a time to sit down with Otis to go over financials, but things keep coming up and we haven't been able to connect. And the roof is just the beginning of the big things that need to be fixed around here."

"Well, I'm better in the kitchen than I am with a hammer, but you know I'm happy to help where I can."

Chad rolled his eyes. Austin Young had made sure not only that all his sons could work on engines, but they could fix just about anything structural as well. "You just don't want to risk injuring your precious fingers," he teased.

"Damn straight," Zach said with a grin, holding up his hands and wiggling his fingers. "These babies are my bread and butter. Gotta take care of them." He began working his way toward the edge of the roof and the ladder. "And . . . women like what I can do with my fingers too."

Chad burst out laughing at the raunchy innuendo and simply shook his head.

The sound of a vehicle coming down the driveway had him turning his head, and his smile grew when he saw Lincoln behind the wheel and Knox in the passenger seat.

Hurrying now, he followed Zach down the ladder.

Zach tackled Knox as soon as he climbed out of the car, and the two were soon rolling around in the grass that made up their mom's small front yard, mock wrestling. Chad chuckled and walked over to Lincoln. He gave him a man hug, pounding him on the back. They'd seen each other at their dad's service not too long ago, but this felt different somehow. All four of the brothers were together again, for more than a brief trip.

"Get 'em!"

Chad heard the words a second too late, and before he was ready, he was taken down by Knox. Zach took care of their oldest brother, and the next thing he knew, all four of them were in a playful scrum, making him feel as if he was a teenager again, roughhousing with his brothers.

A loud whistle froze them all in their tracks, and when Chad looked up, he saw Mom standing in the yard with her hands on her hips, glaring at them. "What are you four doing? Get up! You're causing a ruckus."

Chad couldn't help but chuckle. She sounded exactly like she had when they were younger. He got up and helped Lincoln to his feet. Then all four of them hurried over to their mom and surrounded her, encasing her in a five-way hug.

"You're smothering me!" she complained, but Chad noticed she didn't push them away.

Love and sorrow overwhelmed him. Love for his family, but sadness because their dad wasn't there to join in.

Eventually, they all gave their mom a little room, and she looked teary eyed up at all of them. "Are you hungry?"

Knox and Lincoln chuckled.

"Mom, it's not that far from the airport to here," Knox told her. "We ate on the way."

"You did? But I wanted to feed you," Evelyn protested.

"Chicken and spinach casserole tonight?" Lincoln asked eagerly.

"With your homemade biscuits?" Knox added.

"I was thinking ramen and hot dogs for everyone," their mom said. Silence filled the air for a solid minute before she giggled and said, "Just kidding! I'll make whatever you want."

"But in the meantime, I could eat again," Knox said, clearly not wanting to disappoint their mother.

"Me too," Linc agreed.

Chad was bursting with happiness. He knew his brothers would annoy the crap out of him before long. Of that he had no doubt. They were all too type A to get along perfectly. Too much alike. But for now, all felt right in his world.

For some reason, he glanced over at the body shop, where he'd last seen Britt heading. He just caught a glimpse of her standing by the side door to the office before she ducked inside. But he'd seen the small, wistful smile on her face as she watched the mini reunion in the front yard of the main house from her vantage point.

A vision hit Chad then. Of her watching a group of children playing in this same yard, years from now. Laughing as they roughhoused and got on each other's nerves. His heart rate jumped with anticipation and longing.

He was confused about his feelings for the stranger he'd invited to Lobster Cove. She made him think about things he'd never considered before. It was uncomfortable, yet at the same time filled him with anticipation for the future.

"Come on, bro, help me unload the car," Knox said as he smacked the back of Chad's head. "I brought some stuff for Mom from Florida."

He walked toward Lincoln's SUV and asked, "You and Linc stop by your places yet?"

"Stopped and got the keys to our places before we came here," his brother said. "And Lincoln's place is sweet. He did good. The house isn't huge, but it overlooks the Atlantic from a hill, and while it's no Lobster Cove, it's nice. We unhitched the trailer with all his stuff while we were there. It won't take long to move him in."

To Chad's surprise, their oldest brother had bought a house when he'd made the decision to move back to Maine. It had been on the market for quite a while and needed some work, which their brother wasn't afraid to take on. Of course, they'd all help him however they could.

And his mom was right—Knox was renting an apartment nearer to town. Maine didn't have large apartment buildings like those available in other parts of the country. Mostly people renovated older houses into separate living quarters. Knox had the bottom floor of one such house. It had two bedrooms and one bath and apparently wasn't very large, but since he was single and planned to spend a lot of his time at work, he'd told Chad he didn't really care.

Zach had also found a place to rent. It was a studio apartment—really just one room in a renovated house, much like Knox's place. But more importantly, he'd also bought one of the food shacks downtown. Ironically, as much as he'd protested operating a lobster shack, that's exactly what it was. But Chad had no doubt his brother would put his culinary skills to use and update the menu so it was both high-end and down home at the same time.

His brothers were settling in, and Chad was thrilled. He had no problem staying at Lobster Cove himself. He wanted to be home to look after their mom and make sure things continued to run smoothly, now that their father wasn't there to serve in the traditional role he'd held for half a century.

He refused to acknowledge the small voice in the back of his head telling him those weren't the only reasons he was content to stay in the house where he grew up.

Britt Starkweather.

She'd gotten under his skin. Now that he'd admitted it to his brother, he was forced to acknowledge the fact to himself as well. He wanted to learn everything about her. And what better way to do that than to live with her?

Lincoln shook him out of his thoughts by flinging an arm over his shoulders and tugging him toward the house. "So . . . how bad is the roof?"

He'd asked the question in a low tone so their mom couldn't hear.

"Total replacement," he said with a shrug.

"Figured. Well, we'll get it done before winter sets in again. No problem."

And that was just another reason Chad was happy his brothers were here. Problems shared always seemed less daunting than when faced alone.

Just like that, once again his thoughts turned to Britt. She seemed to have more than her fair share of problems that she'd had to figure out on her own. Well, now she had him, and his entire family, to help solve any issues she might face. The thought made him smile as he climbed the porch stairs.

His family might be rambunctious and loud, but he wouldn't trade them for anything in the world. The Youngs stuck together, no matter what.

CHAPTER SIX

Britt sat in a chair in front of the desk Otis Calvert used when visiting the auto shop, waiting for him to return. She'd been filling out insurance paperwork when Otis apologized and said he needed to run out to his car, where he'd left one of the pages in a folder on the front seat. As she waited for him, a loud commotion outside caught her attention.

Hoping nothing was wrong, she hurried to the door leading directly to the side of the garage, afraid Evelyn was hurt or something. But the sight she found surprised her, then made her smile. Apparently, Chad's other brothers had arrived. There were four men rolling around on the ground in front of the main house, play-wrestling, as their mom walked toward them.

She'd leaned against the doorjamb and watched the reunion, trying not to feel envious of the obviously close relationship between the siblings. She'd never had that. Her mom had been too busy working to even make dinner most nights. In the sixteen years since Britt had graduated from high school and moved out, she'd tried countless times to forge some sort of mother-daughter bond, only to fail miserably.

Her mom was judgmental. And bitter about how her own life had turned out. She'd chosen one bad relationship after another, and she wasn't shy about letting her only daughter know Britt was going to turn out just like her mom had. Britt hadn't gone to college, had been forced to work two jobs to pay for a tiny apartment when she left home. She'd worked in retail her entire life, and while she was good at it, she didn't particularly love it.

What she really wanted was what she'd never had—a family. A big one. A loving husband who worked alongside her to support their children and didn't resent every bite of food they put in their mouths, or every small expense that came up while raising them.

That's how her mom had been. She may have kept a roof over their heads, but she'd resented every penny she had to spend raising a daughter—and it affected Britt to this day.

Remembering the last conversation she'd had with her mom, when she'd told her she was moving to Maine with Cole, was painful. Her mom had laughed—a low, mean, bitter sound—and said that Cole was going to fuck her over, warning Britt not to come crawling home for a handout when it happened.

Which was the main reason she hadn't bothered to call her mom when Cole had done exactly as she'd predicted. Britt wouldn't get any sympathy from her own flesh and blood. And even though she hadn't taken a cent from her mother since the day she'd turned eighteen, Britt still felt the need to prove that she could make it on her own. That she could be successful.

She'd failed spectacularly at that until she'd met Chad.

She couldn't take her eyes off him as he interacted with his brothers. They looked similar, but if he and Zach were any indication, they were probably all very different, personality-wise.

When Chad suddenly looked in her direction, Britt ducked back into the office—only to find Otis standing in the doorway leading into the shop, watching her. She desperately hoped the blush on her cheeks wasn't as obvious as it felt.

The older man's next words made her forget all about her embarrassment.

"All Austin's money went to his wife."

Britt blinked. "Pardon?"

"If you're thinking to snag one of the Young brothers for his money, for Lobster Cove, it's not going to happen."

Irritation instantly spread throughout Britt. "I'm not looking to date *anyone*," she stated.

"That's good. Because the money in this place isn't liquid. It's not as if there are millions of dollars in the bank. It's all tied up in the real estate and investments."

Britt did her best not to get upset. This wasn't her business. Hell, it wasn't Otis's place to discuss the financial success or failure of Lobster Cove with a new employee.

Otis Calvert had been introduced to her as one of Austin Young's best friends. He had been working for the family for around two decades, managed the investments and the financial aspects of the various businesses, acted as the human resources representative for the employees, and did the taxes for Lobster Cove. He was invaluable to the running of the organization, and it seemed clear to her that he was a trusted and invaluable member of the Young family.

But seeing the slight scorn on his face right now made Britt extremely uncomfortable.

The man was sixty-eight years old but looked younger. He was Chad's height, around six feet, and still muscular. He obviously took care of his body. He had blue eyes and grayish-blond hair that could use a cut. Every time Britt saw him around Lobster Cove, he was in dress slacks and a button-up shirt with a tie. He didn't fit into the relaxed atmosphere around the place. He also seemed to enjoy the power and responsibility he'd been given.

But more than all that . . . he simply gave her the creeps. He reminded her of one of her mom's ex-boyfriends. He had a shifty look in his eyes that made her want to immediately leave whatever room he was in. It made no sense, because everyone else seemed to love him.

Deciding she was being unreasonable and she needed to get over her ridiculous feelings about him since he'd be around a lot, she did her best to give him the benefit of the doubt.

Still . . . listening to him talk so openly about the Young family finances made her skin crawl.

"Well, I'm sure Evelyn is going to be around a very long time, so it's a moot point anyway." She tried to keep her voice level and not let her irritation show. It suddenly occurred to Britt that she was alone with this man, essentially a stranger, and he was definitely strong enough to overpower her. It was best to sign whatever she needed to sign and go about her business.

"Just making sure you don't go gettin' ideas in your head that you can get with one of our boys. You won't be the first woman to put them in your sights, and you won't be the last."

Full-on anger now threatened to overwhelm her. "So . . . what? You think they're all going to be single forever? That they'll never settle down, get married, have families?"

"I'm sure they will. But it'll be with someone local, not an outsider who cons her way into the family."

It was taking everything within her not to lash out at this asshole. This was the man the entire family thought walked on water? "What else do I need to sign?" she asked brusquely.

Otis stared at her for a moment, then handed over the paper he'd gone out to his car to grab. He sat, then pulled a pair of readers out of his front pocket and perched them on the end of his nose as he mumbled under his breath while sorting through the rest of the papers.

Neither of them spoke as she read and signed the necessary documents. When she took the time to read each and every paper that was put in front of her, Britt ignored the irritated sighs coming from Otis. She didn't care how long this took. She wasn't about to sign anything she hadn't thoroughly read first.

Everything seemed to be in order, and when she was done, even though she was irritated with the man, she was proud of herself. She'd managed to land on her feet, thanks to Chad and his mom, and she would work hard to keep up the good reputation Lobster Cove had nurtured with locals and tourists alike.

She left the office through the auto body shop, making a point to stop in and say a quick hello to Walt and Barry. They were already hard at work in the bays. She didn't want to be a nuisance, since they were obviously busy, and left soon after to head to the smaller guesthouse. She planned to work on pulling weeds in the backyard while the guests were gone for the day, to clean it up a little and make it look even nicer for the next renters.

Time got away from her as she lost herself in the monotonous yet somehow cathartic work. A bell ringing caught Britt's attention, and she had no idea what it meant. Looking at her watch, she saw it was one o'clock, later than she'd thought. Her belly growled, and she realized the bell probably was a way to let anyone who wasn't at the main house know that lunch was ready.

Britt could imagine that it got a lot of use when the Young brothers were kids. She could picture them running around Lobster Cove, playing in the water or in the woods, and dropping everything to run to the house for lunch or dinner when the bell pealed.

Walking around the guesthouse, she smiled when she saw Evelyn standing on the front porch, waving at her. She quickly headed toward the house to join her. Evelyn looked happier than she'd seen her since the day she'd arrived.

"My boys are here!" she said as soon as Britt got close enough.

"I saw."

"Knox is too skinny. Poor thing was never much interested in cooking and has probably been living off boxed crap and microwave meals. I made a huge lunch for everyone . . . sandwiches, fruit, homemade chips, and chocolate cake for dessert."

Britt's mouth watered. "Homemade potato chips?" she asked as she climbed the porch steps.

"Uh-huh. I slice potatoes really thin, season them up, then bake them in the oven. They're so much better than anything you can get in the stores these days. Come on, I want to introduce you to everyone." Evelyn hooked her arm in Britt's and towed her toward the front door.

For a moment, she considered pulling out of Evelyn's grasp and running away, but that would be stupid. She was nervous to meet the remaining Young brothers. She'd sensed an obvious unease from Zachary and was afraid the older brothers would think the same as Otis—that she was there to somehow harm their mother and their family legacy.

To her surprise, the second she walked into the kitchen, Knox turned and gave her a huge smile. She knew who was who, of course, because Evelyn had shown her tons of pictures of her sons, bragging about them and sharing hilarious stories about each of them as kids.

"So, you must be Britt."

"Uh . . . yeah, that's me," she said uncertainly, her gaze searching out Chad for reassurance.

He was standing in the corner of the kitchen, his hands filled with a large bowl of the homemade chips Evelyn had bragged about. He gave her an encouraging grin just as the man who'd greeted her stepped into her path—and hugged her.

She was even *more* surprised at the exuberant greeting, but she didn't pull away.

The oldest brother, Lincoln, smacked Knox on the back of his head and exclaimed, "You can't go around touching women without their permission!"

Britt was immediately released and staring at the man's smiling face.

"Sorry 'bout that. I'm Knox. We've been hearing how amazing you are from Mom all morning. She says that you've taken over the cleaning of the guesthouses and doing the laundry and stuff. Thank God, because cleaning up after the guests is the worst job ever. Did she tell you about the time she went in to clean after a family had left and discovered they'd apparently adopted an injured raccoon they'd found in the woods?"

Britt gasped in surprise.

"No lie. They'd put it in one of the two guest rooms, along with a ton of pine needles, I guess as a bed or something. But apparently it wasn't as injured as they'd thought, and it went crazy being locked in that room and destroyed it. There was raccoon shit and piss everywhere—and I mean *everywhere*. The bedding was trashed, the walls had claw marks from where the raccoon had tried to climb them, and the damn thing was practically rabid, it was so desperate to escape."

Britt was speechless.

"Mom and Dad had to break the window—because of course it was locked, and they weren't about to enter the room anyway and get clawed to death or bitten—to give the poor thing a way to escape. It took all of us a week to scour and air out that room. That's the year they implemented the no-animal policy for the rentals. Anyway, my point is . . . we're all grateful that you've taken over the cleaning of the rentals."

Britt smiled at him. "You're welcome?"

"We'll help if something like that happens again, though," Chad reassured her as he put the bowl of chips in the middle of the table. "We wouldn't leave anything like that for you to clean up by yourself."

"Of course we wouldn't," Evelyn said. "Britt, this is my third-born, Knox. He was in the Coast Guard, and now he works as a contractor for them."

"It's nice to meet you," Britt said, holding out her hand.

Knox took her hand and instead of shaking it, leaned over and kissed her knuckles. "My pleasure to meet such a pretty young woman."

"Cut it out," Chad griped as he knocked his shoulder into his brother's—hard—making him drop Britt's hand as he did his best not to fall onto the floor.

Chad's oldest brother rolled his eyes and held out his hand to her. "I'm Lincoln. Heard you ran into a bit of bad luck. You're good now?"

Britt shook his hand and felt relief spread through her. She didn't read any negative vibes coming from the brothers. "Yes. Your mom has been awesome. And Lobster Cove is . . ." She struggled to come up with an appropriate word that would explain how she felt. "Everything."

"Yeah, it is."

"Now that the introductions are over, let's eat!" Evelyn ordered.

Everyone shuffled to the large table just off the kitchen, and Britt couldn't help but smile as all the brothers reached for the food their mom had laid out. She found herself sitting next to Chad and was surprised when he took her plate and filled it for her.

"Just wanted to make sure you got some," he told her when he placed it back down in front of her. "I know my brothers, and if you're too polite around here, you'll starve."

She laughed a little. "I can see," she said as she watched the other men pile their plates high.

Lunch was eye opening. Britt already knew that Chad and Zach had a great relationship with their mom, but seeing Evelyn with all her sons, and the affection everyone shared openly and without reservation, was beautiful. There was a lot of laughter and good-natured teasing, which had Britt grinning like a fool.

And the food . . . it was obvious it was made with love. Which sounded silly, because food was food, but somehow it seemed to taste different this afternoon. And watching Evelyn interact with her sons made Britt realize what an amazing group of men they were. They'd understood that their mom needed them after their dad's death. They'd left their homes, jobs . . . their entire lives to move back to Maine simply because it was the right thing to do.

Yes, them being here would be a huge help around Lobster Cove, but they could've simply hired more help to take care of the place. Though that wouldn't have kept Evelyn from being lonely. She was very used to being around men, had been for most of her life here at the family home. Britt had the humorous thought that Lobster Cove should've been named Alpha Cove instead . . . the Young brothers certainly fit that bill.

"What's the plan for the rest of the day, now that we've determined what needs to be done for the roof?" Chad asked.

"I'm tired," Lincoln said bluntly. "I've been driving for three days. Thought I'd head to my new place and get settled. Maybe take a nap before coming back here for Mom's chicken and spinach casserole and biscuits."

"Can you drop me off at my apartment?" Knox asked. "My truck is supposed to be delivered tomorrow, but in the meantime I'm without any wheels."

"You can take Dad's truck if you want," Chad offered.

"Or my Corolla," Britt blurted. She blushed as everyone turned to look at her. "I mean . . . I know it's old, but Walt looked at it and said it's safe."

"Appreciate it," Knox told both his brother and Britt. "But if Lincoln can chauffeur me around for a little while longer, I'll be good until tomorrow."

"You coming back tonight?" Evelyn asked.

"Wouldn't miss it," Knox reassured his mother.

"Good."

"If you guys are all good, I'm gonna go and scope out the competition for my lobster shack," Zach said.

"I still can't believe you actually bought a freaking lobster shack," Lincoln said with a shake of his head.

"It's gonna be *the* place to eat in Rockville. Mark my words," Zach boasted.

"I have no doubt whatsoever. You're amazing in the kitchen," Knox told his brother.

"I'm not sure how much that compliment means coming from the man who burns ramen noodles," Zach joked.

Knox threw his balled-up napkin at his brother.

"Enough," Evelyn warned. "The last time you started something at the dinner table, mashed potatoes ended up on my ceiling."

Everyone chuckled.

Britt found that she'd been smiling so much, her cheeks hurt. Being a part of this was such a novelty . . . a family who loved and supported and teased each other. And she liked it. A lot.

"Get on with you then," Evelyn said as she stood. "Dinner'll be around seven."

Everyone else stood as soon as their mom did, and they all started grabbing plates and dishes. Chad took Evelyn's plate out of her hand. "We've got this, Mom. You cooked, we clean."

The more Britt was around this man, the more she liked him. She couldn't remember one time that Cole offered to do dishes after she'd made dinner for him.

She was shooed out of the kitchen, and she wasn't exactly sure what she should be doing while the guys cleaned up. She grabbed a cloth and wiped down the table while they joked and laughed in the kitchen.

The house felt happy. Looking over at Evelyn, Britt saw that she felt it too. It had probably seemed very empty and a little scary, being in this house by herself after her husband passed away.

When the dishes were done and the kitchen was clean and tidy once again, the three brothers made their way for the door. Knox and Lincoln told her again how nice it was to meet her and how glad they were that she was there, and then they and Zach headed outside.

Britt was sure they'd probably talk about her and her situation when she wasn't around, but that was all right. She understood their need to protect their mother from anyone who might want to take advantage of her.

That was the last thing on Britt's mind. The longer she was around the Young family, the more she *wanted* to be around them . . . and the more protective she felt of Evelyn herself.

"You ready?"

Turning, Britt looked at Chad in confusion. "For what?"

"For that tour I promised you. Of the secret trail."

She'd forgotten about that. "Oh, sure, if your mom doesn't have anything she needs done right now?" She looked over at Evelyn, who was shamelessly eavesdropping.

"No, no, you two go on. I need to go through some of Austin's things."

"Mom, I thought we agreed that you were going to wait and let me help with that," Chad said with a small frown.

"I know you want to protect me from any hurt, but I need to do this on my own, Chad. I miss your father with every molecule in my body, but I refuse to pretend he never existed. I like seeing his things and remembering our good times. Heck, even our bad times. I'm okay. Having you home, and your brothers, and having you here, Britt . . . it all helps. A lot. But sometimes I just need to sit and cry. I'll be fine. You two go on, do your thing."

"If you're sure," Chad said skeptically.

Evelyn walked over to him and put a hand on his cheek. "I love you, son. There are times I look at you and your brothers and I'm amazed at how much of your father I see in you. That's a good thing. He lives on in all of you. *You're* his true legacy. One he was very proud of. And he'd want me to move on. It hurts to see his clothes in our closet and his things on the bathroom counter. Everything has to be sorted through to figure out what needs to be given to charity, what I want to keep, and what can go in the trash. And *I* need to be the one to do it."

Chad hugged his mother tightly, then pulled back, keeping his hands on her shoulders. "We're here if you need anything. A shoulder to cry on, help with sorting through things, carrying bags."

"I know and appreciate it. Go on, you two. I should warn you, though, that trail hasn't been used in a while, and the ticks have gotten worse over the years. Make sure you do a thorough tick check when you get back."

Britt held back a shudder. She hated ticks. They were the *worst*. What was even the point of them? Bloodsucking leeches. Yuck.

"We will. Love you, Mom," Chad said as he kissed her forehead. Then he turned to Britt. "You ready?"

"Um . . . can we use some bug spray before we go?"

He chuckled. "Of course," he said, holding out his hand.

Britt stared at it for a beat, thinking about the warning Otis had given earlier. She'd told him that she wasn't interested in dating, but staring at Chad's hand had her belly doing flip-flops. She wanted to take it. Wanted to feel his skin against her own. Getting closer to him probably wasn't the best idea, but she apparently had no willpower when it came to this man.

She put her hand in his and felt tingles shoot up her arm when his fingers squeezed hers gently.

They walked out of the house hand in hand, and she couldn't remember being more excited. This man . . . she had a feeling he could either crush her spirit and grind it into the dirt, or give her a life she'd only dreamed about.

She hoped it was the latter.

CHAPTER SEVEN

Chad worried about his mom. He hated that she wanted to deal with going through his dad's stuff by herself, but he also understood why she wouldn't want her sons there when she grieved. At least lunch had been good. For her and for all of them.

He loved having his brothers home. It would make things around Lobster Cove so much easier. Even though Knox, Zach, and Lincoln would always have their own lives, he knew without a doubt if he called them and asked for help, they'd give it without a moment's hesitation.

And no matter how hectic things got, they'd be frequent visitors to Lobster Cove. They were drawn there, just as he was. He could see in their faces how much they'd missed their mom, and he hoped they'd never regret upending their lives and moving back to Maine.

For himself, Chad felt as if moving back to Rockville had been a long time coming. He enjoyed Virginia, but there was no place like home. Memories flooded his brain as he led Britt along the overgrown trail that went from the bench at the water's edge and through the trees between Lobster Cove and the next property over.

He'd spent a lot of time out here in the woods when he was growing up. Both with his brothers and by himself. When he needed some alone time, this was where he came. Because as much as he loved his family, they were sometimes a bit much. He'd read books out here, climbed trees, dug holes, battled imaginary dragons, lain in the dirt for hours pretending to track enemies with guns he'd made out of sticks. And when he got older, he brought girls out here to make out.

That last thought made him smile. He'd learned pretty fast that generally, girls didn't like being dirty, so before bringing anyone out here, he'd made the fort more comfortable with bottles of water and a throw blanket. He hadn't lost his virginity out here in the woods, but he'd definitely come close.

"That looks like a good thought," Britt said.

"Yeah," Chad agreed. "Just thinking about how much time I used to spend out here."

"I can see why. It's beautiful. It feels as if we're the only two people in the world. We could be miles and miles away from anyone, and yet the house is just through the trees."

"Exactly. I think that's why I liked it so much as a kid. I could pretend I was on a grand adventure, but if I scraped my leg or got hungry, I could be home in minutes."

"You were lucky to grow up here."

"I was."

"Can I ask you something?"

"You just did," Chad joked. But when he looked at Britt, she wasn't smiling. "Sorry, yes, of course you can. I know we only recently met, but I hope that by now, you know you can trust me a little."

"I do. I just . . . I'm not sure how to approach this."

Chad frowned, wondering what she wanted to talk about. "Is it Mom? Is something wrong?"

"No. And I would definitely come to you if I was worried about her. She's still sad, that's easy to see, but she's strong. And I think you and your brothers being home is exactly what she needs."

The relief Chad felt was almost overwhelming. "That's good. And being here is as good for us as it is for her, I think. This place has a way of grabbing you around the heart and not letting go."

She didn't say anything as they walked, and Chad thought maybe she'd changed her mind about asking her question. Then she took a deep breath and stopped in the middle of the trail.

"Otis . . . he's been with your family for a while now, right?"

Chad's brow furrowed. "Yeah. He and my dad were close friends. They hung out a lot, went fishing together all the time."

She stared out into the trees, obviously not seeing them.

"Why? What happened? Did he say or do something inappropriate?" Chad knew she'd met with him to sign paperwork before lunch.

"He seems to think I'm here because I'm after your family's money. He made it very clear that any money you guys have is tied up in Lobster Cove."

Chad pressed his lips together in irritation. "I'm sorry. He had no right to say that to you."

Britt shrugged. "I mean, I get it. I'm a stranger, and he wants to protect Evelyn and her assets. I just . . . he . . . ." She sighed. "Never mind."

"No, say what you're thinking. Please."

"He just made me uncomfortable. He obviously doesn't like me. Considers me an outsider. Told me that you and your brothers would marry local girls and someone like me shouldn't get any ideas."

"Someone like you?" he asked, holding on to his temper by the skin of his teeth. Otis had no right to treat Britt that way. She'd been nothing but helpful and kind to his mom.

Britt shrugged, obviously uncomfortable discussing it further.

"I'll talk to him."

Britt turned to him with wide eyes and put a hand on his arm. "Oh! Please don't! I have a feeling that will only make things worse. I know he's a family friend, and I can be nice to him for the sake of my job. I was mostly uncomfortable because he was talking about your mom's money situation to a stranger."

Chad was *definitely* going to talk to Otis. It had been a while since he'd done more than exchange greetings with the man. It was time to remedy that anyway. But . . . since it was something his brothers should be involved in, he could at least wait until they'd settled into their new homes. Then they would all sit down with him, their mom too, and discuss the state of Lobster Cove—taxes, investments, and other financial issues. It had already been on his to-do list, after his mom's mention of money being tight.

And then, he'd take a moment or two alone with Otis to address his treatment of Britt.

"I appreciate you telling me," he said, not promising her anything. "And I want you to know that you're one of us now, just as Walt and Barry are. And *no one's* allowed to make you feel uncomfortable in your own home. If anyone says or does anything out of line, you tell me or one of my brothers. That includes the guests staying in the cabins. Okay?"

She nodded.

Unease sat in Chad's belly like a lump of coal, but he took a deep breath and did his best to ignore it. It wouldn't do any good to stress about Britt's interaction with Otis right now. He'd confront the man later and make it clear that Britt was to be treated with respect—and who he and his brothers decided to date, or possibly marry someday, was none of his business.

"You want to see this fort still?" he asked.

"Yes!" Britt said, sounding more like the woman he'd gotten to know over the last week.

"All right. But I'll warn you, it's been out here in the woods, neglected, for a long while now. It's possible with the snow and windstorms, it's nothing but a pile of rubble."

"Oh, that would be a shame," Britt said.

Chad set out on the trail once more, Britt right on his heels. It didn't take much longer to get to the area where the fort had once stood.

But instead of the crude structure he and his brothers had built and played in, there stood what looked like a tiny house. It even had shingles on the sloped roof.

Chad stared at it with his mouth open in shock.

"Um, that doesn't look like a pile of rubble," Britt said with a laugh.

"I don't . . . how . . . What the hell?" Chad said, stumbling over his words.

"Hello?" Britt called out.

He wasn't sure who she thought she was talking to. As far as he knew, there weren't any homeless men or women secretly living in their woods.

But to his shock, someone called out, "Who's there?"

Chad was dumbfounded.

"It's Britt and Chad," she said cheerfully, taking a step toward the small hut.

But Chad grabbed her arm and held her back. "You have no idea who's in there," he hissed.

"I don't, but it's obviously a kid. It's fine, Chad." She shook off his hold and stepped toward the fort once more.

She'd picked up on what Chad hadn't in his shock. The voice *was* that of a kid. Relief made him almost dizzy. He'd had visions of some escaped convict hiding out in their woods, which was ridiculous.

The door, made of scrap pieces of wood, opened slowly, and a boy's head popped out. He was on his knees, probably because the building wasn't tall enough for him to stand in. He had red hair that stuck out in every direction. He was skinny . . . kind of scrawny, actually. Chad estimated he was between ten and twelve. And he'd never seen him before in his life.

"I don't know you," the boy said belligerently.

"And I don't know you. But we can change that easily enough. I'm Britt. Britt Starkweather. And yes, that's my real name, not a nickname. I live at Lobster Cove with the Young family. I'm helping out Evelyn with the guesthouses." She held out her hand to shake.

The boy frowned, looking confused. But someone had drilled some manners into him, because he reached out to shake her hand as if he couldn't help himself. "I'm Kash Bates. I live over there," he said, gesturing to the property next to Lobster Cove with his free hand.

Chad frowned. "That's Victor Rogers's house," he said.

"Yeah. He's my grandfather. Mom and I moved in with him a while ago."

Now his brows quirked up in surprise. From what Chad remembered of Harper, Victor's only child, she was one of the mean girls back in school. Hearing that she'd returned to Rockville was a bit of a shock, since she'd been so determined to get out of this "hick town," as she called it, and make something of herself in Hollywood or New York.

"Chad figured this fort was probably nothing but sticks because so much time had gone by since he'd last been here," Britt said conversationally.

"It was," Kash said with a shrug. "I fixed it up."

"Well, you did an amazing job. This looks awesome. Like a tiny house."

It wasn't hard to see how great her compliment made the boy feel. His chest actually puffed out a bit as he nodded. "It wasn't hard," he said nonchalantly.

Chad continued to let Britt carry the conversation, as it was obvious Kash was more comfortable with her than with him. Every time he looked at Chad, a guarded expression took over his face and he seemed to be on the verge of bolting.

"Can I look inside?" Britt asked.

Reluctantly, Kash nodded. Chad stayed where he was as Britt moved forward and got on her knees to peek into the doorway.

"Oh my gosh, it's awesome. You built shelves! And it was so smart to use these boards as a floor, so you don't have to sit on the ground and get dirty. Is that a telescope in that plastic bin? Do you like to look at the stars?"

It seemed that was the right question, because Kash lit up and began babbling about the Milky Way and the recent eclipse and how he'd seen the northern lights several times.

Chad didn't care that the boy was using the fort. He was glad the forest was giving another child the joy it had given him and his brothers.

But he *did* care about a child hanging out here alone without anyone apparently being aware of what he was doing.

Kash had made a mini house out here, complete with books and bedding, if what he could see from his vantage point was right. He also had a couple of storage bins inside to keep things dry when he wasn't there. He hoped it was simply a fort for the boy . . . but Chad couldn't be sure he wasn't using it as a place to hide from his homelife.

The truth was, Victor Rogers was an asshole. Always had been. Even though several acres and a lot of trees separated their properties, Victor had still put in regular complaints with the sheriff's department about Lobster Cove over the years. Noise complaints, disputes over property lines, questioning their business licenses, and trying to claim the land wasn't zoned for this or that. Chad's dad had done everything by the book, so there had never been any legal action taken against the Youngs, but Rogers had remained a pain in their asses.

He couldn't imagine it would be fun to live with Victor Rogers. He was downright mean. Clearly where his daughter had gotten her attitude back in the day. If she'd moved home with her son, she *had* to be desperate.

Of course, he could be way off base, and the man might be a marshmallow with his daughter and grandson . . . but Chad didn't think that was the case.

"You have snacks in there?" Britt asked Kash.

"Yes."

"Cool. I was going to say if you didn't, maybe you could come over to our house"—she pointed back the way she and Chad had come—"and get some. I'm sure Evelyn would be happy to feed you."

Kash shook his head as his eyes widened. "She's mean!"

"What?" Britt asked, genuinely shocked. "Evelyn? She's the nicest woman I've ever met."

But Kash was still shaking his head. "No, she greets people at the door with a gun! Threatens 'em too. Granddad told me so!"

Chad was shocked. If his mom had greeted Victor at the door with the shotgun his dad kept in the house for protection against bears and moose—which were much more prevalent decades ago, before the coast was built up so much—she had to have been afraid of the man.

He wanted more information about what the hell Victor might've said to his mom to make her threaten him with that gun—if that was even the case—but Britt was already talking again, in the same calm and steady voice she'd been using all along. She could tell the boy was spooked and was doing everything in her power to make sure he didn't bolt.

"Wow, I'm sure that was scary to hear. But I can promise you, Evelyn isn't normally mean. I bet she was just having a bad day. Do you ever have days when everything goes wrong? You get a bad grade on a homework assignment, you drop your sandwich at lunch, or your mom yells at you for something that wasn't your fault?"

Kash nodded.

"Right. So, I bet Evelyn was having one of those days. Was your granddad maybe yelling?"

Kash shrugged, looking away. Which Chad took to mean the boy wasn't a stranger to Victor's foul moods.

"Yelling can be scary. I know because my mom had some boyfriends who did that a lot, and it always made me want to hide. Anyway . . . I just got here a week ago. But I was living in my car, and Evelyn made me a delicious lunch and then invited me to stay. Can you believe that? *I* couldn't. I'm earning my keep, working hard, but still, she didn't have to let me stay in her house. I bet if you came to the house and introduced yourself, she'd invite you in and feed you too."

Chad was mesmerized by Britt's calm. It was clear she was winning the boy over.

"You had to sleep in your car too?"

The simple words were heartbreaking for all that they revealed.

"Yeah. It's not very fun, is it? Kind of scary. I was always afraid someone would pound on the window in the middle of the night and tell me I had to leave."

Kash nodded.

She looked over her shoulder at Chad, and he could see the concern in her eyes. Then she looked back at Kash. "Well, I think you've made a fine little place here. It's comfortable, and you have your books to read. And I bet you can see the stars really well at night."

"Yeah. Especially when I go over by the coast."

"Oh, you be careful over there, especially in the dark. You could get hurt if you fell into the ocean. We're going to get going, leave you to do your thing. But if you ever need help, or get hungry, or even just bored, come on over to Lobster Cove. I'm sure everyone would be happy to meet you. Walt and Barry are usually in the auto shop during the day, working on cars or engines, and now that all the Young brothers are home, they'll be around doing maintenance on the property. You're welcome there anytime. Right, Chad?"

She looked up at him as she said that last bit.

"Of course," he said without hesitation. "We'd love to have you over. Get to know you better."

Kash looked skeptical. "Are you going to tell on me?" The question was aimed at Chad.

"Tell who what?" he asked the boy.

"I know this is your land. I'm not supposed to be over here. Granddad put up that fence to keep you out of his property, but I climbed over it and found this place. I like it. Made it mine."

Chad squatted down so his weight was on the balls of his feet. He did his best to look relaxed and not upset in the least. And he wasn't, not about the boy being on Lobster Cove property. He was more concerned about *why* the boy felt the need to escape his own house and hide out in this little hut.

"As far as I'm concerned, you can stay as long as you want. I used to play out here when I was your age, and I'm thrilled that you've given Fort Bad Assery a new life."

Kash frowned. "Fort Bad Assery?"

"Yeah, that's what we called this place. Used to drive our mom crazy. She wanted us to give it a nicer name. Like Down Home or Fort in the Woods . . . but my brothers and I wanted it to be tough. To be badass. So we named it Fort Bad Assery."

Kash smiled for the first time. "I like that. Fort Bad Assery."

"I'm thinking maybe you shouldn't let your mom hear you call it that," Britt told the boy.

He got serious. "Oh no. She doesn't know I'm out here either. I won't mess up and say it in front of her."

That was one more thing Chad wasn't thrilled about. Yes, Lobster Cove was safe. It wasn't as if anyone would be able to get to the boy when he was out here, but keeping secrets from a parent wasn't the best sign. Not if he was using the fort to hide out from someone or something.

"Okay, enjoy Fort Bad Assery," Britt said, then grinned. "That's really fun to say. *Assery, asssery, assery.*"

To Chad's amazement, Kash giggled.

"Right. Remember what I said, if you get hungry or lonely, come on over. We're just through the trees, and I promise no one will be mean."

Kash didn't look totally convinced, but he nodded.

Britt stood up, gave the boy a little wave, then turned to Chad and hooked her arm with his, practically pulling him away from the newly renovated fort in the woods.

As soon as the trees obscured them from view and they were out of earshot, Britt looked at him. "I don't know what to do."

"Yeah," he agreed. "I don't care that he's using the fort or hanging out there, but I'm worried about why. And I definitely don't like that Mom felt the need to break out the shotgun when Victor came over, if that story is true. Or the fact that he was probably yelling at her."

Britt hadn't dropped his arm, and she leaned into him for a moment, resting her head on his bicep. A jolt went through Chad from the spot where her head lay all the way down to his toes. He stilled, not sure what he was feeling.

"I'm worried. About Kash, Evelyn, Victor . . ."

"I'm on it," Chad reassured her, shifting so he could wrap his arm around her. Holding her felt nothing like holding any other woman. It felt more intimate than when he'd made love to his last girlfriend, which was both alarming and scary at the same time. But he also felt as if he was exactly where he wanted to be. "I'm going to let Lincoln know about his old classmate living next door. Maybe he can go over to say hi, scope out the vibe of the place."

"He's not going to tell on Kash, is he?" Britt asked, lifting her head and staring at him.

"No."

"Are you going to tell your brothers about Kash?" she asked.

"Of course. We can all look out for him. Maybe you can butter him up by bringing him some of Mom's cookies one day."

"Oh! Great idea." She sighed. "Chad?"

"Yeah?"

"Lobster Cove is awesome."

He smiled. "Yeah, it really is."

"Did you really call your fort Bad Assery?"

He chuckled. "Nope. But it sounded like something a preteen boy would love."

"You're right. He did love it."

"You want to go sit on the bench and watch the ocean for a while?"

"Yes. But I can't. I need to go check on the guests. Then I told Evelyn I'd go with her to the grocery store."

Chad was disappointed, but also proud of the woman at his side. She worked hard, didn't shirk her duties, and loved the land as much as he did. Not only that, but she genuinely seemed to care about his mom.

It was a win-win situation all the way around, and he was so thankful he'd stopped by that lumberyard and met her.

He had things to do as well, but for the first time in his life, all he wanted to do was sit and talk with a woman.

He almost snorted. When was the last time he was happy to just *talk* to a woman? His old Army buddies would be laughing their asses off, telling him to get in her pants already. But he was a different person than he used to be. He wasn't out to put another notch on his bedpost. He wanted what his parents had, and he was already way behind the eight ball on making that happen. As were all his brothers.

He had no idea where his brothers stood when it came to settling down and starting a family, if it was something they wanted or not . . . but he'd bet everything he owned that they felt the same as him.

Chad refused to settle. He'd seen the love and respect his parents had for each other. The way they were a team, working together to make their dreams come true. That's what Chad wanted, someone willing to put in the work to build a future together. Someone he could be proud to have at his side, and who'd feel the same way about him.

He couldn't help but wonder if she wasn't already standing right next to him . . .

Telling himself he was being ridiculous, that Britt had only been there a week and he really didn't know her all *that* well, he lowered his arm and very intentionally took a step backward.

Britt blinked at him, then straightened and brought a hand up to brush a lock of her hair behind her ear. "Um . . . we should go," she said.

Chad hated that he'd made her feel uncertain. But he had a lot of shit he needed to do, and getting involved with the woman he'd brought home to keep his mom company and help at Lobster Cove suddenly didn't seem so smart. Hell, they were *living* together . . . sort of. They saw each other during the day and every night, and they had breakfast together every morning. It could be a complete disaster if they started dating and things went south.

He couldn't do that to his mom. He needed to keep his distance. Right?

With his mind in turmoil, he smiled at her and headed back down the path toward the main house. He felt as if he was giving Britt mixed signals, but he could put a stop to that, at least. He'd be nothing but polite. No more touching, no more holding hands. He'd be friendly but professional.

As soon as he had the thought, she let out a gasp.

Chad was turning and reaching for her before his brain could catch up with his body. She'd stumbled over a tree branch in the path, and he caught her, making sure she didn't face-plant onto the ground. And once she was steady and they continued walking . . . he somehow found his hand tightening around hers once more . . .

And the anxiety he'd been feeling about all the things he should or shouldn't do faded away.

Shit.

CHAPTER EIGHT

Over the next two weeks, Britt thought back to the moments she and Chad had shared in the woods more than once. She'd felt as if they were connecting on a deeper level than simply friends, and then on the walk back, it was like a veil had fallen over his eyes, blocking her from seeing any kind of emotion, despite his holding her hand on the way home. It was confusing and disorienting . . . but in a way, she was relieved.

She'd been getting too attracted to Chad. Her time here at Lobster Cove wasn't permanent. Once the summer was over and she'd saved up enough money and there was less to do around the property, she'd be moving out and finding her own place. That didn't mean she wouldn't still visit and help Evelyn, but she couldn't live in the main house forever.

So she and Chad had been keeping their distance from each other since their time in the woods. Which was for the best . . . and easy, since they'd both been busy. She was still learning the ins and outs of Lobster Cove, and Chad was working hard to make as many updates to the place as he could.

One of Britt's favorite things about living and working on the property was getting to know Evelyn's other sons and watching them interact with their mom. The brothers were all very different, but at the same time they were so much alike in some ways, it was scary. For instance, they were all incredibly protective of their mother.

One morning last week, Evelyn fell while she was in the kitchen. She was all right, just got a little banged up. Chad heard the commotion and came running downstairs to see what had happened. Once he was reassured that his mom was fine, just bruised and embarrassed more than anything else, he'd obviously called his brothers to let them know what happened.

It didn't take more than twenty minutes for the other three Young boys to show up. They wanted to see for themselves that Evelyn was okay. It was incredibly sweet and touching . . . and Britt had to go to her room so she didn't make a fool out of herself by bursting into tears in front of everyone. It once more struck her how alpha and protective the Young brothers were. Again, she had the thought that Alpha Cove would've been a better name for the family property instead of Lobster Cove.

The Young brothers might be badass former military men with alpha tendencies, but they were also mommy's little boys. Family oriented. Committed to making sure Evelyn was happy and safe for however long she had left . . . which would hopefully be twenty or thirty more years.

And weirdly, their protectiveness seemed to extend to Britt, which was hard to get used to. She'd been on her own for so long, it felt odd to be cared for by not only Evelyn but also her sons. She was constantly being asked if she was okay, if she had everything she needed, if she could use any help, if she wanted a day off.

It wasn't until she was around the Young family that she'd realized how toxic most of her previous relationships—with men, and with people in general—had been.

In the last two weeks, she'd also met the other part-time employees who worked at Lobster Cove. There was the teenager and his dad who came over for a couple of hours in the evenings and helped Knox with the boats. They assisted the owners who came to pick them up from storage, getting them hooked up to their vehicles and trailers. Or, when preferred, they loaded them into the water at Lobster Cove's deepwater dock, for owners to take home via the water.

There were also a couple of part-time mechanics who were hired for the busy summer season. Not that the auto shop wasn't busy in the winter, but it was even busier once people began to emerge from their houses after the long winters.

One of the part-timers at the auto shop was Camden Calvert, Otis's son. He was in his midforties, and just like his father, he gave Britt bad vibes. It wasn't anything he said, it was simply a gleam in his eye as he stared at people, as if he was always concocting some scheme.

Britt hated feeling that way, especially when she didn't even really know the guy . . . but she still had to admit that she didn't feel comfortable being around him *or* his father.

Thankfully, she hadn't had any more one-on-one chats with Otis, but he was around the property a lot. He often came to the main house for lunch with Evelyn, and he frequently used the computer in the shop's office to manage payroll, pay invoices, and do everything else related to the business. Britt wished he could do it all at his own office in downtown Rockville, but since he was practically family, she wasn't about to suggest it to anyone.

As she walked across the yard toward the auto body shop, she hoped Otis wasn't working in the office today. It had been a few days since she'd seen him last, and that was more than all right with her. She couldn't forget the assumptions he'd made about her and how disrespectful he'd been of all the Young brothers. Who they wanted to date or eventually marry wasn't any of his business.

She was carrying a large bag of glassware containers filled with the chili Evelyn had made for lunch. She'd informed Britt that Walt and Barry loved her chili and she wanted to share it with them. She'd included bowls in the bag, but since they were swamped with a backlog of cars, she'd packed the chili in jars, just in case the guys needed to shove it in the shop fridge until they had time for a break.

As she approached the bays, she heard a lot of swearing and yelling coming from within. She immediately recognized Chad's voice. She'd thought he'd gone into town, but clearly he either had gone and already returned or hadn't left yet.

She cautiously entered the first bay and blinked as her eyes adjusted to the lower light inside. More swearing came from underneath an elevated pickup truck.

Britt cleared her throat. "I'm sorry if I'm interrupting, but Evelyn sent down some lunch."

Almost in unison, three heads peered out from under the truck, making Britt chuckle.

"Lunch?" Walt asked.

"What is it?" Chad added.

"Please tell me that's her chili," Barry pleaded.

"It's chili," Britt confirmed.

Suddenly, she was surrounded by the three men. Barry took the bag from her hand with an effusive "Thanks!" and headed straight for the office, closely followed by Walt.

She laughed and turned to head over to the smaller guesthouse. The renters had left that morning, and she needed to get it cleaned and ready for tomorrow, when a couple would be arriving.

"You eaten?" Chad asked.

Knowing she couldn't simply ignore him—that would be rude— Britt paused, offering a small smile. How a man so dirty could look so good was beyond her. He had on a gray Lobster Cove Auto shirt that had stains on the front, as if he'd wiped his greasy hand across it at some point. He also had some of that same grease on his cheek. His dark hair was mussed, allowing more of the highlights he'd gotten from working outside in the sun to show through.

And his gaze was fixed on her, as if she was the most important thing in his world at the moment, even though they both knew how much work needed to be done in the shop.

That was just one more thing that drew Britt to this man. When he spoke to her, he didn't make her feel as if she was keeping him from more important things, even though he was constantly busy. He focused completely on *her*, which was a heady feeling. She'd always been an afterthought. To her mom, to boyfriends. Even the friends she'd had in the past. But with Chad, he looked her in the eye, didn't fiddle with his phone, didn't look around to see if there was anyone more important to talk to or anything more pressing to do.

"Britt? Did you eat with Mom at the house?"

"Yeah. Lincoln was visiting earlier, but he had to leave, and I didn't want her to eat by herself."

He stared at her for another long moment—even more intently, if that was possible—and Britt wished she knew what he was thinking.

"You have a minute to sit with us?" he finally asked.

A refusal was on the tip of her tongue, but for some reason she found herself nodding instead.

Chad finally smiled and stepped forward, taking her elbow in his hand and turning her toward the office. He dropped his hand as soon as they began walking, but her skin still tingled from the light touch.

Walt and Barry were already eating right out of the glass containers, ignoring the bowls Evelyn had sent down with the meal. Britt couldn't help but smile at that. It felt like the ultimate compliment that they didn't want to wait the few seconds it would take to put some chili into bowls.

"It's still hot!" Barry told Chad as he reached for one of the two remaining containers.

"First one done gets the extra container," Walt said with his mouth full.

Britt suppressed a giggle. The guys were funny, especially the way Barry growled at his coworker.

"There's more where that came from. No need to make yourselves sick by eating too fast," she told them. "Evelyn made a huge stockpot full of it. I thought it was way too much, but I can see that I was wrong."

"I'll go up and grab some more after we figure out what parts we need for the truck," Barry said.

"It seems to me that we're constantly out of the parts we need," Chad muttered as he sat and began to eat a little more sedately than the other two men. Britt had taken the last seat, and she enjoyed the moment of rest before she needed to get to the cabin to start cleaning.

"We are," Barry said with a shrug.

"Why?" Chad asked.

Walt rested the container of chili in his lap and met Chad's gaze. "You want the real answer, or the one that will keep the peace around here?"

"Real. Always," Chad said seriously.

"Your dad never wanted to spend the money on an inventory system. Said it wasn't necessary. That the three of us knew what we used, what we had, and what we needed. He wasn't necessarily wrong, but over the years, we've had more and more business . . . and for the last few, things have gotten kind of out of control around here."

"Wait, you guys don't have a computerized inventory system?" Chad asked, sounding incredulous.

"No. The responsibility falls on us to just take notes and keep up with what we use, but at the end of the day, we need a way to account for what we're using and what we need."

Britt listened intently.

"What do you suggest?" Chad asked.

"An inventory system that creates itemized invoices at the same time. I know it won't be cheap, between buying software and hiring someone to use it, but it'll save Barry and me a ton of time. Time that we could use to service more customers," Walt said. Then he glanced at Barry, who gave a slight nod. "And that's not all. Just to clear the air . . . sometimes when we've tried to order parts, we haven't been able to because of unpaid bills."

"What?" Chad asked, his brows shooting upward. "Are you shitting me?"

"Sorry, but no."

"Fuck," he said, putting his chili to the side. "We need to fix this shit. Lobster Cove will *not* be known for being flaky about paying our bills."

"Um . . . Chad?" Britt said tentatively.

"Yeah?" he asked, obviously distracted.

"Before I moved to Maine, I worked in retail for years. Department stores, fast food, and even convenience stores. I worked with inventory software all the time."

"What are you saying?" Chad said.

"Maybe I can help?"

"You're already run ragged with cleaning, dealing with the guests, helping Mom with reservations, and returning phone calls and emails and baking for guests, *and* being Mom's companion," he told her.

"I know. And there would be a learning curve for me, since I don't know the names of any of the things you guys use to fix cars. But I'm sure with Walt and Barry's help, I could pick it up fairly fast. And I've even taught new employees how the systems work, the invoicing and inventory. I could probably help Walt and Barry figure out that part."

Silence filled the office, and for a moment, Britt thought she'd overstepped. She wouldn't be here forever. And the last thing she wanted was for Chad or anyone else thinking she was trying to get more money out of the Young family.

But apparently the men sitting with her didn't think that. Or they didn't care one way or another.

"That would be great!"

"That's just what we need."

"I don't know."

It was Chad's response that worried Britt. "I promise that I won't mess things up. And I don't even want more payment. I just want to help. I don't think it would take long, actually. Just a couple extra hours each day. I'm not an accountant, and I don't have any kind of business degree, but I'm pretty good at data entry. If there's a program, it's just a matter of plugging numbers and descriptions into the appropriate fields.

And I wouldn't need to know bank account numbers or anything. Otis can input the financial info, and once the system is set up, he should be able to download figures directly into his spreadsheets."

"Breathe, Britt," Chad said, gently reaching over and taking her hand. "I trust you. And if you really don't think it'll be too much, we'd love your help with inventory and other light admin stuff for the shop. It would be a *huge* help. But if you find that you can't keep up with that on top of everything else you've taken on, you need to say something. I can talk to my brothers and figure something out. Maybe hire a part-time admin."

"I can do it," Britt said firmly. If the shop actually had unpaid bills for some reason, she hated the thought of the Youngs having to hire yet another employee to do something she was sure she could handle. It wasn't as if she was busy all day, anyway. She had plenty of downtime, and her salary was already enough, when she factored in her free room and board.

"And I'm not sure if we can raise your salary," Chad told her. "Between my schedule and Otis's, I still haven't been able to sit down with him and figure out what's up with the money situation at Lobster Cove. He seems to be making himself available to everyone but me."

"That's more than all right. You pay me generously enough as it is. I'm happy to help!"

"I'll see what I can do," Chad said, as if she hadn't spoken.

Britt frowned at him as he went back to eating his chili.

"It's no use," Barry told her. "I used to tell Austin that he was overpaying me, but he just ignored me. Said that if he wanted the best, he needed to pay to get it. And . . . just saying . . . Walt and I *are* the best mechanics around. Except for the Young boys, that is."

"Boys?" Chad asked with a raised brow.

The three men chuckled.

Getting a raise wasn't what she'd expected when she offered to help. There was no way she was taking more money from Evelyn. Britt was working hard to build her bank account from the zero it had been when she'd started. And while she didn't have enough to rent her own place yet, especially not with the first and last month's rent and security deposit most places required these days, by the end of the summer, she should have that and more, even without a raise.

It felt great to be earning money again. To know she could support herself. It quieted the voice of her mom and Cole, who'd insisted she couldn't make it on her own in Maine.

"I'll talk to Camden and the others and let them know what's up. That we'll be setting up an inventory-and-invoicing system," Walt said.

Britt's mind spun with ideas for improving the organization of the shop. The computer system would help immensely, even if it would take the mechanics some getting used to.

"You know, Austin ran this place the same way for years. I'm thinking it'll be good to have some fresh blood . . . someone who can help set up a more efficient system. Something we have no clue about," Barry said as he wiped his mouth.

His confidence in her felt good. Britt gave him a thankful smile.

"With that settled, how about we get back to work tackling that piece-of-shit monster in the bay," Chad suggested.

The others agreed and quickly cleaned up their lunch. Even though Walt threatened to go back to the house and get more, he seemed content for now. Before she could blink, Britt had the now much lighter bag in hand, ready to take back to the house. It was time to head to the cabin and see if there was any damage from the last renters and get to work setting it to rights for the next guests.

"Britt?" Chad asked as she turned to leave. "I just wanted to say . . . I might have only met you recently, but I knew then, just as I know now, you're good people. I sensed it in that lumberyard, and you've proven it time and time again with your work ethic and how good you are to my mom. Lobster Cove was lucky to have snagged you before anyone else could."

She wanted to cry at Chad's words. They meant the world to her.

"Two more things . . . one, it's my mom's birthday next week. And she doesn't like to be fussed over, but I wanted to do something nice for her. There's a spa in town where I've made reservations for her to get her nails done, her hair, and I've arranged for some longtime friends from the area to join her there, and then for dinner afterward. But first, I thought it might be nice to start her day with a nice breakfast she doesn't have to make herself. Would you mind helping me with that? I can hold my own in the kitchen, but I'm not an expert. I'd ask Zach, since he's the chef in the family, but he's been working his ass off trying to get the lobster shack he refuses to call a lobster shack up and running."

"Of course I'll help," Britt said. "When's her birthday?"

"Next Tuesday."

Britt blinked in surprise. "Seriously?"

"Yeah, why?"

"That's *my* mom's birthday too."

"Wow! That's quite a coincidence."

Britt nodded. It was, but the differences between the day Chad wanted to give his mother and the birthdays *her* mom celebrated were immense.

"Mom's an early riser, so it'll be hard to surprise her, but I was thinking if we got up and started working on things around five, maybe we could finish before the time she usually appears in the kitchen."

"Sounds good," Britt said. She had no problem getting up that early. She was a morning person as well. She'd learned to be one growing up, since her mom was usually too tired after working the night shift to get up and make sure her daughter had breakfast before heading to school.

"Thanks. I appreciate it. And the second thing . . . if you could maybe help me think of something other than scrambled eggs and bacon, that would be awesome."

Britt giggled. "I think I can manage that. Do you want me to go shopping?"

"No. You do enough around here. Just give me a list, and I'll grab what we need. I can keep the stuff in the fridge here at the shop, so Mom doesn't see it and wonder what we're planning. I'll bring it up that morning."

Making plans with Chad felt . . . homey. As if they were a couple. Which was crazy, but Britt couldn't help the thought. In just three weeks, she'd spent more time with Chad than she had with any guys she'd dated. They ate just about all their meals together, watched TV at night with Evelyn. He usually went to bed around the same time as she did, so he was the last person she said good night to in the evenings, and many times they crossed paths in the hallway in the mornings, when they were getting ready for their day.

Even though they weren't sleeping in the same room—or bed—she felt *closer* to him than she had most of her past boyfriends, as well.

Feeling awkward all of a sudden, and kind of sad that he couldn't be more than a friend and coworker—because getting into a relationship with one of the men who had a say over whether she could stay at Lobster Cove or not wouldn't be smart—Britt gave him one last nod and headed for the door.

The more she integrated herself into life at Lobster Cove, the more it would hurt when she left. This was a temporary job. They both knew that. She knew they'd offered her a job out of pity, despite Chad insisting otherwise, but she'd continue to do right by them before she left. Britt Starkweather wasn't one to flinch away from hard work.

No, the work was the easy part. But this place just might break her another way by the time she left. Somehow, in just a short few weeks, she'd fallen in love with Lobster Cove. With Evelyn. With the smell of the ocean breeze, the sound of the birds obnoxiously singing, or bitching, in the mornings . . . and with Chad.

That last thought had her tripping over her feet, but thankfully she didn't face-plant onto the ground.

Chad was everything she'd ever wanted in a partner. Kind, strong, compassionate, funny, hardworking, and understanding. And he wasn't hard on the eyes either. She'd decided after the fiasco with Cole and the way he'd ditched her in Maine, taking all her money with him, that she was done with men.

But life had a way of laughing in her face. She loved Chad Young, even though she had no idea what to do about those feelings. She suspected she'd end up seriously hurt in the long run if she tried to pursue them.

Therefore, the only thing she could do was pretend nothing was different. That he was nothing but someone she worked with. And when the summer was over, maybe she'd leave after all, head west toward Portland.

Because staying in Rockville and running into Chad and his brothers all the time would be too painful.

Deep down, that didn't feel right. She adored Rockville and the whole Midcoast of Maine. The people, the climate, the beauty of the land. Being by the water was a new experience, and one she loved.

Surely she could find another town, though. There was a lot of water in Maine.

But it wouldn't be Lobster Cove. This place was special. And even if it felt as if she'd been steered here specifically, she couldn't stay and pine for Chad. It would hurt too much.

Her decision made, Britt straightened her shoulders. She had stuff to do. A cabin to clean and a birthday breakfast to plan, and she needed to think of something she could give Evelyn for her special day. The woman had been more a mother to her than Britt's own, and she deserved to have a beautiful day full of love and no stress whatsoever. A day to forget her sorrow and revel in the joy of being with friends.

But as much as she attempted to turn her attention to Evelyn's upcoming birthday, Chad's face wouldn't completely fade into the back of her mind. It was burned there, and Britt was afraid it would never fade.

Swallowing hard, she pushed open the front door of the main house. Being in love sucked, especially when the person you loved had no clue.

CHAPTER NINE

Chad lay in his bed and stared at the ceiling. It was early. Or late. He supposed at two in the morning, it could be either. And he wasn't sleeping. His mind wouldn't turn off. Last night had been . . . perfect. His mom decided she wanted to play gin rummy, and so he'd gotten out the cards and he, Britt, and his mom sat down to play. One game became two, which became five.

Britt turned out to be a ruthless competitor, which was kind of a surprise because she didn't exude a merciless vibe. She was generally easygoing and kind of quiet. But when it came to winning the card game, she didn't hold anything back. And she gloated when she won too. In a good-natured way, but it was clear she wasn't about to let anyone win just to be nice.

It had been a long time since Chad had seen his mom so relaxed. When she began yawning, he'd encouraged her to head off to bed. He and Britt had stayed downstairs, moving to the couch to watch *Deadpool* on TV. It was her suggestion, which once again was a surprise. He supposed he was stereotyping, but that was probably the last movie he would've assumed she'd pick.

When it was over, they talked. About his childhood, about growing up in Maine and on Lobster Cove. Some of the shenanigans he and his brothers got into. She encouraged him to tell her more about his dad, and it felt great to share how much the man had meant to him. It wasn't until after he'd been talking for what seemed like forever that he realized she hadn't reciprocated. She hadn't opened up about her own family.

When he'd asked and she'd abruptly changed the subject to this morning and the birthday-breakfast surprise they were planning for Evelyn, Chad let it drop. If she didn't want to talk about her mother, he wasn't going to force her. But it made him all the more determined to make her stay here at Lobster Cove a good experience.

When they decided it was late and they should get some sleep so they could be up early to make breakfast, they'd ended up standing outside her bedroom door together for a long moment. It had felt an awful lot like walking a woman to her door after a date.

And it hit Chad that he wanted to kiss her. Wanted to take her in his arms, push open her door, and lay her out on the bed.

Which wasn't too surprising. From the moment they'd met, and especially since they'd practically been living together, he'd definitely noticed their attraction. And he hadn't seen one thing about her so far that turned him off. She didn't gossip about people behind their backs. She was insightful, considerate, positive. She didn't let little bumps in the road that came with running a business throw her off.

Britt was great with the guests, taking care of their questions and concerns without needing a lot of guidance from him or his mom. And while cleaning the cabins between guests wasn't anyone's favorite thing to do, she certainly did a thorough job. Didn't cut any corners, wanting each group to feel as if they were getting their money's worth in the hopes they'd come back the next summer.

She wasn't perfect, which would've been a deal-breaker for Chad anyway. He didn't want a Stepford wife. He wanted someone who could laugh at her mistakes, who wasn't afraid to get dirty, who didn't expect everyone around her to cater to her every need.

The first time he'd gotten a glimpse of Britt before she was showered and ready for the day, she'd come downstairs for some coffee in a pair of sweatpants with holes literally all over them. They were ratty as hell and obviously several years old. Her T-shirt wasn't much better. Her hair was sticking up, and she had a mark on her face he assumed was from her pillow. She looked like she'd just been on a weeklong bender.

Instead of being mortified that he'd caught her looking like that, she paused when she spotted him, then simply shrugged and made her way to the coffeepot.

He'd gaped at her as she chatted with his mom for a minute, seemingly unconcerned that she was looking . . . less than her best. She was so comfortable in her own skin—which was a huge turn-on for Chad.

More than that, he loved how she looked people in the eyes when they spoke, giving them her entire attention. How she pitched in to help with just about any job at Lobster Cove. How, when she'd been sprinkling salt on a bowl full of eggs and the top popped off, ruining the food, she hadn't had a meltdown, just laughed and immediately started a new batch.

All that was small stuff, though. It was how she treated people that earned Chad's respect. Walt, Barry, Camden, the little neighbor boy, Kash, Chad's mom and his brothers, the guests . . . it didn't matter who it was, Britt went out of her way to be respectful. To be kind and helpful and compassionate. It might be her retail background, but Chad had a feeling it was simply who she was at her core. Even when she didn't particularly like someone, like Otis, she didn't talk smack about him, was always polite and considerate.

Oh, she got moody. There were a few evenings when she'd been antisocial, going to her room after dinner instead of hanging out. But overall, she was easy to get along with.

So when Chad stood with her in front of her door a few hours ago, he couldn't stop wanting to kiss her. Even after they'd said a somewhat awkward good night and he'd gone to his room, he could see her lips in his mind. Could see the interest he was feeling reflected back in her eyes.

She was an employee. Was living in the same house. It would be wrong to take advantage of that. But it was extremely difficult to see her day after day and not let her know how much he was coming to care about her. How *attracted* he was to her.

A loud clap of thunder shook the house, making Chad jerk on his bed. He knew there was supposed to be a big storm sometime during the night, and now it sounded as if it was almost on top of them.

The longer he listened, the louder the wind howled. Chad couldn't remember when he'd been through a stronger storm. True, he hadn't lived in Maine for a while, but even while growing up, he didn't remember the storms being *this* crazy.

Since he wasn't sleeping anyway, he got out of bed and went over to the window and peered out. It was dark, so he couldn't see much, but the light that his mom kept on all the time over the back door illuminated just enough of the yard for him to see the pine trees around the house swaying ferociously back and forth in the wind. The rain was coming down almost sideways, and he winced, regretting that he and his brothers hadn't been able to get the roof replaced before this particularly vicious summer storm decided to come through.

He was thinking about everything that would need to be done tomorrow—well, later today—to clean up. There would be branches all over the yard. He prayed none of the trees around the property fell onto any of the vehicles waiting to be fixed at the auto body shop. He'd need to check out the roof of not only the main house but the guesthouses as well. And hopefully the kayaks weren't blowing away right that second.

Chad was still lost in thought about all the work ahead of him when a noise at his door caught his attention. Glancing over his shoulder, he saw someone in his doorway. For a second he thought it was his mom, and concern shot through him . . . but then recognition set in.

"Britt?" he asked, turning to face her.

Before she could speak, a bolt of lightning lit up the room, and immediately afterward came a deafening clap of thunder. The raging storm was right on top of them.

Britt clapped her hands over her ears with a grimace, then, without a word, she rushed into the room and headed straight for him.

She flung her arms around his neck and buried her face against his throat.

Instinctively, Chad's arms wrapped around her, holding her tight. He could feel her trembling almost uncontrollably. "Britt?" he asked again. "What's wrong? Are you okay?"

"S-storm," she stuttered, the warmth of her lips and breath seeping into his skin.

It was then Chad realized he wasn't wearing anything but a pair of boxers, and Britt had on only the ratty T-shirt she apparently always wore to bed. Her legs were bare, and he could feel her soft thighs pressed against his own as she plastered herself against him.

His first thought was how good . . . how *right* . . . she felt in his arms.

His second was . . . *Oh shit, this is totally inappropriate.*

She didn't even seem to notice their states of undress. Another bolt of lightning lit up the room, and he felt her stiffen against him right before the thunder cracked. A tiny cry escaped her lips, and he didn't think it was possible, but she managed to burrow even closer.

It finally dawned on him then. She was utterly *terrified*. Of the storm.

Wanting nothing more than to comfort her, Chad backed her up until they were away from the window, then slowly turned to sit on the edge of his bed. To his surprise, instead of sitting next to him, Britt literally crawled into his lap. She straddled his thighs and pressed her chest against his. It was as intimate a position as he'd ever been in with a woman, but it wasn't because she was horny. She was still shaking like a leaf and seemed honestly freaked out.

"It's okay," he murmured, attempting to scoot backward so he could lean against his headboard. A task made all the more difficult because Britt was deadweight against him. She was holding on to him so tightly, not one inch separated them.

Chad was a little freaked out himself now. He was desperate to ease her suffering. Because it was obvious she *was* suffering.

"Shhhhh," he soothed, running one hand up and down her back as the other held her tight. She was making a quiet keening noise in the back of her throat that he had no idea if she even realized she was making. The sound was heartbreaking.

"I've got you," he told her. "Close your eyes, concentrate on me, nothing else." Chad felt helpless. He didn't know what to do or say to help her.

Of course, the storm sure didn't help. Another bright flash and loud boom shook the house, and it made the pace of Britt's breathing increase alarmingly.

Making a decision, Chad scooted down until he was lying flat, bringing Britt with him—not that he had a choice, since she was clinging to him like a baby sloth hanging on to its mother.

He lifted his butt cheek and managed to get the comforter out from under him, then pulled it over both of them, enclosing them in the dark space.

"You're okay. The storm is outside, and we're safe in here. Slow your breathing, Britt."

But his gentle words weren't helping. He put a little more force in his tone.

"I mean it, Britt—slow your breathing down. Do what I do . . . breathe in . . . hold it . . . breathe out. Good. Again."

He felt her making the effort to mimic him, and a bit of his own panic started to fade. One of her hands had made its way into his hair, and he could feel her fingernails scraping rhythmically against his scalp. It didn't hurt, but it underscored her desperation. This wasn't a simple fear of storms. This extreme reaction went much deeper.

Having the blanket over their heads made the air around them humid and warm, but Chad ignored the slight discomfort because it also helped make the lightning flashes less bright. He continued to talk to her, having no idea what he was even saying as he held Britt tightly against him.

Eventually, the scary lightning and thunder began to fade, but the sound of the rain against the window and the wind blowing crazily outside continued. Every now and then, Chad heard a crash, and he prayed again that the trees weren't causing damage to anyone's personal property.

But that was the least of his worries at the moment. The woman in his arms was his priority. She was still tense, still trembling, but at least with the lessening of the thunder and lightning, the distressing keening sounds had stopped.

Chad moved the blanket down from over their heads and took a deep breath of the fresh air. Britt was still lying on his chest, her legs on either side of his, and they were still plastered together. Her T-shirt had ridden up, and the only thing separating most of their bodies was their underwear. He could feel her bare belly against his own. But he wasn't aroused. Not in the least.

"Can you talk to me, Britt? Lift your head and look at me?"

She shook her head against him, and Chad didn't push the issue. "Okay. We'll just lie here and breathe together."

And that's what they did.

To his surprise, even though he could still hear the rain beating against the window, Britt fell asleep in his arms. He could tell the moment it happened because her entire body went limp against his. For a moment he panicked, thinking something was terribly wrong. But when he felt her steady breaths against his neck and her heart beating against his bare chest, he realized that she was getting some much-needed rest.

He didn't dare move an inch, not wanting to wake her up now that she was asleep. Glancing over at the clock on his nightstand, Chad saw that she'd been in his room for an hour. It hadn't felt that long, yet it had felt like an eternity at the same time. But he wasn't close to falling asleep himself. His mind was going a million miles an hour.

First and foremost, what had caused this woman to be so damn terrified of storms? Yes, they made him uncomfortable, made him worry about the aftermath, and many people didn't care for the sounds. But the level of fear Britt had suffered was enough to convince him that she'd experienced some kind of trauma associated with a bad storm like the one that had just blown through. Thinking of what that trauma could've been kept Chad wide awake.

Tomorrow was going to suck. There was no way around that. It was his mom's birthday, they had the special breakfast planned, his brothers would all be over to celebrate, and now he'd need to deal with the aftermath of the storm as well. Doing all that on little to no sleep was going to be extremely difficult. But he'd experienced his share of sleepless nights in the Army. Lying motionless on top of roofs, both in the scorching sun and throughout freezing nights, waiting for the exact right moment to take out his target.

He could deal with exhaustion better than most people.

It was Britt he was worried about. Nothing about the last hour had been fun. He couldn't even enjoy finally holding her in his arms. When he'd had the thought earlier that night about taking her to bed, this hadn't been what he'd envisioned.

Despite that, he wouldn't want to be anywhere else. It hadn't escaped his attention that when Britt was scared out of her mind, she'd come to *him*.

She'd likely experienced many storms in her life, and he wondered how she'd gotten through them in the past. Had she hunkered down in a closet? Listened to music? Huddled in a ball in a corner by herself until they passed? He didn't know. But he was humbled that she'd turned to him for comfort tonight.

Making a mental vow not to let her down in any way from this point on, Chad closed his eyes. He did what he'd ordered Britt to do earlier: he concentrated on breathing. Matching his breaths to hers. And as worried as he was about the woman in his arms, it wasn't long until he succumbed to the lure of exhaustion himself.

CHAPTER TEN

Britt lay still, wondering where the hell she was and why she was so damn hot. When the mattress under her shifted, she froze—and everything returned in a flash. Going to bed after a wonderful night. Feeling horny, getting herself off while thinking about the look in Chad's eyes as he'd said good night at her door . . . then being woken up by a thunderclap that felt as if it was inside her room rather than outside.

And just like that, memories flooded into her brain and she was eight years old again, scared out of her mind. Alone while it seemed the world exploded as a storm raged outside.

Last night, her only thought was to get to safety. To *not* be alone. And she'd gone to the person she'd fallen asleep thinking about, who made her feel safe.

Chad.

She was lying on her side next to him in his bed. She had one leg and one arm flung over his body and was using his shoulder as a pillow. He was on his back, had one arm around her shoulders, holding her against him, and the other resting over his head.

As she lay there, she felt his breathing change. He wasn't sleeping.

She didn't know what time it was, except that it was probably nearing the time they needed to get up and start the breakfast they'd planned for Evelyn's birthday. It had taken Britt a bit to acclimate to the summers in Maine and how damn early it got light outside. Being on the extreme eastern edge of the country meant the sun rose super early in the summer and set very late.

Even knowing she needed to get up, Britt didn't move. For one, other than being warm, she'd never been more comfortable in her life. But more importantly, she was *mortified*. It had been a long time since she'd experienced a storm like the one that had hit last night, and she thought she'd been managing her fear of them just fine in the last couple of years. But apparently she was wrong.

"I know you're awake," Chad said softly, his warm breath wafting over the hair on the top of her head.

"Yeah," she whispered.

"Are you all right?"

She nodded against him, trying to get up the nerve to leave the warmth of Chad's bed and embrace. She hadn't noticed when she'd first woken up, but as clarity returned, she realized he was practically naked. Chest hair tickled her arm, and she could definitely feel skin under her own naked thigh.

For a moment, she panicked, wondering if she'd somehow stripped before climbing into bed with him. Then she sighed in relief when she figured out she was wearing her sleep shirt. But it had ridden up until it was bunched just below her breasts.

"Talk to me," Chad requested.

Talk to him? She was ashamed that her first thought was *Talking when we're both practically naked would be a total buzzkill.* She wasn't in his arms, in his bed, because of some romantic tryst. She'd given him no choice but to care for her. She'd come to his door and barged in, desperate for comfort.

"Britt?" Chad pressed, and she felt him lift his head as if trying to see her face.

Mentally, she sighed. She wasn't going to be able to get out of this without talking to him. And honestly, he deserved some kind of explanation. She was a grown-ass woman who'd acted like a four-year-old.

"I'm afraid of storms," she blurted.

She wasn't sure what she'd expected, but it wasn't for him to chuckle. The sound rumbled through her from the ear plastered against his shoulder, and she realized how stupid that succinct explanation sounded.

"I think I got that, Peach."

The nickname surprised her, and she lifted her head enough to stare at him.

"What?"

"Peach?" she retorted.

He shrugged. "You're from Georgia. It just popped out. Sorry."

"No, it's okay. I just . . . I haven't ever had a nickname before."

Neither said anything for a long while, until he spoke.

"You're afraid of storms . . ." His voice trailed off, obviously an invitation for her to keep talking.

Britt put her head back down on Chad's shoulder so she didn't have to look at him while she explained her fear. "When I was eight, I was home in the trailer we were living in. It wasn't great, but our neighbors were mostly nice. Hardworking people who for the most part minded their own business. It was all my mom could afford.

"Mom was working the night shift, as usual, and it was just me at home. There was a storm. No, that's not the right term—it was actually a hurricane. Much less dangerous and powerful than when it had first hit the coast of Florida, but by the time it got to Atlanta, it was still a Category One.

"The wind was howling, and I think I remember hearing afterward that there were tornadoes too. The trailer started shaking, and it even moved off its foundation. Trees were coming down everywhere, and debris was hitting the sides. The window in my room blew in, which made everything even louder.

"I had no idea what to do. Where to go. The trailer was shaking so hard, I thought it was going to tip over. That I'd be blown away like in *The Wizard of Oz*. I have no clue how long it actually lasted, but as a kid, it felt like hours. I hid under my bed at first, but that seemed like a bad idea if the trailer collapsed. So I ran into the bathroom and got into the tub, like we were taught in school. But the latch on the door was broken, so it kept opening and closing, slamming against the wall. I could literally feel the wind blowing through the house, through all the cracks in the windows and seams.

"When the storm finally passed, I stayed right where I was, too scared to move. To see what had happened. My mom didn't get home until it was light outside, and when she found me still huddled in the bathtub, covered in vomit, shaking like a leaf . . . she laughed."

Britt cringed at the memory that was still fresh in her mind after all these years.

"She what?" Chad asked.

"Laughed," Britt repeated. "Told me I was pathetic, that it was just a storm. A bad one, but a storm nonetheless. Told me to get up and change my clothes because I stank. Then said that she was exhausted, so she was going to bed."

When she paused, Britt realized that the man she was practically lying on was extremely tense. It seemed that every one of his muscles was clenched.

"It wasn't a big deal, I was used to taking care of myself," she said, downplaying how big a deal it *really* was and how relieved she'd been not to be alone anymore. "It took a year and a half for the landlord to get our trailer straightened on its foundation. Granted, it had only shifted about eight inches, but every time I came home and saw how it was askew, it reminded me of that night.

"Anyway . . . I got up and changed, like Mom wanted. Then, because I knew better than to do anything that might wake her, I went outside and started helping our neighbors clean up. Overall, we were lucky. No one was killed or even hurt that badly. There were just some cars that were damaged because of falling limbs and trees."

"And you've been scared of storms ever since," Chad said in a tone Britt couldn't read. It was strangely calm. And unemotional.

She shrugged against him. "Yeah."

"Last night's was bad," he told her. "I forgot how intense they can get here on the coast. Thankfully Lobster Cove is protected, and we don't get a lot of pounding surf on the beach. We do get high and low tides, but that's about it. What do you usually do when there's a storm?"

His change of topic was a bit dizzying, but she answered his question. After what he'd done for her, both last night and in general, she felt as if she owed it to him to explain pretty much anything he wanted to know.

"I usually don't climb in bed with strangers," she said a little flippantly.

But he didn't laugh. Instead, he practically growled, "You and I . . . we aren't *strangers*."

He was right. They might've only met recently, but she knew Chad. And she had a feeling he saw a lot more than she wanted him to when it came to her. "I usually turn up the TV and put in headphones and play music to try to drown out the sound of the thunder. That doesn't help with lightning, but that doesn't bother me nearly as much as the thunder boomers. One thing I *don't* do is go hide in the tub. I have an aversion to baths now . . . which makes sense, I guess, but it's annoying as hell."

"We don't really get tornadoes here in Maine," Chad said. "If we do, they're usually in the southwestern and central parts of the state, not here on the coast."

Britt swallowed hard. He was trying so hard to make her feel better, and it was kind of weird, but it was working. "That's good."

"But even so, anytime you get nervous or feel uneasy, anytime it starts raining, you can come to me. I'll do what I can to distract you, and if it's not working, then we'll hide under the covers together like we did last night."

Even though Britt didn't love talking about her phobia, she couldn't help but squirm a little at the thought of the two of them hiding out together in his bed, in a position much as they were right now. She opened her mouth to thank him, but he kept speaking, cutting her off.

"Your mom was cruel to blow off your fears. To not care that you'd been so terrified, you'd actually thrown up. I get that she was probably working her butt off to keep a roof over your head, but that was uncalled for and completely heartless, and she should've had her damn mom card revoked."

Britt couldn't help it—she giggled at that last part.

"I'm serious," Chad said angrily.

"I know. I have . . . complicated feelings about my mom. Intellectually, I know it was extremely difficult to be a single mother, but for most of my childhood, she wasn't really around much. I had to learn how to make myself dinner, and I packed my own lunches for school. Sometimes she made breakfast, but only if she wasn't too tired from her night shift."

Britt inhaled sharply when Chad rolled her onto her back and hovered over her. She had no choice but to look into his eyes as he stared at her.

"Does this make you nervous?"

Furrowing her brow in confusion, Britt asked, "Does what make me nervous?"

"This. Me and you. In bed. Me *over* you."

"Um . . . no. Thunder is a trigger, not you."

"Good. Because I want to kiss you, Britt. May I?"

Britt swore her heart stopped beating for a moment. "Because you feel sorry for me? Because I was so scared last night?" she blurted.

"Not even close. Because having you plastered against me while we're both almost naked has me on edge. I can't think about anything other than how your lips will feel against mine. Yes, I'm pissed about your upbringing, and the fact that you experienced something extremely scary, and neither your mother nor anyone else in your life saw fit to get you to talk to someone about what happened, so you could get over it. They didn't, did they?"

She shook her head slightly as she stared up at Chad. For some reason, her hands had gone to his waist when he'd rolled them, and the warmth of his skin seeped into her fingers.

"Right. So yeah, I'm pissed at a lot of things right now . . . but I don't feel sorry for you. I pity your *mother*, because she didn't understand what she was losing by treating you the way she did. For not forming a bond that would help her get through the tough times. You haven't told me that you two aren't close, I'm simply assuming, and I apologize if I'm off the mark. I'm also worried about your extreme reaction to the storm, even if I understand where it comes from.

"But I'm so damn impressed with you, I'm practically bursting with pride. You lived a childhood that could've broken you. Instead, it built you up. Made you more resilient. I'm not saying it's right or fair, what you went through. But you being the woman you are today is a miracle. And I want to kiss you because I feel like if I don't, I'll regret it for the rest of my life."

She'd assumed he'd be irritated that she'd acted like a baby last night. Put off that she'd used him as a crutch for her debilitating fears. Instead, he was anything but. She was overwhelmed by everything he'd said. But more than that, she was turned on. It was crazy, but there it was. Hell, she'd masturbated last night to thoughts of him. She was the one who would have regrets for the rest of her life if she didn't experience one of his kisses. But . . .

"I haven't brushed my teeth," she blurted.

He studied her with such emotion in his eyes, it made her blush.

Then he smiled, and it transformed his face. "Right. So . . . how about we both run and clean our teeth, then, and meet back here?"

Britt immediately regretted her words. Talk about a mood killer. She wasn't about to kiss this man for the first time and only be able to think about how bad her breath was, instead of concentrating on him. But she had a feeling that as soon as she climbed out of this bed, reality would intrude, and she'd be too embarrassed to come back to his room and pick up where they'd left off.

"Okay," she said belatedly.

But Chad didn't move. He continued to stare down at her.

"Chad?"

"You amaze me, Peach. I hate what happened to you. I'll say it again, and I'll keep saying it . . . you need a safe haven when there's a storm, you come to me. I'll take care of you. You never have to go through a storm alone and scared again."

She couldn't stop the tears from forming in her eyes as she nodded.

Then Chad rolled away from her and held out his hand as he stood next to the bed.

Britt could only stare. He wasn't wearing anything but a pair of boxers, and while he didn't look like a bodybuilder, didn't have muscles upon muscles, he was definitely in shape. Working around Lobster Cove obviously went a long way toward keeping him toned.

He also had a slight farmer's tan from working outside, and it made Britt smile.

She took his hand and stood next to him a little self-consciously. The shirt she was wearing covered all her intimate bits and came down to her upper thighs. She felt naked, but as his gaze swept over her, from her head to her toes and back up again, she also felt powerful. Beautiful. All because of the look of interest in Chad's eyes.

"Four minutes," he said. "Do what you need to do, then we'll meet back here."

"We should probably get dressed and go start on breakfast . . . if we want to surprise Evelyn, that is," she felt obliged to point out.

"We will. *After.*"

All righty then. Chad squeezed her fingers, then turned and pulled her after him as he went to the door.

There were two bathrooms upstairs, one half bath and one full. He walked them both into the full bath and grabbed his toothbrush and toothpaste, which were sitting next to the sink. Then he dropped her hand and backed out of the small room. "Three and a half minutes now," he told her.

Thankful for something to think about other than last night's storm and how it made her feel, or the way Chad's body felt against hers, Britt reached for her own toothbrush.

CHAPTER ELEVEN

Chad was actually glad for a moment of space from Britt, but not for the reason she might think. He was pissed enough to want to punch a wall. Hearing how she'd been left alone in a trailer, at night, when a hurricane was approaching, at *eight years old*, was bullshit. Negligence. Child abuse. And then to *laugh* at her when she'd so obviously been traumatized was icing on the cake.

Even if she hadn't told him as much, it was obvious Britt had complicated feelings about her mother, simply because she refused to talk much about her. And when she did, she offered excuses for her behavior.

He wouldn't and couldn't give the woman any benefit of the doubt. If he had a wife and kids and was working, he'd find a way to get to them if a huge storm was approaching. Or he'd send someone to the house to be with them. He'd do whatever it took to make sure they were all right.

He could picture a young, terrified Britt huddling in a bathtub, trying to ride out the storm. It infuriated him and saddened him at the same time.

He stood with his head bowed, hands braced on the countertop as he struggled to gain control of his emotions. It was a surprise that he had such a broad range of feelings, as usually he could compartmentalize his emotions and put them in boxes to deal with later. He'd done that a lot as a sniper. Had to. Especially when he was hungry, tired, and hurting as he stared through the scope of his rifle, waiting for the exact right moment to take a shot.

Brushing his teeth helped. Because it made him think about why he was doing it. Without warning, his dick hardened. Simply thinking about *kissing* Britt turned him on more than actually having sex with some women in the past.

And there was something so endearing about her wanting clean breath before kissing him. Chad had no problem acquiescing.

Of course, she might change her mind, now that they weren't in bed plastered together. And if she did, he'd be all right with that. He wanted to kiss her for himself. But he'd also wanted to make her forget about her mother, or any lingering embarrassment she had about what she'd done last night. He wasn't conceited enough to think that kissing him would erase all her fears or make her feel better about what happened, but maybe, just maybe, she'd be able to think about something else for a moment. Preferably *him*.

And he'd seen the interest in her eyes. It was hard to miss. He was pretty sure the same need was reflected in his own gaze.

He ignored the little voice in his head that said it was too soon. That Britt was on the rebound from her relationship with the man who'd left her high and dry in Maine. The electricity he felt between them was strong. Unlike anything he'd felt before. He was thirty-seven years old. He knew the difference between lust and true feelings. He respected Britt. Admired her. Had already been attracted to her.

But after last night and this morning, he wanted her more than he wanted his next breath.

He finished up in the bathroom and headed back to the bedroom. To his delight, Britt was already there. She hadn't gone back to her room. Hadn't changed her mind. He hoped.

Chad walked up to her and didn't hesitate. He put his hands on her cheeks and tilted her head upward. He felt her hands hesitantly brush against his sides before she flattened her palms on his bare skin.

His erection pulsed in time with his heartbeat, and because he didn't want to scare her, he made sure to keep his hips away from hers. Lowering his head, Chad licked his lips, anticipation making this moment almost too overwhelming. This was the first kiss of what he hoped would be many more. He wanted it to be perfect . . . which was another reason he had no problem with the quick break to brush their teeth.

The second his lips touched hers, Chad knew his life had changed forever.

Bolts of what felt like pure energy reverberated throughout his body. Made his fingers and toes tingle. He could physically feel his heart thumping in his chest as he licked the seam of her lips, asking permission for entry.

She opened to him, and the mint on her tongue mixing with her natural taste made him hold her face a little tighter, and he groaned deep in his throat. His cock twitched as he felt her fingers dig into his waist just before she sagged against him.

Britt gave as good as she got, twining her tongue with his and tilting her head, trying to get more. The small moans she made went straight to his dick. Precome leaked from the tip in preparation for burying itself so deep inside her, neither would ever know where one of them ended and the other began.

Every part of him was screaming to put her on her back on the bed and make fast, wild love to this woman. But he also wanted to savor this . . . whatever *this* was.

If he had his way, it was the start of a relationship.

He didn't want to move too fast, push her into anything she might not want. The truth of the matter was, there was still an uneven balance of power between them. Lobster Cove was his home. She didn't necessarily work *for* him, but since he'd brought her here, if things didn't work out, it would be awkward for her to stay. So he wanted to go slow, enjoy the journey, and make sure she knew that what happened between them had no bearing on her job at Lobster Cove.

Of course, that was easier said than done. He'd need to prove to her that if she said yes to dating him, or more, that he wasn't taking advantage. That she could say no and suffer no consequences.

All those thoughts made him ease the desperation in his kiss and eventually pull back. The dazed look in her eyes had him feeling ten feet tall. Made him want to pound his chest in masculine satisfaction. Instead, he lifted a hand and smoothed a piece of hair behind her ear.

"Morning," he whispered with a small smile.

"Hi," she returned.

Fuck, she was adorable. "That was . . . nice," he said lamely.

She grinned. "Not the word I'd use, but we can go with that."

"What would you use?" Chad asked, the question just popping out.

"Fanfuckingtastic?"

He grinned. "I like that better."

Her smile faded. "What are we doing?" she whispered.

Hating the uncertainty he saw on her face, Chad hurried to reassure her. "We're getting to know each other. It's what people do when they're interested in each other, when there's a mutual attraction. When they want to date."

She looked shocked. She hid the emotion, but not before Chad saw it.

"What do *you* think we were doing? Fooling around? Scratching an itch? Because I'm too old for that shit," he told her, just a little defensively. "As far as I'm concerned, I want more, Peach. I want to know all your hopes and dreams, your fears. Hear your laughter, soothe you when you're sad or worried.

"Am I moving fast? Yeah. But I'm old enough to know what I want and what I don't. And *you*, Britt Starkweather . . . I want. But if the feeling's not mutual, that's okay. Your job is safe. *You're* safe. If you want me to back off, just say the word."

She licked her lips, then blew his mind with her next words. "What I want is to climb back into that bed with you and not leave for a few days. But I'll settle for kisses . . . for now. I've had my share of shit relationships, so I know a good man when I see one. And *you*, Chad Young, are almost too good to be true."

He smiled down at her. "So we're on the same page?"

"If that page is seeing where this leads, then yes."

Relief swept through Chad, filling him up. "Awesome," he breathed.

"Yeah," Britt agreed.

Not able to help himself, Chad leaned in and kissed her again. It was just a light touching of their lips, without the passion or the tongue, but no less intimate.

"We should get changed so we can get this breakfast going," Britt suggested.

"Yeah." Everything within Chad protested. He didn't want Britt out of his sight for even a second. But they both had things to do.

She chuckled. "You have to let go of me so we can do that."

It took every ounce of strength he had to drop his hands from her face and take a step backward.

"See you in the kitchen," she said with a shy smile.

It was official—Chad loved that she was living in the same house as he was. That meant he got to spend *way* more time with her than if they'd had more traditional living situations. "See you there," he told her.

He watched her walk out of his room, tearing his gaze from her butt at the last second . . . but not soon enough for her to miss where he'd been looking when she glanced back at him. To his relief, she laughed, and it was the last thing he heard as she stepped into the hall and out of sight.

Chad grabbed a change of clothes and dressed, ignoring his still-throbbing cock for the moment. He wished he had time to take a quick shower and take care of himself, but he'd leave the bathroom to Britt. He'd go out to the auto shop while she was getting ready and grab the food they'd stashed there so his mom wouldn't get suspicious.

By the time he returned, to his surprise, Britt was in the kitchen waiting for him. Her hair was damp, and she smelled like the sweet soap she liked to use. After this morning's kiss, and their subsequent discussion about trying to make some sort of relationship work, all he wanted to do was bury his nose in the crook of her neck and take a bite out of her.

Shit. He'd managed to get control of his dick while he'd gone to get the food, but now it was right back at full mast.

"Um . . . that looks painful," Britt said with a small grin.

"You have no idea, woman."

"I guess you're used to it, though, being a guy and all."

"I've had plenty of erections, yes, but trust me when I say I stopped getting them spontaneously a long time ago."

"Oh," she said with a small blush.

"Yeah, oh," Chad agreed.

"How's it look out there?" she asked, and Chad was glad for the change of topic. He wasn't embarrassed by his hard-on, but talking about it didn't make it go away. Not in the least.

"Not great," he admitted. "There are a few trees down and branches everywhere."

"Do you think the guesthouses are okay?" she asked with a frown.

"No clue. I'll check after breakfast with my brothers. We'll all go out and see what's what."

"Oh! And Kash's fort . . . I hope it wasn't destroyed."

Chad hadn't even thought about that, but now that she mentioned it, he didn't have high hopes. It hadn't been all that sturdy to begin with, and even though the neighbor boy had done a great job reinforcing it, it still wasn't as if it was a house built with safety codes in mind.

"I'll check on that too."

She nodded, but he could tell she was still worried.

Feeling bold, Chad stepped up behind her and wrapped his arms around her waist. He leaned in, resting his chin on her shoulder. "If it's broken, I'll help him repair it," he reassured her.

One of her hands came to rest over his. "I'm sure he'd appreciate that."

Chad wanted to stay there all day, but the food wasn't going to make itself. "If you can start on those cinnamon rolls you found on the internet, I'll get the waffle batter going."

She nodded, and Chad dropped his arms, but not before lightly kissing her on the temple. It felt amazing to be able to kiss her intimately whenever the urge struck. And surprisingly it struck a lot. It wasn't something he'd felt the need to do before—constantly touch or kiss a partner—but since she wasn't complaining, he wasn't going to worry too much about it.

He just had to curb his urges when they were around his mom and brothers. He had no doubt they'd be thrilled that he and Britt were in a relationship, but this was too new—less than an *hour* new—and he wanted to keep things private for now.

Between the two of them, Chad and Britt got everything cooked and baked in time, and his mom's birthday breakfast was a huge hit. And not because of the food, although that was amazing. They'd had cinnamon rolls, waffles, sausage, bacon, sliced fruit and cheese, and donuts from Ruckus Donuts, which Zach had picked up on his way in.

No, his mom had declared it one of her best birthdays ever because all her boys were there to help her celebrate it for the first time in years. She was obviously missing her husband, but thankfully she seemed to be a bit more settled than she'd been when Chad had first arrived home.

"That was some storm last night, huh?" Knox said when they were all sitting around the table, drinking coffee and letting some of the huge breakfast they'd eaten settle in their bellies.

"One of the worst we've had in a while," their mom said.

"It's a mess out there," Lincoln mused. "Trees down all over the county. I checked out the guesthouses before I came in, and the big one that's currently occupied seems good, but the smaller one . . . a tree fell on the corner, taking out part of the roof on one side. But we were actually lucky. If it had fallen a foot in a different direction, it would've gone straight into the house. Thank goodness we didn't have anyone in there last night."

"Oh no!" Britt said with wide eyes.

"Kind of par for the course, living around here with all the trees. And many have super-shallow root systems, so all it takes is wet soil and a hard wind and they can topple right over," Zach said with a shrug.

Britt looked even more alarmed to hear that, and Chad wished his brother would've kept his mouth shut. She already didn't deal well with storms; thinking a tree was going to fall on the house every time they had some wind and rain wasn't healthy. "It doesn't happen a lot," he said, trying to reassure her. "We'll all go out in a bit and survey the damage."

"We're supposed to have renters arriving today," Mom reminded them.

"I know. But Chad's right, let's not get worked up until we check it out," Lincoln said.

"You guys don't seem all that concerned," Britt said with a small frown.

"No need to get stressed about something until we know it's a problem," Evelyn said. "If we need to make alternate arrangements for the people coming in today, we will."

Chad could see that Britt wanted to argue the point, ask more questions—like what kind of alternate arrangements, exactly—but she took a sip of her coffee instead.

This had actually happened once in the past, but that time, a tree had taken out an entire wall of one cabin. All the renters booked throughout the repair process had been invited to stay in the main house instead, at a reduced price. Some had taken them up on it and some had canceled, but everyone who'd stayed gushed about how accommodating their hosts had been and what a good time they'd had.

Of course, this time was different, as Britt and Chad were occupying two of the bedrooms in the main house. If they had to take in paying guests, it would be a full house. But they'd manage . . . the Youngs were nothing if not flexible.

Even though there was a lot of work to be done around Lobster Cove, no one seemed in a hurry to get up and get started. Zach updated everyone on his lobster shack. He hadn't thought of a name for it yet and was considering running a contest on social media to get some ideas. Knox had met with his program manager at the Coast Guard station and would be starting work in the next week or so.

Lincoln hadn't said much about what he was doing, but Chad knew he had a good pension from the Air Force and could afford to take his time finding a job.

Things were so relaxed that, without thinking, Chad opened his big mouth and asked Britt a question that, in hindsight, he really should've waited until they were alone to ask.

"Since today's your mom's birthday too, Britt, have you considered reaching out?"

She'd been smiling and sipping her coffee as his brothers updated everyone on what was going on with their lives, but as soon as the question left his lips, Chad regretted it. It was such a stupid thing to ask, especially when he knew she didn't really have a relationship with her mom. If he could have taken back the words, he would've.

Britt tensed, and the fingers around her mug whitened with the pressure she was exerting, letting him know exactly how badly he'd fucked up.

"Today's your mom's birthday too?" Evelyn exclaimed happily. "Oh! That's so fun! Yes! Call her. We can all sing and wish her a happy birthday like you did for me!"

"Um . . . I'm not sure she'll be up yet," she hedged.

But his mom either ignored or didn't hear Britt as she stood up to grab the cordless phone sitting on the kitchen counter. Knox had bought her a cell phone a few years ago and she was on his cell phone plan, but she rarely used it, preferring the old-school cordless phone she'd had for years.

Evelyn sat back down at the table and held the phone out to Britt. "I'd love to talk to her. Tell her how wonderful her daughter is and how much of a help you are to me," she said in an earnest voice.

Britt reluctantly took the phone but looked about as happy as a fish out of water.

"Mom, maybe we should let Britt call later if she wants," Chad said, attempting to backpedal.

"Nonsense. My gift of this wonderful breakfast and the company of five of my favorite people has me sad that Britt's mom doesn't have her daughter with her for her birthday."

"We don't have the same kind of relationship that you and your sons have," Britt said softly.

"Oh, well . . . that's a shame. But it's never too late to mend fences. And her birthday would be a great time to start."

Chad frowned. He needed to fix this. Now. "Britt, I'm sorry," he said firmly. "I shouldn't have suggested it. I was way out of line. And Mom, if Britt wants to call her mother in private later, she can."

"It's okay," Britt told him.

"It's not. Forget I brought it up," Chad insisted.

He could feel his mom watching their interaction closely. She didn't know the reasons behind Britt's reluctance, but he was grateful she was no longer pushing.

"I think . . . I think I want to try. To talk to her, I mean," Britt said. "You're right. It's her birthday, after all." Then she sighed. "I don't know how she'll react, though."

"Britt, you can call her later," Chad tried again.

She glanced at him. Then she sat up straighter and took a deep breath. "No. I might as well do it now."

Chad had no idea if she was agreeing to the call because she didn't want to hurt anyone's feelings or because she truly wanted to reach out to her mother. Whatever the reason, he could see her uneasiness as she pushed the buttons on the phone. Once more, he wished he'd kept his damn mouth shut.

As she dialed, Chad reached over and put his hand on her thigh in support.

Britt held the phone up to her ear, but everyone at the table could clearly hear the ringing through the handset. Their dad had been losing his hearing, so the volume on the phone was always turned up to its highest level. It obviously hadn't been changed since his death.

Britt didn't seem to notice how loud it was, or that everyone could hear the ringing. She was staring straight ahead, and with every ring, every muscle in her body tensed up more and more.

Chad was two seconds away from taking the phone out of her hand and disconnecting the call, but he was too late. Britt's mom picked up.

"Do you know what the hell time it is?" the woman shouted.

It wasn't a great start to the phone call.

"Hi, Mom. It's me, Britt."

"I repeat—do you know what the hell time it is?"

"Um . . . yeah. Sorry. I just wanted to wish you a happy birthday," she said in a quiet, even tone.

"Happy? What a joke. I'm hungover, I'm broke because my boyfriend cleaned out my bank account, *and* the bastard took most of my food when he left yesterday. I got home from work at the ass crack of dawn to find nothing to eat or drink. Some birthday."

"I'm sorry."

"Yeah, so am I. Heard Cole's back in town. Told you he was a loser. That's all you ever date. I warned you not to believe his lies. Told you he'd fuck you over, but you never learn. Like mother, like daughter."

A muscle in Britt's jaw flexed as she ground her teeth together. "Yeah, you were right," she said after a moment. "But I'm doing okay. I found a job with a wonderful family. They live on the coast, and it's so beautiful here."

"And cold as shit. I don't understand why anyone would live up there in the frozen tundra."

"It's not actually that cold. Spring was lovely. And summer's been great so far—"

"Is there a reason you called? I'm not sending you any damn money. I just told you that I'm broke, and I *also* told you when you left with that dirtbag not to come crawling back to me when he fucked you over."

"No. Just to wish you a happy birthday, Mom," Britt reminded her softly. Her gaze was locked on the table in front of her. "You share a birthday with the woman I'm working for. It's quite a coincidence."

"Well, I hope you aren't being a pain in *her* ass like you were for me," her mom bit out.

Chad was done. It was torture sitting there and listening to one of the nicest, hardest-working women he'd ever met being disparaged by her own mother . . . especially when he'd brought this on Britt himself.

Acting without thought, he did what he should've done earlier. He took the phone out of Britt's hand and brought it up to his own ear.

"Ms. Starkweather? My name is Chad Young, and I want you to know that the way you're speaking to your daughter is despicable. She called to wish you a happy birthday, nothing more and nothing less. And you've done nothing but berate and denigrate her. Britt has been a godsend here. She works hard and has become a part of our family."

"I don't know what the fuck *denigrate* means, but I don't like your tone," her mom bitched.

Chad huffed out an impatient breath. "And I don't like *your* tone. Do you even care that your daughter was living out of her car when I met her? That she was starving? Putting herself in danger because she didn't have a safe place to sleep?"

"No."

One word. That's all she had to say about her own flesh and blood.

Chad wasn't going to prolong this call for another second.

He took the phone from his ear and clicked the off button. He really missed the days when his parents had an old-fashioned rotary phone that could be slammed down. Hitting a button didn't give him the same satisfaction as hanging up forcefully.

Silence hung in the air like the fog that sometimes rolled in from the ocean.

"Yeah, so—"

Britt didn't get anything else out of her mouth before Evelyn abruptly scooted back her chair and stood. She began to collect the empty plates and silverware, muttering under her breath as she did so.

"Stupid, ungrateful *bitch*. Talking about our Britt that way! If I was told one of my boys was homeless and living in his car, I would've asked a hell of a lot more questions. Would've been on a damn plane to wherever they were to help them myself! She doesn't have the right to have the title of mother. What a bitch!"

Chad was afraid Britt might be offended by his mother's rant, even though it wasn't directed at her. She was talking to herself, really. Venting about that awful woman as she cleaned up from breakfast. They all heard her, of course, because the rest of them remained at the table, still sitting in shock over that damn phone call.

When Britt stood, so did Chad. He couldn't let her run out of the room, embarrassed over what just happened. Her *mother* was the one who should be embarrassed. Though he couldn't blame Britt for being upset.

But she surprised him. Instead of leaving, she walked up to his mom, took the stack of plates out of her hands, put them back on the table, then wrapped her arms around her and held on tight as she whispered "Thank you."

Evelyn hugged her back, squeezing extra hard in that mom way that she had. Then she pulled back and took Britt's face in her hands, tilting her head down so she could look into her eyes. "Don't you listen to a word that woman said. You're beautiful, sweet, kind, and I can't imagine you not being here at Lobster Cove. You're the daughter I never had, and I love you."

The mean words her own mother had spewed hadn't made Britt cry, but the compliments and tender mom-words from Evelyn *did*.

"I'm sorry I insisted you call her. I didn't even give you a chance to explain why it wouldn't be a good idea. I just ran roughshod over your protests. Don't let me do that again," Evelyn admonished. "I tend to get a little pushy when I think I have a good idea."

Britt gave her a watery chuckle. "Yeah, I've noticed."

The two women shared a long tender look.

"I have no idea how you turned out so kind after being raised by . . . *her*."

"I was left to raise myself most of the time," Britt said with a shrug.

"And that doesn't really make me feel any better. For the record, you are welcome in *my* home and on Lobster Cove always. I don't care if it's ten years from now or fifty."

"Um . . . as much as I want you to live to be one hundred and twenty, I'm not sure you'll be here in fifty years."

"Even when I'm gone, you'll still be welcome here." Then Evelyn turned to her sons and added sternly, "Right?"

"Yes, ma'am,"

"Of course."

"Not a problem for me."

"Damn straight."

All four brothers answered at the same time. Evelyn turned back to Britt. "My point is, you never have to be homeless again. Forget that bitch. You belong to *us* now."

Britt smiled and hugged Evelyn again.

Chad hovered close to the duo, not sure exactly what to do. He wanted to pull Britt into his own arms and reassure her the way his mom had. He still wasn't sure he wanted anyone to know about the change in their relationship just yet . . . although that call had him rethinking everything.

"I'm thinking now's a good time to go check out the property. See what damage has been done and get to work fixing it. I don't know about you guys, but I wouldn't mind breaking some branches and shit right about now," Lincoln muttered.

"Language," Evelyn scolded.

Linc rolled his eyes. "Mom, you just said *bitch* several times."

"*Bitch* isn't a bad word. *Shit* is."

"There, you just swore yourself," Lincoln said with a smirk.

Their mom rolled *her* eyes this time and turned back to Britt. "I don't know how I survived raising these four monsters."

"We were angels," Knox countered.

Evelyn snorted.

The tension in the air had lifted somewhat, which was a relief.

"You boys go and do your thing. Britt and I will take care of stuff in here."

"I should go and see if anything needs to be recleaned in the cabin," Britt suggested.

"They can check that out and let you know," Evelyn said.

"I also told Walt and Barry I'd get with them and go over the inventory list. I have some questions for them."

"You can do that later. For now, I want to sit with you and enjoy making it another trip around the sun," Evelyn said firmly. "I don't know how many more birthdays I'll have."

Chad knew from experience that when she got that tone in her voice, it was better to just do what she asked. And since she was laying the bullshit on pretty thick, he had no doubt it would work on Britt.

He was right.

"Okay. I'll do the dishes and put away the extra food, and you go sit on the deck. Take the blanket from the back of the couch because it's probably still a little chilly out there this morning."

"You're a good girl," Evelyn said softly. Then she pulled Britt's head down so she could kiss her forehead before she turned and headed for the couch.

Chad waited for his brothers to reach the front door before he moved in closer to Britt. "You okay? That was intense."

"I didn't even realize you could all hear her until you took the phone from me," she said, not answering his question.

"For the record, I agree with my mom. You're amazing. And kind. And smart. And your mom's an idiot."

Britt gave him a small smile. "Yeah."

"I'm so sorry, Britt. And next time, like Mom said, don't let anyone—especially me—talk you into doing something you don't want to do. Okay?"

She nodded.

"I mean it. I should never have brought up your mom, and that whole scene happened because I opened my big mouth. And . . . my mom means well, but she's also lived here in Rockville her entire life. She's surrounded by loving family and good friends and has kind of lived in a bubble."

"It's not a bad way to live," Britt said, defending his mom and her way of life.

"I know, but I don't like that both of you feel bad after what happened, especially when it's all my fault."

"I'm used to it."

"Doesn't mean I like it any better," Chad told her.

"I don't know why my mom's the way she is," Britt told him. "Her life has been hard, and being a single parent didn't make it any easier, but instead of appreciating the things she has, she's become more and more bitter over the years." She gave him a small smile.

"Obviously. So why are you smiling?"

"Because it's nice to know people who have my back. Thank you for sticking up for me with her. I've never had anyone—friends or boyfriends—who've done that for me."

"Then they were weak. Didn't deserve you. No man or woman worth their salt would stand by and let someone they loved, or even liked, get berated like you were. Especially when all you were doing was calling to wish her a happy birthday."

The look on her face was giving Chad all the same feels he'd had that morning. Except he didn't like that he was receiving it because he'd stood up for her. Because he'd hung up on her horrible mother.

Leaning forward, he kissed her on the forehead, just as his mom had done . . . though he was one hundred percent sure the thoughts in his head were the complete opposite of his mom's. He wanted this woman.

Wanted to spoil her. Pleasure her. Show her what having someone at her back *really* meant.

He had a feeling if the men she'd dated never had the balls to stand up for her, they probably never had the patience or sexual prowess to make sure she was satisfied in bed either. If she gave him the chance, he'd show her how a true partner took care of his woman—in bed and out.

"What's that look for?" Britt asked as she stared up at him.

"How comfortable are you with letting my family know what's up with us?" he asked, instead of answering her too-observant question.

"What's up with us?"

"Yeah. That we're dating. We're a thing. Boyfriend, girlfriend."

"We are?"

Chad frowned. "Aren't we? I thought we discussed it this morning. I asked if we were on the same page, and you said, and I quote, 'If that page is seeing where this leads, then yes.' Have you changed your mind? Do you not want to date?"

"I haven't, and I do. I just . . ."

"Just what? You can talk to me about anything," Chad told her, feeling anxious.

"I don't want anyone to think I'm a gold digger."

Chad chuckled. "They won't."

"Otis did. *Does.*"

Chad frowned at that. He'd known she and Otis hadn't gotten off on the right foot and that the man thought she was after whatever money she could get out of Lobster Cove . . . but he'd hoped once Otis got to know Britt, he'd see how his first impression was way off the mark. "He's wrong. And my brothers won't think that. Not for a second. And neither will my mom. If you don't want them to know, I can attempt to keep my hands to myself, but I have to warn you, Peach . . . I have a feeling they'll figure it out pretty damn fast anyway."

"Okay."

"Okay, what?"

"I don't mind if they know we're seeing each other."

Chad beamed. "So that means I can hold your hand and kiss you and call you Peach in front of everyone?"

She gave him a shy smile and nodded.

"Good." He leaned down and kissed her lightly on the lips. Then he went in for a longer, more intimate one. By the time they pulled apart, they were both breathing hard . . . and his damn erection was back.

"I need to get this food put away," she told him.

"And I need to join my brothers in reconning the property."

"You'll be in for lunch, though?"

"Probably. I'll text you if we aren't."

"Okay."

"This is going to work," Chad told her firmly.

"I hope so."

"I know so," he retorted. He kissed her once more, hard and fast, then backed away before he lost his head and took her in his arms and brought her right back to his room. He hated that the storm had scared her so badly, but he couldn't be upset that it had led them to this point.

He gave her a chin lift, then turned and walked toward the door. He had a sappy smile on his face, but he didn't care. Not in the least. Coming home to Lobster Cove had turned out better than he'd hoped. Than he could've ever dreamed. He was reconnecting with his brothers once again, rediscovering the joys of living on the coast of Maine, and spending time with his mom, and somehow he'd lucked out and met a woman he could seriously see himself being with for years to come.

Nothing could ruin his good mood today.

CHAPTER TWELVE

How wrong he'd been.

Victor Rogers could ruin his good mood.

Their neighbor had been a thorn in the Young family's side for as long as Chad could remember. When the boys were growing up, he'd been a jerk about Chad and his brothers being on his property. He'd call and yell at their parents when he found them playing on his shoreline. When they'd created a dirt path through the trees for their bikes and accidentally made part of it on his land, he'd come over ranting and raving and insisting they "fix" the rut in the ground they'd made on his property. Which seemed just as ridiculous now as it had then. It wasn't as if Victor had ever used the heavily forested area between his house and Lobster Cove.

And when Evelyn and Austin had built the boat storage facility, he'd protested the use of the land for commercial business with the county. Chad's dad had solved that issue by putting in a request to change the designation of Lobster Cove from residential to commercial and then commenced to create not only the auto body business but the rental cabins as well.

Victor had retaliated by building his own rental cabins on *his* property, obviously hoping to steal business from Lobster Cove. But he'd built his rentals closer to the road than the shoreline, not giving his guests the beautiful views he could have. Every now and then, Chad looked up the neighbor's rentals online, and he wasn't surprised to see that they were cheaper and didn't have near the number of positive reviews that Lobster Cove Rentals did.

But Chad wasn't the kind of man to gloat about that sort of thing. There had been a sort of unspoken agreement that they'd each mind their own business, and as far as Chad knew, that had been working for the last decade or so. It wasn't as if his mom and Victor would ever be best friends, but at least they were civil.

Still, he'd never given up trying to convince his parents to sell some of their land. That's why it wasn't too surprising to see Victor's old Subaru Outback pull down the driveway into Lobster Cove.

Their neighbor parked near the house, then strode toward where Chad and Lincoln were prepping to repair the damage the tree had done to the smaller guesthouse. He and his brothers had already used a chain saw to cut up the tree and stack the wood near the firepit, so it could be used for future bonfires for either their guests or the family, if they got the urge to chill outside one evening.

Knox and Zach had gone into town to get what they needed to replace the gutter and see if they could get metal roofing materials as well. They'd discussed it and decided they might as well replace the roof now, rather than put in a temporary patch over the damage done by the tree and replace the roof later.

Chad had already gone to the house to talk to his mom about the rental, letting her know it would be out of commission for a few days. It should only disrupt one booking—possibly two—but he hated to inconvenience anyone. It wasn't fair to the renters, but it couldn't be helped.

"Just came over to see what kind of damage you all had from the storm," Victor drawled. He apparently wasn't offering to help, he just wanted to be nosy, which raised Chad's ire.

"We were lucky, just this one cabin," Lincoln said, sounding more diplomatic than Chad would've if he'd responded.

"Your mom home?"

Chad's hackles rose. "Why?"

149

The fake offended look on Victor's face wasn't doing anything to help Chad calm down in the least.

"I just want to check on her. It's what good neighbors do," Victor said.

"Good neighbors don't call the city to try to get businesses shut down. Good neighbors don't complain about kids playing and accidentally stepping onto their property. Good neighbors don't come over to gloat when something goes wrong," he retorted between clenched teeth.

Victor glared at him. Chad had never been his favorite person. Especially since he'd never been one to back down, even as a kid. When Victor yelled at them to get off his property, Chad was always the one to plant his butt on the imaginary line that Victor had drawn between Lobster Cove and his land—then proceed to sing at the top of his lungs, just to be a jerk.

Without another word, Victor turned and headed for the main house.

Chad wanted to follow, wanted to tell him that he was trespassing and order him to go the hell home. But he bit his tongue. His mother was the one who'd been dealing with this man for years, and she was much better at it than he was. She'd told him more than once that you caught more flies with honey than vinegar. But Chad had always wondered why the hell anyone would want to catch flies in the first place.

Then he remembered what the boy, Kash, had said when he and Britt had met him. That he thought Evelyn was mean . . . and that she'd met his grandfather at the door with a shotgun. Hell, so much had happened since then that he'd forgotten all about that. And he hadn't even told his brothers about Kash using their old fort. He needed to get his head out of his ass.

He almost ran to the house to make sure his mom was all right, but he had no doubt if something happened, Britt would scream her head off and alert them that there was a situation.

And the more he thought about it, the more he doubted Kash's story. His mom didn't like guns. Never had. Didn't get on Dad about having them, but he couldn't see her picking up the shotgun and actually threatening someone with it. He doubted it was even loaded.

No . . . probably a story Victor had made up to scare Kash away from their property. It would really get under his skin if his grandson made friends with the neighbors.

Still, Chad was glad that Britt was inside the house to run interference if needed. She was as protective of his mom as he was. She'd also be able to report back as to what Victor actually wanted. Chad didn't believe for a second that he was just checking on them after the storm.

"Something's up," Lincoln mused after a moment.

"No shit," Chad responded. "I don't trust him."

"Me either. We'll ask Mom what he wanted when we're done out here."

Chad nodded, his thoughts returning to their neighbor's grandson and the old fort in the woods. He recalled the books, telescope, and bedding Kash had in there and knew if the plastic bins leaked, or if the boy had forgotten to put everything away, it was all a pile of mush after that severe wind and rain.

Now was the perfect opportunity to tell Lincoln about the boy. "While we're waiting for Knox and Zach to get back, I'm gonna run into the woods and check something real fast."

"Check on what?" Linc asked.

"Our old fort," he told his older brother.

"That thing? It's got to be a pile of debris by now."

"It was, but Kash claimed it as his own," Chad said.

"Who's Kash?"

"Victor's grandson."

"Wait, wait, wait. Harper had a *son*?"

Chad wasn't surprised Lincoln connected the dots so quickly. He and Harper were in the same grade growing up, and she'd been pretty mean to him. He was bound to remember her. "Apparently."

"Is she living over there too? Or just her son?"

"No clue. Didn't get into it with Kash. I just brought Britt out there to see where our old fort was, and we found Kash had rebuilt it and was using it. He was afraid I'd kick him out, since he was on our property, but since I'm not a dick like his grandfather, I reassured him I wouldn't. Besides, it's not like he was making bombs or playing with fire in there or something. He had a ton of books. He also likes astronomy, and he has a pretty nice kids' telescope out there too. I lied and told him we'd named the place Fort Bad Assery when we were young, so if you ever see him and he says something about it . . . go with it."

"Hold on. I thought Victor put up a fence between our properties?"

"He did. Kash climbed over it. Britt was talking to him about how she had to live in her car for a while . . . and apparently Kash could really relate to that."

Lincoln frowned. "Harper and her son were homeless?"

Chad nodded. "Sounded like it, but the boy was uncomfortable with the topic, so neither of us pressed. There's more."

"*More?* Fuck," Lincoln swore.

"When Britt invited him to come to the house sometime, he was petrified. He immediately said no, that Mom was mean. Said that she held a shotgun on his granddad once."

"That's bullshit!" Lincoln exclaimed.

"I agree. But why would Victor tell his grandson that?"

"Because he's a dick. And probably because he doesn't want him getting close to any of us. How old is this kid?"

Chad shrugged. "Ten? Eleven? Twelve? It's hard to tell. He's a scrawny little thing. But not any older than that, I don't think."

"Right. Come on then. Let's go visit old Fort Bad Assery and check on his stuff. Then we'll head to the house and see what Victor wanted."

"I told Kash I wouldn't let his granddad know he was on our property," Chad warned.

"I have no problem with the kid using the fort. I'm more concerned about what the hell is happening with his mom and why they were homeless, and what she's doing now that she's back in Rockville. She swore never to come back here once she graduated, so life really had to have gone to shit for her if she's home again."

"I thought you hated her. That she went out of her way to make your life miserable in high school. Why do you care?" Chad asked. He didn't know the details about his older brother's relationship with their neighbor, but he knew there was a lot of strain there.

"I don't hate her. She's not my favorite person in the world, but if she has a son who's hiding out in our fort . . . something's going on, and I want to make sure he's safe."

Chad couldn't argue with that. He and Linc headed into the woods toward Kash's fort. He was surprised when he spotted it in the distance and it looked like it was still standing.

"Damn, the kid did a good job rebuilding it," Lincoln said.

There was some damage from the wind, and the back wall would need reinforcing, but it was still usable. Getting to his knees to look inside, Chad saw that Kash had put his books and, of course, the precious telescope in one of the large plastic bins, and had then covered it with sticks to try to protect it. As far as he could see, everything was intact.

He backed out of the doorway and let his brother look inside.

When he stood, Lincoln whistled. "It's solid. Nice shelves, decent floor . . . kid's pretty smart. Smarter than *we* were when we built this place."

"We were more interested in using sticks as swords and playing war with each other than having a place to sit and read a book," Chad said with a laugh.

"True. Think the kid has any interest in engines? It would be kind of fun to have a youngster around to teach, like dad taught us when we were kids."

Chad was surprised. "No clue. But I'm sure Victor won't like that at all."

Lincoln smiled. It was more of a smirk than a genuine smile. "That's the point."

He chuckled. "I like it."

"Come on. Let's get back to the house. Knox and Zach should be back soon. I want to check on Mom before we start working on the cabin."

They walked back through the trees to the main house. Victor's Outback was nowhere to be seen, and Chad was relieved he wouldn't have to see the man again. At least today. He and Linc walked into the house, and he called out for his mom.

"We're in here!" she said in return.

Walking into the living area, Chad saw his mom and Britt on the couch, drinking coffee and looking calm and composed. Whatever Victor had wanted couldn't have been that upsetting, since neither woman looked concerned.

"What'd Victor want?" Lincoln asked, not beating around the bush.

"He said he was concerned about damage we might've had from the storm and wanted to check on us," his mom said.

"And how often has he 'checked on us' in the past when we've had storms?" Chad couldn't help but ask.

"Well, never. But that was . . . before. When your dad was still alive."

Those words still had the ability to make Chad's heart hurt. He could only imagine what his mom felt every time she had to say them.

"He also wanted to know if we had guests who were scheduled to stay in the cabin that was damaged, and when Evelyn said yes, he offered to let them stay at his rental instead," Britt added.

Chad was honestly shocked. "He did?"

"Yes. It was a nice thing to do."

It kind of was—but it was also Victor trying to take advantage of a shitty situation by stealing their business. Victor Rogers definitely didn't do anything out of the goodness of his heart.

"Of course I said no, because anything that man wants comes with strings. Big, fat, hairy ones," his mom said, with a huge smile on her face.

Chad was relieved his mom had seen through their neighbor's "nice" offer to help.

"And after she politely declined his offer, he turned nasty and told her she was an idiot. Said if she turned renters away, they'd stop coming, and then he questioned your mom's ability to keep Lobster Cove going. Said Austin was the businessman, not her, and he insisted that ultimately, he wouldn't need her to sell to him. He could just buy the property after she went bankrupt."

Chad's mouth fell open.

"What the fuck?" Lincoln exclaimed.

"Language, Lincoln," their mom admonished, then calmly took a sip of her coffee.

"Why aren't you spitting fire?" Chad asked.

"Britt asked the same question. And the answer is because Victor Rogers is a pathetic, angry man. But he wasn't always that way. Before his wife died, he was tolerable. It wasn't until she passed, and he had to figure out how to raise a daughter on his own while keeping his business going, that he turned bitter and ornery."

Ornery. What a joke. The man was an ass.

"Heard a story about you pointing Dad's shotgun at him," Chad blurted. "Any truth to that?"

His mom smiled into her cup, then she looked up at him and Lincoln and shrugged. "That was blown out of proportion. He came over here a few days after your father passed and got pushier than normal, wouldn't take no for an answer when I told him I wasn't interested in selling Lobster Cove, to him or anyone else. Since he refused to leave until I discussed selling, I decided to clean up a little. I merely picked up Austin's shotgun and moved it from behind the front door so I could sweep. I wasn't *pointing* anything at anyone. It's not my fault if Victor thought I was threatening him."

Chad didn't want to, but he couldn't stop the snort of laughter that escaped.

"Mom. You didn't," Lincoln groaned.

"Didn't what? All I was doing was moving the gun so I could sweep."

Chad wasn't surprised at all to hear that Victor had tried to bully their mom into selling Lobster Cove. The man had actually approached her when she was at her most vulnerable—at their father's funeral. He had no shame.

The value in Lobster Cove was the land itself, not necessarily the businesses they were running. Property values had skyrocketed in Maine in the last couple of decades, especially coastal property. His parents had bought the place fifty years ago for practically nothing. Today, it was worth millions.

But Chad could no sooner see his mom selling Lobster Cove than he could see her falling in love with another man and getting remarried. She and Austin Young were soulmates, and nothing and no one would ever replace the love she'd had with her husband—or the home they'd created together.

Grateful all over again for making the decision to move home, Chad mentally vowed that his mom wouldn't have to so much as *look* at Victor Rogers from now on. The man could deal with him or one of his brothers going forward. And he told her as much.

But their mom wasn't having it.

"I love you both, and Knox and Zach too, more than you'll ever know, but I don't need you to run interference with Victor for me. I've lived next to the man for years, and I can deal with him. Did you know his daughter moved back home? And she has a young son too."

"We know, Mom," Chad said. "But I don't think—"

"No," she said firmly.

"You don't even know what I was going to say," he protested.

"Yes, I do. You were going to tell me that I'm elderly and fragile and I shouldn't have to deal with the pressure from Victor to sell. Well, forget that. I *am* elderly, yes, but I'm perfectly healthy, and I plan on being around for at least thirty more years, so I can see my grandchildren grow up and enjoy Lobster Cove as much as their fathers did when they were kids."

Chad shared a look with his brother, and they both rolled their eyes. Their mom wanted grandchildren more than anything, but since none of them had found the right woman, someone they wanted to spend the rest of their lives with, she was still waiting.

But now . . . he looked at Britt. She was sitting next to his mom, looking at her with concern in her expression. He remembered how great she'd been with Kash. How she hadn't hesitated to get on her knees in the dirt and compliment him on his fort. She'd be a wonderful mom.

And suddenly, all he could envision was Britt lying in their bed with an infant on her chest, smiling up at him.

Shaking his head, focusing back on his mother, Chad looked to Lincoln for help.

"We'll back off, but if he keeps pressuring you, we're going to step in," Lincoln said firmly.

"Okay."

"Okay?" Lincoln questioned.

"Uh-huh. To be honest, I feel sorry for the man. He's got a beautiful piece of land of his own over there, and yet all he can think about is getting his hands on Lobster Cove. And for what? If he put half that energy toward his own place, he wouldn't be so consumed with what's going on over here."

She wasn't wrong.

The familiar sound of the chime that announced the arrival of a car coming down the driveway pealed from the front hallway. Linc walked to the front window and looked out.

"It's Knox and Zach. Have you talked to the renters, Mom?"

"Britt did."

Both Chad and Lincoln glanced her way.

"I explained the situation and told them they could either get a refund, a credit to be used for a future date—which included a twenty percent discount—or they could stay in the main house in one of the extra bedrooms. I warned them that the house had two family members and an employee living here, but that we're all easygoing and friendly. They were actually kind of relieved, because one of their sons decided he wanted to play soccer this summer and he has a tournament this weekend they were going to have to miss. So they took the credit and will come back later this summer," Britt explained.

Chad sighed in relief. That gave them two uninterrupted days to get the repairs done.

"Great," Lincoln said. "Since they postponed, that will give us time to replace the roof so no one else should have to delay their trip. Thanks, Britt."

"Of course."

"I'll go meet the others and catch them up," Lincoln said, before heading for the door.

Chad's mom shook her head in exasperation. "This place is worse than one of those soap operas I used to enjoy watching. Gossip spreads like wildfire."

"We just want to make sure you're safe and happy," Chad protested. "And if you're being harassed to sell, that's not cool."

"I can handle Victor," Evelyn repeated firmly. "Besides, Britt was at my side, glowering as hard as you two were when you heard what happened."

A flash of lust hit Chad hard, taking him by surprise. God, he was so strange. He had no idea why hearing how protective Britt was toward his mother was such a turn-on. But there was no denying it made him want her all the more. Appreciate her. Thank his lucky stars that he'd been in that parking lot at the exact right time to overhear her being yelled at by that stupid employee.

"Britt, can I talk to you for a second before I go join my brothers?"

She looked concerned and stood immediately. "Of course. Evelyn, I'll be right back. Oh, and don't forget to work on your grocery list. I need to do some more inventory work at the shop, but how about we run into town after lunch?"

"That sounds perfect," Evelyn said as she sat back against the couch cushions. "I'm just going to sit here and relax and enjoy the view for now. I love when the sun comes up after a storm. It reinforces the fact that no matter how dark a day, the sun eventually always rises again."

Chad had heard his mom's idioms so many times, this one barely registered. But he could see that it resonated with Britt.

When she reached him, he grabbed her hand and headed for his dad's office at the side of the house, out of his mom's eyesight.

"Chad?"

His mom's voice stopped him in his tracks. He turned to look at her. "Yeah?"

"Treat her right . . . or you'll deal with me." Her voice was uncharacteristically stern.

"Of course. And for the record, we're dating. I hope that's not a problem."

"Nope. As long as you're good to her."

"I am."

"He is."

He and Britt spoke at the same time. He grinned at her, and she returned his smile.

He continued toward the office. As soon as he shut the door behind them, he took her face in his hands and kissed her. Backing her against the closed door to devour her properly, Chad didn't miss how she enthusiastically returned his ardor.

Their heads tilted left and right as their tongues dueled. Britt's hands slipped under his shirt, caressing his lower back and using her fingernails to urge him closer. They were plastered together from chest to hips, and there was no way Chad could hide how much he wanted her.

They were both panting when he tore his lips from hers a minute or so later.

"Good Lord, woman," he exclaimed.

She shyly smiled at him as she licked her lips, making Chad want to kiss her again.

Taking a deep breath, he said, "Tell me what happened."

She was on the same wavelength, and he didn't have to explain what he meant.

"It was interesting. They were both pretty polite, and their voices didn't rise. They could've been having a conversation about the weather . . . despite your neighbor's words getting nastier the more she refused. He was telling Evelyn that she couldn't possibly think she could run the businesses by herself, that she'd be better off selling to him and moving into something called Summit Place."

Chad curled his lip. "That's a retirement home up in Belfast. It's nice enough, but Mom would hate it. All her friends are here in Rockville, and she'd go stir crazy sitting around with nothing to do. Besides, this is her home. Where she lived with Dad for decades. She'd hate only having a small room to live in."

"Which is what she basically told Victor. And that he could take his lowball offer of one million and shove it up his ass."

Chad gaped. "She said that?"

"Yup. Very politely. She also told him that we were doing just fine, thank you very much, and that *he'd* be better off putting all the energy he was exerting on harassing her toward his daughter and grandson. That finally seemed to piss him off, and he left pretty much right after that.

"For what it's worth . . . Evelyn can take care of herself. She wasn't upset, wasn't surprised that he was asking for what I assume is the hundredth time for her to sell. She knows how to deal with him, and that's by staying calm and meeting his rude comments with a few snarky ones of her own. She's pretty amazing."

"She is," Chad agreed. "As are you. Are you all right?"

"Me? Yes, why?"

"Because that had to be a little awkward. And Victor's a big man, and you don't know him."

"It was actually a little entertaining. At first, I didn't understand what was happening. I was thinking everyone's opinions about the neighbor had been blown out of proportion. He seemed genuinely concerned about the damage to the cabin. It's almost impressive how he can be so nasty without changing the inflection of his tone in the least. How's the fort? Is Kash's stuff okay?"

Chad wasn't sure he wanted to change the subject. He was still worried about his mom and concerned with how Britt was handling all the drama. She'd had a hard night, still looking a little pale after the scare she'd had, and then the conversation with her mom. But he didn't want to keep asking her if she was all right. She was a grown woman.

"It's good," he finally answered. "Kash did a great job building it. Just a bit of damage that shouldn't be too hard to fix. And his stuff is all safe."

"Good. I told your mom about the fort and Kash, and she's determined to make him some cupcakes."

"That'll *really* stick in Victor's craw."

"Yup. But I think she cares about the kid. She isn't looking to befriend him just to spite Victor."

"Of course she isn't. That's not how my mom's made. And considering how badly she wants grandkids, she'd befriend *any* strange kid that shows up at Lobster Cove."

He watched a slight flush bloom in Britt's cheeks.

"You want kids?" he blurted.

The pink deepened. "Yeah. Three. You?"

"Three as well. It seems like a good number. And I want them closer together than me and my brothers were. I loved playing with all my brothers, but Zach and Lincoln aren't as close, since they're ten years apart."

Britt licked her lips again, and all Chad could think about was giving this woman children. Watching her play with them. Spoil them. Go mama bear when there was some perceived threat.

"I'm both sad and relieved I don't have any brothers or sisters. I wouldn't want anyone else to experience what I did growing up. I'm determined to do better for any children I might have. I might not be the richest person in the world, but my kids will never go a day without knowing they're loved and wanted. They'll never feel abandoned. I'll never make them feel as if they're a burden, the way my mom did to me."

Chad's heart broke for her. He framed her face in his hands and tilted her face up to his. "You're going to be the best mother. Your experiences will actually make you a better mom than most."

"I hope so," she whispered.

"I have a secret," he said.

She smiled and lifted a brow but didn't pull out of his embrace.

Chad ran his thumbs along her cheekbones. "The closet in your room? There's a small access panel in the back."

"I saw that," she told him, looking confused now.

"It leads to *my* closet. That was Knox's room when we were growing up, and we begged dad to put in a secret passage so we could play together in the morning without waking anyone else up."

He could see the heartbeat in her neck speed up. "Yeah?"

"Uh-huh. It might be a tight fit, but I think you could probably manage."

"Why would I want to do that?" she asked, mock innocently.

"Because after holding you last night, after you being in my bed, in my arms, I'm not sure I can ever sleep without you again."

Britt licked her lips once more. They were shiny and plump, and her light-brown hair fell in tousled waves around her shoulders. She'd filled out a bit since she'd been at Lobster Cove because of his mom's cooking, and while beauty was totally subjective, to him, she was gorgeous.

"No pressure," he hurried to say. "I know it might be awkward to be sneaking around in my mom's house, especially as an adult."

"Before you and Linc arrived, she not so casually told me that since her room was on the other end of the house, on the first floor, she couldn't hear anything that happened upstairs. She said it was a blessing when the four of you were growing up that she couldn't hear any arguments or roughhousing."

Chad chuckled. "I should be surprised my mom is trying to interfere in my sex life, but I'm not."

"She's something else," Britt agreed.

Wanting to beg this woman to come to his bed tonight, Chad kept his mouth shut. He'd extended the invitation. The ball was in Britt's court now. He wouldn't pressure her into doing anything she wasn't completely on board with. But he wanted to do more than share a hallway and bathroom with her—he wanted it all.

The ring, the house, the kids. It was unreal how fast his feelings were developing, but they felt so right. Moving back to Maine, living back on Lobster Cove, meeting Britt. It all felt like fate. And he was there for it. He just had to have the patience to let Britt catch up. She'd faced a lifetime of trauma, and he'd rather cut his wrists than add to that stress.

"I'm gonna head out and help the others. If you need anything, you know where we are," he said.

Britt nodded, then went up on her toes and kissed him again. It wasn't a short peck either. She took control, sweeping her tongue into his mouth and knocking his socks off. He wasn't the kind of man who normally enjoyed giving up control in a relationship, but he could handle *this* woman taking charge.

"Evelyn's making lasagna for lunch. See you then?" Britt asked when she lifted her head.

"Yup. And yum. It's my favorite."

"That's what she said."

Chad reluctantly dropped his hands from her face and stepped back. Britt moved away from the door, brushing her own hands down her sides, as if trying to straighten her shirt.

"You look perfect," he told her. And she did. Her lips were deep red and her cheeks equally rosy, and she had a satisfied look in her eyes. Chad *loved* it. He couldn't wait to see what she looked like after he'd made her come.

"See you later," she said quietly.

"Later," he agreed, then forced himself to open the door and head down the hall.

Britt Starkweather had stormed into his life, and he was more than happy to have her there. Time would tell if the chemistry they had would morph into a long-term relationship or not. He hoped like hell it would, because so far there wasn't a damn thing about the woman he didn't like.

CHAPTER THIRTEEN

The rest of the morning felt surreal to Britt. She kept remembering that kiss in the office and how . . . different it felt. And she couldn't stop thinking about that secret passageway in her closet that led to Chad's room. He'd made it more than clear that he wanted her in his bed . . . but was that smart?

No, definitely not—but that didn't keep Britt from wanting to be there. She'd never felt as attracted to any man as she was to Chad. But was that just because of their proximity? Was it because she'd felt safe in his arms last night while the storm raged? Was it because she was so starved for love that she'd latched on to the first seemingly good man she ran across after being abandoned by Cole?

She didn't think her feelings were a result of any of those things. But what if she was wrong? She didn't have the best track record when it came to guys. But Chad felt different from anyone else. Living and working side by side with him gave her a perspective she hadn't had on any of the other men she'd dated.

If she'd been able to live down the hall from Cole and eat every meal and be with him twenty-four seven, she never would've moved to Maine with him. He said one thing but did another. He promised her the world, and failed to deliver on every front.

Seeing Chad interact with his family was one thing, but seeing him treat Walt, Barry, and Camden with respect told her more about the man's character than anything else. He also went out of his way to be helpful to everyone who came to pick up their boats. Even though it wasn't in the contract—she'd asked Evelyn about that—he helped each and every customer get their boat hooked up to their vehicle or into the water.

He interacted with their renters as if they were the most important people in the world. He was patient with their questions and made sure everyone understood the importance of wearing life jackets while they kayaked, even if they were good swimmers.

And when he'd told her that he wanted three kids? Her ovaries almost exploded, and she'd been about two seconds away from asking him to take her against that door and give her a baby right then and there.

It was crazy, and Britt felt completely out of her element. She didn't think it was just lust. Chad Young was a wonderful man, and she had a gut feeling that if she messed up and let him go, she'd regret it for the rest of her life.

But did that mean she was ready to take the leap and change their intimate friendship into something more? If she slept with him, she'd be all the way in, and that scared her. She already loved him for his kindness and decency, but she knew without a doubt that if she slept with him, she'd be totally head over heels. The intimacy that came with making love would cement the connection she felt with Chad.

And the last thing she wanted to do was lose herself completely in a man. She'd screwed up so badly with Cole, and she hadn't even been this emotionally invested. She didn't want to have her heart ripped out if things went south again. She'd absolutely have to leave Lobster Cove, which would be almost as painful as losing Chad.

It wouldn't be smart to go all in so fast . . . but Britt honestly didn't think she could say no. Not when everything she'd always wanted in a partner was within her grasp.

Screw it.

She didn't want any regrets. And not taking Chad up on his offer to share a bed would be one *huge* regret.

It was hard to keep the excitement off her face. But if she went into the living room right now, Evelyn would know something was up. She'd be giddy with excitement and would somehow get Britt to spill all the beans, and the last thing she wanted to do was talk about sex with Evelyn. Especially since the sex would be with one of her sons.

Feeling a little cowardly, she called out from the hall, "I'm going to head over to the auto shop to meet with Walt and Barry about inventory!"

"Okay!" Evelyn called back.

Feeling relieved she wouldn't have to face Chad's mother yet, not when she had so many X-rated thoughts about the woman's son swirling through her head, Britt headed toward the side door. The weather was beautiful today, as if the terrifying storm never even happened. But the limbs strewn all over the ground were proof that it had.

Thinking about the power of the storm made her shudder. She hated that she had such a deep phobia. She'd tried everything to avoid being so damn scared of them, to no avail. Cole had thought her fear was funny. She should've broken up with him after the first storm they went through together, when he couldn't understand why she was so freaked out. The difference between Cole and Chad's reactions was night and day.

Cole made her feel ashamed of her fear. Chad made her feel safe and understood, without even knowing the root of her problem.

Well . . . *safe* wasn't exactly the word, but at least she hadn't felt as if she was two seconds away from dying, like she usually did.

Looking over at the guesthouses across the vast property, Britt smiled. She couldn't see what the Young brothers were doing, but she could hear hammering, the occasional swear word, and laughter. Seeing the brothers interact was pretty much exactly what she envisioned when she thought about a "big happy family."

She heard Walt, Barry, and Camden talking as she approached the auto shop. Britt hadn't been able to get a better read on Otis's son since their first meeting, though he still made her a little uneasy. Camden hadn't said or done anything offensive, but she was pretty sure he didn't care for her much, even though she hadn't said more than two dozen words to the man. She assumed he was standoffish because, like his father, he considered her an outsider.

Or maybe he was upset that she'd offered to help out with inventory and some of the admin work for the auto shop. But he might not know that she wasn't being paid anything extra for the work.

Determined to be friendly even if he wasn't, Britt plastered a smile on her face and stepped into the first bay.

"Good morning!" she called out.

"Britt!"

"Hi!"

Walt and Barry both greeted her with smiles and genuine pleasure in their voices. It didn't escape her notice that Camden didn't even look up from the engine he was bent over. He was in the corner, working on a riding lawn mower that someone had brought in because it wouldn't start.

"That was some storm last night, huh?" Walt asked.

"Yeah," she said, feeling as if that was the understatement of the century.

"My youngest crawled into bed with my wife and me," Barry said. "My oldest wanted to go up on the roof to get a better view of the lightning, so he could get some good pictures. And the middle one slept through the whole thing. I can't believe how different they are."

Britt shuddered thinking about being outside in a storm like that. But on a roof? *Closer* to the lightning? Where you could get hit by it even easier? That was literally her worst nightmare come true.

"Take it you're not a fan of storms," Walt boomed with a laugh, though it didn't feel like he was laughing *at* her.

Britt gave him a small shrug. "No. Had a bad experience when I was little."

She surprised herself by admitting that. She didn't usually admit to anyone that she was terrified of storms, but something about the mechanic made her feel as if he wouldn't make light of her fears. And she was right.

His smile dimmed and his brows furrowed. "You okay?"

She gave him a nod. "Yeah."

"If it makes you feel any better, storms like that aren't common. Yes, we get rain and wind, but those huge thunder boomers and the lightning? Not as much."

Relief swam through Britt's veins. "Good."

"Was there much damage to the guesthouses?" Barry asked. "Saw the boys heading over there this morning, and we can hear them working on it."

"A little. The reservation that was supposed to check in today was okay to cancel, so now they think they can fix it before the next couple is scheduled to arrive," Britt told him.

"That's good. Was hoping to head over and see if they needed a hand later, but we're up to our eyeballs in repairs down here."

Britt nodded. "Do you have time to sit with me and go over more inventory? Or should we do it another time?"

"No, now's good," Walt told her. "Barry, if you can finish up here, I'll help Britt. If we take an hour or so, I figure we can get another good chunk done."

"Sure thing," Barry said amiably.

"Camden, while Britt's helping out with inventory, I'm also gonna place an order. Is there anything you need?"

He looked up from the lawn mower. "You know she's just going to fuck it up, right?"

Britt was a little taken aback at his nasty words.

"She knows nothing about engines or cars. She doesn't know a carburetor from a proportioning valve. How do you expect her to be able to manage inventory?"

Britt pressed her lips together in irritation. She opened her mouth to defend herself. To mention her experience in admin. To explain that she didn't need to know what the parts did, just ensure that they were properly coded in the inventory system and that it was calculating the parts as each one was used and invoiced.

But Walt spoke before she could.

"Are you shitting me?" he asked, his voice booming throughout the bay. "We've asked you at least a hundred times to help us out in the past, to inventory the parts you've used before you leave work, and every damn time you came up with excuses. Either you don't have time or you don't get paid for that shit. Now we have software that'll manage it for us, and Britt's offered her expertise for free. And I bet she won't make any more mistakes than *you* do. How many times have you asked us to order the wrong shit? Or punched in the number wrong so we got ten bottles of oil instead of a hundred? Either cut her some slack, Cam, or shut the hell up!"

If looks could kill, Walt would've been obliterated into a million little pieces. But rather than respond, Camden slammed down the wrench he was holding and stormed out of the building.

"*Fuck* he's annoying," Barry muttered.

"Don't listen to him," Walt told Britt. "He's just an asshole. Always has been, always will be. Austin would've fired him a long time ago if he wasn't Otis's son. And Evelyn is too nice to cut him off. You're doing just fine. Come on, we'll go into the office and fire up the program, and you can show me more about how it works."

Thankful that at least Walt and Barry seemed to want her help, Britt headed into the office.

An hour later, her head was spinning. She'd truly had no idea there were so many different parts when she'd started this venture. Which was stupid, because engines were complicated machines. And the engine on a Honda was different from the engine on a snowmobile, which was different from an engine in a lawn mower. She really *didn't* need to know exactly what they did or how they were used, but since she was logging each part into the inventory program one by one, it was taking a bit more time than she'd thought.

She was confident she'd become familiar with the parts they ordered most frequently soon enough. But Camden wasn't exactly wrong when he'd said that not knowing anything about engines would make the job more difficult.

"You're doing great," Walt praised. "You're gonna be an engine pro in no time. And I can't believe how fast you type! You're also a great teacher. We'll all have the hang of this system before you know it. It's going to make things so much easier around here."

He really was a nice man, and Britt was grateful for his patience.

"I need to get back out there and help Barry. We good in here for now?" he asked.

Britt nodded quickly. "Of course."

He smiled and gave her a nod, then stood and headed for the door.

"I'm just going to create another mock invoice or two before I go," she told him. "Check to make sure the invoices still work as expected, charging the right prices and stuff. Then make sure the inventory and the billing systems are integrated properly."

Walt didn't even turn around. He waved his hand and said, "Sounds good" as he exited.

It took her just a few minutes to create a simple invoice for random parts, and she was thrilled to see the prices were correct, the sales tax was applied, and the parts were automatically deducted from their inventory. Just like the first test she'd run a couple of days ago. She sighed in relief.

She clicked on a different icon on the computer. She'd also been happy to discover she was familiar with the accounting software Otis used for Lobster Cove Auto Body.

It was pretty intuitive, and her experience helped her navigate the spreadsheets quickly. But unlike last time, the longer she poked around in the program, trying to figure out if it was pulling the correct data for the parts she'd invoiced, the more confused she became.

She was finding recent bills for parts that she hadn't entered into the system.

Frowning, she sat back in her chair.

There were also a lot more vendors in the system than just a couple of days ago. Names she didn't recognize. Businesses she'd never heard of. Not *too* alarming; after all, she didn't have every vendor memorized. But the amounts that were being charged to Lobster Cove were . . . substantial. And she hadn't heard Walt, Barry, or even Chad mention any large orders they'd placed recently. Nothing that would account for such big vendor invoices.

Scanning another spreadsheet, she saw that last month, there were thirty-two bills that had been paid. This month, she only saw twelve. That was a pretty large difference.

"Maybe most of these vendors bill late in the month?" she muttered. So in addition to some rather large bills already paid . . . there could be almost two dozen more coming in?

Looking up, Britt made sure she was still alone in the office. Of course she was. But her guilty conscience was kicking in. She was looking at stuff she technically shouldn't be. But her curiosity had been piqued—and she was suddenly worried.

Clicking on some of the vendor names only confused her further. Digital records of the previous month's bills were dated throughout the month, not just toward the end.

Most confusing of all—when she compared what was listed on the vendors' invoices, the parts weren't listed in the new inventory software . . . and they weren't on the spreadsheet Walt had put together for her of the parts used most often.

For example, one bill last month was for a hydraulic booster unit, whatever that was, but she didn't see it anywhere on Walt's inventory list.

The more she clicked, the more discrepancies she found.

Twenty brake rotors—one of the first things she and Walt had put into the inventory system—were paid for, but she'd only logged in ten. Had they actually used *another* ten in the last few weeks, before she'd started inputting data? She doubted it.

There was also an SAE J1772 type 1 connector, an engine cradle, a water pump pulley, a resonator, an intake manifold, a steering arm . . .

More parts the shop had paid for that either didn't exist on the inventory sheet Walt gave her—whether as stock or as having been used in the last few months—or had way more listed on the bill than were on hand.

Had any of that wonderful, special breakfast Britt had eaten five hours earlier still remained in her belly, she might have thrown it up right there and then. What was going on? Was this just a matter of sloppy administrative work, Walt not knowing what parts they had . . . or something else?

It wasn't a simple matter of an extra part being ordered here and there. The difference was far too great. *Thousands* more dollars going out to vendors than parts actually being received.

Sitting back in the chair, Britt glanced at the corner of the computer screen and realized that she'd been digging around for over an hour.

She felt seriously sick. Something was very wrong here. But she didn't know exactly what. And she wasn't sure what to do. She was new to Lobster Cove. And she wasn't even supposed to have anything to do with the financial side of things. She'd only logged in to that system to reconcile the mock invoice. The last thing she wanted was to accuse anyone of being deceptive. Of *stealing*.

But she couldn't just sit back and keep her mouth shut either, especially with the amount of money she now had a feeling was missing from Lobster Cove's accounts.

"Britt?"

She recognized Chad's voice as he called her name. For some reason, she panicked. She clicked out of the programs on the computer, then gathered the papers she'd jotted her notes and thoughts on and shoved them into the bottom drawer of the desk.

She stood and turned to face the door just as Chad appeared.

"Hey, you've been down here a while. Everything good?" he asked.

Britt nodded. "Yeah, it's good. I was just checking everything out. Trying to get a feel for the programs. It's fine. Good." She was talking too fast and repeating herself, but she couldn't help it. She hadn't decided the best way to explain what she'd found, or even who to talk to. It might be nothing, and she didn't want to make any wild accusations.

Was Barry or Walt fudging the books? Was Otis scamming the system and pocketing money? Were they innocent mistakes? Maybe she didn't understand what she was looking at. Or the charges were correct and the missing inventory was just parts that weren't used very often and stored somewhere she didn't know about. Or Walt simply forgot to add them to his spreadsheet.

"What's wrong?" Chad asked with a frown.

It was crazy how well he could read her after such a short time.

"Nothing," she said quickly, feeling as if she was being more than obvious that something was *definitely* wrong. But there was too much she didn't know. She couldn't make him worry over nothing, if that turned out to be the case.

He stared at her for a long moment, then held out his hand. "Come on, time to break for lunch."

Thankful he wasn't going to push—Britt had a feeling if he had, she would've cracked—she took his hand. Instead of walking toward the door, Chad yanked her forward, making her stumble and fall into him. He wrapped his arm around her waist until they were plastered together.

"I don't want you to be afraid to tell me anything. If something's bothering you, no matter how small you think it is, I want to know about it."

Gah. This man. He was killing her. "Okay," she whispered. The burden of holding in her suspicions was heavy, but again, she really didn't want to accuse anyone until she was sure that something was wrong. This was her second day of helping out with the admin stuff. It was too soon to be pointing fingers.

Chad stared at Britt for a long moment before nodding. Then he slowly leaned in, giving her time to refuse his advances. But Britt had no intention of doing that. She met him halfway, almost desperate to get lost in his kisses once more.

It wasn't until a wolf whistle sounded from the doorway that they pulled apart. Britt had been two seconds away from begging him to take her right there on the desk. She could feel herself blushing furiously as she turned toward the door. Chad didn't lower his arms from around her, though. He simply smiled at Walt, who'd been the one to whistle.

Britt's lust died when she saw a frowning Otis at Walt's side.

"Just getting Britt for lunch," Chad told the two men.

"Is *that* what that was?" Otis muttered.

"Good," Walt said at the same time as Otis's snarky comment. "She's been in here working for hours."

"Doing what?" Otis asked, standing taller, his gaze going from her to the computer on the desk.

"Inventory," Britt blurted, that sick feeling in her gut returning. "Just trying to get everything entered into the system."

She saw the older man's shoulders visibly relax at her words.

Shit, shit, shit. She had a very bad feeling the Youngs' oldest and dearest friend was responsible for the inconsistencies in the accounting. The very last thing she wanted to do was call him out and hurt his relationship with the family. But how could she not? From what she could tell, thousands of dollars were going missing every month. And if Otis was stealing, she *had* to say something.

"Come on, we're doing Mom's cake after lunch," Chad said. "And you're all invited. Say in about forty minutes or so? Come up to the house and we'll do the singing thing."

"Awesome!" Walt exclaimed, rubbing his belly. "Please tell me it's German chocolate."

"Would it be anything else? That's her favorite," Chad said. "And Zach made it."

"Hot damn!" Walt said with a huge smile. "That boy's magic in the kitchen."

"He is," Chad agreed. "Otis, you'll join us, right?"

"I've got a lot of invoices to input," the older man hedged.

"Come on. Please?"

"All right."

"Good. Come on, Britt. I don't know about you, but I'm starving."

She wasn't. At Otis's words, she felt even sicker. Was that why the number of invoices for this month had been fewer than previous months? Because he hadn't gotten around to putting in the rest? She had a feeling that when she next looked at the accounting software, it would more closely match the previous months . . . but would the inventory match the bills?

She doubted it. And the Youngs' bank account would be that much lighter.

It didn't escape Britt's notice that Walt stepped between her and Otis when Chad pulled her out of the room. She hated that the older man's dislike of her was so obvious . . . but she couldn't help thinking of how much *more* he'd hate her if she could prove he was embezzling money from Lobster Cove.

And with a start, she realized that it might go even deeper. He was in charge of all Evelyn's finances. Taxes. Investments. The question of how much money he could've stolen over the years without anyone knowing was mind boggling—and terrifying.

Chad walked them halfway to the main house, then stopped and turned to face her. "I know we're just starting our relationship, and you've had some not-so-great experiences in the past when it comes to men, but I'm not like them."

Britt stared at him with her heart in her throat.

"You can trust me to have your back. If someone is bothering you or harassing you, we'll deal with it. If you changed your mind and don't want to help with the admin stuff, no one—especially me—is going to be upset. If all this is too much and you need to find another job, put some distance between yourself and my crazy family, that's all right too. It can be a little overwhelming to live and work at the same place. I'm feeling a little of that myself. It's difficult to go from living on my own to moving back in with my mother.

"All I'm saying is, whatever's on your mind, you can share it with me when you're ready. I won't judge, I'll listen, and we can figure out how to fix whatever it is . . . *together.*"

Britt wanted to cry. This man . . . he was . . . pushy, confident, moving forward at the speed of a bullet train . . . but she didn't hate it. "I need to mull something over for a bit. I don't like making split-second judgments," she told him. "But I'll talk to you. Soon. I promise."

"I can live with that." Then Chad leaned down and pressed his lips to her forehead. "I can be intense."

Britt couldn't help it. She laughed. That seemed like the understatement of the year.

Chad chuckled a little. "Yeah, I know. Mom always tells me I'm like a runaway train coming down the tracks at a hundred miles an hour. But all you need to do is tell me to back off, and I will. I just want what's best for you, Mom, my brothers, Lobster Cove. And believe it or not, I do have a ton of patience . . . had to as a sniper in the Army. There were times I had to lie unmoving for hours to wait for the perfect moment to take my shot. I just like to cut to the chase when I can."

Britt hadn't thought much about what he'd done before she'd met him. But she couldn't deny she was curious. Being a sniper couldn't have been easy, physically or mentally. It made her admire him even more.

"Come on, everyone's waiting on us."

Britt frowned. "They are? Why'd you stop me, then? We need to get inside!"

Chad laughed but obediently followed behind her as she hurried toward the house.

CHAPTER FOURTEEN

Lunch was fun. Chad was happy to once again recapture moments they'd enjoyed until the boys started leaving home after graduating from high school. Every birthday, they'd gather around the kitchen table with a huge cake and sing to whoever was turning another year older. It was such a simple thing, but it felt as if it had more meaning now than in the past. Dad was missing, of course, but that just made every second the family could spend together a little more important.

And having Britt at his side was an added bonus. It was scary how much this woman had come to mean to him in such a short period of time . . . and how easily he could read her.

Something had happened while she was at the auto shop, but he had no idea what. Walt and Barry seemed fine, their usual selves. Camden had been there earlier, but he wasn't in the shop when Chad had gone to get Britt. Otis had just arrived, so he couldn't have said anything to Britt to put that look of worry and concern on her face.

Whatever it was, he hoped she'd confide in him sooner rather than later. He didn't want her time here at Lobster Cove to be concerning or stressful.

There was still a lot he needed to learn about her, and vice versa. He hated that he hadn't known about her fear of storms before last night, but now that he did, he'd keep an eye on the weather and do what he could to mitigate her fears. He never wanted to see her as scared as she was when she'd barged into his room. She'd practically been in a terror-induced trance, and if he hadn't been around, he hated to think about how she would've coped . . . or not coped.

He wanted her to know that she could lean on him for anything. To get through storms, to talk through her feelings about her mother, to rant and rave. He wanted a real relationship, not just the bright and shiny parts. He wanted the warts, slogging through the mud, dealing with any darkness that might arise—and he wanted to do it all together.

That wasn't something he'd ever felt before. He'd been satisfied with simple relationships in the past. Going out to eat or to the movies, having sex. He'd never felt the need to share his burdens or deep dark thoughts with a woman before. But he did with Britt.

He had a feeling she'd understand the complicated emotions that came from being a sniper. How proud he was of his record . . . and how disgusted at the same time. Killing human beings wasn't something to brag about or talk about in polite circles, or even with his family, but he could see himself unburdening his soul and telling Britt about some of his more gnarly missions.

In return, he wanted her to open up to him as well. Her childhood had been shit. She'd practically raised herself, and that couldn't have been easy. Listening to her mother harangue her that morning was painful . . . almost as much as watching Britt pretend it didn't bother her.

But he was grateful she didn't need her own awful mother anymore . . . because she had *his* now. Britt had gone with his mom to the store after lunch, and when they'd returned, they'd both been laughing—he and his brothers could hear it all the way from where they were working on the cabin.

On that front, they'd made great progress on the new roof today, and Chad felt confident they'd finish up in time to welcome the next renters. Zach, Knox, and Lincoln had left for their homes an hour ago. Evelyn had left shortly before her sons, back to town for her spa appointment and birthday dinner with some of her oldest friends.

He and Britt had the house to themselves, and Chad was thrilled. He wanted nothing more than a quiet night to relax and hang out, just the two of them.

Many people would think his life was damn boring, and they certainly wouldn't understand why in the world he'd moved back in with his mother at thirty-seven years old. But he didn't care. He loved his mom, and he loved Lobster Cove. It was in his blood, and he felt more at home here than anywhere he'd ever lived.

And Britt being with them was icing on the cake. He didn't have to convince her that he wasn't a weirdo for living at home. Didn't have to try to talk her into moving in with him . . . she was already here. He grinned at the thought.

"What's that smile for?" she asked.

Chad glanced over at her. They'd eaten leftovers for dinner and were now sitting on the couch, watching TV. Some show about people being dropped into isolated places and competing with others, who they couldn't see or talk to, to be the last one to quit and go home. It was interesting, but not as interesting as the woman next to him.

"I was just thinking about how much I love this."

"This?" she asked.

Chad waved a hand to indicate the room. "This. Sitting at home. Waiting for my seventy-one-year-old mother to get home from a dinner date. Watching TV. Relaxing after a long day of honest work. Being with you."

Britt rested her head on the cushion behind her. "Yeah. I like not being alone."

Chad nodded. She'd hit the nail on the head. "Yes. The hardest part about being single was coming home to an empty apartment after work or after being deployed. Not having anyone to talk to, to share my day with, to eat with."

"Being here has been . . . enlightening," Britt said.

He glanced over, feeling the intimacy of the moment. There was only the large-screen TV and a small light in the kitchen illuminating the room. She had a blanket over her legs, and they were sitting close, but not quite close enough to touch.

"How so?" he asked.

"Growing up, I was always alone, since my mom worked so much. I came home from school to an empty apartment, ate dinner by myself, put myself to bed. In the mornings, Mom was usually sleeping when I got up. There were some weeks when we barely said two words to each other, since our schedules were so opposite."

"That's sad," Chad said softly.

Britt shrugged. "I didn't know any different."

"Doesn't make it any less sad."

"My childhood wasn't necessarily *bad*," she said. "At least, it could've been a lot worse. But after seeing this place, the love you and your family have for each other, I realize that I missed out on so much."

Chad reached for her hand. He didn't pull her into him, although he wanted to. He simply wanted her to know that he was there, that she had his support.

"It wasn't always easy growing up with three brothers and having so many businesses here on the property. We didn't go on a lot of vacations because we needed to be here for customers. Dad worked a lot . . . yes, he was here on Lobster Cove, but he was always doing something. But I don't think I would've changed anything about my childhood. We had everything we needed right here."

Britt squeezed his hand. Then she sighed and turned her head to stare into space.

Chad wanted to reiterate that she could talk to him. That she could tell him anything. But he didn't want to push.

A couple of minutes passed as the TV show played in the background.

He felt Britt tense a moment before taking a deep breath and turning her head back toward him. "I think someone is stealing from you. From Lobster Cove. And I think it's Otis."

Chad blinked. That was so far from what he imagined was wrong, it wasn't even funny. His first instinct was to deny it. Tell her there was no way. But he forced the words back. It was obvious Britt had seemed distraught since before lunch. And it was no wonder she'd needed some time to think before telling him what was wrong.

"Why?"

Her head came up off the cushion and she tilted it in a questioning way. "You aren't going to disagree? Tell me I'm wrong? That there's no way he'd do something like that?"

"I don't have enough information to say any of that," Chad said calmly.

He felt her relax a little through the grip he had on her hand. She was still tense, but it was as if getting that first sentence out released a lot of tension she'd been holding on to since this afternoon.

"I don't know for sure. But when I was helping with the inventory at the auto shop, I noticed some stuff that looked hinky."

Chad didn't want to believe it. But Britt had no reason to lie. Not about something like this. Besides, she knew how close Otis was to their family. How much he'd done for them, was *still* doing for them. So she'd also know accusing him of something so egregious was a huge deal.

"At first I didn't think too much about it. Figured it was just data entry errors. There seemed to be a lot of inventory ordered and paid for that wasn't actually in stock . . . or at least, Walt didn't have it on his spreadsheet. It was weird. I thought I was probably just confused, since I'm still learning what the different parts are. But when I looked at the accounting program—which I only did because I was making up some fake invoices to test the system—I also noticed there were double the amount of bills the previous months than there are for this one."

"It's possible with Dad's death, the shop simply hasn't been as busy as it was before, so we've ordered fewer parts," Chad said gently, still not wanting to believe what he was hearing. He wasn't making excuses for anyone, per se, just trying to come up with some kind of reason for the discrepancies.

"Yeah."

Chad waited for her to say more, and when she didn't, he was kind of disappointed. "What else? If someone is stealing from my mom and Lobster Cove, it's a big deal, and my brothers and I need to know about it so we can do something."

She sighed. "Well, despite all those bills . . . what the shop has paid for in parts doesn't match the inventory list Walt gave me. There are things that were apparently purchased that it seems were never delivered. And it's not just a few things. I'm not talking about ten bucks here and there. It's thousands of dollars' worth—*every* month, Chad. It looks to me like someone is making up bills for parts that don't exist, then pocketing the money."

"And you think that's Otis."

Britt nodded. "I don't know who else it could be. He's the only one, up until now, who's used the accounting program. Unless one of your brothers has been helping?"

Chad shook his head. What she was accusing Otis of doing was serious. Felony serious. Thousands of dollars a month added up to a hell of a lot of money, no matter *how* long it had been happening.

And his mother had mentioned money was tight . . .

He'd wondered in recent years why his parents had refused to retire at least *some* of their businesses. He'd casually suggested over a year ago that maybe they shut down the rental houses, let themselves slow down a bit and enjoy life a little more. But his dad had basically blown him off, said they liked to stay busy . . . but now he wasn't so sure that was the reason.

Then another thought struck him. If Otis was skimming off the top from the auto shop, what was he doing with their taxes? And their investments?

His stomach dropped.

"I'm sorry," Britt said, sounding upset.

"No," Chad said a little too forcefully. "You have nothing to be sorry about. If you're right, we all owe you a huge debt of gratitude."

But she looked as miserable as Chad felt. His mind was reeling. He needed to talk to his brothers. See if they could find an independent auditor to take a look at not only the auto shop books but their taxes and investments as well. And maybe have a conversation with his mom without letting on about what might be happening. Not yet. Not until they were positive.

If Otis was guilty of what Britt suspected, it would destroy Evelyn. Losing her husband was devastating. Losing one of their oldest friends on top of that would be another huge blow.

"Come here?" Chad asked, letting go of her hand and holding out his arm, inviting her to scoot over.

Thankfully, she didn't hesitate, moving into his side. She leaned into him and curled her arms in front of her chest as she snuggled closer.

Chad wrapped his arm around her shoulders and arranged her blanket over both of them. Just having her near made him feel so much better.

Neither said anything for a long minute or two.

"That couldn't have been easy to tell me. Thank you," Chad told her.

"I feel awful about it. When I realized what I was looking at, I felt sick," Britt said quietly. "I admit that Otis and I didn't hit it off, but I wouldn't lie about this. And I wouldn't accuse him of something this horrible if I wasn't sure something was off."

"I know. And in case you're worried he'll turn around and try to blame everything on you . . . if he's guilty, there will likely be years' worth of data. Long before you arrived."

She nodded. "I know. I was actually thinking about that all day, and it's one of the reasons I felt brave enough to come forward. I wanted to wait until I had proof, but I figured the longer I waited, the more time he had to find a way to blame me. Say I messed with the software and screwed things up or something."

She wasn't wrong.

As the minutes ticked by, Chad felt Britt relaxing against him, which was a relief. He wasn't quite as relaxed, but with her in his arms, he was getting there.

When the current episode of the TV show ended, the next one started. But Chad wasn't paying any attention. Everything he'd have to deal with tomorrow was eventually pushed to the back of his mind as he continued to hold Britt. Slowly but surely, his senses tuned in to her. The way her warm breath felt against his chest. How close her hands were to his nipples. The feel of her body. Every time she shifted, he imagined turning them so she was on her back beneath him.

He wanted her. Having her in his bed last night felt so right . . . even though the circumstances sucked. And he'd extended an invitation for her to use the secret door in the back of her closet to join him again tonight . . . but he didn't want to sneak around. They were adults, and his mom was perfectly fine with the fact they were dating. She loved Britt, already considered her a part of the family.

But he wouldn't pressure Britt into doing something she wasn't ready for. She was relying on his mom, and him and his brothers, for a place to live and her salary. He didn't want her to agree to do anything out of a sense of obligation or because she felt she had to in order to keep her job.

Needing some space before he did something he'd regret, Chad lifted his arm in preparation for getting up. He opened his mouth to make some excuse about needing something to drink from the kitchen, when Britt moved.

She turned into him, hitching her leg up and over his thigh while grabbing his shoulder. Then she lifted her head and kissed him. It wasn't a tentative kiss either. It was aggressive and almost desperate—and it communicated exactly what Chad was feeling.

He moved without thought, pushing her backward without lifting his lips from hers until she was just as he'd envisioned in his mind seconds earlier. On her back, beneath him. His hands roamed her body as he took control of the kiss and devoured her.

But Britt wasn't passive. Her hands were just as busy, one second clutching him to her and the next shoving up under his T-shirt to rake up and down his back. She arched into him and lifted her knees until her feet were flat on the cushions and she was cradling him between her thighs.

Chad's dick was hard, and he couldn't stop himself from grinding into her soft belly as they made out. He felt like he was sixteen again and making out with his girlfriend while pretending to watch a movie, hoping against hope his parents or brothers wouldn't come downstairs and interrupt.

Desperate to touch her bare skin, Chad thrust a hand under her shirt. He roughly pulled one cup of her bra down, and they both groaned when he palmed her naked breast. Her nipple hardened under his touch, and he felt a spurt of precome leak out of his cock.

This woman had him ready to blow, and they were still mostly dressed. He lifted his head and stared down at Britt, in awe at her power over him. At how much he wanted her.

Her chest rose and fell with her rapid breaths, pushing her tit into his hand with each inhale. One of her hands was clutching an ass cheek, holding him against her as close as she could get, and the other was digging into his bicep, her fingernails lightly stinging through the cotton of his shirt.

She licked her lips, and Chad swore he was two seconds from coming in his pants right then and there, because all he could think of was how those same lips would look wrapped around his cock as she swallowed him down.

"The invitation to stay with you tonight is still open, right?" she whispered.

"Tonight. Tomorrow. And every day after that," he said truthfully.

"I'm scared things will change. Once it comes out that I was the one who told on Otis."

Giving her nipple one last tweak and loving how she arched into his touch, Chad reluctantly removed his hand from under her shirt. He palmed her cheek and leaned down to kiss her gently. "Nothing is going to change. You've got my mom wrapped around your little finger, Walt and Barry adore you, the rental guests think you're amazing, and my brothers already see you as part of this family."

"And you?" she whispered.

"You don't know?"

She shook her head.

"I can't imagine you not being in my life. It's as if I've known you forever, except I'm pissed that I haven't. That we've missed out on so much time. You're different from every woman I've ever known, Britt. I feel it deep inside. We were meant to be in that parking lot at the same time. You were meant to be here at Lobster Cove. With me."

Chad held his breath. He had no idea if he was freaking her out or not, but he couldn't keep quiet about his feelings anymore.

Hell, he'd come this far . . . he might as well be completely honest.

"I love you, Britt Starkweather. It's too fast. I know. But my feelings aren't going to change. For the first time in my life, I understand the kind of love my parents had for each other. But I have no intention of rushing you or forcing you to be with me if you don't feel the same way."

"I do," she whispered. "And . . . rush me. Please."

Chad lowered his head and kissed her hard. His dick was pulsing and his balls were drawn up so far toward his body, they hurt.

He was seconds away from yanking her pants down and taking her right then and there when he heard a noise at the front door.

He pulled his head back and swore. "Shit, Mom's home."

The next few seconds were almost comical as they both sat up quickly and tried to right their clothes and act like they hadn't been about to make love right on the couch.

They were sitting two feet apart and staring at the television when Evelyn walked into the room. "I'm home!" she said. "What have you two—"

Her words cut off abruptly, and Chad turned around to look at her, praying she wasn't as good at reading him as she used to be.

"Well, crap. My timing is shit, isn't it?" she asked with a huge grin on her face.

Chad wanted to laugh. It seemed he still couldn't hide anything from his mom.

"I'm just going to go to bed. I had a wonderful birthday, and I'm beat. You two carry on with . . . you know . . . whatever you were doing. Don't mind me. I'll be in my room on the other end of the house . . . far away from anything going on out here. And I sleep like a rock, so don't worry about the . . . *TV* bothering me or anything."

With that, she turned and headed for the hallway that led to her room.

Chad caught Britt's eye, and they both burst out laughing. He stood and held out a hand. "What do you say we take this upstairs?"

To his relief, she took his hand and let him help her up. "I'd like that," she said, sounding a little shy, but eager at the same time.

Chad leaned down and kissed her on the lips, keeping his tongue to himself this time. If he didn't, he'd end up bending her over the couch and taking her there and then. And as much as his mom was apparently thrilled with the idea of the two of them together, he didn't think she'd enjoy knowing they'd had sex in her living room.

He turned off the TV and led Britt toward the stairs, then stopped. "Shit. I want to make sure the house is locked up. My mom sometimes forgets to lock the door. Dad always used to complain about that. Wait for me? Better yet, you can go up and use the bathroom first and meet me in my room?" It was as much a question as a suggestion.

"Okay."

Relief swam through Chad's veins. His cock was still hard, and the thought of her waiting for him in his bed wasn't helping the situation.

She backed toward the stairs slowly, smiling at him, and it wasn't until she'd gone up three steps that she finally turned around and hurried up the rest.

Chad watched her go, his gaze locked on her ass until he couldn't see her anymore. Then he quickly headed for the front door to make sure it was secured.

Things had taken a strange turn tonight. He'd wanted to know what was bothering Britt, but never in a million years would he have thought she'd tell him Otis might be stealing from his family.

He'd had no intention of admitting so soon that he loved her, but he hadn't been able to hold back.

And now he was going to get to make love to her, something he'd thought about almost constantly recently. Tonight, he wasn't going to have to be content with masturbating to the thought of Britt; he'd get the real thing.

Smiling, Chad forced himself not to rush as he made sure the windows and doors were all secured. He wanted to give Britt time to get ready. Because as soon as he set foot inside his bedroom and saw her there, going slow was going to be a thing of the past. He'd waited too long for this moment . . . to make love to a woman he loved.

CHAPTER FIFTEEN

Strangely, Britt wasn't nervous at all. She was excited. Keyed up. Horny.

Chad Young loved her. It was a miracle. She still couldn't believe she'd heard him right. She'd always hoped to find a man who would love her for who she was, and it was hard to wrap her mind around the fact that Chad felt the same way about her as she did for him.

She'd thought about this moment for quite a while now. Masturbating to the thought of his hands on her was nothing compared to the real thing. His calloused fingers on her breast had almost made her come. She was relieved Evelyn had arrived when she had, because Britt had been two seconds away from pulling Chad's pants off and going down on him right there on the couch. How embarrassing would it have been if Evelyn had walked in and seen *that*?

As hard as she and Chad had tried to act like nothing was going on when she'd arrived, his mom had known anyway. But thankfully she hadn't seemed upset. The way she'd fled to her room was obvious and hysterical. Almost as funny as how fast she and Chad had gone upstairs.

Britt got ready for bed in record time. She kind of wanted to check out the secret panel in the closet, but it was quicker to just use the regular door. She'd have time later to inspect it, pretend she was a teenager sneaking into Chad's room. For now, she wanted to be ready and waiting when he came upstairs.

She heard him on the steps, then entering the bathroom in the hall. Anticipation swam through Britt's veins, and she second-guessed her decision to come to his bed wearing nothing at all. She probably should've at least tried to be a little demure. Maybe put on the oversize T-shirt she usually wore to bed. He might've wanted to undress her himself.

Shit, the last thing she wanted was to look like a whore.

But it was too late to go to her room and grab something to put on, or even to grab a shirt from Chad's drawer. She heard him in the hall seconds before the door opened. Britt had left on the light by the bed, as it gave the room an intimate feel, more so than leaving the bright overhead light on would've.

She was sitting in the middle of the bed when he entered, with her back against the headboard, the covers at her waist, her upper body exposed.

Chad's eyes widened, then he turned quickly and shut the door, locking it in the process.

Swallowing hard, Britt prayed she hadn't made the wrong decision in her clothing choice . . . or lack thereof.

Then he was walking toward her. It didn't take many steps since the room wasn't that big, yet by the time he reached the side of the bed, he'd peeled off his shirt, dropping it on the floor. His gaze locked on her breasts as his hands went to the fastening of his pants.

He shoved his jeans and underwear off at the same time, then stood there, letting her look her fill as he did the same.

Britt took a deep breath and felt her pussy gush. The man was *gorgeous*. His cock was hard and bobbing in front of him as he widened his stance a little. He was muscular, though Britt couldn't help but smile at the little pooch of his belly, which matched her own. She liked that he wasn't hard all over like a bodybuilder. He had a bit of chest hair but not too much. The hair at his groin was trimmed, enhancing the size of his dick.

Her mouth watered. She wanted to taste him.

Britt loved blow jobs. Loved how it made her feel when the guy she was with moaned and groaned and begged to be sucked deeper. How his hands tightened in her hair, and how he tasted as he got close to the edge. And she enjoyed swallowing. A lot of women didn't, but she never felt so powerful in her life as she did when she made a man come by using her mouth.

"Look at me," Chad ordered in a dark, hoarse tone.

Tearing her gaze away from his dick, she looked up.

"When I get in that bed, you're going to do what I tell you, how I tell you to do it, and when. You have any problems with that?"

Britt's heart beat overtime. She'd never considered herself all that submissive. She liked what she liked in bed and had no problem expressing those desires. But the thought of Chad taking control had her literally dripping.

"Britt? I'm on the edge here, and I need you. Hard and fast. I'll make it up to you after our first time. Okay?"

In response, she flipped the covers back, exposing herself to Chad. To emphasize her consent, she spread her legs a little, showing him how wet she was for him.

"Damn," he swore, then he was lying next to her. He grabbed her and pulled her down with him, but instead of pressing her to the bed, Chad surprised her by rolling them until he was beneath her. She felt a smear of wetness when his cock brushed against her belly.

His hands came up and cupped her breasts, squeezing and pushing them together. Britt had never been all that impressed with the size of her tits, but with Chad, she felt as if she was perfect. His hands fit her just right. And when he used his fingers to pinch both her nipples at the same time, she groaned and straddled his waist, undulating against him.

"Chad," she moaned.

"That's it. Show me how much you need me," he said, moving his hands to her hips and encouraging her to rub herself against him.

Britt could feel his dick against her ass as she moved over him, spreading her wetness on his skin. It was dirty and raunchy, and she'd never felt more empowered. She didn't feel as if she needed to hold back with this man. She could be exactly who she was. And she was a woman who loved sex and had too often been let down by it.

Britt had no doubts that Chad wouldn't let her down. He would take her over the edge, *force* her over it in fact, again and again.

"You're so fucking wet," Chad said. "I can smell you. You smell so damn good. Come for me, Peach. I want to feel you come on my stomach before I let you fuck me."

Before he let *her* fuck *him*? Oh yeah, she wanted that. So badly.

She had no doubt who was in charge here, though. He was. Yes, she was on top, but he was controlling every step of their lovemaking. And she liked it.

He moved one hand between her legs and began to aggressively strum her clit. Britt squeaked and began to rock against him harder.

"That's it, Peach. Give it to me."

It didn't take long for her to come. Not when she'd dreamed about being exactly where she was right now, and when Chad was staring between her legs as if he'd found nirvana.

She froze for a single second before every muscle in her body began to shake. Then she couldn't hold herself up anymore as she exploded.

"So damn gorgeous," Chad murmured as he drew out her orgasm by continuing to stroke her clit. Even when she was too sensitive and tried to shift away from him, he tightened his hold on her hip and kept up the motion of his thumb on her bundle of nerves. That caused her to scream a little as she came again, spilling more of her wetness onto his belly.

"*That's* it. That's what I wanted."

His hands dropped from her body entirely, and Britt had to brace herself on his chest to keep herself from falling over. She felt as if she were floating, and she fought to catch her breath as he leaned to the side and reached into the nightstand, taking out a condom.

She didn't think she could love him any more, but with that gesture, she realized she did. He was protecting her, them, without having to be asked. Hell, at that moment, she was more than ready to take him bare, even though she'd never had sex with anyone without a condom before.

His hands went around her sides as he rolled the condom on without having to see what he was doing. Then he put his hands right back where they'd been, one on her hip and the other between her legs.

Britt jerked a little when, without warning, he pushed his index finger deep inside her body. She came up on her knees a little, giving him more room.

"So hot and wet. Squeeze my finger," he ordered.

Britt tightened her inner muscles around him.

"*Damn.* Yeah, you're going to be a tight fit. Stay there for a second."

Britt hovered over him as he added another finger inside her. He didn't shove them in roughly, didn't push them in and out of her as if he was jabbing a fucking elevator button. No, he was gentle but steady. And it felt amazing.

"One more," he warned, before adding a third finger. It was a little uncomfortable, but given how thick his cock was, Britt knew she needed to be stretched a bit before she was able to take him. She moved up and down with shallow thrusts, taking it upon herself to fuck his fingers.

"I've never been so hard in my life," Chad told her, moving his gaze up to hers. It made the moment even more intimate. "I want you, Britt. So damn much. And not just here and now. I want you in my bed, my life, every day. I love you."

Shit, he was going to make her cry. How often had Britt longed to hear those words? Not only hear them, but truly feel as if the person saying them meant it? She couldn't remember the last time her mother had told her that she loved her. And a few of the men she'd dated had said the words, but she'd never truly believed them. She'd always felt like they were saying the words to get something from her, or because they thought they were expected.

"I love you too," she whispered, trying not to let her voice break.

Chad pulled his fingers out of her body and brought them to his lips. He stuck all three into his mouth and groaned. "Damn, I can't wait to get my mouth on you. I'm not going to let you up for at least an hour while I feast. But first . . . I need inside you. Take me, Britt."

His hand dropped from her hip, not helping her at all. She understood. This was up to her. If she wanted him, she was going to have to do exactly as he said—take him.

He was leaving the ball in her court. On a visceral level, she got that once she took him inside her body, that was it. She was his. Just as he was hers.

Scooting back on her knees, Britt reached between her legs and took hold of his cock. It was *so* thick. Thicker than any she'd had before, and she couldn't wait to know how it would feel inside her. He twitched under her hand, and she took the time to briefly run her pinkie finger over his balls.

"Stop fucking around," Chad growled.

Feeling happier than she could ever remember being, Britt giggled. But she did as she was ordered and lifted up a little higher. She rubbed the head of his dick against her still extremely sensitive clit and jerked at the intense feeling.

"Put me inside, Peach. Do it. Now."

Her belly clenched at the thought of using his cock as her own personal sex toy, getting off solely by rubbing it against her clit. But she pushed that idea aside for another day and notched the head at her opening. Then she began to lower herself over him. Even with how wet she was, it was a tight fit. And it stung a bit. Pressing her lips together, Britt took a deep breath.

Chad remained still as a stone under her, letting her take the lead, which she appreciated more than he could know. Still . . .

She didn't think she could do this on her own.

"Help me?" she whispered.

"How?" he asked, still not moving.

"Touch me. I need you to touch me."

"Touch you how? Tell me," he demanded.

"I don't know! I need you. I love you. You're just . . . big! Bigger than I've ever had."

He didn't hesitate, easing his hand between them and stroking her clit.

The second he touched her, she jerked—and that pressed his cock inside her a little more. Closing her eyes, she began to move the way she had earlier, when she'd gotten off by rubbing against him.

"Open your eyes. *Please*. Look at me," Chad said gruffly. "I want you to see who loves you. Who's inside you."

Britt's eyes flew open, and she stared down at him as she continued to try to feed his monster dick inside her body slowly, bit by bit, as he strummed her clit. "Last night before the storm, after you left me at my door, I masturbated," she said softly. "I imagined you kneeling over me, fucking me hard. I came so damn fast."

"Show me how you imagined it. Move your hips, show me how I fucked you."

That wasn't a hard order to follow. Britt began to move her hips back and forth. Up and down. She was so lost in the lust and love she saw in his eyes, the way she was feeling, the memory of her fantasy from last night, that she didn't realize she'd taken all of him until she felt his pubic hair rubbing against her own. His hand had moved out of the way, and she hadn't even noticed.

"Look down, Britt. See how well you've taken all of me."

She did, and the sight of him buried so deeply inside her body made her clench around him.

"You okay? I'm not hurting you?" Chad asked.

Britt shook her head.

Then he was touching her again, and she let out the breath she hadn't even known she was holding. "I'm going to fuck you now. You good with that?"

Honestly, the way he kept making sure she was on board with this, that she wanted him, was both endearing and annoying at the same time. "Yes, Chad. I'm good with that. Please, take over."

"With pleasure," he breathed—then he gripped her hips hard, pulled her up his dick, and slammed her back down.

Britt let out a quiet screech. He rubbed places inside her that had never been rubbed before. The strength he showed in manipulating her body was equally impressive. All Britt could do was hang on and feel.

"Hold yourself there," he ordered after a few minutes of lifting her up and down on his dick. Britt didn't know if she could hold herself up, but she tightened her thigh muscles, determined to at least try.

Then, as she hovered over him, he fucked her from below. Watching his cock repeatedly appear and disappear into her body was as erotic as any sexy video she'd ever seen online.

He suddenly grabbed her hips and hissed, "Sit."

She wanted to complain about being given an order like she was a dog, but deep down, she loved being told what to do. It took the pressure off. She didn't have to think about her next move or wonder if it would please him.

Without hesitation, and feeling relieved that she didn't have to try to hold herself up anymore, Britt lowered herself onto him slowly.

"Fuck me from the inside, Peach."

Grinning, Britt did as asked. She tightened and loosened her inner muscles around his cock over and over. He grimaced, and if she didn't feel him actually swell inside her, she might've thought she was hurting him. Then he gripped her almost painfully, groaned loudly, and came.

Power swept over her. *She'd* done that. She'd made him come with just her pussy muscles. She was smiling huge but didn't even care. But before she could revel in her victory, his eyes popped open, and he reached up and pinched one of her nipples tightly, at the same time using the thumb on his other hand to rub circles over her clit.

She came almost immediately, her body confused about whether it was experiencing pain or pleasure.

His second groan as she rippled around his dick was almost as satisfying as the orgasm he'd given her. She wanted to collapse onto his chest in a sweaty, satisfied heap, but he held her up with a hand on her upper arm.

"I need to remove this condom," he told her gently.

Shit, she'd almost forgotten. With a small moan, she started to lift herself off him, but before she finished the move, he rolled until she was under him. Then he pulled out of her, making her whimper with disappointment . . . and a bit of relief. He really *was* thick.

He straightened to his knees as he deftly removed the condom and tied it off. Then he nonchalantly placed it on the bedside table and lowered himself over her.

But Britt couldn't stop looking at the used condom on the table. That was . . . gross.

"Um . . ."

He chuckled, and she felt it against her chest.

"You want me to get up and throw that away?" he asked.

"Do I want you to get up? No. Do I want to have that thing staring at me all night? Also no."

"Need to put a trash can next to the bed," Chad murmured. "Stay put. Don't move. I mean it. Not one muscle."

She nodded.

Chad got up, grabbed the condom, and wrapped it in a tissue. Then he walked butt-ass naked to the door and into the hall.

Britt was shocked. She stared at the door with her mouth open. When he returned, he had a washcloth in his hand. His cock wasn't hard anymore, but it was no less impressive. It hung between his legs, swaying back and forth as he walked toward the bed.

"I can't believe you went out there like that!" she exclaimed.

Chad chuckled. "My mom knows better than to come upstairs at night. Especially after what she walked in on tonight."

"We weren't doing anything," Britt protested.

"We would've been if we'd had five more minutes. You know it, I know it, and my mom knows it. She's thrilled. Trust me. If she wasn't, she would've finagled you into having tea with her and made it clear she didn't like the idea of the two of us together."

Britt had a feeling he was right, but still.

"Open," Chad ordered, as he held the washcloth over her pussy.

She could wash herself, but she did as he asked, sighing in pleasure at the feel of the warm cloth against her folds. She would be sore, that was for sure, but sex with Chad had been worth every second of discomfort.

He dropped the wet washcloth on the floor next to the bed—making Britt roll her eyes—maneuvered her onto her side, and snuggled up behind her, spooning her as if they'd done it every day of their lives. It felt right. Natural.

And Britt arched her back, pushing her butt into his crotch a little snugger.

"Wait, you didn't wash yourself," she said. It was easier to talk about this while she wasn't looking at him.

"I know. I like how you smell on me. Didn't want to wash you off."

She didn't know if she should be turned off by that or not. She decided she wasn't.

They were quiet for a long moment before he nuzzled her hair. "Thank you," he said softly.

Britt smiled. "You're welcome."

She felt as if she should be thanking *him*, but she was too tired. She couldn't remember how many orgasms she'd had, but she felt as if she'd been turned inside out. It had been a long day after a crappy night's sleep because of the storm. She was half-asleep when she felt Chad kiss her shoulder. It was an intimate and sweet gesture that was a perfect end to the day.

CHAPTER SIXTEEN

Chad's mind was in turmoil. On one hand, he was thrilled to have woken up with Britt in his arms. He'd slept like a rock, and she said she'd done the same. He loved hearing her giggle when she went back to her room through the closet. They'd tried to keep things as normal as possible at breakfast, but Chad had no doubt his mom was pretending to be oblivious to the big change in their relationship. She already knew they'd decided to date, but being intimate with Britt had already altered things drastically.

For one, he couldn't keep his hands off her if he tried. Brushing against her every time he passed, keeping a hand on her leg as they ate or on the small of her back when he stood next to her. His mom wasn't an idiot, and if the silly grin on her face was any indication, she was just as happy as he was.

Which was why he hated to burst that happy bubble by telling her about Britt's suspicions about Otis. Sticking to the decision he'd made last night and choosing not to tell her until he'd spoken with the man himself, Chad felt stressed about the confrontation ahead of him. He'd already texted Otis and asked if he could talk to him that morning.

Which wasn't an unusual request. He'd been wanting to have a family meeting with him after his brothers settled in. But with all the work needed around the property and how busy they'd all been, he hadn't made the time. And that was totally on him. He should've made it a priority.

Chad himself had been on the verge of switching his own investments over to Otis, and he'd planned to have the man do his taxes next year. Now the thought of him having access to his accounts made his skin crawl. And he hated that he felt that way.

He also needed to have a talk with his brothers and let them know about Britt's suspicions, but again, he wanted to see what he could figure out first.

The meeting with Otis hadn't gotten off to a great start when the man tried to put him off entirely, saying he wasn't sure he could get to Lobster Cove today. But Chad wasn't willing to take no for an answer. He told Otis that he'd be glad to meet him at his office in Rockville, which was what they finally agreed upon.

His brothers had arrived to hopefully finish work on the rental cabin, and Chad felt bad that he was bailing on them. But this meeting with Otis couldn't be delayed. Not if he was stealing from his mom and Lobster Cove.

Britt knew where he was going this morning, and why, and she was concerned. Not for his safety so much as for the excuses Otis might have to explain the accounting discrepancies.

She walked him out to his dad's pickup, and they stood by the driver's side door.

Chad took her face in his hands and rested his forehead against hers as she held on to his wrists. "It's going to be fine."

"I know. I just . . . What if I'm wrong? I'll feel horrible about accusing him of something so heinous if you find out that he's innocent."

"I have a gut feeling you aren't wrong," Chad told her, trying to sound reassuring.

"But I don't know all the ins and outs of things around here yet. And it's possible I just don't know enough about automotive parts to understand what I was looking at."

Chad dropped his hands to her shoulders. "From everything you've told me, you don't *need* to know what the parts are for. Numbers are numbers, and if they don't add up, something's wrong."

She bit her lip.

"I'm not going to accuse him of anything, even if I find out for sure that you're right. I want to be certain all our ducks are in a row and that we're covered. All I'm doing today is feeling him out. Asking him to explain a few discrepancies. I want to see what he says. Okay?"

Britt nodded. "Be careful."

Chad frowned slightly. "This is Otis. He's not dangerous."

But the worry in her eyes didn't abate. "Anyone can be dangerous if they're cornered," she countered.

She wasn't wrong. Chad nodded solemnly. "Yeah. I'll be careful."

"Good. Because it would be really sad to never get to show you my cock-sucking skills."

And just like that, Chad's dick hardened. "Damn, woman," he breathed.

She gave him a coy smile. For such an innocent-looking woman, she was sure able to push all his buttons. What did people sometimes say? Lady in public and vixen in the bedroom? He was a damn lucky man, and he knew it.

Chad pulled her against him, letting her feel what her words did to him. "What are your plans today?"

"Your mom wanted to head into town to that quilting store."

Chad chuckled. "My mom can't quilt."

"Well, apparently she wants to learn."

The thought was hilarious, because his mom had done just about every craft there was . . . and failed spectacularly at each and every one. But if she wanted to try quilting, he wasn't going to be the one to dissuade her.

"I also thought I'd go out to Kash's fort and see if he's there before Evelyn and I head into town. Check on him. If he's not, I can check on his stuff. I'm also meeting with Walt and Barry again later, and then I need to clean the cabin once your brothers finish up, to make sure it's ready for the next renters."

"Busy day," he said, trying desperately to think about something other than her sinking to her knees right there and taking his dick into his mouth.

As if she knew where his mind was, she smiled at him and ran her hands up and down his chest. "Yeah."

Damn. He needed to go if he was going to meet Otis on time. A glimpse of his future flashed through his head. Of sneaking around to find time to be with her without getting caught by their kids. Talking about their upcoming days every morning, much as they were doing right now. Holding her in his arms when they were both old and gray and reminiscing about their lives.

A pang of longing so strong it made his knees weak hit Chad, and he tightened his arms around Britt.

"Are you okay?" she asked.

"Yeah. Just feeling lightheaded because all the blood in my body is in my cock right about now."

She giggled.

"Be careful driving into town," Chad told her.

"I will."

"You taking your car or Mom's CR-V?"

"I think your mom's."

"Okay. I'll text when I'm done with Otis and on my way home."

And just like that, the worry came back into her eyes, and Chad wanted to kick himself for putting it there.

"It'll be fine," he reassured her again.

She nodded and went up on her toes to kiss him. They kept their embrace light and easy, and before he was ready, Chad was getting into his truck and waving at Britt as she stood in the driveway, watching him drive away.

Taking a deep breath, he turned his attention toward his upcoming meeting. He was going to be as nonconfrontational as possible, just see what Otis had to say. See if he could explain some of the discrepancies Britt had discovered without coming right out and accusing him of anything. It was still almost impossible to believe his dad's best friend might be stealing from the family.

But money could make almost anyone do things they might not otherwise do in the name of greed. Chad had no idea what Otis's money situation was. He'd always assumed he was doing fine, but that might not be the case. He could have any number of vices . . . gambling, drinking, drugs.

Or he could simply be jealous of what the Youngs had built at Lobster Cove. It wouldn't be unheard of. From what Chad knew, Otis and his son lived in a small house close to Rockville. He hadn't been there in years, but maybe it was time to drive by and check it out.

Hating that he felt the need to spy on their family friend, Chad straightened his shoulders. He'd do whatever it took to safeguard Lobster Cove. Losing it would destroy his mom, and that wasn't going to happen. Not if he could do anything about it.

Deciding he was getting ahead of himself, that he still didn't know if Otis was doing anything nefarious or not, Chad did his best to relax. But deep down, he had a bad feeling that Britt was right. She wouldn't have said anything if she wasn't sure herself that something was wrong. As it was, she'd had a difficult time speaking up. But she did, because she loved Lobster Cove and his mom as much as he and his brothers did.

Chad pulled into the small parking lot in front of the older house, which held several offices. Otis had rented one for years for his tax and investment business. He got out of the truck and strode up to the door. In this part of Maine, there weren't many strip malls or big office buildings. Most businesses were located in older houses just like this one, which had been retrofitted.

Otis's office was on the first floor near the back. It was basically one room with a small half bath and an outer space to greet clients, with a tiny office in the back. A bell tinkled over the door as Chad opened it, and Otis appeared in the doorway to the office.

"Chad," he said politely with a small nod. "Come on back."

He followed the older man to the office and sat in a small chair in front of a desk that took up most of the room. He perched on the end of the chair, not wanting to do this but knowing he had to. He placed the folder he'd brought with him on the desk and rested his elbows on the hard surface.

Leaning forward, he said, "I haven't had a chance to talk to you much recently. How've you been since Dad died?"

"It's been tough, but being able to take care of your mom has helped."

Chad forced himself not to react to that. It was clear he was setting the stage from the get-go. Trying to show how invaluable he was to both his mother and to Lobster Cove.

"My brothers and I appreciated you being around until we could get here."

"It's a good thing you've done. All of you. Coming home to help around Lobster Cove."

"Yeah," Chad agreed.

Done with pleasantries, he opened the folder he'd brought and cleared his throat. He'd thought about this before the meeting; he wasn't going to tell Otis that it was Britt who'd found the damning evidence against him. The last thing Chad would knowingly do was put a target on her back.

"I know you're busy, and I need to get back and help my brothers with the guesthouse, but I wanted to talk to you about some inconsistencies we found at the shop . . ."

Thirty minutes later, Chad was getting back into his truck—and he had no doubt whatsoever that Britt's concerns had merit.

Otis had done his best to explain away the things she'd found, but he'd been visibly stressed throughout the meeting and had talked in circles more than he'd actually answered Chad's questions.

When asked about the missing inventory, he'd blamed that on Walt not accurately writing down what they had on hand for Britt to put into the new inventory system. When asked about the number of invoices in the system, he'd acted like he didn't know what Chad was talking about, and sure enough, he'd produced evidence of twenty-seven invoices in the system—fifteen more than Britt had noted just the day before.

On the surface, everything he said seemed aboveboard, if a little shady—especially putting the blame on Walt—but it was his body language that stood out the most to Chad. As soon as Chad started asking questions, Otis began sweating and wouldn't look him in the eyes. He also fumbled his words constantly, when Chad had *never* known him to be anything but well spoken and concise.

Everything about their awkward meeting screamed that something was wrong. And Chad didn't know enough about what to look for in the money trails to figure out what that something was. He needed to talk to his brothers and see if any of them had a contact who could take a deep dive into Lobster Cove's financials. They needed an independent audit of *everything*. And that could take a while . . . because they'd possibly have to go back twenty years.

This sucked, and Chad hated it. But he wasn't going to let it go. *No one* fucked with his family. Even if that person had been best friends with his father.

Otis Calvert peered out the tiny window in his office and watched as Chad pulled out of the parking area. He dropped the curtain and wiped his brow with a handkerchief before he sat down and took out his cell phone.

This wasn't good. Not at all.

And it was all that bitch's fault! She'd barely been there a month, and everything was going to shit. He knew she was going to be trouble the second he'd met her. Just *knew* it.

She had no business poking around in his files. And he had no doubt it was her . . . no doubt *she* was the one who'd gone running to Chad with what she'd found.

The problem was—she wasn't wrong.

He'd been skimming money from Lobster Cove for years, using his friendship with Austin Young to his advantage.

Turned out, he was a skilled accountant but bad with investments . . . and unfortunately, most of his clients had dumped him years ago, unhappy with the way he'd managed their money. But since Austin and Evelyn Young were such close friends, they'd always trusted him. Never questioned *anything*.

Being in charge of the money for all the businesses on their property had made it easy to create fake invoices and pay himself, making up for his loss of income. And every year when tax time came around, he simply told them they owed more than they did and pocketed the difference.

Lobster Cove was easy pickins, and he hadn't expected anything to interfere with that for years to come. Not even Evelyn's sons, who were too busy and too trusting to question Otis.

Until that outsider bitch started sticking her nose where it didn't belong.

There was only one solution—he needed a distraction. Something to take the heat off himself while he did what he could to cover his tracks. He'd gotten too confident over the years, too lax, and now that Chad was suspicious, he needed to clean up the books.

For a moment, Otis felt bad about what he was about to do, but tough times called for tough measures.

"Come on, come on," he muttered. "Answer."

As if his son could hear him, he picked up.

"What do you want, Dad? I'm busy."

Otis's lip curled. His son was a lazy son of a bitch. He only worked at Lobster Cove Auto Body because Otis needed him on the books legitimately so he could pay him . . . way more than he actually earned, of course. Camden was paid a full-time salary for part-time work every month, thanks to Otis and his creative accounting.

That particular fraud wasn't on Chad's radar yet, but if he dug into payroll, it would only be a matter of time.

"I need you to do something for me. If you don't, the money train stops."

"What are you talking about?" Camden asked.

"They're suspicious. And if I lose *my* job, you lose *your* job."

"Fuck," Camden swore.

Otis nodded. "Right."

"What do you need me to do?"

After Otis explained his idea, as he expected, his son didn't have any protests. He'd do what he was told because if he didn't, they'd both lose the house they lived in, and Camden would have to find a real job—which Otis knew his son didn't want to do. He enjoyed hanging out with his deadbeat friends and smoking weed too much. His entire lifestyle relied on his old man paying him under the table for work he didn't actually do.

"It needs to happen today," Otis warned.

"Today?" Camden whined.

"Yes. The sooner the better."

He sighed. "Fine. I'll go find Evelyn and tell her that I saw some oil under her car or something. Tell her that I need to take a look at it."

"Perfect. Don't fuck this up, Camden."

"I *won't!* Damn, Dad, ease up."

But Otis couldn't. If this failed, he had no doubt things would go bad for him in a huge way. He'd *never* be able to pay back the amount he'd taken over the years. He'd be thrown in jail, and that would be the end of him.

"I expect to get a call later today, confirming this worked."

"You will. Later."

Otis hung up and stared into space for a long moment. He wanted to immediately start manipulating the computer system, deleting and manipulating files, but if he did that, it would be even more obvious that something was up.

No, the only thing he could do was stay the course and pray Camden didn't screw up. That attention would be turned from him to . . . more important matters.

CHAPTER SEVENTEEN

Britt's day had turned on its head after saying goodbye to Chad. She and Evelyn were supposed to go to Rockville that morning, but something was wrong with her car, so they'd had to switch around their plans.

Britt *did* check on Kash's fort and was impressed all over again at how well it had fared in the storm. It didn't look like it needed anything, so she took a moment to sit just inside the small door and breathe in the quiet of the morning and the fresh air. A porcupine even waddled by, totally ignoring her.

Chad had texted when she was on her way to the auto shop to meet with Walt and Barry to work some more on the inventory. He'd kept his text short and sweet, saying he'd be back in a bit and not to worry, that he'd tell her all about his meeting when he returned.

She understood that he probably couldn't go into detail in a text, but she was still anxious to hear what was said and what Chad thought. Did he think she was being paranoid? Had Otis explained everything in a way that assuaged Chad's concerns? She didn't know, and she didn't have the bandwidth to stress about it right now. She had to concentrate on entering car parts.

While she was working at the computer with Walt, explaining more about how the software worked—while he explained to *her* what they used various parts for—Camden pulled Evelyn's car into the shop and slid beneath it. She had no idea what was wrong—it seemed fine yesterday—but she felt better when Barry ambled over to talk to Camden, presumably about the vehicle.

She finished up with Walt at the same time Camden finished with the CR-V. He backed it out of the bay and parked it near the house.

"Have fun in town," Walt told her as she prepared to leave the office and head to the house to see if Evelyn was ready to go.

Britt looked back at him with a raised brow.

He chuckled. "The woman loves to shop. Doesn't matter if it's for groceries or fabric she'll never use."

Britt smiled. "Woman's prerogative," she told him with a wink.

He nodded. "Got to say . . . it's nice having another woman around for Miss Evelyn to talk to. She's had to deal with nothing but testosterone most of her life."

"She's a doll," Britt returned.

"That she is. Later, Britt."

"Later."

As she walked toward the house, the familiar sound of Chad's truck hit her ears. Turning eagerly, she grinned as she saw him pulling down the driveway. She waited for him to park and get out, then threw herself at him.

He caught her and hugged her hard.

"Is everything all right?" she asked, hating the stressed-out look on his face.

"Yes. And no. I need to talk to my brothers."

Britt frowned. That didn't sound good. She desperately wanted to ask if he believed her. If he thought there was something wrong, as she did, but she held her tongue.

As if he could read her mind, Chad whispered in her ear, "I think your suspicions are more than founded."

Britt's heart felt as if it was in her throat. She was both relieved and sick to her stomach at the same time. "I'm sorry."

"Don't be. If it wasn't for you, who knows how much more money would be stolen. You been to town and back already?"

It was an abrupt change of topic, but Britt didn't mind. She was impressed he'd remembered her schedule, considering everything he was dealing with. "No. Something was up with your mom's car. The guys looked at it, fixed whatever it was, and I was just going to the house to get Evelyn so we could head out."

Chad frowned and looked over at the Honda CR-V. "What was wrong with it?"

Britt chuckled. "You're asking the wrong person. Sorry."

He glanced over to the auto shop, probably thinking about heading over to find out what they'd done with his mom's car, but Lincoln shouted from across the way, near the rental.

"About time you got back. Get your butt over here!"

"Are they upset that you weren't here to help them?" Britt asked.

Chad shook his head. "No. But they like to pretend they are. They'll milk this, call me a slacker, and make fun of me for weeks, insist that I purposely skipped out on helping. It's what brothers do."

Britt didn't think that sounded fun, but she'd never had brothers or sisters, so what did she know?

"Have fun with Mom. Be safe."

"I will, and we will," Britt told him.

The more she was around this man, the more she *wanted* to be around him. He kissed her. Long and deep, right there in the middle of the driveway for everyone to see. But Britt wasn't embarrassed. When he pulled back, they were both a little breathless.

A loud wolf whistle sounded from where his brothers were working. Chad grinned down at her. "Now *that* is something I'll happily take a ribbing over."

Britt was glad he had something to smile about, because she had a feeling once he told Lincoln, Knox, and Zach what was going on with Otis and the finances of Lobster Cove, no one would be in the mood to joke around or smile for a while.

"Love you," Chad said almost nonchalantly as he backed away from her.

The casual way he threw that out there startled Britt for a moment, then she smiled. "Love you too."

If she could freeze a moment in time, this would be the one. The look on his face was everything she'd ever dreamed about. He looked at her as if she was the most important person in the world. As if the sun rose and set with her. She'd never been looked at that way in her life. It made her feel cherished . . . and loved.

She watched his butt for a moment when he finally turned and walked away, then headed into the house.

"Evelyn," she called when she opened the door. "You ready?"

"Finally!" the older woman said as she stood from her chair in the living area. "I've been waiting forever."

Britt chuckled. She was being dramatic, but in a cheerful way. "Well, get your stuff and let's go check out this quilting store."

It took ten minutes for Evelyn to get everything together that she needed for the outing, then they were on their way.

The drive into Rockville was gorgeous. Lobster Cove was south of the city, and there was a narrow, winding, miles-long back road they had to navigate to get to the main road into Rockville. One thing Britt loved about the route was all the water. Everywhere she looked throughout the drive, there was a pond or a glimpse of the ocean, a cove or a bay. Sometimes even a river.

There was just something so calming about looking out the window and seeing the sun glint off water at almost any given time.

After turning onto the main road, it was a straight shot into town. It took a bit to find a parking space; now that summer had arrived, there were a lot more people in town. The two women walked arm in arm toward the quilting shop, stopping to talk to several people Evelyn knew along the way.

Their time in the shop was hilarious, as neither of them even knew what they were looking for. The woman who owned the store was very patient and sweet, and she helped Evelyn pick out a project she could start on that wasn't too difficult. It took longer to pick out the fabrics Evelyn wanted, as she kept getting sidetracked by each pretty pattern and changing her mind.

An hour after they'd arrived, they left with several bags of supplies and smiles on their faces. Evelyn decided she was hungry and needed a snack, so they stopped at a local pub. Thankfully it was after the lunch rush, so they got a seat quickly. Britt ordered some gooey, yummy cheese fries, and Evelyn enjoyed the seafood chowder.

It was later than she expected when they headed back to the car. The weather had also changed. The sun was nowhere in sight, and a light drizzle had moved in. By the time they got to where they'd parked, they were both a little damp.

Evelyn asked Britt to drive, and she got into the driver's seat without hesitation. She turned on the heat once she got the car started, so Evelyn wouldn't get a chill. Even though it was warmer than it'd been when she'd arrived in Maine, here on the coast, it was still in the lower seventies despite July being just a few days away . . . which Britt loved. She wasn't a hot-weather girl, so the climate here in Maine was perfect for her.

They began the drive home as Evelyn babbled happily about starting her wall hanging and where she wanted to put it when she was done.

They'd just turned off the main highway, onto the back road that would lead them to Lobster Cove, when Britt felt the vehicle acting funny. It wasn't anything she could put her finger on, but the steering felt . . . sluggish.

Not wanting to worry Evelyn, just deciding to say something to Chad when they got home, she did her best to control the vehicle as it went around the twisting curves.

She was already driving slower than she normally would because of her uneasiness, when all of a sudden, she lost all control of steering.

"Shit!" she swore, struggling to pull the wheel to the right as they headed toward yet another curve. But it was no use. The car wasn't responding. Britt stomped on the brake.

And to her horror, nothing happened.

How the hell could both the steering *and* the brakes go out at the same time? Especially right after it had been in the shop this morning?

"Hold on!" she yelled, giving up on trying to control the car and throwing herself toward Evelyn as they headed straight for the curve.

It was awkward, since she had her seat belt on, but out of the two of them, the older woman was far more vulnerable.

As if in slow motion, Britt watched the CR-V go off the road, bounce over some of the huge rocks lining the shoulder, then tilt forward drastically, headed down the steep embankment and straight for the water in the bay below.

Thankfully the car had crapped out where it had and not a mile earlier, where the drop-off to the water was even steeper. As it was, the trip was bone jarring. But the water in the cove was at high tide. If it was low tide, they would crash headlong into the hard mud.

The impact with the water was still painful, and Britt felt her seat belt tighten just as the airbags exploded in their faces. Then she felt water lapping over her feet and quickly looked down. The water might have cushioned their impact somewhat, but now they were in trouble of a different kind . . . because it was quickly filling the vehicle.

Feeling as if she was watching the scene from above, Britt moved quickly, reaching for the window breaker one of Evelyn's sons had mounted on the driver's door. It was held there by a piece of extra-strong Velcro that had been glued to the side of the door. She tugged hard, and it came off in her hand. Using the seat belt cutter built into one end of the tool, she freed herself, then leaned over and got Evelyn's belt undone.

"We need to get out of here," she told the woman who'd come to mean so much to her.

"Oh my . . . ," Evelyn said, sounding as if she was in shock. She had some blood on the side of her head, where Britt assumed she'd smacked against the window when they'd crashed into the water.

They both seemed to be all right for now, but the CR-V was actually drifting away from the shore, and if they didn't get out right now, they'd be in big trouble. Either from the car sinking or hypothermia. The water in Maine was nothing like the water at the beaches in the South.

Chad had told her the other day that the water temperature was usually around forty-three degrees or so at the end of April, so it was probably much warmer now, but still way too cold.

Britt tried to open her door, but as she suspected, it wouldn't budge. The water pressure was too much. She'd have to use the window breaker and get Evelyn out that way.

She wasn't looking forward to this. Not at all.

Still, without hesitation, Britt swung the pointy end of the tool at the driver's side window, and it immediately shattered, showering her with glass. Using her elbow, she did her best to clear the frame so she and Evelyn wouldn't get cut as they crawled out.

"Okay, I'm going. Scoot over to my seat and follow me. I'll help you out," Britt said in a no-nonsense tone, praying Evelyn followed her directions. Taking a deep breath, Britt got up on her knees in the driver's seat and put her upper body through the window. It was a bit awkward and took some contorting, but she managed to get herself out.

She fell headfirst into the water, taking her breath away with the immediate chill that filled her completely.

Not wasting time, she stood and turned back to the window. The water was at her thighs and climbing as the car drifted farther into the bay.

"Now, Evelyn! Give me your hands and I'll help you out."

Thankfully, the older woman complied. When she was almost all the way out, Britt had an epiphany. "Wait! Let me turn around. Get on my back," she told her.

Staggering under Evelyn's weight, Britt prayed she wouldn't fall as she slowly made her way toward shore.

To her surprise, she heard someone shout Evelyn's name.

Looking up, she saw two men carefully navigating the ruts in the mud that the CR-V had made on its way into the water.

Seconds later, there were two more people scrambling down the hill toward them.

The relief she felt, knowing they weren't alone, almost made Britt's knees buckle. But she couldn't fall apart until Evelyn was safe.

It took several more steps, then one of the men closest reached out and grabbed her elbow, steadying her.

"Wow, you got out in the nick of time," someone said.

Glancing over her shoulder, Britt saw the back end of the CR-V bobbing in the water just before it disappeared altogether. She was shocked at how quickly the car had sunk, but her attention was yanked back to where she was and what was happening when someone got on her other side, supporting her, and they all walked out of the water and mud toward firmer ground.

"I saw you go over," the man to her right said. "Good job on getting out so fast. You were already crawling out the window by the time I reached the side of the road. Here, let me help you."

The last words were said to Evelyn. The man helped her off Britt's back and onto the muddy bank.

Looking at the woman, Britt saw she was shivering. From the chill of the water that had soaked her feet and lower legs or from shock, she didn't know. Then she registered the far-off sound of sirens, and she hoped they were coming for them. Britt felt okay, but she was worried about Evelyn.

"I'm fine," the older woman said. "I can stand on my own."

Relieved that she seemed to have retained her spunk, Britt sighed. Personally, she felt a little wobbly.

"Britt! Mom!"

At the sound of Chad's voice, Britt's head whipped up, and she stared in disbelief as he and his brothers scrambled down the incline toward them, almost falling in their haste.

She had no idea how they'd gotten there so fast, but she assumed one of the bystanders must have called them. Everyone knew everyone in Rockville, especially this close to Lobster Cove, and Britt had never been so glad to see anyone in her life.

It took seven seconds exactly for him to get to her—Britt counted. The second Chad had her in his arms, she felt more like herself. Stronger.

"You're freezing," he muttered, tightening his arms around her.

"I'm okay. Check on your mom," she said, even as she clutched him closer.

"My brothers have her. Let go for a second, I need to check you over," he said.

Britt didn't want to let go, but she did anyway. The bank of the bay seemed crowded now with bystanders and all four of the Young brothers, but Britt was more than thankful they were all there.

"You're cut," Chad said, looking at her forearm. "And you have a bruise on your cheek."

"Airbag, probably," Britt mumbled.

Just then a fire truck rolled to a stop at the top of the embankment, followed closely by an ambulance and a police car.

"Hang tight!" one of the firefighters called down. "We'll get the rope system set up to get everyone back to the road."

"No need!" Lincoln called back, picking up his mom and cradling her in his arms. "I've got her." Then, with the help of Zach and Knox, he began to walk up the hill, holding his mother tight.

Chad started to pick up Britt, but she stopped him. "I can walk," she told him.

"Are you sure?"

She wasn't, but she nodded anyway.

With Chad on one side of her, his arm around her waist, and with the two men who'd originally stopped for her and Evelyn helping as well, they made their way up the slippery slope. The firefighters were at the top to give them a final hand.

Chad ushered Britt to the ambulance, where his mom was already seated on the gurney in the back.

"Is she okay? Are you okay, Mom?" he asked, tension in his tone.

"I'm fine. Barely even wet, thanks to Britt. Are *you* okay, honey?" Evelyn asked.

"Cold, a few bruises, but I'm fine," she reassured her.

"I hate this damn road, always have," Knox muttered from next to her. "I've always been afraid someone's gonna go off the side, especially in the winter. I'm guessing because you're new and aren't used to it, you must've misjudged the curve."

Britt looked at Knox and said firmly, "I didn't misjudge the curve. The steering stopped working. As did the brakes."

The silence around them was heavy.

"Are you sure?" Zach asked, frowning.

Britt nodded.

"Fuck."

"Language, son," Evelyn scolded Lincoln.

"Mom, I'm thinking if there was ever a time to swear, this is it!" he protested.

"If you'd all step back, we need to get Mrs. Young to the hospital to be checked out."

"I don't need to go to the hospital."

"Yes, you do, and we don't want to hear anything else about it," Lincoln told his mom firmly. "You too," he said, nodding at Britt.

"Me? No, I'm good."

"Nope. You're soaking wet, the airbag went off, and you're going," Zach said with a shake of his head.

"Another ambulance is on the way," the paramedic said.

"I'll take her," Chad informed him. "It'll be faster."

"We'll need you to sign an AMA form then. Saying that you're going against medical advice to be transported," the paramedic argued.

"Fine. Just give us the form so she can sign and I can get her to the hospital," Chad growled.

He sounded as if he was on the verge of either biting someone's head off or hurting someone. Britt hated how stressed he was on her behalf. She put her hand on his arm and leaned into him. "I'm okay, Chad. Cold, sore, but nothing's majorly wrong."

"I swear I think I lost ten years off my life when Lincoln got that phone call."

It didn't take long for the necessary forms to be signed and for Chad to hustle her into the back seat of Knox's SUV. They'd left after the ambulance but arrived at the emergency room at almost the same time.

Hours after they'd arrived at the hospital—after they were warmed up, tests were done, Britt's arm got two stitches, she answered the police detective's questions while Chad and his brothers were talking to the doctor about their mom, and Evelyn had been appropriately fussed over and deemed well enough to go home—they were on their way back to Lobster Cove. The sun had dipped below the horizon, but Britt could see the CR-V still sitting on the bottom of the small cove as they went past the curve where she'd gone off the road, not quite covered with water, now that it was low tide.

Shivering with the memories of the split second when she realized they were going to crash, Britt closed her eyes and felt Chad's arm tighten around her. He hadn't left her side. Not even for a second. His mom had been in the room next to hers, and yet he hadn't left Britt to check on her. He'd relied on his brothers for updates.

The last few hours had been stressful and scary, and Britt wanted nothing more than to be home. She hadn't spoken any more about what happened to any of the Young brothers, and no one had asked. But the time was coming when she'd need to explain more about her claim that the CR-V had lost both its steering and its brakes.

Knox pulled up as close to the front steps of the main house as he could get, with Lincoln on his tail, their mom in the front seat of his truck. They all entered the house, and Lincoln turned on lights as Zach headed to the kitchen, hopefully to whip up something to eat. Britt was starving, as the fries she'd had earlier had long since digested.

Everyone was quiet and subdued as they sat down to eat at the table. The grilled cheese sandwiches Zach made were the most delicious thing Britt had ever tasted. She had no idea what he'd done to the bread or the cheese, but they tasted gourmet and nothing like the ones she'd made for herself in the past.

"So . . . brakes and steering?" Knox finally said after everyone had eaten.

Britt sighed and nodded. It was time, and honestly, she was glad. She didn't want anyone thinking she was just a bad driver and that's why she'd gone off the road.

"The car felt . . . off on our way back from town, but nothing I could put my finger on. The steering just felt a little sluggish. It wasn't until we were on that back road that I suddenly stopped being able to steer at all. We were heading for the curve, so I put my foot on the brakes, but the pedal just went all the way to the floor, and nothing happened. I couldn't stop, couldn't steer out of the curve, so I didn't have time to do more than lean over and grab Evelyn before we were bumping down the embankment toward the water."

"Thank you for that, honey," Evelyn said, reaching out and taking Britt's hand in hers.

"Of course."

"Thank goodness you remembered the window breaker," Zach said.

"It was the first thing I thought of when we hit the water," Britt said.

"It's so weird, because the boys looked over the car right before we left," Evelyn mused.

Chad straighten next to her. "How did that come about?" he asked his mom.

"Camden came to the house and said he was worried because he saw some fluid on the ground under my car, and he asked if he could take a look at it," Evelyn explained.

Every muscle in Britt's body tightened at hearing that. Chad had pulled his chair close enough to hers that their thighs were touching . . . so she felt it when his body did the same.

"Who worked on the car?" Chad asked, his tone dark.

"I don't know. Why?" Evelyn asked.

"Yeah, why? What aren't you telling us?" Lincoln asked, narrowing his eyes at his brother.

Chad sighed. "This isn't how I wanted to tell you guys about this. It's going to come as a shock."

"As much of a shock as our mom and Britt almost dying because someone might've tampered with their fucking car? I doubt it," Knox bit out.

"Knox. Language," Evelyn scolded in her familiar way, but she didn't sound all that upset.

"Spit it out. Was it Camden? Did he do this?"

"Apparently." Then Chad went on to explain *everything*—Britt's suspicions after what she'd found, his meeting with Otis, his belief that their family friend was stealing from them.

Tension filled the room when he was done. No one said a word, each clearly trying to process what they'd been told.

To Britt's surprise, it was Evelyn who broke the heavy silence.

"That *bastard*! I've always wondered how Austin could work so damn hard every year, and yet we were barely breaking even."

"Mom—" Lincoln started, but she put a hand up.

"I'm tired. I'm sore. And I'm pissed. I need some time to think about this. Who's arranging for my car to be towed, and who's going to look into it to see if it was tampered with?"

This assertive woman was a surprise to Britt. Evelyn was usually so mild mannered. And admittedly, she was more than a little relieved that she hadn't been made out to be the bad guy here, since she was the one who'd first brought her suspicions to Chad.

"I'll take care of the car," Knox said.

"Linc and I will look at it when it gets here," Zach said. "And if anything seems hinky, we'll call the police so they can file a report."

"Do we really think Otis did this? Or more accurately, convinced his son to tamper with Mom's car?" Lincoln asked.

"He wasn't happy with my questions today," Chad answered. "If he thought he was about to be found out, or if his money train was ending, he could've been desperate enough to try to put our attention elsewhere."

Everyone was quiet as they considered that. Even Britt was having a hard time wrapping her head around a family friend doing something so awful as trying to hurt—or even *kill*—the matriarch of the Young family, just to get the attention off himself and his illegal activities.

Evelyn pushed her chair back, and Zach, Knox, and Lincoln were immediately on their feet, reaching out to help her.

"I can walk," she snapped. Then she sighed. "Sorry, I'm just stressed. I appreciate you all being here and staying at the hospital with me. Britt, thank you for saving my life today. I mean it. If you hadn't been there, I'm not sure I would've been able to get out of that car as fast as we did.

"Everyone, go home. Get some sleep. Things are going to get shaken up around here very soon, but we can't do anything tonight. Tomorrow, we'll regroup and discuss next steps. And no one will do *anything* without me being involved. This is my home, and if I'm being stolen from, it will stop. Immediately. Understand?"

"Yes, ma'am."

"Of course."

"We won't do anything without your say-so."

Everyone spoke at the same time, and Britt was even more impressed with Evelyn than she was before . . . and that was saying something, because she was already damn impressed with the woman.

Knox held out his elbow for his mom, and she allowed him to walk her toward the back of the house to her room.

"Evelyn, do you need any help getting ready for bed?" Britt called out.

"Thank you, child, but no. I'll let you know if I need anything."

"You good?" Lincoln asked Chad.

"Yeah."

"You *were* going to tell us today about your meeting with Otis, right?" his oldest brother asked.

"Of course. After we'd finished up with the rental, I was going to sit you all down so we could come up with a plan."

Lincoln nodded, then jerked his head toward the door. "Come on, Zach. Want to come to my place tonight to crash?"

"Yes." The one word was firm and almost . . . eager.

Britt had a feeling the brothers would be up late into the night, figuring out a plan that they'd then bring to their mom for approval before executing. The brothers' time in the military had guaranteed they wouldn't go into any situation without a plan A, plan B, and probably a plan C, as well.

She looked over at Chad, wondering if he felt left out, if he would've preferred to be going with his brothers to talk about their options. But she found him staring right back, and all she could see in his eyes was concern . . . for *her.*

"You ready for bed?" he asked quietly.

Britt nodded.

Chad helped her to her feet, then urged her toward the stairs.

"I'll clean down here and lock up," Knox said as he returned from the direction of their mom's room.

"Appreciate it," Chad told him with a small chin lift.

Britt found herself in the hallway bathroom before she could blink.

"Take your time. I'll be in our room."

She didn't know when his room had become "our" room, but she wasn't going to complain. "Okay."

By the time she'd stepped through the door, she was dead on her feet and barely able to keep her eyes open. The stress of the day, and especially the last few hours, had caught up to her. Britt didn't think she'd be able to string two coherent words together.

Of course, Chad noticed. "In," he said, standing by the bed and holding up the covers for her. Britt climbed into bed and sighed in contentment as her body was finally able to relax.

"I'll be back in a bit. Sleep, Peach."

"Thank you for being there today," she murmured.

"Nowhere else I would've been," Chad said as he leaned down and kissed her temple.

That was the last thing Britt was cognizant of before she fell into a deep healing sleep, content in the knowledge that she was safe. That Chad would protect her from Otis and Camden sneaking in to try to hurt her or Evelyn.

CHAPTER EIGHTEEN

Chad woke with a start. He'd been having a wonderful dream about being on a honeymoon with Britt, lying in the sun on a private balcony as she went down on him.

Looking down, he realized he wasn't dreaming. Not about Britt being between his legs, at least.

She was on her knees, bent over his crotch, and she had his cock in her mouth.

She looked up at him when he stirred, and it was all he could do not to come right then and there. Her hair was falling around her shoulders, brushing against his groin, and her lips stretched around his dick was erotic as hell.

Then he remembered. The accident.

"Britt, no," he murmured, reaching for her. But she brought an arm up and blocked him—and sucked harder.

Chad groaned. *Damn*, her mouth felt amazing.

She doubled her efforts, now that he was awake, squeezing the base with her hand as she bobbed up and down on him. Her saliva and his precome gave her plenty of lube, and Chad couldn't help but flop back down against his pillow as she greedily devoured him. As soon as he closed his eyes, he opened them again and lifted his head. He wasn't going to miss this. No way.

It was obvious Britt was into what she was doing. She wasn't sucking him because she felt obligated. The effort and energy she put into blowing him was genuine. And that was a *huge* turn-on.

"Come up here," he cajoled, wanting his mouth on her pussy as she sucked him off.

But she shook her head, even as she continued to bob on him.

It wasn't going to take him long to come, and he told her as much.

In response, she sucked faster, taking him to the back of her throat and swallowing.

"Fuck," Chad gasped as he threaded his fingers through her hair, holding it back from her face so he could see his cock disappearing into her mouth.

"I'm close," he warned. "Pull off now if you don't want a mouth full of my come."

She didn't let go, simply raised her gaze to his as she sucked harder.

That was all it took. Chad exploded. His vision went dark and he saw stars as Britt swallowed every drop of his release.

It was a full thirty seconds before he could think again, and when he looked down, Britt's head was resting against his thigh as she gently caressed his now-flaccid cock.

"Damn, woman," Chad murmured.

"Good morning," she replied with a saucy grin.

Chad leaned over and pulled her upward until she was resting on his chest. "Are you hurting? Why'd you do that? You have to be so sore." He couldn't decide if he was pissed or pleased with her right this moment.

"I'm okay. A little sore. Too sore to make love, but I wanted to show you how much I love you. How thankful I am that you're in my life."

"I loved that, and you, but at no time will I ever put my own pleasure above your safety and comfort."

"I'm fine, Chad. I promise. I love giving head. The control it makes me feel. And I needed that after yesterday, when I had none. At that moment, when I realized we were going to crash, that we were going into the water, I felt so helpless."

Any ire he had about her possibly hurting herself disappeared into a puff of smoke. "I'm so sorry, Peach."

But she shook her head. "Why? You didn't cut those brakes or make the steering not work. You were there when I needed you. When your *mom* needed you."

Thinking about what happened threatened to destroy Chad's mellow mood after the best blow job he'd ever received. Rolling until Britt was under him, he leaned on his elbows and stared down at her for a long moment.

"What?" she asked with a small smile.

"I'm trying to decide if you're being honest with me about how you feel. How sore you are."

"I don't think anyone can be in an accident, be restrained by a seat belt, have the airbag go off in their face, and *not* be sore," she replied.

"Does it hurt to lie on your back?"

"No. Mostly when I twist too far one way or another. And my shoulder hurts. I think it probably took the brunt of the airbag's impact."

"You need one of the painkillers the doc prescribed?" Chad asked.

"No."

"Sure?"

"I'm sure."

"Okay. Then how about you just lie there. I'll do all the work," Chad told her.

"All the work— Oh!"

When he began to slide down her body, it clearly dawned on her what he meant. Chad was pleased when she eagerly widened her legs, giving him room and inviting him in.

For the next twenty minutes, he teased and pleasured his woman. She'd had a hell of a day yesterday, and he wanted to start this one out as amazingly for her as she'd done for him. Eating her out was a feast for his senses. His dick got hard two minutes after he licked her for the first time, but he ignored it. This was for Britt.

After her third orgasm, she begged for mercy.

Smiling, Chad rested his cheek on her thigh, much as she'd done after he'd orgasmed, and inhaled deeply. Her scent was ingrained in his psyche, and he wouldn't want it any other way.

"I'm dead," she said, her eyes closed as she lay limp and sated under him.

Chad chuckled. "I hope not. Because if I'm not mistaken, I smell bacon. And I heard my brothers arrive not too long ago."

Britt sat up abruptly, then let out a small groan of pain. "They're here? Why didn't you say anything? What time is it?"

"Yes. Because I was busy, and so were you. And I don't know and don't care."

"Chad!" she complained. "We need to get downstairs and see what's happening."

"We will." He scooted up and gently pushed Britt back down. He stared into her eyes for a long moment, trying to read her.

She gave him a small smile. "I'm okay. That was a fantastic way to wake up."

"I agree. You want to shower?"

"Of course."

"Sorry, I should've been more specific. You want to shower with *me*?"

She frowned a little. "Won't that be . . . weird? I mean, your family might know."

"Do you care? They already know we're dating. And for the record . . . I know it's too soon, but if things continue to go as well as they are with us . . . my plan is to make this, *us*, permanent."

Her eyes widened. "What?"

"I want it all with you, Peach. A ring, a wedding here at Lobster Cove, kids, maybe a dog or cat, the whole shebang. I'm doubting we'll live with my mom forever, but for now, I think she needs us both here.

I'm not willing to pretend that we aren't in a serious relationship. I want this. Mornings with you in our bed. Intimate showers. All of it."

Chad held his breath. He was showing all his cards, and he hoped like hell he and Britt were on the same page.

"I want that too," she whispered after a moment. "And yes, I'd love to shower with you. I've never gone down on anyone in the shower, but I'm thinking it would be fun. We can make a mess and not have to worry about laundry afterward."

And just like that, Chad's cock was stiff as a board once more. He had a feeling it was going to be a normal occurrence with Britt around. His brain conjured an image of coming on her tits as she knelt in the shower, smiling up at him.

"Fuck yes," he breathed, then forced himself to roll away from her and stand. She was sore, and if he stayed in bed with her another second and listened to her say such dirty things, he'd end up doing something he'd regret. And he'd never ever do anything that would hurt this woman.

"No going down on anyone again today. We need to shower and get some breakfast before we hear the plan my brothers came up with last night, then execute said plan."

"You really aren't upset that you weren't included?" Britt asked with a small frown.

"Not in the least. I trust them. Whatever they came up with will be perfect."

Britt stood, and Chad took her hand. She was wearing one of his T-shirts that she'd put on the night before, with nothing on under it. She was sexy as hell . . . and all his. He was a lucky bastard, and he'd spend the rest of his life making sure he spoiled this woman shamelessly.

He'd spent his teens watching his dad do the same for his mom. He'd had the best role model, and he vowed to make his dad proud, even if he couldn't be here to see it. For a moment, Chad was sad that his father never got to meet Britt. But if he *was* still around, Chad never would've met her. He wouldn't have had a reason to move home, wouldn't have been in that parking lot at the exact moment Britt needed him.

Austin Young had to have had a hand in them meeting. Everything happened for a reason, and while Chad hated that his dad had to die in order for him to find Britt, he was coming to terms with it. Besides, he had no doubt his father was watching over his family from wherever he was.

Their first shower together was cramped and a comedy of errors. The shower/tub combo wasn't exactly made to hold two people at the same time. They made it work, but Chad vowed at some point to give them a roomy and comfortable shower more conducive to sharing.

They made their way downstairs hand in hand and found his three brothers and Evelyn sitting at the kitchen table. Everyone was frowning, which wasn't a great sign.

"Thank goodness you're here. Your brothers are being stubborn and irritating!" his mom declared.

Looking from her to the others, he saw without anyone saying a word that they thought their mom was being just as stubborn and irritating.

"Something smells amazing. Zach, please tell me you made whatever it is."

"Egg tarts, jalapeño bacon, fruit bowls," Zach informed her.

"Yum," Britt said. "Good morning, Evelyn. Lincoln, Knox," she said, nodding at his brothers and going over to his mom to kiss her on the top of the head. "How do you feel this morning?" she asked in the same sweet, easy tone.

"Sore. Mad. Ready to kick some butt," Evelyn responded.

Britt chuckled. "Can I grab something to eat before we get out the pitchforks and head out to hunt for people's heads?"

Her words seemed to snap his mom out of the funk she'd been in. "Of course. Here, let me get up and—"

"Nope. You stay," Britt told her. "I can get it."

"No, *I* can get it," Chad countered, pulling out an empty chair next to his mom. "Sit."

"Woof," she teased as she looked up at him, sitting where he'd indicated.

Chad heard one of his brothers try to stifle a laugh. He leaned down and kissed Britt right on the mouth before heading into the kitchen. "Anyone want anything while I'm in here?"

"Bring the plate of bacon. We saved you some, but now that you're here, we can finish what you and Britt don't want," Lincoln told him.

The amount of bacon sitting on a paper towel–lined plate was staggering. Stuffing one of the pieces into his mouth, Chad barely held back the moan that threatened to escape his throat. His brother was a fucking genius in the kitchen. The bacon held just the right amount of heat from the jalapeños. It wasn't overwhelming, but left a nice tingle in his mouth.

He loaded up two plates for him and Britt and carried them to the table. Then he went back into the kitchen for the bacon. As soon as he placed it on the table, his brothers reloaded up their own plates with the delicious meat.

Chad was grateful his brothers gave him and Britt a chance to eat before discussing what was on everyone's mind. As soon as Britt finished her egg tart, Lincoln spoke.

"Right, so before you guys came downstairs, we were telling Mom that we wanted to talk to Otis this morning," Lincoln said without preamble.

"And I was telling *them* that isn't going to happen. Like I said last night, no one will do anything without me being involved. And *I* want to be the one who sits down with Otis. And if I'm not satisfied with his answers, I'll fire him," Evelyn said firmly.

"Mom, I don't think—" Knox started, but Evelyn interrupted.

"I appreciate you all being here. I do. But this is something I have to do. Otis and your father were best friends. At one time, we were as close as any three people could be."

Chad frowned at that. "At one time?" he questioned.

His mom sighed. "Yes. At one time. We used to do everything together. But even before your dad died, Otis . . . started to rub me the wrong way. He changed. Anytime he met with us about the businesses, he became condescending. When we questioned him about our taxes or how our money was being invested, Otis made it seem as if we were questioning his integrity. He made the conversations personal. I'm thinking now that he did that to keep us from delving deeper into what he was doing with our money. I feel like an idiot."

"Mom—"

But Evelyn cut Chad off. "We were *both* idiots. We didn't want to rock the boat. We valued our friendship with Otis more than our own financial well-being. Which was stupid. He was clearly smart about it, leaving us enough to run our businesses but not enough that we could really get ahead. We should've asked a lot more questions. Should've had someone else look at things years ago. But we didn't. And now here we are."

"Mom, we don't know for sure that he's been embezzling," Zach said gently.

Evelyn turned to Britt. "You've been here for two point three seconds, and the first time you got a good glance at the Auto Body accounts, you had your suspicions. What do you think? Is he stealing from Lobster Cove?"

Britt shifted in her seat, obviously uncomfortable with being put on the spot.

"Mom, I don't think—"

She held up a hand, cutting Chad off again, her gaze fixed on Britt. "I'm sorry . . . but yes," she said after a moment.

"When he arrives today, I'd like to see him in Austin's office here at the house. If one of you—and I *mean* one of you, not all four—could escort him to the house, I'd appreciate it," Evelyn said firmly.

Chad wasn't thrilled about his mom wanting to confront Otis, but he had a hell of a lot of respect for her.

His mom had never backed down from injustice. He remembered when he was in middle school and she found out that there were kids who weren't eating lunch because their accounts hadn't been paid by their parents, because they couldn't afford it. The school said they couldn't get any more lunches until the bills were paid. She was outraged, and she took it upon herself to berate the school board for denying children food.

Then she rallied the citizens of Rockville and, with their help, raised enough money to pay off the overdue bills for students in not only the middle school but the elementary and high school too . . . with money to spare.

"What about Camden?" Chad asked.

"I checked the schedule, and he's supposed to work this morning," Knox said. "Zach and I will meet him when he arrives and tell him his services are no longer needed at Lobster Cove."

"Are you going to ask him about Mom's car?" Chad asked.

"Oh yeah," Knox said, with an angry glint in his eye. "I called a friend at the PD, and he's interested in talking to him as well. He also doesn't want us to touch the CR-V. He's already working on getting it towed to the PD this morning, and they'll check it for fingerprints and to see if the brakes and steering were tampered with. If they were, Camden's going to be invited down to the station to answer some questions."

"I already talked to Walt and Barry this morning," Zach said. "They both said Camden seemed especially motivated yesterday, and he refused to let Barry help with Mom's car . . . which was very unlike him. If necessary, they're both willing to testify that Camden worked on the car before Mom and Britt left for their errands."

Chad's hands clenched, thinking about what could've happened to both his mom and Britt. It was hard to believe anyone who worked here at Lobster Cove would actually try to hurt or kill the women.

He felt a touch on his fist in his lap. Looking down, he saw Britt had covered his hand with her own, and she was looking at him with concern.

"Fine, it's settled. I'm going to do dishes," Evelyn said, putting her napkin on the table next to her plate.

All four Young brothers stood at the same time.

"I've got it."

"No, you aren't."

"Sit, Mom."

"Not a chance."

Evelyn smiled and sat back in her chair. She looked at Britt. "I've got such good boys."

"You've raised them well," Britt said in return.

Britt kept his mom company as Chad and his brothers made quick work of the breakfast dishes. He kept one eye on the table and was relieved to see that neither woman seemed to have any adverse effects from the accident yesterday. Both seemed a little stiff, but not in pain, which was a relief. Once more, he was grateful for Britt's quick thinking and ability to crash the car in the one place that was likely to do the least damage . . . the water instead of a tree.

When Chad returned to Britt's side, she looked up at him and said quietly, "All the passwords for the accounts Otis has access to need to be updated. Like the accounting software, the bank accounts, even the online tax system."

Chad nodded. She was right. Hell, they should've done that last night. At this point, he wouldn't put it past the man to try to drain all their accounts completely. If he could steal from his best friend for years, why wouldn't he take as much as he could before he was fired? And he had to know that his time here at Lobster Cove was done. That Chad and his brothers and his mom would eventually put two and two together.

Of course, without Britt . . . they might not have.

Guilt filled him at the thought. Why had he and his brothers never thought to question Otis long before now, even when their father was alive? Maybe out of respect for the relationship the man had with their dad? Because they didn't want to risk upsetting their parents? Because none of them were interested in taxes, accounting, or investments?

Considering just one man had been in charge of it all for so long, it was a *huge* mistake—and one that may have devastated his mother's financial future.

They'd all moved home to help their mom secure Lobster Cove's future . . . and they'd failed spectacularly so far. Thinking about how much money Otis might have stolen from his parents over the years made Chad physically ill.

"I'm going to head to the shop. I want to be there when Otis arrives. Camden too," Lincoln said.

Evelyn nodded and stood. "I'll be in your dad's office. Bring Otis up as soon as he arrives," she ordered, before turning and heading down the hall.

Britt was frowning, and Chad could see the angst practically pouring off her.

"My mom's tough," he told her.

Looking up at him, Britt nodded and said, "I know that. She raised the four of you. She had to be. But the most dangerous time for a woman is when she tells her partner she's leaving. I know this isn't quite the same, but I'm worried about her being alone with Otis."

"She won't be alone," Lincoln said. "While Knox and Zach take care of Camden, I'll be in the office with Mom and Otis."

"I thought she said she wanted to talk to him on her own," Britt said.

"No. She said she wanted to be the one to *talk* to him, not that she wanted to do it on her own. Even if she did, there's no way any of us would agree to that, and she knows it."

Britt let out a relieved breath. "Oh, good."

"Chad, you want to join me?" Lincoln asked.

"Hell yes," he said. Otis had tried to harm not only his mother but the woman he'd fallen for in a big way. He definitely wanted to be there when the man was confronted.

"Forgot my coffee. That man has me turned every which way," Evelyn said as she stomped back into the room toward the kitchen.

"What can I do?" Britt asked.

Chad's knee-jerk response was to get her as far away from Otis and Camden as he could get her. Before he could say anything, his mom spoke from the kitchen, where she was pouring a cup of steaming-hot coffee into her mug.

"The boys finished the work on the rental yesterday, and with everything that happened, we haven't been able to make sure it's ready for the next guests. Do you think you could go out there and make sure it's clean?"

Britt's eyes narrowed. "You're just trying to get me out of the house," she accused.

Chad was thankful his mom had made the suggestion and not him, because the daggers shooting from Britt's eyes were definitely lethal.

"Of course I am," Evelyn told her sweetly. "I appreciate more than you know that you immediately brought your suspicions about Otis to Chad. But this is a Young issue . . . no offense. I don't want him to see you and think he can accuse you of lying or planting evidence against him just because you're not a local. I mean, he could still do that with you at the cabin, but I want to spare you from having to see him or hear whatever accusations he might make."

Britt's shoulders relaxed. "I can understand that. And we do have the renters coming today. All right, I'll head out there and get the cabin ready."

"Thank you, child."

"I'll walk you over," Chad volunteered. The sooner he could get Britt out of the house, the better he'd feel. Not that he honestly thought Otis was a threat, but like his mom, he didn't want him saying anything that might make Britt feel bad or suggest that anything that happened was her fault.

He was ready to get this done. Get Otis off Lobster Cove property, talk to the police, press charges, move on.

Feeling antsy, not knowing when Otis or Camden would show, Chad turned to Britt, wanting to get her safely into the rental *now*. "Ready?" he asked.

She glanced at him with a confused look. "Yeah. I guess so."

He held out his hand.

Britt looked like she wanted to protest, stall, *something*, but thankfully she just took his hand and stood. "Okay. Thanks."

Once she was standing, she walked over to Evelyn and kissed her on the cheek. "Be careful, okay?"

"Of course. Otis isn't going to hurt me."

Chad wanted to snort at that. He'd *already* hurt her. First by stealing from her for years, then by having his son tamper with her car.

He wasn't surprised Britt was thinking the same thing.

"You have no idea what a desperate man might do. If he's been stealing from you and then suddenly gets cut off, there's no telling how he'll react."

Evelyn nodded. "I know. Which is why I won't be alone. Just in case."

Reluctantly, Britt backed away, and Chad took her hand once more. They walked out of the house, and he saw her look around a little cautiously.

"He's not here yet," Chad said, understanding what, who, she was looking for.

She wrinkled her nose. "I was that obvious, huh?"

"A little," he said with a shrug.

"It's just . . . this feels so unreal. Do you really think Otis had a hand in what happened yesterday?"

"I don't know for certain, but my gut says yes. Camden could have acted on his own. But to me, it's too much of a coincidence that right after my meeting with his dad, Camden found a reason to work on Mom's car. At the very least, Otis didn't discourage whatever he did."

"You think Camden is involved in the embezzling?"

"Probably. He's most likely benefited by getting handouts from his dad. And if Otis is canned, that also stops. Camden isn't the hardest-working individual I've ever met. If Otis told his son about my visit yesterday, Camden might have decided to take matters into his own hands. Or Otis could've told his son what to do. We might never know, because I doubt either will confess to anything. Otis has had years to perfect his lies."

"I'm sorry."

"For what?" Chad asked. "You didn't cause any of this."

"I know, but I still feel as if I brought it all down on everyone."

Chad stopped in his tracks and turned to Britt. He took her face in his hands and tilted her head up so she had no choice but to meet his gaze. "Do *not* feel guilty. You were able to see something that's been right under our noses for years. We owe you, Britt. Big time. Whatever happens to those two is on *them*, not you. Got it?"

She nodded.

"Good," he said, dropping his hands and turning them toward the guest cabin. He wanted to continue to reassure her, but he also wanted to get back to the house and prepare himself for the impending confrontation with Otis.

"I'm also sorry," Britt added as they continued toward the cabin, "that you and your family have to deal with a betrayal like this. I've experienced it with my mom and with Cole, and it sucks."

It hit Chad then that she probably really *did* understand. The one person who was supposed to support and love her unconditionally, her mom, had let her down over and over again. And then to be abandoned in Maine without any money and apparently without a second thought by her ex was another huge blow.

They'd arrived at the cabin, and Chad opened the door, pulling Britt in behind him. He did a quick walk-through of the house to make sure everything was as it should be, then pulled Britt into a long hug.

"Don't overdo things. You were in an accident yesterday," he said.

"Yeah, I remember," she said with a grin.

"Stay in the house. No matter what," he ordered.

Her grin faded. "Sorry, but if I hear yelling or worse . . . I'm not hiding in this house like a coward."

"Britt, I was in the Army, Zach was in the Navy, Linc was an Air Force pilot, and Knox was in the Coast Guard. I think we've got this."

"I know, but . . . I'll never be the kind of woman who hides under a bed when shit's going down. Well . . . not since I was eight. You should know that about me by now."

"And I love that about you. But I don't want you in danger."

"Chad, I could be in danger walking down the street. Or in the woods because the ticks around here are horrible and they carry that Lyme disease. Or I could trip walking up the stairs. Or—"

"Can we please stop talking about you getting hurt?" Chad asked, feeling a little sick inside.

"I'm just saying if you think there will ever come a time when I hide in a closet while you or someone in your family is in danger, you're so wrong it's not even funny."

"If anything happened to you, it would destroy me," he whispered.

"If something happened to *you* and I was sitting around doing nothing, it would destroy *me*," she countered.

Chad frowned. He understood what she was saying, but it still went against everything within him to let her charge into any kind of unstable or dangerous situation.

"How about this?" she said. "How about if I promise to not run willy-nilly into whatever's happening? I'll analyze, take stock, figure out what's happening and the best course of action before I act."

He still didn't like it, but that was better than the alternative. "All right."

"All right," she echoed. "And for the record . . . I don't like violence. I don't like confrontation. Or yelling. So I'm happy to stay in the background and not get involved if at all possible."

"I promise this is an anomaly. Things around Lobster Cove are usually easygoing and smooth sailing."

"I know. I've seen it for myself. Go. Get back to your mom. I know you're chomping at the bit to get to the house. You'll let me know when it's safe to return?"

"I'll come get you myself."

"Thanks. Be careful, Chad. Desperate men do desperate things. Even sixty-eight-year-old men who have been family friends for decades."

"I know." And he did. He'd learned from his time in the Army and as a sniper that when backed against a wall, people could do just about anything. He wasn't going to let his guard down around Otis. He didn't care if he was sixty-eight, a hundred and eight, or eighteen.

Leaning down, he kissed Britt long and slow. He needed this memory to get him through the confrontation with Otis. His mom would be in charge of the meeting, but it would take every ounce of control he had not to demand answers himself.

"Love you," Britt whispered.

The two words seemed to travel throughout Chad's body, giving him the strength he needed to get through whatever was to come. It would be unpleasant, but after today, they'd all have a new start.

They'd find a new accountant, someone else to check his mom's investments, and maybe one person who could oversee all the Lobster Cove businesses. He and his brothers would convince his mom that having one person do literally everything related to money was no longer a good idea . . . but maybe after everything with Otis, she wouldn't need much convincing after all.

"Love you too," Chad said, then backed away. She gave him a small smile and adorkable wave.

Grinning, Chad headed for the door. He closed it firmly behind him, took a deep breath, then headed for the house and the impending confrontation.

Deep down, he had no doubt that Otis was behind yesterday's accident. He'd panicked after Chad confronted him. It would be interesting to see what the man had to say. How he'd defend himself. But no matter what, the result would be the same. Otis Calvert and his son would no longer be working or associated with Lobster Cove after today.

CHAPTER NINETEEN

Chad's respect for his mother grew tenfold as he observed her meeting with Otis. She was a rock. Standing tall and not giving an inch.

Otis had arrived at the house with Lincoln by his side, both men frowning. Evelyn had met them at the door and led the way to the office. It was where her husband had conducted all his official business, and as she sat in Austin's leather chair behind his large wooden desk, inviting Otis to take a seat, she set the tone by taking charge.

Lincoln and Chad took up positions against the wall by the door. Both had their arms crossed over their chests, and they didn't miss the uneasy glances Otis kept giving them as he fidgeted in the chair across from Evelyn.

She didn't beat around the bush. Jumped right into the matter at hand. "Are you embezzling money from Lobster Cove?"

Otis had stuttered and stumbled over his immediate denial.

But Evelyn didn't let up. She asked about one specific item after another that Otis had a hard time explaining.

She'd obviously done her research the evening before. Instead of going to bed, as they'd all thought, it was clear she'd pulled up the Lobster Cove Auto Body financials and inventory. Had researched for herself the things that Britt had brought to light.

She'd also researched the Lobster Cove tax returns for the past several years. His mom might not be an accountant, but she was doing a damn good job of asking the right questions—questions Otis was clearly surprised by and didn't have good answers for.

The man was sweating and answering in general terms, not incriminating himself but not giving any details that could be verified either. He was lying by omission, trying not to say anything that might bite him in the ass later.

Finally, Evelyn seemed to have enough. She pushed a stack of old tax returns to the side and leaned forward, putting her elbows on the rough wooden desktop. She met Otis's gaze straight on.

"You've been my friend for decades, Otis. We've laughed together, cried, had good times and bad. I don't know how I would've made it through Austin's death without you. And yet I have a feeling it all meant *nothing* to you."

"What? That's not true."

"Yesterday, I could've died. If it wasn't for Britt's quick thinking, we both would've drowned. Or died in a head-on collision with another car or a damn tree. Tell me to my face that you had nothing to do with my car being tampered with. That you didn't talk to your son and tell him the jig was up. That the money you've been stealing from me, from Austin, from my sons, was drying up."

"I didn't."

Otis didn't hesitate to say the words, but even to Chad's ear, they sounded insincere.

His mom sighed and sat back in her chair. "You're fired, Otis. *Done.* You and your son aren't allowed on Lobster Cove property anymore. For any reason. Our friendship is over. You let greed win. I'm disgusted and disappointed. Oh, and I'll be filing restraining orders against both you and Camden. If you come within one hundred yards of me or Lobster Cove, you'll be arrested. All the passwords to the accounts you had access to have already been changed."

All the blood drained from Otis's face. He looked shell shocked. As if he couldn't believe he'd actually been fired.

Evelyn stood then, bracing her palms on the desk as she kept eye contact with one of her oldest friends. "Austin is rolling in his grave right now. I'm glad he's not around to learn what one of his best friends has done. How you've been screwing over his family. Austin worked his tail off for Lobster Cove. I *knew* we should have had a lot more to show for it than we did. And now we know it's because you were stealing his hard-earned money, you bastard! Get out. I'll see you in court. I'm gonna do whatever I have to in order to recoup every penny you stole. Not for me. But for my boys. For the legacy of Lobster Cove."

"Evelyn—" Otis began in a pleading tone.

But she was having none of it. "Out!" she ordered, pointing at the door with narrowed eyes.

If Chad hadn't been looking at Otis at the exact moment he turned to leave, he would've missed the sheer hatred that flashed in his eyes. As it was, Chad wasn't sure he'd truly seen what he thought. Because as soon as the emotion flared to life, it was gone.

Otis paused at the door. "I know you don't believe me, but I had nothing to do with your accident. And I've been nothing but honest with you and Austin. I'd never steal from you."

"Get out," Evelyn said again, this time sounding bone-deep weary.

Without another word, he left. Lincoln followed him out, Chad staying behind with his mom.

"Mom?"

But she shook her head. "Not now, Chad. I need a moment. Alone."

He hated to leave her when she looked so . . . broken. But if that's what she needed, that's what he'd give her. She'd rally. She always did. His mom was the strongest woman he knew.

Chad walked over to where she sat back in the big leather chair and kissed the top of her head. "I'm proud of you," he said softly, wanting her to know how he felt. "That wasn't easy, and you were awesome."

She nodded but didn't speak.

Chad left her and went to the window at the front of the house, watching as Lincoln, Knox, and Zach stood with their arms crossed, glaring at Otis as he got into his car, with Camden already in the passenger seat, and pulled away.

It was done.

Hopefully that would be the last any of them saw of the Calverts on Lobster Cove.

As soon as he had the thought, Chad's stomach churned. He had a bad feeling this *wasn't* the last they'd see of the pair. He just hoped whatever happened in the future would be in a courtroom and not in any other capacity.

～

"We're done for," Otis told his son.

"This is bullshit! They have no proof of anything," Camden seethed.

"They will. They've changed all the passwords to the accounts, so I can't cover my tracks."

"*Fuck.* And Zach and Knox made sure to tell me that the cops have towed the CR-V. They're gonna find the cut brake lines and see that the steering was tampered with. What are we going to do? How will we find enough money to live on?"

"You could try actually getting a full-time job," Otis muttered under his breath. He was pissed. More about getting caught and less about losing a decades-long friendship.

In all honesty, he hadn't *always* stolen from the Youngs. It started fairly recently . . . like in the last ten years or so. It was too easy because Austin was so trusting. When Camden moved in after doing his last stint in prison—this time for involuntary manslaughter—Otis needed a little extra cash. He had another mouth to feed, and all the other expenses that came with supporting Cam. He felt bad in the beginning, but Austin and Evelyn had plenty of money back then. They certainly wouldn't miss a few thousand dollars a year.

As the years passed, it became harder and harder to control himself. And Camden pushing for more and more money from his old man hadn't helped. Otis had given in to temptation and started taking as much as he wanted. More than was smart.

But Otis wasn't blaming his son. He could've said no. He could've put his foot down and kicked him out and forced him to make his own way. But he hadn't. And thanks to his ugly divorce, Otis partially blamed himself for the way his son had turned out—hot tempered, quick to use his fists when provoked, and greedy as hell.

And now . . . here they were.

"It's all that dumb bitch's fault. If it wasn't for her being so goddamned nosy, none of this would've happened," Camden growled.

Otis nodded. This *was* all Britt Starkweather's fault. She had Chad so wrapped around her finger that he'd believed *her* over someone he'd known his entire life. It was a massive insult—even if Britt was right.

"I'm not going back to prison," Camden vowed.

Panic blossomed in Otis's chest. He didn't want to go to jail either. But he'd encouraged his son to mess with Evelyn's car, and he'd been embezzling money from the Lobster Cove accounts for years. He'd be found just as guilty as his son. And the thought of spending the rest of his life behind bars was terrifying. At his age, he'd be easy prey.

"No one's going to jail," he vowed.

"So what are we gonna do?"

"I don't know. If Evelyn had been by herself when her brakes failed, things would be different. If Britt wasn't with her, those boys probably would've been engrossed in funeral plans and grieving. I'd have time to cover my tracks. And they might love Lobster Cove, but if their mom died suddenly, I doubt any of them would actually *want* to stay in the middle of bumfuck Maine. They came here specifically to help Evelyn with the property, and if they didn't have a reason to stay . . ." His voice trailed off suggestively.

"I don't know. Chad seems pretty content living there," Camden said skeptically.

"Shit!" Otis fumed, his mind spinning. "If I can just get Evelyn away from her damn sons for a talk, I know I can convince her that everything's fine," he insisted.

"How are you going to do that? She *fired* you, Dad. And she's getting a restraining order."

Otis shrugged. "It's just a piece of paper. It doesn't actually keep me from *doing* anything. I'll give her some time to cool down, then approach her."

"And if she doesn't want to talk? If she calls the cops? Or if they come for you before you can talk to her? What then?"

"I don't know!" Otis yelled, sick of Camden's questions. "But I have to try *something*! I'm going to fix this."

"Yeah, right. I think you should leave this to me, Dad."

Otis snorted. "What would *you* do, smarty-pants?"

"I think we're beyond talking at this point. And if there's no one around to press charges at all, we'll be off the hook."

Otis blinked. "What're you going to do? Kill them all? Evelyn, Knox, Lincoln, Chad, *and* Zach?"

"If I have to," his son said calmly.

Stopping at the end of Lobster Cove's long drive, Otis stared at his son for a long moment, hardly believing they were having this conversation.

"You think that'll get me off the hook?" he finally asked quietly.

"Maybe. Maybe not. I'm sure there will be some cops that still think you're guilty. But if you can delete files or tamper with them, without the Youngs to testify, there might be enough doubt to make it hard to prosecute," Camden said.

Otis wasn't sure about that . . . but the idea of getting rid of the people who had completely upended his life was shockingly tempting.

"Besides," he went on, "I *hate* that bitch. The new chick. She thinks she's so smart? She's not. Things were operating just fine before she stuck her nose where it didn't belong. If she wasn't driving, we would've taken care of Evelyn, and things would be very different right now."

His son wasn't wrong. Still . . . "I don't know, Cam—"

"I do. You got us into this mess. *I'll* get us out," he interrupted. "We have that money you transferred last week. We'll use it to leave the state. Start fresh somewhere. Maybe Alaska."

Otis wasn't opposed to starting over on the other side of the country. If it could possibly keep him out of jail, he was good with going far, far away.

With a sigh, he met his son's gaze. "What can I do to help?"

Camden smirked. "You're a pain in the ass, old man, but I love ya."

"I love you too," Otis said. "What's the plan?"

They spent the rest of the ride home strategizing. Desperate times called for desperate measures—and Otis Calvert wasn't going to go to prison. He felt a pang of remorse for what he and Camden were planning for the Youngs, but it couldn't be helped.

The easiest target was Evelyn. She'd be the lure for the rest of the family.

With any luck, by this time next week, he and Camden would be on their way to Alaska and the start of a new life, with a clean slate.

This would work.

It had to.

There was no alternative.

CHAPTER TWENTY

The rest of the week was . . . strained. That was the only way Britt could describe it. Everyone was on edge. The police detectives came out to Lobster Cove to talk to Britt and Evelyn about the accident. After Britt was done telling them everything she could remember about what happened, they confirmed her suspicions, that the brakes and steering had both been tampered with.

Walt and Barry had reiterated that they'd testify in court that it was Camden who'd suggested Evelyn's car had something wrong with it and he'd been the one to work on the vehicle, refusing their help. The lack of any fingerprints other than Camden's on the car confirmed their stories.

The independent financial consultant that Lincoln had hired was working through the years of tax returns and other financial documents, and had preliminarily confirmed that all the Youngs' suspicions were correct. Large amounts of money each month had been embezzled, most likely by Otis. It would take a while to determine how much exactly, from which accounts, and for how far back.

The DA wasn't ready to press charges yet, but they were coming. It was inevitable.

And while everyone at Lobster Cove was relieved that Otis and Camden would face charges for everything they'd done, there was also an air of grieving around the property for the second time in just a few months. Otis was as much an institution around the place as Austin

Young had been. Evelyn had trusted him. Hell, everyone had. And he'd broken that trust in the worst way.

Britt did her best to keep the things she could running smoothly, to take the stress off Evelyn and the others. She completely took over everything having to do with the guest cabins, greeting the renters, and making sure they had everything they needed. She answered the email inquiries and kept on top of the website they used to book stays. She cleaned the cabins, baked for the guests, and generally became the face of Lobster Cove Rentals.

She also continued to help out with inventory at the auto shop. Walt and Barry were subdued but busier than ever now that Camden was gone. True, he was only part time, but even the few hours he'd worked had taken some of the pressure off the two men.

Lincoln had stepped up to help out around Lobster Cove where he could. Zach was busy trying to make his lobster shack profitable, and Knox was working with the Coast Guard every day.

Everyone was busy, but the pall of Otis's betrayal hung over Lobster Cove like a shroud. Despite being fired, the damage he'd done was still front and center in everyone's mind.

Britt was making muffins in the kitchen to put into the two-bedroom cabin as a welcome gift when Chad entered the house. He was sweaty and dirty, and he had a determined gleam in his eye.

"We need a break," he declared.

"What?"

"A break," he repeated. "You haven't been swimming in the cove yet."

"Chad, the water's freezing," Britt told him.

"It's chilly. Not freezing. We've had some warm days recently, and it's time you were given a proper welcome to Lobster Cove."

Britt frowned. "And what's that?"

"The lobster swing."

"The what?"

"The lobster swing. It's a swing hanging from a tree near the shore. It's tradition for everyone who lives and works at Lobster Cove to take a turn. Everyone's done it but you. Hell, even some of the guests at the cabins have used it."

"I'm good," Britt told him, not liking the idea of getting into the water. Yes, it was warm now, but that didn't mean the water was warm. For someone used to southern waters and beaches, it wasn't even warm-*ish*.

"Come on, it'll be fun," Chad cajoled.

The front door opened, and Knox and Zach walked in.

"Heard it's lobster-swing day!" Zach exclaimed. "I left the shack to my employees for a few hours because I wasn't going to miss opening day for the swing!"

"Same," Knox agreed. "It's been forever since we've been on that thing."

"So how do you know it's not going to break? The rope might be rotted," Britt pointed out.

"Not a chance. Besides, Lincoln is out there now, checking it."

"Mom!" Knox yelled down the hallway. "It's lobster-swing time!"

Two seconds later, Evelyn peeked her head out of the office. "Woo-hoo!" she exclaimed. "Britt, you're going to love the swing. Let me go change. Don't leave without me!"

Britt turned to gape at the brothers. "Your *mom* is doing it?"

"Yes, so you have no excuses as to why you can't," Chad said with a chuckle. "Go on. Go upstairs and get changed. I have no idea if you have a suit or not, but if you don't, you can wear a pair of shorts and a tank top or something."

As Britt made her way up the stairs, she wondered how in the world she'd gotten roped into this. She could swim, but she also vividly remembered how cold the water was less than a week ago, when she'd crashed Evelyn's car and gotten submerged after escaping the wreck.

But if Evelyn could do it, and was apparently looking forward to it, so could she.

Britt changed and made her way down the stairs, shaking her head as she heard the brothers talking about years past, when they'd spent hours playing on the swing and in the waters of the cove.

By the time they all headed out of the house toward the infamous lobster swing, Britt realized the mood of the Young family had taken a turn for the first time since Otis had left the property. Everyone was in high spirits, laughing and reminiscing about good times on the swing. It was a nice change.

They walked along the shore, past the bench, and up through the trees on a path that took them about ten feet above the water. They went down a second, barely visible path, if it could be called that, and meandered back toward the water.

The path abruptly ended at a large tree where two long, thick, sturdy ropes holding a wood-plank seat hung from one of the large branches. The ropes were currently looped around big hooks that had been screwed into the tree trunk, obviously to secure the swing when not in use, to keep the ropes from getting tangled in the tree during the winter or any windstorms.

There was maybe a ten-foot slope that led down to the water, and Britt could see someone had made a crude set of wooden steps over the rocky slope, so whoever was in the water could make their way back up to flat ground fairly easily.

Finally, there was a platform made out of wood standing near the tree. Britt couldn't figure out exactly what it was used for. Maybe for someone to stand on, to make sure whoever was swinging was safe?

She didn't have to wait long to find out. Knox was eagerly stripping out of his T-shirt as he yelled, "I'm calling dibs on first swing!"

The other Young brothers grumbled good-naturedly but didn't seem too upset that Knox wanted to go first. She stood by a smiling Evelyn as they watched Knox climb onto the box. Zach unhooked the ropes from where they'd been secured against the tree and handed the swing to his brother.

Knox tugged on it hard a few times. Apparently satisfied that it was secure and would hold his weight, he put his ass on the thick wooden board affixed to the bottom of the ropes. It looked like any swing in a kids' playground or schoolyard. Except for the extremely long ropes and the ocean water lapping against the shore.

Knox stood on his tiptoes and leaped backward. He let out a loud *whoop* as he swung forward over the water. Lincoln stepped up, and when gravity swung Knox back toward land, Lincoln pushed against his back—hard—making his brother go much higher when he next flew out over the water.

That happened a few times, and on perhaps the fourth swing, Knox propelled himself off the board when it reached its peak. His arms and legs flailed a bit as he let out another joyous shout and fell toward the water below. He landed with a huge splash and came up laughing, shaking his head, water flying in every direction.

"Ooooh boy! This water is nothing like in Florida!"

Everyone laughed.

"Baby!"

"You've been gone from Maine too long! Gone soft!"

"Don't be a wuss!"

Knox's brothers didn't hesitate to make fun of him for implying the water was cold.

Of course, that made Britt nervous. If *Knox* thought the water was cold, it was probably freaking freezing. How much could it have warmed up since the accident? She figured not much.

Then again, Knox wasn't exactly spending a lot of time swimming. He immediately made his way to the shore and used the crude stairs to walk/crawl back up to where they were all standing.

One second Britt was smiling at everyone's good-natured teasing, and the next, she was letting out a girly screech as Knox made a beeline for her and wrapped her in a giant bear hug—soaking her clothes in the process.

"Knox!" she protested, trying to wiggle away from him.

"Just trying to get you ready for your turn," he said with a laugh.

Chad ended up pushing his brother away. "Mine," he declared with a mock growl and scowl.

Everyone laughed again, and any lingering tension they'd been feeling because of the events of the last few days was officially nowhere to be seen.

Britt hadn't even noticed Knox holding another rope when he came up the bank, but apparently it was attached to the bottom of the swing, and that was how it was prepared for the next person. Lincoln pulled the swing back toward the tree and held it for Zach as he climbed up on the box.

"Why the box?" Britt asked Chad as she leaned into him. He had his arm around her, and it felt nice. He was warm, and even though the air temperature was bordering on hot in the sun, her clothes were now damp thanks to Knox, making her feel chilly.

"It gives extra leverage. Gets the swing going faster and higher than if we got on it on the ground."

"I'm not sure I'd be able to even *get* on it from the ground," Britt observed.

Chad chuckled. "That's the other reason. When Dad put it up, he miscalculated and made the ropes a little too short for Mom to be able to get on. He tried to pretend he'd done it that way on purpose, that his plan was to use the box all along, but we all knew differently."

Not for the first time, Britt wished she could've met Austin Young. He'd raised some fine sons, and it was more than obvious how much love he had for his little corner of the world here at Lobster Cove.

Zach let out a Tarzan yell as he flew through the air after launching himself off the swing and into the water. Britt had to admit that everything about the swing looked fun.

"Why is it called a lobster swing?" she asked Chad as Zach grabbed the rope used to pull the swing in and headed for shore.

"Everything around here is called lobster something or other," he told her. "It's kind of a running joke. Mainers know that lobster anything sells to tourists, so they use it as much as they can. And since this is Lobster Cove, we figured *lobster swing* was an appropriate name."

"Tell her the real story," Evelyn chided her son.

To Britt's surprise, Chad's cheeks turned pink.

"Oh, this I *have* to hear," she teased.

But Evelyn didn't give Chad a chance to explain. She told the story herself. "When Chad was around eight, before Austin put up the swing and about a year after Zach was born, he and Lincoln were playing in the water here. As you can see, there's a small protected area where it's not as deep. Lincoln was around eleven, and he knew he was in charge of keeping his younger brother safe. They had to adhere to the buddy system when they were playing. Anyway, he came running into the house screaming that Chad was being attacked.

"I, of course, panicked, and Austin and I ran to see what was happening. Chad was standing down there in the water, crying hysterically—with a lobster attached to his penis. They'd been skinny-dipping, as our boys did all the time, and somehow this lobster mistook his . . . you know . . . for something it wanted to eat.

"Austin and I did our best not to laugh, because we knew poor Chad had to be in a lot of pain, but after we got the lobster detached and realized he was just bruised and not truly hurt, we couldn't hold back our laughter anymore. It wasn't too much later that Austin put the swing up. We started calling it the lobster swing because of where it was and what happened to Chad. The name stuck."

Britt tried really hard not to laugh, but it was impossible not to, especially when all Chad's brothers were practically rolling on the ground. Zach and Knox were too young to remember the incident, but it was obviously a well-loved story that had been told over and over.

"I'm sorry," she said as she tried to control her mirth, "but I can just picture you standing down there, trying not to move, scared to do anything that might make that lobster pinch even harder."

"I was literally afraid it would cut off my dick," Chad said with a small smile and shrug.

"I have one question . . . ," Britt asked. It was taking all her control not to burst into giggles.

"What's that?" Chad asked.

"What happened to the lobster?"

"Austin took it home and we had it for dinner, of course," Evelyn said.

That did it. Britt burst out laughing. Everyone joined in, including Chad. She was glad he wasn't upset that they were essentially laughing at what had to have been a traumatic experience for him.

"My turn!" Evelyn exclaimed as she stepped toward the box. Lincoln helped his mom climb up, while Knox steadied her from behind.

Britt was in awe of the woman. She didn't have any hesitation, and the joy on her face as she stepped off that box and flew through the air was contagious. This was a woman who loved the little things. Who would never be content to sit in her house and hibernate away from life and all it had to offer. She might not be the most well-traveled woman in the world, having spent most of her days right here on Lobster Cove, but she was content with who she was. With what she had. And from where Britt was standing, it seemed as if she had everything anyone could ever want.

Lincoln pushed his mom when she swung back toward shore, but not quite as hard as he'd pushed his brother. After a few swings, when she felt she was high enough, the matriarch of the Young family leaped off the swing. She laughed loudly as she flew through the air and landed in the water.

Chad moved from Britt's side and headed down the bank, holding out his hand to his mom as she came toward shore. The love he and his brothers had for their mother brought tears to Britt's eyes. Yet again, she thought about the kind of relationship she had with her own mother, and how much they'd both missed out on for years.

A slight noise behind her had Britt turning, and to her surprise, she saw a little boy peeking around a tree next to the path that led back into the trees. Stepping toward Lincoln, she nudged him with her elbow and gestured subtly to where the boy was watching Evelyn and Chad climb up the crude steps.

It was Kash. His red hair was sticking up all over his head, and he had a look of longing on his face that made Britt's heart hurt. She knew all too well the feeling of being on the outside looking in at others having fun. Birthday parties she wasn't invited to, neighborhood cookouts that her mom hadn't been asked to attend, or couldn't attend because she was working. Staring at an amusement park full of people as she and her mom drove by.

It wasn't a secret that the Youngs didn't get along with their neighbor. That they thought Victor Rogers was a grumpy asshole. Britt wondered for a split second if that dislike would extend to his grandchild, but to her relief, Lincoln didn't seem upset that the boy was spying on them.

"Hey, you must be Kash. Heard you'd moved in next door. Also heard you've taken over our fort in the woods. That's cool," Lincoln said, keeping his voice low and friendly as he spoke to the boy.

"Fort Bad Assery," Chad said as he stepped back onto the flat area around the tree. "Hey, Kash. Good to see you again. I'm impressed that you did such a good job securing the fort and your stuff so nothing was damaged too much in the storm. That's awesome."

The men's casual banter and welcoming words had Kash stepping out from behind the tree he'd been using as a hiding spot. "Yeah. Some of the books were a little damp, but nothing too bad," he said.

"That's good. Great. Do you know my brothers?" Chad asked.

The boy shook his head.

"This is Lincoln, he's the oldest. I'm next. Then there's Knox, and Zach is our baby brother. And this is my mom."

"Hello, sweetie," Evelyn said.

"You went on the swing," he said, staring at Evelyn.

"I sure did. And it was *fun!*" she told him with a smile.

"My granddad says you're mean. That you're a stick-in-the-mud."

Britt tensed, but no one took offense to the boy's words.

Evelyn chuckled. "That's because your granddad's a grump. He doesn't seem to like anything or anyone who doesn't fit into his idea of what he thinks they should be. For example, he thinks I should be forever wearing an apron and standing in the kitchen. Which is ridiculous. For one, there are so many other things to do here on Lobster Cove than stay inside cooking all day. And two . . . I don't think I've owned an apron in my whole life."

Kash looked at the ground briefly. "He thinks I should be on the football team. Or baseball. But I'd rather read and look at the stars."

Evelyn smiled. "Reading and looking at the stars is awesome. I like that stuff too."

Kash nodded eagerly, and Britt wondered if that was the first time in his life he'd heard someone tell him it was okay to be himself. It made her wonder about his mother. Where was she? Was she as grumpy as her father? Did she also wish her son was more athletic?

"You want to take a turn?" Lincoln asked Kash.

The boy's head whipped around as he stared up at Lincoln. "Really?"

"Sure. It's tradition that anyone who lives or works at Lobster Cove has to swing. Britt hasn't gone yet, but she will, since she's living here now and dating my brother."

"I don't live or work here," Kash said.

"You're hanging out in our fort. That counts," Lincoln said with a shrug.

Kash looked from him to the swing in his hand, then back the way he'd come on the path. "I don't know," he said, biting his lip. "I'm not supposed to be over here. If Granddad knew . . ."

"How about if you just watch, then?" Lincoln said, not putting any pressure on the kid.

"Maybe for a while."

Britt turned her head so Kash didn't see her smile. She had a feeling it was only a matter of time before he'd be giving in to his obvious desire to take a turn on the swing. How could any little boy resist?

"Okay, Britt. Your turn," Lincoln said firmly, looking in her direction.

The smile dropped from her face. "Oh, um . . . I'm not sure."

"Come on. It's a blast!" Evelyn said.

Britt wasn't convinced. She liked swings, of course she did, but she'd never been all that good at jumping off one. All her friends had done it when she was little, but to Britt, it always seemed a little dangerous. And when Becky Coleman had done it when they were in fourth grade, and misjudged her landing and fell on her face, scraping it all up and needing three stitches in her chin, it solidified her desire to use the swing as it was intended . . . and keep her butt planted at all times.

But she found herself moving toward the box even as everything inside her was screaming to back away. To run to the house and hide. *If Evelyn can do it, so can I.* That was what she told herself as she took a deep breath and lifted her leg to the first step of the box.

Before she was ready, she was standing on top of the box and lifting her ass onto the swing. Her heart was racing, her hands were clammy, and it felt as if she was hyperventilating.

"You got this. Push backward, then lift your legs. You'll swing out over the water, and when you come back, Lincoln will push you so you go a little higher. Around the fourth or fifth swing, at the highest part of the arc, jump off. It'll feel just like you're flying," Chad coached.

Britt nodded, holding on to the ropes on either side of her with a death grip. There was so much wrong with this, she didn't know where to start. She had no idea how deep the water was, but no one else seemed concerned, so she shouldn't be either. But what if momentum pitched her forward and she belly flopped onto the water or landed on her face? What if the water was so cold she stopped breathing when she hit?

She couldn't help but remember the story of the lobster attaching to Chad . . . What if there was a giant lobster under the water, pissed because its home had been disturbed by the others who'd swung before her, and it attached to *her*?

Britt was well aware she was being ridiculous, but she couldn't help it. This was so far outside her comfort zone it wasn't even funny.

Before she could get even further into her head, Lincoln was counting down.

"Three, two, one . . . go!"

Her body automatically obeyed, and Britt found herself flying through the air. The first swing, she didn't breathe and she squeezed her eyes shut, but when she felt Lincoln's hands on her back as he pushed her, she took a deep breath and opened her eyes.

The feeling of being weightless was exhilarating. She could do this part forever. Simply swing back and forth over the water, then back toward land.

"You're high enough now, Britt! Next time, jump!" Lincoln ordered.

"You got this!" Evelyn shouted.

"Woooooo!" Kash whooped, obviously getting into the excitement of the moment.

"Do it, Britt!"

It was Chad's words of encouragement—okay, his order—that had Britt taking a deep breath and letting go of the ropes as she propelled her body forward when she was over the water the next time.

For a split second, it really did feel as if she were flying—then reality hit as she plummeted toward the water. It was too late to change her mind now! Her arms and legs flailed as she struggled to keep herself upright as she fell.

It took only seconds to hit the water, and as she sank and her body felt as if it were immediately encased in ice . . . Britt realized she was smiling.

Her head bobbed to the surface, and it felt as if her limbs weighed eight hundred pounds, but she couldn't help but exclaim "That was fun!" as she saw Chad standing on the bottom step, waiting for her.

He smiled back and held out his hand. Britt made her way over to him and sighed in satisfaction as his fingers closed around hers.

Something came over her then. She had no idea what. Maybe it was his warm hand when she was so cold. Maybe it was his bossiness as he'd yelled "Do it" when she was swinging. Maybe it was the "I told you so" smirk on his face.

Whatever it was, she yanked his hand toward her, pulling him off balance and making him fall into the water with her.

Laughter rang out from the shore above them as a soaking-wet Chad emerged from the water. For a split second she was afraid she'd made him mad, but then he laughed and shook his head, much as a wet dog might. Water went flying everywhere, and Britt stopped breathing for a moment as her thoughts went right back to the last shower they'd shared, when his hair had been wet just like it was now, and he'd smiled at her while she'd been on her knees in front of him. He'd just come all over her chest, and the happiness on his face had been just as clear as it was now.

"Hold that thought," he murmured, as if he could read her mind. "My turn!" he called out as he climbed onto the first step and reached back to help Britt once more.

Some men wouldn't put themselves in the exact same vulnerable position as he was doing now. But Britt had no desire to pull him into the water again. She gratefully accepted his help, as it wasn't easy to get up onto that first step, and they climbed back up to the tree.

Chad took his turn on the swing, flying higher and farther than anyone else had so far. Which of course started a good-natured competition among the brothers. Britt even found herself wanting to go again, and now that she knew what to expect, she wasn't as freaked out as she'd been the first time.

Evelyn didn't jump again, just contented herself by sitting on the ground, her back against a tree, as she watched her boys enjoy themselves.

Eventually, Kash agreed to take a turn. The joy on his face and in his scream as he flew through the air was easy to see and hear. After that, he was insatiable. He swung twice as much as anyone else.

Two hours went by before the group decided to call it a day.

Lincoln knelt in front of Kash and put a hand on his shoulder. "You have fun today?"

The boy nodded enthusiastically, a big grin on his face.

"That's great. You've now officially christened the lobster swing. But I need you to listen to me carefully. Are you listening?"

"Yeah."

"Under no circumstances are you to come here and swing by yourself. Understand? I know you want to, because it's fun. But it can also be dangerous. The water current today is almost nonexistent. And we swung at high tide. The rule of the lobster swing, and just about *everything* that's done on Lobster Cove, is that it has to be done with a buddy. Any one of us is happy to be your buddy, but you absolutely cannot swim or swing or do anything else on Lobster Cove without someone by your side. Got it?"

Some of the pleasure on Kash's face faded, but he nodded.

"I know it sucks, bud, but if something happened and no one was around to help, it could be bad."

"Okay."

"How about this . . . how about if we plan to swing again in a week? You can come back and join us."

"Yeah!" Kash's face lit up once more.

"Great. It's a plan. You gonna be okay going home in your wet clothes?"

He was wearing shorts and a T-shirt. He'd taken off his shirt to swing, but it was damp around the bottom where it had touched his wet shorts and around the neckline from his dripping hair.

"I think I'm gonna sit in the fort for a while," Kash said.

"All right. Next time, we'll bring towels. We were so excited we completely forgot this time," Lincoln told him. "And Kash?"

"Yeah?"

"You need anything, anything at all, you come on over to Lobster Cove. To the house. I don't live here, but my mom, Chad, and Britt do. Not to mention Walt and Barry, who work at the auto shop. Any of them will help you with anything, no questions asked. You just need to get away . . . if you're hungry, bored, whatever . . . come on over. Now that you've swung on the lobster swing, you're a part of Lobster Cove."

"Cool," Kash said, a little uncertainly.

"Yeah, it *is* cool." Lincoln stood and ruffled the boy's red hair. "Go on now. Off to the fort and your books. It's a great way to wind down after all this excitement."

"You like to read?" Kash asked, his eyes wide.

"Love it. I think I have about ten books stacked on the nightstand next to my bed right now."

"Awesome!" Kash breathed.

The boy turned to head down the path, and Lincoln called out after him. "And make sure to check yourself for ticks before you go to bed! They're awful this time of year, and being in the woods means you've probably got at least one trying to suck all your blood out."

Kash's forehead wrinkled in disgust, and Britt agreed with him. Ticks were the devil. There was absolutely no point to them at all. She'd read a story just yesterday about how baby moose—mooses? meese? moosi?—actually died from having so many ticks attached to them that they literally couldn't withstand all the blood loss.

And now that she was thinking about ticks, it felt as if they were crawling all over her. She was ready to go home, shower, and do a thorough tick check of her own body.

"I put some dog collars around the inside of Fort Bad Assery, and I usually put them around my ankles when I walk through the woods," Kash told Lincoln.

"Don't see them on you now, bud. So do a tick check when you get home, okay?"

"Okay! Bye, Lincoln! Bye, Knox, Zach, Chad, Britt, and Ms. Evelyn. You're not mean like my granddad always says!" And with that, Kash disappeared into the trees.

"Glad I'm not as mean as Victor claims I am," Evelyn muttered with a roll of her eyes.

Knox finished securing the rope swing to the large tree, and everyone began the trek back to the house.

Chad held Britt back so they were bringing up the rear, then he leaned down and whispered into her ear, "I'm going to need to inspect you verrrrrrry carefully for ticks when we get back to the house."

Britt giggled. "I know you're trying to sound sexy, but"—she shivered—"news flash. Any mention of ticks isn't the *least* bit sexy."

Chad snort-laughed. "Noted." He held her hand as they walked back toward the house. "You had fun today."

Britt nodded. "I wasn't sure about this, and I was terrified that first swing, but it turned out to be fun. And your mom . . ." She sighed. "I'm in awe of her."

"She's pretty awesome," Chad agreed.

"Your whole family is. Did you see how great Lincoln was with Kash? I know he has history with the boy's mother, and *no one* really likes his grandfather, but he didn't take any of that out on Kash. Which I think is awesome."

"You can't choose your family. And he's a kid. A lonely one at that. Lincoln would never be a dick to a kid. It's not how he's wired. How any of us are wired."

"I know. I just think it's great, that's all. Do you think Kash will tell his mom about today? About what he did?"

"No clue. I hope so. Because the last thing we want is someone else from over there hating us."

"I can't imagine anyone hating you, or any of the Youngs. You're all so . . . nice."

"We aren't always nice," Chad told her. "When push comes to shove, we'll defend what's important to us. Our family. Our friends. Our legacy."

Britt nodded. "I can see that. You all have a huge sense of honor and loyalty."

"Which was part of why we all made such good members of the military."

Britt thought about that as they made their way back to the house. Chad was right. He and his brothers would've made excellent lifers in their respective military branches, if circumstances had been different. But the country's loss was Rockville's gain. This little part of the world was better off because the Young brothers had come home. Britt felt that down to her toes.

They said goodbye to Zach, Knox, and Lincoln, and as Evelyn headed toward her room to shower and change, Britt gave Chad a coy look. "Coming?" she asked.

"Not yet. But we both will be soon."

Britt rolled her eyes at the cheesy comeback, but her pulse sped up all the same just thinking about what the next hour would hold for them both. Ticks be damned, she was more than ready for a full-body inspection.

CHAPTER
TWENTY-ONE

Two days later, Chad lay in bed and stared at the ceiling as he listened to Britt shower in the hall bathroom. The pipes ran down the wall right next to his head, and when he was growing up, it used to annoy the crap out of him. Sharing the bathroom with his three brothers was a pain, and someone was always showering at the ass crack of dawn . . . waking him up with the damn water whooshing down the pipes inches from his head.

But this morning, the familiar sound simply made him smile. Knowing it was *Britt* who was naked under the spray, the noise didn't bother him one bit.

He'd had no idea being in a relationship could make him feel this way. Content. Happy. Looking forward to each day.

He didn't even mind that they were living with his mom. She had her side of the house, and he and Britt had theirs. The bathroom was tiny, and he would've preferred to have an en suite, but they were making it work. Which was another thing Chad loved about Britt. She didn't complain. About much of anything. He supposed it was because she'd had such a difficult upbringing, one where she'd been overlooked and had to fend for herself—which sucked. But he couldn't deny he appreciated that precious little got her riled.

What he *didn't* like was how hard Britt was currently working. He couldn't even fathom how his mom had done so much on Lobster Cove by herself. Running every aspect of the rentals was a full-time job in itself . . . as he'd found out from watching Britt do it every day. On top of that, she was helping in the auto shop as often as she could, and still finding the time to look out for his mom.

He'd hit the jackpot, and Chad knew it. He vowed right then and there to do whatever he could to not screw up this relationship. If Britt felt forced to leave Lobster Cove because they were no longer dating, it would be a blow to his mom. And the property had worked its magic on Britt as well. Leaving would hurt her just as much as it would everyone else.

Chad had a long day ahead of him. He was going over to Lincoln's house to help his oldest brother with some renovations. He wanted to rebuild his back deck. The wood was rotted in places, and he planned to replace it with composite. He also wanted to build a firepit, but that might have to wait for another day.

Barry was coming over to help as well, glad for a very rare day off from the auto shop, and after Zach got his lobster shack open for the day, he said he'd also stop by. Knox was working, but he promised to come over afterward to check out the progress and lend a hand if necessary.

Britt wanted to come too, but both rental cabins were being turned over today. The current guests were leaving, and she needed to clean both houses, wash all the sheets and towels, and make muffins as welcome treats for tomorrow's incoming renters.

Just as he was thinking about his woman, Britt walked back into the room with a towel wrapped around her. And any thoughts of the upcoming day flew from Chad's mind. He was up and moving before he thought about what he was doing.

He stopped in front of her and put his hands on her hips. "You smell delicious," he said, leaning down and burying his nose in her neck.

Britt tilted her head to the side, giving him more room, her hands resting on his chest. Her fingers were warm from the shower, and suddenly Chad needed her more than he could remember ever needing any woman in his life. His hands went to her towel and tugged it loose.

"Chad!" she exclaimed with a small laugh.

"You are so beautiful," he told her reverently, his gaze taking her in from the top of her head to her cute pink-painted toenails.

"Thanks," she whispered a little shyly. They were working on her taking compliments better. She used to deflect attention away from herself whenever anyone said something nice, which Chad hated. He wanted her to see herself as everyone else did. Strong, beautiful, a necessary part of Lobster Cove.

He maneuvered them until her back was against the closed door she'd just walked through, and his hand went between her legs, caressing, teasing, probing.

"Chad," she said on a moan, her head going back to thunk against the wooden door. Her hands gripped his biceps as she widened her stance.

Lord, he loved this woman so much. She had a million things to do, and yet she wasn't opposed to delaying the start of her day for him.

His cock was hard and dripping behind his boxers. Awkwardly, he used his free hand to push them down, not willing to move the one currently buried in Britt's silky heat. He stepped out of the material, giving himself a few more minutes to play before reluctantly removing his fingers from Britt's pussy.

Bending his knees a little, grateful they were close to the same height, he lined up his cock and slowly pressed into her dripping sheath.

She inhaled and lifted one of her legs, pressing her inner thigh to his hip.

After enough of his cock was inside her, Chad moved his hands to her ass and gasped, "Up."

Thankfully, she realized what he wanted and immediately gave a little hop. It was all the leverage he needed to pick her up. Her legs clamped around his hips even as her pussy clenched around his cock, now buried as deep as it could get inside her.

They both moaned.

Chad braced her against the door and held her still as he began to pump in and out of her body. Her skin was dewy from the hot shower, and the smell of their combined arousal was an aphrodisiac.

He'd never had sex standing up before. Hadn't really wanted to. Had never been so desperate for a woman that he couldn't wait to get her horizontal. Britt was changing all the rules, and he loved it. Loved *her*.

Her tits shimmied each time he bottomed out inside her. Her pupils were dilated, and he had no doubt her fingernails were leaving little half-moon indentations in his skin.

"Chad," she moaned as she took everything he had to give.

It didn't take long for him to reach the brink. Everything about Britt turned him on. He had no idea how long it would take before he got to the point when he could see her naked and *not* immediately want to be inside her. Maybe never.

He was desperate to come, but he wanted Britt to find her pleasure too. Even though it hurt, he stopped thrusting. Buried his cock as far inside her as he could go, then leaned back a fraction, just enough to get his fingers between them so he could reach her clit.

The second he touched it, she jerked in his grip. He didn't have a lot of room to maneuver, so Chad settled for rubbing the bundle of nerves hard and fast. He felt her hips undulating as much as she could, which wasn't a lot, considering she was smooshed between him and the door.

"Yes, there. Oh, right—"

She didn't finish her sentence because her orgasm hit. Her mouth opened in a silent moan as she stared into his eyes.

Chad didn't hesitate to move his hand back to her ass and thrust in and out of her hard, even as she was still shaking from her orgasm. Nothing had ever felt as powerful and amazing as fucking her when she came. The ripples of her inner muscles around his cock were indescribable. It didn't take long before he exploded himself.

They were both panting by the time Chad regained his equilibrium. Thank goodness he hadn't dropped her. He grinned and bent his knees a little so she could drop her legs from around him. The second his cock slipped out of her body, she whimpered.

The sound was so adorable and sad, he immediately wanted to shove himself right back inside.

"You okay?" he asked, running his hands up and down her arms.

"More than. I need another shower now, but I don't have time."

"You don't. You're perfect."

She rolled her eyes. "I probably look like I was just fucked against a wall."

Chad grinned again. She *did* look like that, but he knew better than to agree with her. He couldn't stop himself from ogling her body if his life depended on it. Her upper chest was red and blotchy, she had a bead of sweat on her temple, and her hair stuck up at the back where it had been pressed against the door.

But it was the thin line of fluid leaking down her inner thigh that had Chad's attention freezing in its tracks. He couldn't tear his gaze away.

"Fuck. I'm so sorry. I didn't even think." He forced his gaze back up to her face. "I forgot a condom. I *never* forget. Ever. No wonder that felt so amazing. No wonder I could feel every single ripple of your orgasm around my cock."

She blushed and licked her lips, but didn't comment.

His gaze was drawn back between her legs. His come had slid down to her knee now, but she made no move to pull away from him. Chad knelt and blindly reached for his boxers. Reverently, he used the cloth to slowly clean from her knee up her inner thigh, then between her legs. When he was done, he leaned forward and gently kissed her stomach, right below her belly button.

The scent of their combined arousal was stronger down here, and it was all Chad could do not to lick her slit from bottom to top. His dick twitched. Even though he'd just come, he was ready to go again.

He didn't want to think about an accidental pregnancy because of his carelessness . . . but how could he *not* at the moment. He pictured himself kneeling in front of her just as he was now, kissing her swollen belly, talking to their unborn child, whispering about how excited they were to meet him or her. It was too soon to be thinking about all that . . . wasn't it?

"Get up here," Britt ordered as she tugged on his hand.

He stood and gathered her into his arms. It was scary how much she meant to him. How much he loved her.

"Thank you," she said, nodding to the hand that still held his now-soiled boxers. Then she kissed him. It was a long, sweet, intimate kiss. Not a prelude to anything sexual, but one that still held so much promise.

Chad was relieved she wasn't upset about the condom thing. He knew that if there were unintended consequences from this morning, he'd take care of both Britt and their child. Hell, he'd marry her today if he could, but he'd never want her to think it was only because of an unplanned pregnancy.

No, when he married this woman, she'd know down to her bones it was because she was the only woman he ever wanted to be with, because he wanted to love and cherish her to the end of their days. He wanted a relationship like his parents had, and he believed with everything in him that Britt was the woman who would make that dream come true.

"I need to get changed. Go downstairs and start the muffins. See what your mom needs help with today before I head over to the cabins."

"You work too hard," Chad said with a frown.

She laughed in his face. "Pot, meet kettle."

He chuckled. She wasn't wrong. "Right. Text me and let me know how your day is going?" he asked.

"If you want me to."

"I want you to," Chad reassured her.

Knowing he could stand there with her in his arms all day, Chad took a step back and leaned down to pick up the towel he'd removed earlier. He wrapped it back around her and tucked the end in, making sure to cop a feel as he did.

As expected, she rolled her eyes at him. "You're such a guy."

"I am," he agreed, then leaned down to kiss her lips briefly. "I'm gonna jump in the shower while you change. You good?"

"I'm perfect," Britt said with a happy grin.

Warmth spread through Chad at her words. He believed her. Everything about this woman glowed. She looked and acted so differently than she had when he'd met her not so long ago. He was proud of her for her perseverance.

He was two seconds away from saying screw it and ripping that towel back off her, taking her back to bed for the rest of the morning, but they both had things to do, people who were counting on them. So he settled for tucking a lock of hair behind her ear, then gently moving her to the side so he could open the door.

He headed to the bathroom naked as the day he was born, not concerned that his mom might suddenly appear. As he'd told Britt before, she knew better than to come upstairs without some kind of warning. She was well aware that her sons liked to wander around without a stitch of clothing on.

By the time Chad got downstairs, Britt was in the kitchen putting a pan of muffins into the oven and his mom was sitting at the table, doing her morning crossword and drinking a cup of coffee.

"Morning," he said cheerfully as he entered.

He didn't have a lot of time before he needed to head out to Lincoln's place, thanks to his impromptu lovemaking session with Britt. They wanted to get an early start before the sun got too hot. Many people thought Maine was cool year round, but it could get brutally hot in the summers, especially in the direct sunlight.

He had enough time to wait for the muffins to finish cooking so he could pilfer one before he left. As he pulled out onto the road and headed toward his brother's house, Chad was content. For the first time since his dad had died, he felt as if things were settling down. Despite the setback with Otis, he was counting his blessings. Life was good, and he felt optimistic about his future, and about the future of Lobster Cove.

~

Britt couldn't stop smiling. She hadn't intended to start her day with a monster orgasm and the man she loved being so desperate to make love to her that he took her against the bedroom door. But man oh man had that been *hot*.

And when he'd knelt at her feet and cleaned up the aftermath of coming inside her? Her ovaries had just about exploded. She hadn't thought about a condom in the heat of the moment either, and she didn't blame Chad in the least. She'd wanted him, right then and there, and she probably would've been annoyed if he'd taken the time to walk across the room to grab one anyway.

The encounter had been perfect in every way. She'd never felt so . . . feminine as she had when he'd picked her up. She'd never been a tiny, dainty woman, but in Chad's arms she felt that way. She didn't think it was the right time of the month to get pregnant, but she supposed anything was possible.

Was she upset at the thought of getting pregnant? She should be. She and Chad were still in a new relationship. But the thought of having his baby made her insides swirl with excitement. He'd be an amazing father. And the baby would have three awesome uncles to spoil him or her rotten as well. And Evelyn was always talking about how much she wanted a grandbaby.

Shaking her head, Britt tried to pay attention to what she was doing. She'd cleaned the smaller cabin hours ago, but the renters in the two-bedroom guesthouse had checked out late—and they were total slobs during their stay. They'd had two small children, and it was as if they'd had a food fight or something. Britt found Cheerios and food crumbs all over the place—under the beds, in the couches. She'd even found a smear of what she thought was peanut butter on the wall next to the door.

Sighing, she grabbed another wipe to try to get the sticky food off the wall.

Thirty minutes later, she'd just turned off the vacuum cleaner when a sound outside caught her attention. Normally she'd have her headphones in, listening to an audiobook as she cleaned, but she'd forgotten to charge them last night . . . so the raised voices were easy to hear.

Not sure what was happening, Britt went to the window and glanced out. What she saw confused her for a moment—then panic set in, and she dropped the handle of the vacuum and ran for the door.

Camden's truck was in front of the main house, and from the window, she'd seen him pulling Evelyn toward his pickup. The older woman was yelling at him and trying to pull her arm out of his grasp, with no luck.

By the time Britt got the door of the cabin open, Camden was climbing into the driver's seat after shoving Evelyn into the vehicle through the same door and forcing her to scoot over.

She acted without thinking, running toward the long gravel drive between the main road and the house. If she could get in front of Camden's truck, block his way, she could maybe get him to stop and find out what was happening. Her shoes weren't exactly made for running, but she didn't slow down for a second. Something inside her was screaming that if Camden left the property with Evelyn, it wouldn't be good.

As she ran, Britt kept her eye on the truck. She wasn't going to make it. Camden was going to race right by her before she could get out in front of him. Of course, there was no guarantee that he'd stop even if she *did* manage to jump in front of his truck—but she had to try.

And apparently, luck was on Britt's side.

In all the time she'd been at Lobster Cove, she hadn't seen any animal larger than a porcupine or wild turkey. She'd wanted to see a moose since she'd moved to Maine, but Chad had informed her that it was extremely rare for them to come this far south, especially in a populated area like Rockville and by the coast.

It wasn't a moose that had Camden slamming on his brakes and swearing so loud she could hear him through the closed windows of his truck—but a black bear.

It ambled across the gravel drive as if it didn't have a care in the world. It barely turned its head when Camden's wheels skidded on the path as he desperately tried to stop from running into the huge animal.

The bear showing up right when and where it did gave Britt just enough time to reach the pickup before Camden slammed his foot on the gas once more. She managed to grab the tailgate and jump on the back bumper as he took off again.

For a moment, Britt thought she was going to lose her grip and fall, but she awkwardly swung one leg over the tailgate and threw herself into the bed.

Of course, Camden didn't have a nice clean truck like Chad did. There were car parts, trash, bags of salt, and who the hell knew what else in the bed. Something poked Britt's side as she struggled to get up onto her knees and regain her balance, but Camden had obviously seen her climb into the back of his truck. He was weaving all over the drive, apparently trying to get her to fall out.

Britt's determination took over. She was stubborn as hell, and there was no way she was leaving Evelyn to whatever this lunatic had in store for her. It was clear the woman hadn't willingly gone with Camden. Not with the way she'd been struggling to get out of his grip and yelling at the top of her lungs.

The sounds of Camden swearing could be heard yet again through the closed windows, and when Britt met his gaze in the rearview mirror, she saw nothing but hatred.

She and Evelyn were in big trouble.

It was then that Britt realized she didn't have her phone. It had been in her back pocket when she'd left the rental cabin, but it must have fallen out. Either as she ran or while she was trying to climb into the bed of the truck.

She couldn't call for help. Couldn't let Chad or any of his brothers know that their mom was being kidnapped.

Fear chilled her blood, but she swallowed hard and vowed to do whatever was necessary to help Evelyn. The Young family had been through enough. She'd get Evelyn home safe and sound if it was the last thing she did.

Although she really, *really* hoped it wasn't the last thing she did . . . because she desperately wanted a long life with Chad by her side.

Camden reached the end of the driveway that led to Lobster Cove and didn't even slow down to look for oncoming traffic as he took the turn onto the back road. The one that twisted and turned through a rural part of Maine along the coast. She worried that he was driving so recklessly, he'd end up in the water . . . but maybe that wouldn't be so bad. Britt would probably die from being thrown from the bed of the truck, but she'd seen Evelyn put on her seat belt, so chances were good she'd survive.

The truck sped up, going way over the twenty-mile-an-hour speed limit for the road. Britt prayed there was a cop somewhere that would pull Camden over, but it wasn't likely, since she'd never seen any patrols on this road.

It was taking all her strength to hang on, to not get thrown out of the truck as Camden continued to swerve to try to knock her out of the truck bed and she stumbled over piles of trash. Trees were whizzing by, and the air in her face made it difficult to keep her eyes open. Britt wanted to pay attention to where they were going, but for now, she bowed her head and tried to hunker down behind the cab to block some of the wind.

She had no idea what was going to happen when they got to wherever Camden was heading, but he was going to find that when someone she loved and respected was in danger, she'd become more of a threat than a mama moose protecting her baby.

She just had to hang on until then.

~

Waiting to pull out onto the road, Victor Rogers frowned at the pickup speeding toward him.

"Damn kids," he mumbled. People sped down this road all the time, and it pissed him off. Hell, most things these days irritated him, but that truck was going way too damn fast for the curves. The driver was probably drunk. Maybe the same person who'd thrown out all the beer cans he'd recently seen on the side of the road.

It was pathetic.

Stupid.

Irritating.

As the truck got closer, Victor's eyes narrowed. He recognized the vehicle. It belonged to one of the Lobster Cove employees. He'd seen the man around now and then.

Figured. The Youngs were a pain in his ass, and it wasn't surprising that someone they employed was acting like an irresponsible idiot.

As the truck sped past the road that led to his property, Victor caught a glimpse of something that had his eyebrows shooting up in surprise. He couldn't have seen what he thought he saw. But he did.

In the back of the truck was a girl. He recognized *her*, as well. She was the new one . . . the girl dating one of the Young boys. He wasn't sure which. To him, they were all the same. Thorns in his side.

But the look on the girl's face wasn't that of someone on a joyride. She was terrified. And even as he watched, the truck jerked back and forth on the road, as if the driver was purposely trying to toss the girl from the vehicle.

And that wasn't all. Evelyn Young had been in the front seat—and she'd stared right at him as they passed. Waving her hand as if to get his attention.

The entire encounter lasted only seconds, but there was no mistaking what Victor had seen.

Something was wrong. He felt it deep in his bones. The same way he'd felt it when his daughter had called and asked if she could come home to live with him.

He might have a reputation for being a grumpy asshole, but he wasn't totally unfeeling. Even if everyone thought he was.

He thought about following the truck, but at the speed it was moving, it was already well out of sight, and Victor didn't want to chance wrecking as he tried to catch up.

Instead, he reached for his cell phone.

He dialed a number, one he'd never called before, never had a reason to; it wasn't as if he was going to invite the guy over for dinner and a chat. But he'd programmed it into his phone all the same when Evelyn had texted it to him. Because there was a chance someday he'd need help with something, she'd said. And neighbors helped neighbors . . . even if they didn't like each other.

"Hello?"

"Chad Young? This is Victor Rogers. Something's wrong. I just saw one of your employees driving down the back road going at least fifty miles an hour."

"Are you kidding me? You called me to bitch about someone speeding on the road? Give it up, Rogers. We all know you're an asshole, but this is going a bit far—"

"Shut the hell up and listen to me!" Victor yelled, feeling frustrated. He knew he hadn't been very nice to the boys since they'd moved home. He actually approved of them coming back to Maine to help out their mom. Even though he wanted Lobster Cove for himself, he'd been where Evelyn was. Feeling lost after the death of a spouse. "That new girl was in the bed of the truck, holding on for dear life while the driver swerved around, trying to make her fall out. And your mom was in the passenger seat."

"*What?*"

"I don't know the name of the driver. Never cared enough to learn. But since it's your mom and that young woman with him, I thought you might want to know."

"What direction were they going?"

"Toward town."

"What color was the truck?"

"Brown."

"Did it have a white stripe?"

"Yes."

"Fuck! Camden. My mom was inside the cab? Did she seem okay?"

"I don't know what you mean by okay, but she was waving at me like she was trying to get my attention. But they were going so fast, I couldn't see much else."

"Can you please go over to Lobster Cove and check on Walt? I'm gonna call the police and have them go out, but if he's hurt, I want to get him help as soon as I can."

"I don't know anything about first aid," Victor protested, not sure he wanted to get any more involved in whatever was happening than he already was.

"*Please*, Victor. I know you hate us, but if Camden was able to take Mom, he had to have done something to Walt, because he *never* would've let that man get anywhere near her if he could help it."

Surprisingly, Victor didn't consider how he could use the situation to his advantage. Because suddenly, at that moment, all he could think about was how he'd feel if something happened to his daughter or his grandson . . . and he asked for the Youngs' help and they said no.

"Okay. I'll go on over."

"Thank you. Text me and let me know what you find."

"I will. And Chad?"

"What?"

The boy sounded impatient and eager to hang up, which Victor couldn't blame him for. "I hope your mom and that girl are okay." He didn't know where the words were coming from. He'd never officially met the girl, only seen her when he'd gone over to Lobster Cove after the storm. He'd actually assumed she was probably a gold digger looking for a free place to live. But that didn't mean he wanted anyone to get hurt.

"Me too. Let me know about Walt."

The phone connection ended.

Victor put his truck in gear and pulled out onto the road after looking both ways. The last thing he wanted was to get T-boned by the idiot driving like a bat out of hell if he happened to come back.

As he turned down Lobster Cove's private drive, Victor's hands tightened on the steering wheel. He began to sweat. Why had he agreed to this?

Oh yeah, because having the Youngs owe him wasn't a bad position to be in.

Ignoring the voice in the back of his head that told him he wasn't checking on Walt because he wanted the Young family to owe him anything, that he was helping because it was the decent thing to do, Victor drove slowly down the dirt road until he came to the huge open area around the house and all the businesses. He turned right, toward the auto shop . . . but not before he saw the door to the main house was standing wide open.

His gut rolled. Something bad *had* happened here, and he wanted nothing more than to turn around and leave. He could call the police. Hell, Chad probably already had. They could figure out what happened. But he'd promised . . .

Victor parked outside the auto shop and got out. It felt eerie. No birds were chirping. No insects buzzing. The wind wasn't even blowing, which was unusual for the coast. He walked toward the one open bay and called out. "Hello?"

He got no response.

Stepping into the shade of the work bay, Victor couldn't help being impressed. Lobster Cove Auto Body was obviously doing well. The space was clean, not cluttered at all. He supposed things could look a lot worse. There could be dozens of rusted-out old cars sitting around the property, lowering everyone's property values.

"Hello?" he called again, a little louder.

A sound around the back of a car in the last bay made the hair on the back of Victor's neck stand up. Reluctantly and cautiously, he made his way toward the sound.

When he rounded the front bumper of the vehicle, he saw a man in a pair of blue overalls lying on the ground . . . with a small puddle of blood around his head.

Quickly, Victor pulled his phone from his pocket and called 9-1-1. The man—Walt, if the name tag on his shirt was any indication—clearly needed more help than Victor knew how to give him.

"Nine-one-one, what's your emergency?"

"I need help. I have a man down. Looks as if he was hit over the head with . . ." Victor looked around and saw a tire iron lying on the floor not too far from Walt. "A tire iron. There's blood everywhere."

"What is your address?"

Victor gave it to the dispatcher.

"Is he breathing?"

"Yes. He's moaning and in a lot of pain. I don't know what to do!"

Victor *hated* feeling helpless. He'd felt this way when his wife died. When his daughter was getting in trouble in high school and he couldn't stop her destructive behavior. When she'd called to let him know she was pregnant . . . and then a few years later, when she called and begged him to let her move back home with her son.

Maybe that was why he was such an asshole. Because he couldn't help the ones he loved the most. Because he'd let them down so badly. But he was who he was; he wasn't going to change now.

The dispatcher walked him through some basic first aid, and the longer the young woman spoke, the calmer Victor became. Walt opened his eyes and stared up at him as he held a clean shop towel against the wound on his head.

"Evelyn," he whispered.

"I called Chad. He's on it," Victor told him.

"Good . . ."

Then his eyes closed, and for a second, Victor thought he'd died. But his chest still rose and fell, and the relief Victor felt at seeing it was almost overwhelming.

Sirens in the distance were one of the best sounds Victor had ever heard. He wanted to be done here. Wanted to be on his way, go to the store like he'd planned—twelve-year-old boys ate way more than he ever expected—and get back home. He didn't like when his world was upended, and he especially didn't like to think about the Youngs as anything other than irritation.

He wasn't ready to be friends with his neighbors . . . but he couldn't help but pray that Evelyn was all right. As well as the girl.

CHAPTER TWENTY-TWO

Britt was terrified. Camden hadn't driven into Rockville, as she'd hoped he would. She'd been planning to scream her head off, get someone's attention, enough that they'd call the cops and Camden would get pulled over. But that hadn't happened. He'd taken back roads that were unfamiliar to Britt, and she was completely lost. Even if she *did* get access to a phone, there was no way she'd be able to tell anyone where she and Evelyn were.

The ride in the back of the pickup had been petrifying. Camden had driven recklessly and never stopped trying to get her to lose her balance. Britt's fingers hurt from gripping the metal. She wanted to leap out, grab Evelyn, and run off with her the second they came to a stop, but she found her legs weren't working properly. If she tried to run anywhere, she'd fall flat on her face.

Besides, where would they go? From what she could tell, they were literally in the middle of nowhere. She hadn't seen any neighboring houses as they pulled down the dirt road, and the last thing she wanted was to be lost in the woods with a pissed-off Camden hunting them down.

"Bitch!" he shouted after he'd finally stopped and ripped open the driver's side door, glaring at Britt as he turned toward her.

Even as she crawled out of the bed of the pickup on the passenger side, Camden reached back through the door and yanked Evelyn toward him. She awkwardly scooted over the console, and if it wasn't for Camden's hold on her arm, she would've fallen out of the truck.

"Son—" she started, but he didn't let her get another word out.

"I'm not your son!" He screamed this time, the sound echoing around the trees in the clearing.

At the shrill sound of his voice, Britt frowned. He didn't seem . . . normal. She made sure to keep the truck between her and Camden.

"I'm not going to jail," he fumed, more to himself than the two women. Then he turned and headed for the ramshackle cabin in front of the truck, dragging Evelyn with him.

Britt was confused. He hadn't ordered her to do anything, had pretty much ignored her after calling her a bitch. Scared but not willing to let Evelyn out of her sight, Britt followed behind the duo at what she felt was a safe distance, struggling to come up with a plan. She wasn't sure how to get Evelyn away from Camden, and even if she managed that, he was stronger than both of them.

Tears formed in her eyes, but she angrily blinked them away. This was no time for crying. She and Evelyn were on their own. They had to figure this out.

"Camden, can we talk about this?" Britt tentatively asked.

"Sure, we can talk."

He sounded so reasonable now. So calm. It made Britt even more confused.

"Inside," he added as he opened the cabin door and practically shoved Evelyn through the door. She stumbled but didn't fall, thank goodness. Camden held the door open and turned to Britt, who'd stopped about ten feet away. "You coming?" he asked with the strangest smile on his face. It reminded Britt of a horror movie she'd seen once. One where a crazed psycho killer lured people into his home like flies to a spider.

Looking around, feeling as if she should run away from here as fast as she could, Britt hesitated. She couldn't leave Evelyn. She could feel Camden's anger. It was a tangible thing. There was no telling what he'd do to the older woman if Britt left.

Knowing she was probably making the wrong decision, especially since every self-preservation molecule in her body was screaming at her to flee, Britt took a step forward.

Making sure not to touch Camden as she passed, she entered the cabin.

The second she was inside, the door slammed shut.

Spinning around, Britt instinctively reached for the door handle.

It didn't move.

Looking down, she realized the knob had been installed backward, with the dead bolt outside. She and Evelyn were locked inside the cabin.

"Camden! Let us out!" she yelled.

His laughter rang through the door. It was muffled, but the glee in the tone was still easy to hear.

"Thanks for making my job easier. I was only gonna use the old broad as bait, but now, I think having both of you is even better. I mean, I wouldn't have been sad if you'd fallen out of my truck and gotten run over on the road, but this'll work too. Sit down, make yourself at home. I'm sure the Young boys will figure out where you are soon enough and come running to your rescue . . . and I'll be waiting to pick them off one by one."

His maniacal laughter made Britt's blood run cold.

She turned and found Evelyn standing right behind her. If she thought the woman she'd come to love as her own mother would be cowering in fear, she was way wrong.

The anger on the older woman's face was easy to read. "What an asshole!" she seethed.

Genuinely shocked, Britt blurted, "Language."

Then she chuckled. And the chuckle turned into giggles, which morphed into full-out belly laughs. Hearing the usually proper Evelyn call Camden an asshole was surprising and so out of character, it was hilarious.

Evelyn joined in, and for thirty seconds or so, both women laughed their heads off. Then they slowly sobered as the severity of their situation kicked in.

Britt reached out and hugged Evelyn hard. The other woman held on tight.

"Are you all right?" Evelyn asked. "I was so worried about you." She loosened her hold and pulled back just enough to glare at Britt. "That wasn't smart. Why'd you get into the truck?"

"I saw him forcing you into the front seat. I tried to cut you guys off. I was going to stand in front of the truck and force him to stop—which in hindsight probably wasn't the best idea, he probably would've just run me over—but I wasn't fast enough. I wasn't thinking, and when that bear came along and I was able to grab the tailgate, instinct took over and . . . in I went. I wasn't going to let him take you, Evelyn. No way."

Evelyn hugged Britt again. For a moment, she was overwhelmed with emotion. She loved this woman. As if she were her own flesh and blood. Lord knew she'd been more of a mother to her than her own had ever been.

Guilt swamped Britt for just a moment. Her mom had worked her ass off to keep a roof over their heads . . . but honestly, she would've preferred to have been homeless with a mother that gave the smallest shit about her daughter.

From outside, they heard the sound of Camden's truck starting, then moving away, but Britt had a feeling he wasn't going far. Just far enough to hide the vehicle somewhere. If she and Evelyn truly were being used as bait to get Chad and the others to this remote spot, so he could do harm to them, he wouldn't want his truck to be visible when they pulled up.

Britt felt Evelyn take a deep breath, then she stepped back once again. "Now what? What's the plan?"

Looking around, Britt frowned. She'd hoped to find something to use to jimmy the lock on the door. Or even smash the whole thing down. But the cabin didn't have much in it at all. A woodstove with no firewood, a ratty-looking couch that was probably at least forty years old, a table with some rickety chairs . . . and that was about it.

Britt wandered over to the kitchen and opened a few drawers. There was some cutlery. No knives sharp enough to do damage to anyone, but maybe they could still use one to try to break the lock on the door. There were cups, bowls, plates, and a pot and pan or two.

It looked as if the cabin hadn't been used in a very long time . . . except by any critters who'd managed to get inside. There was no bedroom, no bathroom. It was literally one big open space. A true open-concept design. She supposed if someone had to pee, they did so outside. She hadn't seen an outhouse, but she hadn't really been looking either.

There were two windows, and Britt hurried over to one to try to open it . . . with no luck. It had been nailed shut, and there were boards hammered across the windowpanes on the outside. The cabin had obviously been modified to keep someone from getting out, rather than keep the occupants safe from anyone trying to get inside.

But Britt wasn't giving up. She wasn't willing to sit there and endure whatever sick plan Camden had devised. She had no idea how Chad or his brothers would find them, but Camden had made it clear that they would. She couldn't let them rush into an ambush.

Britt wondered about Otis's role in his son's kidnapping plot. Camden said she wasn't supposed to be there, only Evelyn. But why? And while she should be happy that he hadn't simply shot her or Evelyn outright, she was certain his plan *was* to get rid of them both eventually. It wasn't as if he could force Evelyn to give him or Otis their jobs back as if nothing had happened, or just let her go after killing her sons.

The bottom line was, she and Evelyn had to get out of this prison. *Now.* If they could find their way back to civilization, someone would help them, of that she had no doubt.

Taking a deep breath, she turned to Evelyn and opened her mouth to speak, but the older woman beat her to it.

"We need to get out of here. I'll start on this side of the cabin, you take the other. We'll see if we can't find any loose boards or something we can use to break that lock on the door. Figures it's the only new thing in this entire place."

Impressed all over again at Evelyn's determination, at her unwillingness to sit around and throw a pity party or wait to be rescued, Britt made a mental vow to be just like her when she was in her seventies.

"Sounds good," she told her, turning back to the kitchen. There had to be *something* they could use to break out of the cabin. They just had to find it.

~

Chad paced furiously. Back and forth. Back and forth. Every molecule in his body was screaming at him to *do* something. Not stand in the house and listen as Lincoln spoke with the police officers who'd shown up after getting both his and Victor's 9-1-1 calls.

Walt was on his way to the hospital. He'd been hit over the head pretty hard and had a concussion, but the EMTs on scene hadn't seemed overly . . . rushed as they were loading him into the ambulance. Which Chad was taking as a good sign.

But the fact that no one had any idea where Britt or their mom was made Chad's belly churn. He'd been in precarious situations before. All his brothers had. But this was different. It was personal. This was their *mom.* And the woman he loved. He'd just found Britt; he couldn't lose her already.

Done waiting, Chad headed for the door.

Knox and Zach immediately joined him.

"Wait, where are you going?" one of the officers called out.

Chad ignored him. There was only one person who could shed some light on what the fuck was happening. Otis Calvert. His son had kidnapped Mom, and Chad had no doubt Otis was actually behind whatever was going on. If not directly, he had information.

His plan was to go to Otis's small house and do whatever it took to get the intel he and his brothers needed to get their mom and Britt back.

To his shock, a car came down the driveway as Chad was heading toward his truck.

Otis's car.

"What the fuck?" Zach mumbled from behind him.

Chad didn't hesitate. He headed straight for Otis. Their former family friend had barely shut the engine off before Chad had his door open and was yanking him out.

"Where are they?" he growled.

"Easy, Chad," Knox said, grabbing his shoulder.

Chad shrugged it off.

"Where's who?" Otis asked with wide eyes. "I saw on the local social media page that there were a bunch of emergency vehicles here and I got worried, so I came down. I know we've had some tough times recently, but you're all still my family. Where's Evelyn? Is she all right?"

He was lying through his teeth.

Chad saw red.

Knowing if the police got involved, he wouldn't get the information he needed, he hauled Otis toward the huge aluminum shed they used in the boat storage area of the property. It was big enough to fit maybe three lobster boats side by side, and it cost an arm and a leg for customers to rent it for the winter, but for those who wanted their boats to be under cover, it was a price they were willing to pay.

It was empty at the moment, as the owners had long since picked up their boats for the summer. It was the ideal place to question Otis, away from the prying eyes of the cops.

"Wait, Chad . . . Where are we going? Is your mom okay? Stop!"

But Chad ignored Otis's stammering. Relief swept through him when he reached the huge building without being stopped by any of the officers inside the house. He was grateful Lincoln was dealing with them, keeping them occupied.

Knox and Zach were right there with him as he entered the building, and his brothers shut the door as Chad practically flung their former employee into a nearby chair.

The chair tipped but didn't fall. Otis stared up at him with terrified eyes.

Good. He *should* be scared.

"Where is he? Camden. Where did he take my mom?" Chad barked.

"What? Camden? You think he's with your mom? I don't know what's going on."

Chad wasn't in the mood for this. All he could think of was how scared Britt and his mom must be at the moment. He hoped they weren't hurt, but it was likely they had been. And anyone involved in whatever this scheme was would pay for every bruise, every scrape, every damn mark he found on his family.

"Cut the shit," he growled. "I want to know what the plan is. Why your son came onto Lobster Cove property and kidnapped our mother!"

"I don't know!"

Chad was done.

He whipped out a hand and grabbed Otis by the throat, tipping the chair backward. The older man instinctively grabbed Chad's wrist with both hands, keeping himself from falling as he stared with bulging eyes. His pupils were dilated with fear, and the scent of piss wafted up from his lap.

Chad wasn't hurting him. Wasn't squeezing his throat, wasn't cutting off his air. Was simply making a point. Making sure Otis was well aware that he held no cards here. He might be fit and strong for his age, but at the moment . . . he was at the mercy of the Young brothers.

Chad had no doubt that either Knox or Zach would step in if they thought it was necessary. But he also knew none of them would back down until they had the info they needed to go and get their family members back.

"Listen to me, and listen hard. We trusted you. You were my dad's best friend—and you stole from him for *years*. Stole his hard-earned cash and made him question his skills as a businessman. All the while eating at his table, spending holidays with him, and acting as if you had his best interests at heart. And if we didn't come home to help Mom? You would've bled her dry. Forced her to sell Lobster Cove. You threw away *decades* of friendship—and for what? Money!

"You're the lowest of the fucking low, and I couldn't give a shit about your problems or the reasons behind why you did what you did. But your fucking son drove up to our house today and kidnapped my mother. I want to know why, and I want to know where he took her—*now*."

He held Otis's gaze. Letting him see the darkness that lived in his head.

Chad had seen a lot of bad shit. Had killed for his country. He loved his family more than he loved his country—and he'd *definitely* kill to protect them.

Apparently, whatever Otis saw in Chad's eyes convinced him to give up the charade of concern he'd tried to hold on to since first opening his mouth upon his arrival.

"I just wanted a chance to talk to Evelyn! To explain! I need this job!" Otis babbled. "I don't know how it started . . . it was fifty bucks here, a hundred bucks there. But things spiraled. Camden moved in with me, and money got tight. She and Austin had so much more than they'd ever need or use. They wouldn't miss the money!"

"Where's Mom?" Knox asked in a low, menacing tone. "Forget about you being a fucking asshole and a shit friend. Where. Is. Our. Mother?"

"We can't go to jail! I won't do well in jail," Otis cried.

Something inside Chad snapped. He tightened his grip on the man he'd once thought of as an uncle. A second father.

The pressure on his neck seemed to finally do the trick. Otis broke. "We have a camp! He was supposed to take her there! I was gonna go out and talk to her. Convince her to drop the charges."

"Bullshit!" Zach said in an explosion of breath. "There's no way our mom would agree to drop charges against you and come home like nothing happened, as if she hadn't been *kidnapped*! Where is this fucking camp?"

Chad abruptly let go of Otis and backed away. The chair thudded down on all fours, surprising the older man, and he fell forward onto his hands and knees on the concrete floor.

Chad's fingers flexed as he glared down at Otis. He'd had to let go. He was too close to the edge. It would've been too easy to kill the man with his bare hands. And that wasn't the kind of person he was. Yes, he'd killed while he was a sniper, but every life he'd taken was a stain on his soul. He wasn't going to add one more.

Not only that, but killing Otis wouldn't give him and his brothers the info they needed. It would only add to their problems. Spending decades behind bars would take him away from Britt. Would end any chance he'd have of asking her to marry him. Of having a family with her.

"I didn't agree with him!" Otis added quickly. "I just wanted to talk, I swear! But Camden, he . . . he thought he could use her as bait. Get you and your brothers to come after her. Then take you all out. He thought we could start over in Alaska. Without anyone to press charges against me, I'd have time to destroy files. Any embezzlement charges would have to be dropped!"

Chad curled his lip in disgust. "How was he planning to lure us to wherever he's got Mom stashed?"

Otis stared at the floor, his shoulders slumped, suddenly looking every second of his sixty-eight years. "He said he'd wait a while, make sure you were good and freaked out over Evelyn being gone, so you'd be willing to do anything to get her back. Then he'd call you one at a time. Tell you he saw someone he knows take your mom and give you the address. When you arrived, he'd take each of you out."

Chad blinked. "That makes no fucking sense!" he exclaimed. "We'd *never* go somewhere one at a time. The first thing we would've done is call each other. What the hell? You *had* to know this asinine plan was totally illogical."

"And you went along with this stupid plan?" Knox asked.

"No! No, no, no! I just wanted to talk, you have to believe me!" Otis swore.

Yeah. He was *talking* out his ass. They all knew it.

"So why come here now? Just to put on this show? To play the part of the concerned friend?" Zach asked.

Otis hung his head and didn't respond.

Chad was done. "You two were planning on killing all of us. Me, my brothers, Mom, Britt . . . and for what? The cops would know you did it, Otis. They found Camden's fingerprints all over Mom's car. A consultant is already digging through our accounts, finding evidence of your embezzlement. You wouldn't have gotten away with *anything*. Did you show up here to gain sympathy? Or so the cops would see you here, give you an alibi? The police aren't that stupid. *We* aren't that stupid."

"You're pathetic," Knox added with a shake of his head. "Where's this damn camp of yours?"

For a second, Chad didn't think Otis was going to give up the location. But he sighed—a long, defeated sound—and told them the address.

Then finally, his head came up and he met Chad's gaze. "Don't kill him. He's my boy. The only thing I have left."

Knox snorted. A disgusted sound that Chad felt down to his soul. This man was going to kill his entire family without a second thought . . . and he was begging for mercy for *his* son? Screw that.

Chad turned to leave the garage without another word. He wasn't promising shit. Especially not to Otis. He'd do whatever needed to be done. If his mom and Britt were hurt in any way, there was nowhere Camden Calvert could hide. He'd find him and exact his own form of justice.

He stopped at the door to the storage building and took a deep breath. He heard his brothers hauling Otis to his feet. He turned and saw the older man was weaving unsteadily between Knox and Zach, who both had a firm grip on his upper arms as they towed him toward the door.

"We're going to the house, and you're going to tell the cops everything you just told us. Word for fucking word. Understand?" Knox ordered.

"I can't go to jail!" Otis wailed yet again.

"You should've thought of that before you stole from Lobster Cove. Before you schemed with your son to kidnap two innocent women. Before you betrayed your best friend by turning on his family," Chad said coolly.

Now that he had an address, the calm he'd perfected from being a sniper had begun to take over. He was focused on what needed to be done. Camden was lying in wait for him and his brothers with the intent to kill, but that wasn't going to happen. Not a chance in hell. Camden was an incompetent piece of shit. No way would he get the drop on the Young brothers. They'd all spent too much time in the trenches in their various branches of the military.

Chad was more worried about what shape he'd find Britt and his mom in than any threat Camden might pose.

Still, he and his brothers needed to be smart. If one of them was forced to take Camden's life, they had to be sure they wouldn't end up behind bars as a result. Taking a contingent of officers to the Calvert camp wasn't ideal, but he'd do whatever was necessary to have a long, happy future with the woman he loved.

He left the storage building, striding across the property toward the main house. The police and Lincoln needed to be updated on the situation, Otis needed to be detained, and their mom and Britt needed to be rescued.

Hopefully before the day was out, their family would be back at Lobster Cove, safe and sound.

CHAPTER
TWENTY-THREE

"Britt! Over here!"

Turning her head, Britt looked across the room to Evelyn, kneeling on the floor of the old cabin. She was pulling on something in the corner opposite from the kitchen. Britt rushed over and crouched down—and excitement blossomed in her chest.

Evelyn was tugging on a loose piece of board on the wall near the floor, grunting with the effort she was putting forth to try to dislodge the wood.

Going to her knees, Britt added her strength to Evelyn's.

Just when she didn't think they were going to be able to get the board up, it broke, sending both women flying backward. Britt popped back up and stared at the hole in the side of the cabin.

The *literal* hole.

"Holy crap," she said, turning to look at Evelyn.

"Wow, whoever built this place ought to be ashamed of themselves. What a piece of shit."

Hearing Evelyn swear again brought another smile to Britt's face. But she was right. There was nothing between the board and the outdoors. She turned her attention to the hole and tested the wood planks around it. "They're all rotten," she said, realizing for the first time they might actually be able to get out of this damn cabin.

She had no idea where they'd go or how they'd find help, but getting one over on the horrible Camden would feel amazing.

They worked on the corner for what seemed like ages. And with every minute that passed, fear that Camden would return increased. The man was clearly unstable, and there was no telling what he'd do if his plans didn't turn out the way he'd hoped.

Britt was skeptical that Chad or his brothers would be able to figure out where they were on their own. Yes, the most likely people to have a beef with Evelyn were Otis and Camden, but that didn't mean anyone in the Young family knew about this cabin.

Camden might contact one of the brothers and *tell him* where to find their mom. Which was scary, because he'd be ready and waiting to ambush the brothers when they arrived. The worst-case scenario.

Of course, Chad and his brothers were all smart, capable ex-military men, unlikely to be taken out by an asshole like Camden. Maybe all she and Evelyn had to do was sit tight and wait to be rescued.

But everything within Britt immediately rejected that idea. She'd never been the kind of woman to play damsel in distress. Lord knew there were enough times in her life when she could've wished for just that. Someone else to determine her fate. Rescue her. But time and again, she'd been forced from a young age to rescue herself, to forge her own way in life.

Today would be no different.

Her hands were scratched up and full of splinters, but eventually she and Evelyn were able to widen the hole just enough for them to get through . . . she hoped.

"I'll go first," she told Evelyn, mainly because if Camden was out there and saw what they were doing, she didn't want him to hurt the older woman. "If Camden sees me, I'll try to lead him away. You get out and go in the opposite direction, okay?"

Evelyn frowned. "No."

"No?"

"No. If you think I'm leaving you to deal with him on your own, you haven't been paying attention."

"Paying attention to what?" Britt asked, genuinely confused.

"To the fact that you're one of my own now. You came into my home, a woman who needed a helping hand, and morphed into the daughter I never had. And don't think I've missed the way you and my son are all doe eyed with each other. I have no doubt you'll soon be my daughter for real, by marriage. But you'll always be the daughter of my heart, even if my son is an idiot and lets the best thing that's ever happened to him get away."

Britt's eyes filled with tears. Words had never hit her harder than Evelyn's did at that moment.

"No crying!" Evelyn declared with a small sniff. "Badass women who can rescue them damn selves don't cry!"

Britt chuckled. It was a bit watery, but she managed to stem most of her tears. "Right. And don't think I'm not going to tell on you to your sons about all the swearing."

Evelyn winked. "My husband always loved that I was a lady in public, and his own potty-mouthed sex demon in bed."

"La la la la," Britt singsonged as she put her hands over her ears.

Evelyn giggled and reached for one of her hands. "Come on. Let's get out of this dump. I need to pee, and I'll be damned if I pee in the woods. I'm too old for that anymore. I need my heated toilet seat and my cottony-soft toilet paper."

Britt didn't think she could love this woman any more than she did right that moment. This situation should've been horrific, but somehow she found herself laughing more than worrying about what their kidnapper might be planning.

"All right. Let's do this. I'm still going first. I'll scope things out. Then I'll help you out and we can decide which direction to go."

"North," Evelyn said firmly. "I don't know exactly where we are, but Camden drove south when we left Lobster Cove, and I can smell the water. So we go north and hope we run into someone. Anyone. A cabin, a car, even a damn tourist out moose hunting."

"I thought there weren't any moose this far south?" Britt said with a frown. "That's what Chad told me, at least."

"There aren't. But that doesn't keep unscrupulous shop owners from selling naive tourists moose hunting permits. If they're stupid enough to not know Maine has a lottery for moose hunting permits, and the seasons for hunting are in September and October, they deserve to get fleeced."

Not sure if Evelyn was kidding or not about tourists wandering around in the woods, trying to bag a moose, Britt decided it didn't matter. If they came across anyone other than Camden, it would be a good thing.

"Okay, here I go. Wish me luck," she mumbled as she got down on her belly in front of the hole in the wall.

"No luck needed. We have goodness on our side."

Britt hoped Evelyn was right.

She wiggled forward, sticking her head out of the hole to quickly look around, then slowly crawling out. The position was awkward, but as soon as she got far enough that she could brace herself on the ground with her arms, things got easier.

Before she knew it, Britt was squatting on the ground on the outside of the cabin. It didn't look any better from outside than it had on the inside.

It wasn't dark yet. In the summer, Britt had discovered that it got light around four-thirty in the morning and didn't get dark until around nine-thirty. She didn't have a watch on, but she guesstimated it to be around seven o'clock or so. It was midafternoon when she'd seen Evelyn getting snatched by Camden, and they'd driven for a while to get to this cabin. Then there was the time it had taken them to search the place and break out.

Looking around, Britt still saw nothing. No Camden. No animals. Even the birds were silent. The quiet and the waning light gave the area an eerie feeling. Not to mention the fact that, even though she couldn't see him, Camden was certainly out there . . . somewhere.

Urgency made Britt turn around and whisper, "Come on out."

Evelyn's hands and arms appeared in the hole, and Britt helped her wiggle out of the cabin. In moments, she was standing next to Britt, their backs against the wall of the cabin.

"Which way is north?" she whispered.

Evelyn glanced at her, brow raised. "I thought *you'd* know."

Britt couldn't help but chuckle softly. "Me? I'm like a fish out of water here in Maine. You're the one who's lived here your entire life. You tell *me*."

"I was kidding," Evelyn said with a huge grin.

Once again, Britt was blown away by this woman. Evelyn had every reason to be freaked out. Instead, it almost seemed as if she was having fun.

"It's that way," Evelyn said with confidence, nodding to her left.

"Are you sure?"

"Absolutely. Austin taught me everything there is to know about navigation. It drove him crazy when we were first married and I'd give him directions like, 'Turn left at the stop sign with the bullet hole in it, then when you get to the Allens' house, go right.'" She chuckled. "After that, he insisted I learn which way was what so I could give him 'proper' directions, as he called it. I spent many a day and night in the woods and on the water, instructing my sons as well."

"Right. Then to the left we go. Slowly and silently," Britt warned.

"Of course," Evelyn said, sounding almost offended.

Britt felt like an idiot. Of course they were going to be quiet. Even though she wasn't nearly as scared as she'd been when they'd first arrived, an air of danger was still palpable around them.

As they set out, careful not to step on any loose twigs and always on the lookout for Camden, Britt couldn't help but worry about Chad. He and his brothers had to be frantic by now. And she hoped if they *did* somehow figure out where she and Evelyn had been taken, they wouldn't get hurt.

Camden was clearly unhinged, and his plan to use them as bait might work exactly like he hoped. She had confidence in her boyfriend and his brothers, that their military backgrounds would ensure they didn't run into a trap, but Camden was such a loose cannon, there was a chance he could still manage to kill someone before he was stopped.

"They'll be fine," Evelyn whispered, as if she knew exactly what Britt was thinking.

She hoped so. She really, *really* hoped so.

The four brothers had all piled into Knox's SUV. It took way too long to get to the address Otis had given them, but as they drove, the brothers planned. They assumed Camden would be expecting them, but since none of them had received a call from him, as was apparently the ridiculous plan, they had no idea what awaited them.

The real question was . . . Did Camden have the patience to sit and wait for the amount of time that had passed since he'd taken Britt and Evelyn?

Chad didn't think so. Camden was a hothead. Impulsive. Lazy. He was also a stoner. He'd probably found what he thought was a perfect spot, sat there for a while. Then got bored. Second-guessed himself. Moved. Then moved again.

Chad had little doubt he and his brothers could find him and mitigate any threat.

But could they do it before the police officers arrived?

They'd been able to leave Lobster Cove ahead of the cops, as they'd had to call in for officers from nearby towns with SWAT experience. Chad and his brothers would likely get in trouble for lying to the police and telling them they wouldn't go to the cabin, but they'd all agreed to do it anyway, despite the consequences.

They had probably about ten minutes to find and neutralize Camden before the police descended on the area. If that happened, their target would probably flee like the coward he was. Regroup. Possibly decide to strike again another day.

Which was unacceptable. They needed to end the threat from the Calverts today. Here and now. And they had limited time to do so.

Piece of cake.

Chad and his brothers had spent hours playing soldiers in the woods around Lobster Cove. As young boys, they'd learned how to be quick and stealthy. They'd only honed those skills during their time in the military. Camden was as good as caught.

Zach had volunteered to be bait. Knox, Lincoln, and Chad would all get out of the SUV a ways from the cabin, and Zach would drive in by himself. He'd hopefully draw Camden out so the other brothers could sneak up and subdue him.

Chad's adrenaline was spiked, and he wanted nothing more than to march up to the cabin and wrench open the door, hopefully finding both Britt and his mom safe and sound . . . maybe a little scared, but okay. And even though none of them thought Camden had combat experience, or the smarts to be able to outmaneuver them, no one was taking any chances with the lives of the missing women. They knew better than to underestimate a desperate man.

By the time Chad, Lincoln, and Knox got out of the SUV and Zach slipped into the driver's seat, they were all more than ready for a confrontation. The three brothers stealthily made their way through the woods toward the cabin, splitting up to be able to cover the area more thoroughly.

It wasn't long before voices could be heard through the trees, causing Chad to break into a jog.

Peering around a large tree, he saw Zach standing in a small clearing in front of the cabin, with Camden before him—holding him at gunpoint with a shotgun.

Chad's blood ran cold. They all knew Otis's son had to be unbalanced if he thought kidnapping two women to use as bait to kill the entire Young family was the best way to stay out of jail . . . but actually seeing him holding his youngest brother at gunpoint flipped a switch in Chad.

No one hurt his family. His mom. His brothers. Britt.

"Calm down," Zach said, holding his hands up, showing Camden he was unarmed.

"Where are the others? I know you didn't come here alone!" Camden yelled.

"They're on their way. I was the first to leave," Zach lied.

"You're lying! Why are you in Knox's car?"

The bad thing about Camden working at Lobster Cove was that he knew a lot about the family . . . including what vehicles everyone drove.

"Camden, where's Mom? Is she okay?"

"Shut up! Just *shut up*! Get over there," he ordered, using the shotgun to indicate where he wanted Zach to go . . . a spot in the trees to one side of the dirt drive, about twenty yards from the cabin . . . that had what looked like a giant bonfire prepared and ready to burn.

Chad wanted to roll his eyes. The last place to set up a fire was in the middle of a freaking forest, but no one had ever claimed Camden was all that smart.

But the *reason* why he wanted Zach closer to the bonfire made Chad extremely wary.

Did the man seriously think he could burn all evidence of murdering six people?

He was totally insane—and it was time to end this so they could get into the cabin and find their mom and Britt.

Chad saw Lincoln peek around the other side of the cabin, and Knox was heading through the woods directly opposite the firepit. They were closing in on Camden, surrounding him.

The four men moved as if they'd rehearsed the moment.

Facing the dirt road that served as a driveway, Camden slowly followed Zach as he inched backward toward the firepit, not taking his eyes off the weapon or the man holding it.

Camden was so focused on Zach that he didn't notice the danger coming up from behind him.

Chad and Lincoln closed in as Camden pumped the shotgun in preparation for shooting Zach.

His brother wisely hit the dirt the same time Knox let out a loud *whoop* as he darted out from the cover of the trees to Camden's left.

As they'd hoped, Camden turned toward the sound, swinging the shotgun around.

Lincoln got to Camden first and went for the gun. He jerked it up and out of his hands, and Chad was there to take over. He punched Camden in the face as hard as he could, needing and wanting him out of commission as soon as possible. No one wanted to chance him having a second weapon hidden on his person.

The sound of his knuckles making contact with Camden's face was obscenely loud in the otherwise quiet woods. Much to Chad's disappointment, Camden went down like a ton of bricks. Lay motionless on the leaf litter and pine needles covering the clearing.

Chad waited for him to move, to get up, to continue the fight . . . but all he did was moan a little.

"Good shot, bro," Lincoln said.

Chad was already moving toward the cabin. As soon as he saw Camden wouldn't be a problem anymore, his focus turned to finding his mom and Britt. Knox was right on his heels. Chad's momentum had him hitting the front door hard.

"Britt! Mom!" he yelled as he stupidly tried to turn the doorknob. Of course it was locked. "Stand back!" he shouted. "I'm going to break the door down!"

The fact that neither woman answered made panic sweep through Chad's body. It was an odd feeling. Normally he was the calm one. Being a sniper had taught him to keep control over his emotions in extremely stressful situations. But all the training in the world wasn't helping him at this moment. All he could picture in his head was one or both of the women he loved lying hurt, or worse, within the walls of this piece-of-shit cabin.

He took a step back and kicked the door.

It didn't budge. All it managed to do was send pain up Chad's leg and knee.

"Fuck!" he muttered. "Is this door steel or what?"

"Let me try," Knox insisted, pushing him to the side. But he had as much luck as Chad.

"How about we try the key?" Lincoln said dryly from behind them.

Spinning, Chad saw his oldest brother holding up a key. He must've searched Camden's pockets.

Feeling a little stupid that he hadn't even thought to do that, Chad held out his hand for the key. Lincoln immediately handed it over.

Thankfully, the key worked. As Chad turned the knob, his heart was in his throat.

The door slammed open and he stepped inside, followed by Lincoln and Knox. Zach was probably watching over Camden, making sure he didn't regain consciousness and either run or come after them once more.

As much as he'd dreaded finding either of the women hurt, it felt worse when Chad got inside and found . . . nothing.

No one was there. The one-room cabin was sparsely furnished, and the place obviously hadn't been used in what was probably years. A musty scent filled the air, but under that, Chad swore he could smell the coconut lotion Britt always wore.

She'd been here, but she wasn't any longer.

Thoughts of the fire Camden had planned overwhelmed Chad. Were they too late? Had he taken his mom and Britt out and shot them already? His emotions careened from sorrow to frustration to grief, and then anger, in mere seconds.

His muscles tightened as he prepared to go back outside and end Camden Calvert's life before the cops arrived, when his brother spoke.

"Look!" Lincoln said, heading for one of the corners of the small cabin.

Chad rushed over and saw what he should've seen at first glance. A damn hole in the wall! Broken boards that had once served as part of the wall were strewn around the floor.

"They got out," Chad breathed, relief making him dizzy.

In tandem, the three men spun and headed for the door. Camden might've locked the women inside the cabin, but they hadn't been cowering in fear, waiting for rescue. No, they'd been doing everything in their power to get themselves out of the situation.

Pride filled him. His mom was a badass. He'd already known that, but she'd just proved it once again.

And Britt? So much love filled him at the thought of her that he felt shaky with it. She was exactly the kind of woman he'd dreamed of finding. Of spending the rest of his life with. Strong. Resilient. Resourceful.

Lincoln, Knox, and Chad burst out of the cabin.

"Mom?"

"Britt?"

"Hello?"

They all called out at the same time, pausing to listen for a response.

But the woods around them were silent. *Too* silent. As if every creature that lived there was holding its breath.

"Which way do you think they would've gone?" Knox asked.

"Not south," Chad said without hesitation. "Mom would know he'd taken them south of Lobster Cove, and she'd figure there'd be more people to the north than south to the coast."

"I agree . . . but what if she's hurt? Not thinking straight?" Knox asked, playing devil's advocate. "Would Britt know which way is north?"

"I don't know. I'm thinking probably not," Chad said.

Susan Stoker

"Right, so we'll split up," Lincoln ordered. "Just in case they wandered in a direction we don't expect. I'm not leaving anything to chance. Chad, you go north. I'll go west. Knox, you go east."

"I'll tie this asshole up and go south," Zach said from beside Camden, who was still lying unmoving in the dirt.

"No. I don't trust him. The police should be here soon. If you can tell them what's going on and which directions we're already looking, *they* can go south," Lincoln said.

Chad had no problem letting his brother take charge. It was a role he was born into, being the oldest, and being a fighter pilot meant he had to make split-second life-or-death decisions every time he got behind the controls of the multimillion-dollar planes he used to fly.

And frankly, Chad was too worried about his missing mom and girlfriend to think straight himself.

He turned and headed north, hoping to find that the most important women in his life were safe and unhurt.

CHAPTER
TWENTY-FOUR

Britt was done.

She was hot. Sweaty. Scared. And she'd already found three ticks crawling on her arms and legs. There was no telling how many more had gotten under her clothes and were even now putting their infected fangs into her flesh to suck her blood. Did ticks have fangs? She had no idea, but they had to be able to pierce human skin, and animal skin, somehow.

There was no doubt the area they were walking in was beautiful, but at the moment, Britt had had enough of pine trees, the sound of the wind in the leaves high above their heads making her incorrectly think she'd heard cars, and nature in general.

She had no idea how long they'd be walking, but her feet hurt—it wasn't as if she'd had time to put on a pair of sneakers or hiking boots—and the adrenaline she'd had coursing through her body since jumping into the back of Camden's pickup truck had long since worn off.

She could see that Evelyn was in the same position. Her steps were slower, and she'd almost tripped and fallen on her face at least three times. There had to be someone out here, *somewhere*. Maine was rural, but it couldn't be *this* rural. They were near the coast, where people loved to build cabins like the one they'd been locked in, and multimillion-dollar homes. It was ridiculous that they hadn't heard or seen any sign of anyone since they'd snuck out of the cabin.

And Britt couldn't help but wonder if Camden had figured out they were gone yet. If he was even now hot on their trail. He could easily shoot them and leave their bodies out here in the middle of nowhere, and no one would ever find them. Until maybe a few years from now, when those same stupid tourists Evelyn had talked about were hunting in the area, and they found some curious-looking bones.

Realizing how morose her thoughts had gotten, Britt took a deep breath. They were much better off now than they were not so long ago. They'd outsmarted Camden, and all they had to do was stay positive and keep walking. Eventually they'd run into a cabin, a person, a road.

After Evelyn stumbled for the fourth time, Britt decided it was time for a break. They were both tired and unsteady on their feet. It wouldn't matter if they took five minutes to rest . . . she hoped.

"Evelyn, look. There's a boulder we can sit on for a second," Britt said, taking the older woman's arm and steering her toward it.

"Maybe we should keep going," she said worriedly.

"We will. But I need a second to sit," Britt said. "I think I scraped my leg on something and want to check it out."

"Oh, you're hurt? Come on, sit, sit," Evelyn tutted.

Britt didn't like lying to the woman, but she wasn't sorry if it got her to rest. Evelyn might be amazingly strong for someone her age, but she wasn't a machine.

Brushing leaves off the rock, Britt waited for Evelyn to sit, then eased to her butt next to her. The rock wasn't exactly soft, but it did feel good to get off her feet for a moment. Britt made a show out of checking her leg for the imaginary scrape and pretended to be relieved when she didn't find anything.

"What do you think he's doing?" Evelyn asked softly.

Britt knew who she was talking about. "Probably freaking out, wondering how he got outsmarted."

Evelyn chuckled. "Bet he didn't think we'd be able to go through the wall."

"Nope. Do you think Chad and the others know we're gone yet?" Britt asked.

"Oh yes. I'm sure of it."

"How?"

"My sons . . . they're protective. And nosy as hell. Austin used to worry that I was raising them to be mama's boys . . . and I totally did. When they were scared, they wanted their mom. When they did something they were proud of, I was the first person they wanted to share with. They spent a lot of time with Austin. He taught them everything he knew about engines and cars. No one can say my sons are anything but strong, loyal men's men. But deep down, when push comes to shove, they're all still mama's boys.

"When Camden kidnapped me, I believe they all felt something wrong in their bones. I fell down the stairs and broke my arm once, after all my boys had left home after high school. We didn't have time to call them and tell them what happened, since we were at the hospital and dealing with everything that entails. But one by one, they all called Austin with the urge to check on me. Somehow, they knew I'd been hurt. So I truly believe they had to know something was wrong at Lobster Cove when I was taken."

Britt felt tears fill her eyes, and she desperately blinked and swallowed hard, trying to keep them at bay.

"Anyone who thinks men should grow up to be tough and emotionless is *wrong*. Men should be protective and empathetic. They should be able to cry when a situation warrants it. They should be just as emotional as they are stoic. It's part of being human. And anyone who raises a boy to be nothing but an unfeeling macho man is doing that kid a disservice . . . as well as humanity."

"You've raised some amazing boys," Britt told her.

"I have," Evelyn said with a hint of pride. "And they know what happened. Maybe someone saw you in the back of that pickup, holding on for dear life—getting in wasn't smart, sweetie, but I appreciate it all the same—and got a hold of one of my boys. Or maybe it's like I said, they'd just felt it in their bones that something wasn't right. But I know without a doubt they're coming to our rescue. Even if we rescued ourselves first."

"We did, didn't we?" Britt said with a small smile.

"Damn straight."

"Language," Britt teased once more.

Evelyn chuckled. Then she turned to Britt and said almost casually, "So . . . how soon do you think you and Chad are going to make me a grandmother?"

Britt blinked in surprise. "Um . . . we just met."

"And you love each other. I have eyes, child. I can see it. And I'm not stupid or naive enough to think you two are watching movies, then giving each other chaste pecks on the cheek when you say good night."

Britt knew she was probably blushing bright red.

Evelyn simply chuckled. "Just sayin', my son loves you. Don't doubt that. I've never seen him so happy in my life. His eyes follow you whenever you're in the same room, and I can see the same love in his eyes when he looks at you that I used to see in my Austin's eyes. Chad might be a mama's boy, but he takes after his father when it comes to falling in love."

Her words made Britt's heart swell. "I love him too," she blurted.

"Good. And . . . grandbabies?"

Britt couldn't help but laugh. "Has anyone ever told you that you're stubborn?"

"Austin. All the time. So?"

Britt smiled at the woman who'd found her own permanent place in her heart. "I want them. But I don't want to rush things."

"Bah," Evelyn said, waving her hand. "Rush them. Lobster Cove needs babies and kids running around once more. And I want to live long enough to enjoy them."

Britt opened her mouth to reply—she wasn't sure what she was going to say—but a sound to their left had both women freezing and turning to look in that direction.

Expecting to see Camden coming after them, Britt was genuinely shocked to see a large moose casually walking through the underbrush. She had a baby behind her. Neither paid attention to the two humans sitting on a rock just twenty feet away.

"I thought you said moose don't come down this far south," Britt whispered in a barely audible tone.

"They don't," Evelyn replied.

The moose walked as if they didn't have a care in the world. They stopped briefly to munch on the leaves of an aspen tree before continuing on.

The two women turned to stare at each other with big eyes when the creatures were out of sight.

"Holy cow! That was . . . amazing," Britt said.

"Beautiful," Evelyn agreed. "And a sign. We were talking about grandbabies, and along comes a creature that definitely shouldn't be in this area with her calf."

Britt couldn't help but shake her head and roll her eyes. "I love Chad. I want to have his babies. I want to marry him and live forever here in Maine with him. But we aren't going to rush things simply because you want grandbabies, Evelyn."

She sighed. "I know. But I can hope, can't I?"

Britt couldn't be upset with her. "Yes," she said, putting her arms around Evelyn and giving her a side hug. "You ready to continue on? I'm ready to get the hell out of these woods. I swear I can feel ticks crawling all over me."

"Yes, and me too. Yuck. Damn ticks."

Britt couldn't believe she was laughing. She'd been essentially kidnapped, even if she'd been the one to jump into the bed of Camden's truck, and now she was lost in the woods in the middle of nowhere with the possibility of their kidnapper giving chase to hurt them, or worse. And she was actually *laughing*. It was crazy. She was beginning to think with the Young family, she should probably get used to chaos and uncertainty. But along with that would come love, happiness, and the family she'd always dreamed of having.

They'd just stood up to continue walking when they once more heard something in the woods. This time it was coming from behind them. Afraid of seeing a pissed-off bull moose who wanted to protect his baby and mate, Britt spun. What she was going to do if it *was* a moose ready to charge, she had no idea. But she wasn't going to stand there and do nothing, that was for sure.

Or worse, it could be Camden. Pissed that they'd escaped and ready to follow through with his evil plans for them.

Instead, a voice rang out through the trees.

"Briiiiiiiiiitt? Mooooooom?"

Britt and Evelyn shared a look.

Holy crap—that was Chad!

"Here!"

"Chad!"

They yelled at the same time, and relief made Britt feel a little wobbly.

The sounds got louder, and within seconds, a frantic-looking Chad burst through the trees, running straight for them.

For a split second, Britt worried that he was being chased. But she didn't see anyone behind him. She realized it was relief that made him look so out of control.

He ran up to them and reached for his mom. Britt wasn't offended in the least. She recalled what Evelyn had said about her children being mama's boys and realized how right she was. The relief Chad's body language projected was clear.

He pulled back and looked his mom in the eyes as he asked, "Are you all right?"

"I'm fine. We're fine," Evelyn said with a huge grin on her face.

Then Chad turned to Britt. The next second, she was in his arms, and he was squeezing her so hard it was almost painful. But it was a good pain. She held him just as tightly.

Since escaping from the cabin, she hadn't allowed herself to think about how stressed and afraid she was. How she might protect Evelyn if Camden found them. But now that Chad was there, she could let some of the responsibility for Evelyn and the situation go. He'd take control.

She began to shake, unable to stop.

Being in Chad's arms made her feel safe. At last. She'd *always* felt safe with him, even that first day when he was a stranger who'd invited her back to his house. Most normal people would've immediately said no and gone on with their lives. But instead, she'd felt an innate trust in Chad. And he hadn't let her down. Not once.

"Britt," he whispered into the crook of her neck, where he'd buried his face. To her surprise, she realized Chad was shaking too. He might be a strong, relentless protector, but it was more than obvious how emotional he was that they were all right.

"I'm okay," she told him.

It took several long moments before either was able to let go of the other. The relief they felt, the overwhelming emotions coursing through their veins, made it impossible to speak, to do anything other than hold each other.

When Chad finally lifted his head, Britt saw that his eyes were filled with tears. Evelyn's words came back to her once more. She'd done an amazing job teaching her children that emotion wasn't a bad thing. "I love you," she told him.

"Not more than I love you," he countered. Then he took a deep breath, framed her face in his hands the way he loved to do, and kissed her. It was a long, soft kiss. It wasn't passionate, it was a sensual sharing of relief, love, and respect between a man and a woman.

"I give it two months," Evelyn said from behind them, sounding extremely satisfied.

"Two months for what?" Chad asked, turning to his mom but keeping an arm around Britt's waist.

"Nothing. Just an inside thing between Britt and me."

Britt found herself rolling her eyes. She knew exactly what Evelyn was referring to. The thought of getting pregnant in the next two months was overwhelming and ridiculous . . . but then, she recalled how Chad had forgotten to use a condom that very morning.

Maybe her prediction wasn't that far off after all.

"Can you two walk? Are you okay going back to the cabin? I can run back and get help if I need to. The police should be there by now."

Britt blinked. She hadn't even thought to ask him what was happening back at the cabin. She'd been so relieved to see him, she didn't even think about Camden. "The police? Where's Camden? He was the one who took us," she belatedly told him.

"We know. Victor called me and said he saw you hanging on for your life in the bed of his truck."

"*Victor* called you?" Evelyn asked.

"Yeah. I was surprised too. He might be an asshole, but he seemed genuinely concerned. When the police arrived at Lobster Cove, they found Walt hurt but alive. Then Otis showed up while we were all there trying to figure out where Camden could've taken you. He told us about the cabin. We got here as soon as we could."

"Otis told you about the cabin?" Britt asked, shocked.

"With a little encouragement, yes. Now, can you two walk? Or do I need to go get help?"

"We can walk," Evelyn said firmly.

"It's okay to need help now and then," Chad said softly to his mom.

"I realize that. And when I need help, I'll ask for it. Now, lead the way, son. I need to pee, and I'm *not* doing it in these woods again."

"Yes, ma'am," Chad said with a small chuckle. He took Britt's hand in his and squeezed before dropping it and turning to his mom. He wrapped an arm around her waist as he began leading them back through the woods, toward the cabin they'd escaped what seemed like days ago.

Britt could only smile as she walked behind mother and son. It melted her heart to see Chad so worried about his mother. She was glad he was helping her, not coddling her.

She had a flash of their future. Of Chad teaching his own sons to love and respect their mother . . . *her*. She hadn't been sure she wanted children so soon, but now? With Chad? She definitely did. Because she knew without a doubt he wouldn't leave her. That she wouldn't have to try to raise a child on her own like her mother did.

Life was full of ups and downs, but it was all the good things that happened that made any bad times seem not quite so awful. There were still a lot of unknowns about the future, about what would happen with Otis and Camden, about whether Walt would be okay, about the financial stability of Lobster Cove after all the money that had been stolen. But Britt had no doubt the Young brothers would band together and persevere.

They were stronger together than they were on their own. And she felt blessed to be able to be a part of it.

It was almost two in the morning, but no one seemed ready to leave Lobster Cove. They'd received word that Walt would be fine. He was staying in the hospital tonight but was already chomping at the bit to get home . . . and back to the shop.

Camden and Otis had both been transported to the Knox County jail. Otis was cooperating fully with authorities, while his son was protesting his innocence, blaming everything on his father.

Chad hated that both his mom and Britt would be dealing with what happened for months to come, with the inevitable court appearances and meetings with the DA. But to his relief, both women seemed to be handling what happened to them with amazing resiliency.

The living room of the main house was currently full of people, despite the late hour. All his brothers were there, as was Barry. Chad was on the couch with Britt snuggled into his side. She was exhausted, but she insisted she didn't want to go upstairs yet. The more time that passed since he'd found her, the more bruises and scrapes appeared on her pale skin. The same with his mother.

It infuriated Chad. He wished he could get to Camden and beat the shit out of him again.

He'd heard the entire story of what happened when his mom met with the officers at the Calverts' cabin. Both she and Britt would have to go to the station tomorrow for an official interview, but from what he understood, Camden had come to Lobster Cove, stopping at the auto shop first and taking Walt out of commission so he couldn't come to their mom's assistance.

Then he'd driven up to the house as brazen as ever and walked straight inside. He'd grabbed Evelyn by the arm and dragged her out, not even pretending he was there to talk, to beg her to reconsider pressing charges against his dad.

It was hard to believe that none of the Youngs had even known about Camden's criminal history. The fact that he'd done time for involuntary manslaughter was a huge shock. Apparently, the man had a violent streak that simmered just under the surface, and when the chance arose for him to take revenge on the Young family, he'd acted.

Britt had seen Camden shoving Evelyn into his truck, and she'd tried to stop him. It was stupid . . . and brave as hell. And Chad couldn't be more proud of her.

Hearing about Britt's harrowing trip to the cabin in the bed of Camden's truck made Chad nauseous. She could've easily been thrown out and badly hurt or killed. And when his mom and Britt heard that Victor had not only called Chad but also gone to Lobster Cove to check on Walt—and called for help after finding him injured—they were both floored.

Britt more so than his mom; Evelyn always said the man hadn't always been the grump he was today.

"I'm going to head out," Barry finally announced with a yawn. "Ms. Evelyn, I'm so glad you're all right. You too, Britt. I'll be here bright and early to see what's what at the shop."

"I can help," Zach offered.

But Barry shook his head. "No, you're busy with your lobster shack."

"I've got it," Chad said.

Barry smiled. "If I know Walt, he'll probably stop by tomorrow afternoon after he's discharged."

"Stupid old goat," Lincoln mumbled. "He'll take a week off if we have to hog-tie him to his bed."

Everyone laughed.

With that, Barry nodded at everyone and headed for the door.

After he'd left, Evelyn cleared her throat. "There's something I want to say."

Chad looked over at his mom. She was sitting in what he considered "her" chair. A light-brown recliner that had definitely seen better days but she insisted was "perfectly fine" and that she'd "finally broken in" to be exactly how she liked it. She had a blanket over her lap, the blue fuzzy robe that she'd had for as long as Chad could remember wrapped around her, and a cup of tea sitting on the small table to her left.

She looked relaxed and happy . . . but he couldn't shake the image of her crawling out of that filthy cabin through a hole she and Britt had made with their bare hands.

Anger threatened to overwhelm him again, but apparently Britt could read his mood, and she snuggled into him a little deeper, tightening the arm that was around his belly. Just having her next to him made him feel a little calmer.

"What's that, Mom?" Zach asked. He was sitting on the floor, leaning against the other end of the couch. Lincoln was standing, leaning against the wall, and Knox was in what had been their dad's recliner.

"I'm going to close the rental cabins after this summer."

No one said a word for a long moment. Chad was genuinely shocked. As long as he could remember, the two small guesthouses on Lobster Cove had been his mom's passion project.

"Why?" Knox asked, breaking the silence.

"I've been thinking about it ever since I learned that Otis was stealing money from us. I've always been frustrated because your dad and I worked our butts off with the three businesses, and I never understood why we didn't have more money saved up. Well, we know the reason. Because Otis was stealing it out from under our noses. Now I'm old. And tired," she said.

Chad and the other four people in the room immediately protested her words, but Evelyn held up her hand, stopping them. "Without the income from the rentals, our taxes will go down. Insurance too. I don't know exactly what the income will be from the auto shop and the boat storage, but now that Otis isn't skimming off the top, Lobster Cove should still be plenty profitable."

"But what are you going to do with the cabins?" Zach asked.

His mom glanced at Chad. "Well, I was thinking that maybe Britt and Chad could move into the two-bedroom."

The room was so quiet, the humming of the dishwasher in the kitchen sounded loud.

"That is, if none of you other boys object. Lincoln just bought a house, and Zach, you seem content to be near your lobster shack. Knox, if you wanted to, you could move into the smaller house."

Knox shook his head. "I'm good where I am. Thanks, Mom."

"I'm good with Chad and Britt moving into the big cabin," Lincoln said.

"Me too."

All eyes turned to Chad and Britt. He honestly didn't know what to say. He loved Lobster Cove. Always had. And he truly didn't mind living in the main house with his mom. Many people would roll their eyes at a man who lived with his seventy-one-year-old mother, but he loved and respected her. And . . . she wasn't hard to live with at all.

But he couldn't deny that having his own space with Britt sounded like heaven. Though he'd never pressure her to do anything that might make her uncomfortable. Their relationship had moved at lightning speed.

"Besides, eventually you'll need the extra room for my grandbaby," his mom said with a smirk.

"Jeez, Mom, lay off the grandbaby stuff already," Zach complained.

Their mom turned her gaze to her youngest. "You aren't getting any younger, Zachary. It's about time you got serious about finding a woman to settle down with and start your own family."

"Whoa! I'm only thirty!" Zach protested, throwing his hands up as if he could physically block their mom's words.

Everyone chuckled at his obvious horror over the thought of having babies of his own.

"Don't laugh too hard," Evelyn warned Lincoln and Knox. "Lincoln, your sperm probably isn't as viable as it once was. The clock is ticking."

His brother choked on the sip of coffee he'd just taken. When he was able to breathe properly, he said, "Can you please not talk about my sperm? Ever again?"

Once more, laughter rang out through the room.

Chad took a deep breath and closed his eyes for a moment. Tonight could've ended so differently. They could've been in the hospital sitting by either Britt or their mom's bedside, hoping they'd be okay after getting hurt by Camden. Or any of them could've been shot by their former employee.

Instead, they were together, laughing and kidding around just like they'd done so many times as they'd grown up. He wished their dad was here, but he wasn't. Life moved on, whether you wanted it to or not.

"So? What do you think?" Evelyn asked. "About moving into the cabin. If you need to expand it in the future . . . you know, to hold more babies . . . that would be more than all right."

Chad opened his eyes and turned to Britt. She hadn't said a word, and he worried that she'd feel put on the spot. Her life had been turned upside down in the last couple of months, and he didn't want to agree to anything that would add to the stress she might be feeling.

But when he looked into her eyes, he saw nothing but excitement for the future . . . and love.

Chad turned to his mom and said, "We'll talk about it. We don't need to make any decisions tonight. I want to make sure if we decide to move that everyone is all right with it."

"I'm cool," Lincoln said.

"Me too," Knox chimed in.

"Me three," Zach agreed.

Their mom beamed.

"As I said, Britt and I need to talk about it. It's a big decision."

"It's not really," his mom said conversationally. "You're already sharing a room, and neither of you leave Lobster Cove all that much. Not that you need anything else to do, but fixing the place up how you want it would give you something to stay busy this fall and winter."

The more his mom talked about him and Britt moving into the cabin, the more excited Chad got about the possibility. He was the brother who'd always loved Lobster Cove the most. He was the one who'd first brought up the idea of everyone moving back to Maine to help out with the businesses and their mom. And he was the one who actually spent the most time here. His brothers all had their own jobs and lives, separate from Lobster Cove.

"And having a built-in babysitter right across the way would be ideal," his mom pushed.

Britt chuckled next to him, but Chad kept a stern expression on his face as he repeated, "Britt and I will get back to you, Mom."

"Okay, okay," she said with a huge smile on her face.

"I'm fucking beat," Zach said out of the blue. "I think I'm gonna head home."

"Language," Evelyn scolded.

For some reason, Britt burst out laughing. Chad turned to her and raised an eyebrow. But she simply smiled up at him. Then she shared a long look with his mom, who giggled, though he couldn't figure out what was so funny.

"I'm going to head out too," Lincoln said.

"You gonna need more help with your place?" Chad asked him. "We were interrupted before we finished today."

"I think I'm good. We got a good chunk done, so I can finish up by myself."

"All right, but if you need me to come back over, just let me know."

"I will, thanks."

"I'll come over tomorrow afternoon after going down to the docks and seeing what fresh seafood has come in," Zach told their mom.

"And I'll be here in the evening after my shift," Knox said. "I want to hear how the meeting with the detectives goes, and what's going to happen next with Otis and Camden."

Everyone stood, and each of his brothers gave Chad a huge hug, complete with slaps on the back. Britt's hugs were just as heartfelt, if not quite as boisterous. Chad noticed that everyone hugged their mom a little longer than usual. A little tighter. All of them clearly grateful she was still with them.

Every day was a gift, and Chad, at least, was determined to live each one to the fullest.

Finally, it was just Chad, Britt, and his mom left in the house.

"How are you doing, really?" he asked his mother.

"I'm fine, son. Really. I was more worried about Britt being in the back of that truck with the way Camden was driving. And then we were concentrating on finding a way out of that filthy cabin, so I wasn't thinking about the what-ifs."

Chad studied his mom for a long moment, trying to ascertain if she was being truthful or not. Her next words made him think she really *was* all right.

"I'm going to do everything in my power to make sure both of them pay for what they've done. I'm glad your father isn't here to see how low his best friend has sunk. If he knew what Otis had been doing, he would've been just as furious as I am. And for Camden to do what he did? How he turned so rotten, I have no idea."

She sounded pissed, which Chad supposed was better than depressed or scared.

"About the cabin—"

"*No*, Mom," Chad chided gently. "I appreciate the offer more than you know, but Britt and I need time to discuss it."

"Okay. Fine," she huffed.

"Are you really sure about stopping the rentals? It brings in good money every summer."

"And it ties us all to Lobster Cove in a way the auto shop and the boat storage don't. Takes up too much time. We have to deal with a lot of disrespectful renters and cater to their every need. I want to cater to *my* needs. To the needs of my family. Now that you're all here, I want to spend time with you and your brothers, especially in the summer. I want to be able to go to town and eat at Zach's world-famous lobster shack. Not be stuck in the house because I have to make muffins, greet incoming renters, or hold my breath to see what kind of shape they left the cabins in when they checked out."

She had a point. Chad nodded.

"Besides, like I said, now that Otis isn't stealing money from me, from *us*, I think we'll be just fine without that income. Now . . . it's late, or early. Britt is barely keeping her eyes open. Take her upstairs, and make sure you both sleep in tomorrow."

"Yes, ma'am," Chad told her. Then he leaned in and kissed her forehead and hugged her. He could've lost her today.

She returned his embrace just as tightly. Then she turned to Britt, and they shared an intimate look that could only come from shared trauma. The two women hugged, and it seemed that both were reluctant to let go.

"You sleep in too," Britt told her.

"Oh, I plan on it. Chad's got things under control around here."

She wasn't wrong. And her confidence in him made Chad feel good. Really good. "Good night, Mom," he told her.

"Night," she returned. Then headed down the hall toward her bedroom. She turned at the last minute and said, "It's days like today that remind me how important family is. Thank you for being there for me today, Britt. And Chad, thank you for coming to our rescue. Raising kids is a crapshoot. You can do everything right and they might still turn out to be self-centered, nasty men or women. But you and your brothers are incredible men. I love you, and I'm extremely proud of you."

And with that, she stepped into her room and closed the door.

Chad swallowed hard. He knew his mom loved him and his brothers. Knew she was proud of them. But hearing the words felt amazing.

Britt looped her arm through his and tugged him toward the stairs.

After they'd settled into bed together, she propped her chin on her hand, which rested on his chest, and stared at him. "Talk to me," she said quietly.

"About what?"

"About what's going through your head. Today was hard for you. How are you doing?"

"I'm pissed. And proud. And relieved."

She nodded. "Me too."

"How do you feel about Mom's offer? About the cabin, I mean."

Britt's gaze dropped. But this was too important a conversation for him not to be able to see her eyes as they talked. He put a finger under her chin and gently lifted her head so she was looking at him once more.

"For the record? I want to take her up on it. There's nothing I'd like better than to move into that cabin with you. To be able to make love to you whenever and wherever I want without worrying about my mother walking in on us. I want our own space. Our own kitchen. I love my mom, though I wouldn't mind some evenings with just us.

"But I'm willing to wait as long as it takes for you to be ready. I can move out there, and you can stay here. We can go on dates, continue to get to know each other. My feelings for you aren't going to change, and the last thing I want is for you to do something you aren't ready for."

"Your mom really wants grandbabies."

Chad blinked. That wasn't what he'd expected her to say. "Yeah. She's kind've obnoxious about it."

"I love Lobster Cove. I love your mom. And your brothers. And Maine. It's so darn beautiful here. Even with the ticks."

Chad grimaced. When they'd gotten home, he'd come upstairs with Britt so she could shower, and he'd picked off her body at least a dozen of the bloodsuckers that she'd picked up from crawling out of the cabin and her flight through the woods.

"You know what I thought of when I was in the bed of that pickup, holding on for dear life so I wouldn't get thrown out and smashed like a bug on the road?"

Okay, *that* wasn't a pleasant thought. Chad pushed it down. "What?"

"The future. With you. Here. How we'd watch our kids running around Lobster Cove like heathens. Swinging on the lobster swing. Playing in Fort Bad Assery. You teaching them everything you know about cars. I kept those images in my head, and it helped me hold on a little longer.

"I want a future with you, Chad. I love you. There's nothing I can think of that would be more perfect than living in the cabin with you, right here at Lobster Cove. We can see your mom every day, make sure she's okay. And if she needs any kind of medical attention in the future, we can be here for her. But I don't want to rush *you* into anything either."

Chad rolled until Britt was under him. The love he felt for her was almost overwhelming. "Rush me," he said firmly, echoing words she'd once said to him.

She smiled. "I think if your mom wants grandkids . . . maybe we should do what we can to oblige her."

He stared down at her, at a complete loss for words.

Her smile faded. "You told me to rush you," she whispered almost accusatorily.

"How do you feel?"

"What?"

"How do you feel?" Chad repeated. "I know you're probably sore. Do you hurt anywhere?"

"I don't hurt anywhere. Yes, I'm sore. And tired, but I also feel wired, as if I could stay up another two days before finally needing to crash."

"It's the aftereffects of adrenaline." Chad shifted so he was lying more next to her than on top of her, and he ran his hand from her collarbone down the middle of her chest, then slipped under the T-shirt she was wearing and back up to cup one of her breasts.

She inhaled and arched into his touch. "Yes," she hissed. She reached up and wrapped her hand around the back of his head and pulled his mouth to hers.

The next ten minutes were both loving and frantic. Their clothes went flying, and Britt was more aggressive than she'd ever been, even as Chad attempted to be gentle. She wasn't having it.

By the time Chad buried himself in her soaking-wet folds, she was whimpering with need. Their lovemaking was fast and hard, but he was still careful not to hurt her as he took her.

It didn't take long for either of them to orgasm. She squeezed his cock harder than ever before as she exploded, which triggered his own release.

Coming deep inside her body was satisfying on a level Chad had never known. He hadn't been able to consciously enjoy it last time, but he did now . . . and the thought that they might have made a baby was exhilarating.

"So . . . should I tell Mom we're going to move into the cabin in the fall after this rental season is over?" Chad asked, pushing himself up to his elbows. He was still buried deep inside her body and didn't want to move for fear his cock would slip out.

"Yes."

"Then I have just one more question for you."

"Yeah?"

"Are we going to get married before we give my mom a grandbaby, or do you want to wait?"

Tears immediately filled her eyes, but Chad could tell they were happy tears by the huge smile on her face.

"Was that a proposal?"

"Hell no. I'm going to get you a big-ass ring, take you down to the beach while my brothers and Mom are all watching from the deck of the main house, go down on one knee, and beg you to marry me. It's going to be a huge production. There might be boats in the cove all blowing their horns, a lobster dinner afterward, and a huge celebration with our family."

"I don't need any of that. I just need you."

"You have me," Chad told her, feeling the words down to his soul. "I think you had me from that first day in the parking lot of that lumber store."

"There's a chance it could take a while for me to get pregnant."

"Nope. I knocked you up tonight."

Britt rolled her eyes. "You have no idea if the timing's right or not."

He shrugged. "My sperm's determined. Yesterday and just now are the only two times it's ever had a chance to do what it was made for . . . to fertilize an egg. And I've always been an overachiever."

Britt giggled, and his soft cock slid from between her folds.

"Damn," he complained.

Britt took his face in her hands and licked her lips. "I love you."

"I love you too. Thank you for looking after my mom today. Thank you for being strong. Thank you for not giving up. For rescuing yourself. For doing what needed to be done to keep yourself and my mother safe."

"You're welcome," she whispered.

"But never again. My heart can't take anything like that happening to you a second time."

"Deal."

Chad moved to her side and pulled Britt into him. Her head lay on his chest, and their legs were intertwined. Nothing felt better than holding this woman in his arms. His life had changed so much in such a short period of time. If someone had told him when he moved back to Maine that he'd find the woman he wanted to marry—and he'd be trying to impregnate her—all within a couple of months, he would've rolled his eyes and told them they were delusional.

And yet . . . here he was. Happier than he'd ever been and looking forward to their future.

He turned his head to ask if Britt needed to get up to use the bathroom, or if she wanted him to get a washcloth so she could clean up, but her eyes were closed and she was already fast asleep.

Deciding not to disturb her—she needed to rest after the long, hard day—Chad tightened his arms around her and closed his own eyes. He was sure the future wouldn't be all sunshine and roses, but together—at least if today proved anything—they could face whatever obstacles life put in their path and come out stronger on the other side.

EPILOGUE

Zach sighed.

He was tired. If he'd thought he worked hard while he was in the Navy, it felt like *nothing* compared to this. He'd always dreamed of owning his own restaurant. His idols were Gordon Ramsay, Anthony Bourdain, David Chang, and Julia Child.

But buying a shack in his hometown and serving lobster—how cliché—wasn't ever on his radar. He was thirty years old, in the prime of his life, and his days consisted of getting up at the ass crack of dawn—which came really early in the summers in Maine—heading to his new restaurant, the Lobster Buoy; doing inventory; coming up with the special of the day; and starting prep.

Of course, the cooking part wasn't very different from when he was in the Navy, except now he wasn't cooking for thousands of people at one time.

He'd been vehemently opposed to opening a lobster shack. They were a dime a dozen on the Maine coast, and many lasted no longer than a few summers. It was hard work with not a ton of payoff. But when his dad died and his older brother had brought up the idea of all of them moving home to help out around the family property and be around more for Mom, the idea truly appealed.

Zach had always loved Maine. And . . . since getting out of the Navy, he'd been floundering a little. Trying to decide what he wanted to do and where he wanted to go. Coming home had taken the huge decision of what to do with his life out of his hands.

He'd actually had dreams of opening a restaurant like the Lost Kitchen, a place where people would clamor for reservations, making him a million dollars in the first year. Operating a hole-in-the-wall lobster shack like the Lobster Buoy wasn't anything close to what he'd envisioned.

It had taken him a while to switch gears in his head from the rural five-star restaurant he'd envisioned, but despite the hard work and bone-deep exhaustion . . . the Lobster Buoy was growing on him.

It was actually fun to come up with new and innovative recipes using lobster. Things that other restaurants weren't doing. Under no circumstances was he ever going to have a "boring" menu that included things like plain ol' lobster rolls. He wanted to wow his customers. Wanted to be able to sell enough to stay open through the slower winter months, and not just cater to tourists coming through the coastal town on their way to Acadia National Park and Bar Harbor.

With every day that went by, he felt he was getting closer to that goal. Of course, it would take longer than one summer to figure out if he could make it or not. But the reputation of his little lobster shack was growing faster than even he'd thought possible. He'd actually been interviewed by *Bon Appétit*, and he'd seen an uptick in business ever since.

He'd also just hired a social media content creator, which seemed ridiculous, but he knew if he wanted to make a success of the Lobster Buoy, he needed all the advertising he could get, and the things she was posting were amazing. Videos, still shots, interviews with satisfied customers. If he didn't own the business, *he'd* want to come and check it out.

Things were going well, but he was crazy busy. Opening the shack in the morning, visiting his mom whenever he had a spare moment, meeting with the fishermen in the afternoons to check out their fresh catches and to buy the lobster and other seafood he needed to make his custom meals.

The situation with the Youngs' longtime friend, Otis Calvert, and his son had put a pall on what had otherwise been a very good homecoming. To know Otis had been stealing from his mom and dad for years was infuriating. And then Camden actually kidnapping his mother and Britt last week? It was as shocking as it was eye opening.

Zach had always felt extremely safe here in Rockville. He'd forever seen it as kind of a backwoods town where nothing interesting ever happened. And no, the town's annual summer Lobster Fest didn't count.

That was part of the reason why Zach and his brothers had all joined the military. To get out, see the world, experience more than just their little corner of Maine. And yes, find some excitement. Now that they were all back, he'd looked forward to the slower pace.

But then they'd learned about Otis's embezzlement. And his mom had gotten fucking *kidnapped*. It put a very different perspective on Rockville for Zach. He wasn't an idiot, he knew bad stuff happened all over the world—he'd seen more than his fair share of it—but he'd always felt as if there was a protective bubble over Lobster Cove, the property where he'd grown up.

Until Camden Calvert had driven right up to the front door and taken his mother in broad daylight.

But Otis and his son were in jail, and Lobster Cove would hopefully bounce back. His mom and Britt would have to appear in court at some point, but for now, things were back to normal.

Well . . . mostly. Chad, the second-oldest Young brother, had fallen in love and would likely be getting married in the not-too-distant future. He and Britt would take over one of the rental cabins . . . well, it wouldn't be a rental any longer. His mom had decided to stop renting to guests after this season.

Changes were happening all around him, and Zach wasn't sure how to feel about that. He was happy for Chad and Britt . . . but change made him nervous.

"Zach, if you're going to get to the docks to meet the lobster boats, you need to move your ass!" Jack yelled.

He was the first person Zach hired after moving home, and he'd hit pay dirt with the guy. He was older, around fifty-five, but could outwork any younger kid, any day of the week. He was a veteran who had an aversion to talking about his time in the Marines. He also wasn't great with customers.

But he was a maestro with a spatula and in the kitchen. Zach needed people who could recreate the dishes he concocted without a lot of supervision. And Jack was able to follow his recipes to a T, and even come up with his own ideas about how to improve the occasional dish.

Zach had a handful of other employees who took orders and schmoozed with customers, but Jack was definitely in charge when Zach couldn't be there.

"I'm going," he told Jack. "I'm thinking lobster and asparagus risotto as the special tomorrow. What do you think?"

"I'm thinking you're the boss and that's going to be fucking fantastic," Jack said with a grin. He was missing one of his lower front teeth and one of his upper canines, and with his longish graying black hair pulled back in a hairnet, he looked a little maniacal, but Zach didn't care what he looked like. As long as he kept the shack clean and continued to cook as well as he had so far, all was good.

Zach waved at the high schooler running the front of the shack and headed for his Explorer. He had to walk through town to get to the parking lot behind the studio apartment he was renting. It wasn't the ideal living situation, but it would do for now. It was close to the Lobster Buoy—only around five blocks down and one block back; about a five-minute walk—and he was a man who was used to living in small spaces, as he'd done while deployed on ships with the Navy.

From the restaurant, he could also walk to the dock where the fishermen came in every afternoon to off-load their catch. But since he planned to purchase a large quantity of lobster, he needed a way to transport it.

There was nothing in the world like fresh lobster. And he could get it at a much better price buying it straight from the boats than from a store or distributor. He also liked to take a look at everything else they'd caught. Many days he was inspired simply by taking a walk down the dock and checking out all the fresh seafood.

Zach parked and pocketed his keys as he headed for the row of lobster boats unloading their catches of the day. He went straight for his favorite lobsterman. Eliot Sullivan was nearing fifty and had been working a lobster boat since he was around twelve years old. His son, Jonah, was closer to Zach's age. He'd always worked right alongside his father.

Lobstering was hard work. They usually started their day around the same time Zach did—very early. Most days they didn't return until late afternoon, so it was hours and hours of hauling traps, sorting lobsters, making sure they threw back small or egg-bearing ones, keeping records of how many they'd caught, and tracking the movements of the creatures for future trapping opportunities.

"Hey," Zach said as he approached the boat.

"Zach!" Jonah called out in greeting when he saw him.

"How was the day?" Zach asked.

"Great. We found an awesome honey hole. Got some beauts today. Wanna see?"

"No, I'm just out for a pleasure walk on the dock because I can't go a day without the smell of dead fish and seeing the seagulls fight over fish guts."

Jonah laughed uproariously, as if Zach was the funniest man alive. One of the reasons why Zach liked Jonah so much was because of how upbeat and positive he was. If they'd had a tough day, he was always pragmatic, saying tomorrow would be better. He made Zach smile, and he appreciated that.

"Hey, Zachary. How are you?" Eliot asked. He'd been bent over a bunch of papers, probably tallying the take for the day, and Zach hadn't wanted to interrupt. The last thing he needed was to report his numbers wrong to the Maine Department of Marine Resources.

"Good."

"Your mom okay?"

"She's great. Thanks for asking."

"Heard your brother's getting married soon."

Zach couldn't help but smile at that. The gossip network in Rockville was alive and well. "It's not official, but yeah, I'm guessing it won't be long before Chad and Britt tie the knot."

"That's great. Oh, did you hear? We've got a new employee. Here she comes now."

Zach turned in the direction the older man was indicating and saw a woman walking toward them. His eyes widened in surprise. She looked *nothing* like he imagined a crew member of a lobster boat could ever look like. He knew he was stereotyping, but Zach couldn't help it.

The woman walking toward them was tiny, especially compared to his own six foot six inches. He doubted her head would reach his shoulders. She had pale-blond hair that was almost white. There were small wrinkles around her eyes, which told Zach that she probably smiled and laughed a lot.

She waddled a little as she walked, but he didn't think it was because of her weight. It was because of all the gear she was wearing—oilskins to protect herself from ocean spray, sturdy rubber boots, a pair of insulated waterproof gloves tucked into the thick tool belt around her waist.

For some reason, watching her walk toward them made Zach's heart speed up, and he couldn't stop staring. She paused at the side of the *Wave Rider*, which was Eliot's lobster boat.

"Hi!" she said cheerily.

"Marit, this is Zach Young. He's a local boy who recently moved back home after doing a stint in the Navy. He owns the Lobster Buoy."

"Oh my gosh, really? I *love* that place," Marit gushed. "I had the lobster-stuffed avocado the other day, and it was soooooo amazing."

The feeling of accomplishment and pride he felt when people told him how much they enjoyed his food never failed to make Zach smile. "Thanks."

"Marit's only been working with us for a week, but I already don't know what we ever did without her," Eliot said with a wink.

"Whatever," she said with a small laugh.

"No, seriously. She's from Portland, and she's been working on lobster boats all her life. Right, Mar?" Jonah added, smiling. It was easy to see that Eliot's son had a crush on the newest crew member.

"I'm not sure about *all* my life," she said easily, holding out a hand to Zach. "Marit Phillips. It's nice to meet you," she said.

The second Zach's hand closed around Marit's, something sparked within him. He didn't believe in love at first sight. Or Bigfoot, the Loch Ness monster, or conspiracy theories in general. He was too levelheaded for any of that nonsense.

And yet, at the first touch of his hand to hers, Zach was suddenly envisioning sitting on the back deck of Lobster Cove with this woman, watching their kids play in the water down at the beach.

The smile on her face faded a little as he gaped at her like an idiot, feeling shell shocked. She gently pulled her hand out of his grip and took a minuscule step back, which sliced at Zach as if he'd dropped one of his filleting knives onto his foot.

"So . . . what do you want today? Lobsters?" Eliot asked, oblivious to the undercurrents between his newest deckhand and his best customer.

Clearing his throat, Zach tried to concentrate. Thankfully, he'd already done the mental calculations on how much lobster he'd need to make the risotto. "Yeah, lobsters. I'm trying out some simple recipes for meals easy to eat on the go, for the Lobster Festival next week."

"Good idea. Heard the weather's supposed to be awesome. Sunny but not too hot. They're talking record crowds this year," Eliot commented, as Jonah and Marit got busy packing up Zach's order.

"Great," he replied absently, forcing himself to take his gaze off Marit.

He wasn't sure what was happening here, but he wasn't going to read too much into his reaction when he'd touched the woman. Chad and Britt's overwhelming happiness was probably rubbing off on him. That was all. He was too young to settle down. Didn't want to. Didn't even want a girlfriend. He was too busy, had too much going on in his life right now.

A tiny voice inside him warned that he was protesting too much. He quickly tried to push it away.

But when Marit turned to him and hefted a large, heavy crate with a smile and seemingly little effort, saying, "I'll help you load up. Lead the way," Zach had the feeling that his life had just changed in a huge way.

This tiny dynamo of a woman was going to upend *everything*. Of that, he had no doubt. But would it be in a good way? Or bad? Only time would tell.

RETURN TO ALPHA COVE IN

THE SAILOR

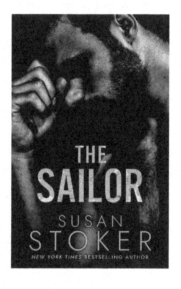

A former Navy chef meets his match in a woman who holds her own in a man's world . . . and he wants her to be a part of his.

Like his brothers, Zach Young has recently moved home to Maine after the untimely death of his father. In addition to helping his mom maintain Lobster Cove, the family's beloved property, the Navy cook has big dreams of opening his own restaurant . . . but, for now, has reluctantly settled for a lobster shack. Not exactly what he had in mind, though a new lobsterwoman in town has made his daily trips to the docks worthwhile.

Having been literally bullied out of her last port city a little farther down the coast, Marit Phillips isn't in Rockville long before the familiar grumblings begin . . . hardened lobstermen thinking a petite woman can't possibly do the job, no matter how experienced. Fortunately, her new boss judges her based on work ethic . . . and the handsome cook who visits their boat every day? He seems to see things in Marit that even she doesn't.

But as much as Zach builds her up, there's another man in town, his polar opposite, trying to tear her down. And he proves more determined than the couple thought possible . . .

ABOUT THE AUTHOR

Susan Stoker is a *New York Times, USA Today,* and *Wall Street Journal* bestselling author whose series include Badge of Honor: Texas Heroes, SEAL of Protection, and Delta Force Heroes. Married to a retired Army noncommissioned officer, Stoker has lived all over the country—from Missouri and California to Colorado, Texas, and Tennessee— and currently lives in the beautiful wilds of Maine. A true believer in happily ever after, Stoker enjoys writing novels in which romance turns to love. To learn more about the author and her work, visit her website, www.stokeraces.com, or find her on Facebook at www.facebook.com/authorsusanstoker.

Connect with Susan Online

SUSAN'S FACEBOOK PROFILE AND PAGE

www.facebook.com/authorsstoker

www.facebook.com/authorsusanstoker

FOLLOW SUSAN ON INSTAGRAM

www.instagram.com/authorsusanstoker

FOLLOW SUSAN ON TIKTOK

www.tiktok.com/@susanstokerauthor

FIND SUSAN'S BOOKS ON GOODREADS

www.goodreads.com/susanstoker

EMAIL

susan@stokeraces.com

WEBSITE

www.stokeraces.com